UNFORGIVABLE
LUST & FIRE

UNFORGIVABLE LUST & FIRE

Shay Lee Soleil

Soleil Publishing
Belle River, Ontario,
Canada, N0R 1A0
www.shayleesoleil.com

Copyright © 2016 by Shay lee Soleil
Second Edition—2016

All rights reserved.

No part of this publication may be reproduced in any form, or by any means, electronic or mechanical, including photocopying, recording, or any information browsing, storage, or retrieval system, without permission in writing from the publisher.

This is a work of fiction. Names, characters, places, and incidents either are the product of the author's imagination or are used fictitiously, and any resemblance to actual persons, living or dead, business establishments, events, or locales is entirely coincidental.

Library and Archives Canada Cataloguing in Publication
Soleil, Shay Lee, author
    Unforgivable lust & fire / Shay Lee Soleil. -- Second edition.

(Unforgivable ; book 1)
Previously published: Victoria, BC : Friesen Press, 2015.
Issued in print and electronic formats.
ISBN 978-0-9952342-0-8 (paperback). ISBN 978-0-9952342-3-9 (ebook)
    I. Title. II. Title: Unforgivable lust and fire.
PS8637.O4223U44 2016   C813'.6   C2016-906587-1
                                        C2016-906588-X

ISBN 9780995234208 (Paperback)
ISBN 9780995234239 (eBook)

1. Fiction, Erotic Romance
Distributed to the trade by The Ingram Book Company

Dedication

To my brother in-law Norm (May 8 2012)

I started to write this book on his birthday, January 5 after he died. Thanks for the incredible journey, you made me realize life is short. To my husband and my children, thanks for putting up with me when my mind was elsewhere. Thank you for letting me follow a dream.

Acknowledgements

*To Chrissy, Damon, and Benjamin at Damonza.com
You have gone above and beyond to help me save this
file and re-format it for me, when I was losing my mind
over this. You saved me and my book. I can't say enough
good things about the Damonza team. You are all amazing!
My appreciation is endless. Thank you so much!*

1

I'M LEISURELY STROLLING through the grocery store with a song stuck in my head that I'd heard on the drive here. For some strange reason, it has me singing it out loud. "She don't love you she's just lonely. She wasn't once upon a time." Jeez, story of my life. Suddenly I stop singing as I'm stretching to reach my spaghetti sauce on the top shelf, because in my peripheral vision is someone at the end of the aisle staring at me.

The thought crosses my mind that it's the guy who follows me around town. I guess you can call him my stalker. He watches me from a distance, but has never approached me. I don't even know his name and in a small town like Huntsville, you'd think I'd know who he is. What's strange is that I'm not getting that feeling of utter disgust like I usually get when I catch my stalker staring at me. This time it's a delicious tingle travelling down my spine, so I automatically stop what I'm doing and look. I'm riveted to the same spot, staring back as intensely as he is to me. "Oh. My. God!" When I realize I said that out loud, I quickly close my mouth.

Standing at the end of the aisle is a tall, dark and gorgeous hunk of a man that exudes power and confidence in his stance and he's staring directly at me. Or I think he's staring at me? I look over my shoulder one way and then the other to see if anyone else is behind me. Nope. He's staring at me.

Not just staring, burning a hole right through me kind of stare. My eyes do a once over inspecting his beautiful body from head to toe. My thoughts running away from me, fantasizing of how hard his body is beneath those clothes, how would it feel pressed against mine? What exactly is he packing in those jeans? I can't take my eyes off of him. I feel this indescribable feeling running through my whole body and a gush of wetness between my legs. What the hell? I squeeze my thighs together, shifting my stance, trying not to make it look so obvious of what he's doing to me.

I'm secretly pleased with what I'm wearing. It's seasonably warm for being so late in September. There's not many days left like this before the cold weather gets here, so I've got on my stone washed little cut off jean shorts and a white tank top, which makes my boobs look bigger. God blessed me and I'm quite happy with what I have, but at this moment, every little bit helps. I really do like the way these shorts hug my bubble butt too, which my friends say they'd sell their soul for. I can hear my best friend Leena in my head right now. 'Keera, that ass of yours should be plastered all over magazines. It's perfect.'

My friends make comments on the attention they get when they're out with me because people stare a lot. They say I look like a Barbie doll and they'd kill to look like me. I consider myself being average with a lot of flaws. Yes, I have the long blonde hair, but that's it. I'm not even that tall, only five foot four, must've got that from my mom's side of the family.

We stare each other up and down for a minute or two. His friend steps in beside him, stops, and looks at him. His friend follows his line of sight to me and then back to him. The friend shakes his head in disbelief and then grabs his arm, pulling him away, but Mr. Tall, Dark, and Gorgeous shakes his arm free and returns to the end of the aisle to stare at me once again. A smile forms on his beautiful face, but then quickly diminishes when his friend gives him attitude and pulls him away for the second time.

I'm flustered, standing with my spaghetti sauce in my hand. What was that all about? And who was that?

I wander around the store dazed and confused, forgetting what else I need, thinking about him and how good looking he is. I can't explain it, but I have an awful urge to see him again and find myself struggling with the thought of searching for him. I could make up some kind of excuse, so I can talk to him?

No. let's not make an ass out of yourself. Jeez Keera, like you've ever done that before. What's wrong with you? I finally break out of my daze and remember what I need.

My phone rings and I answer it with the usual greeting. "Hey, girlfriend."

"Keera, what are you doing?" Leena asks.

"Getting groceries."

"Let's go dancing with Katie and get our drink on."

"Sure, I'd love to."

"Meet us at eight tomorrow night. The Lodge."

"K, sounds good. See you tomorrow." I picture in my head all the good times my best friends and I have had at that bar, dancing the night away and it makes me smile. But when I think of Mr. Tall, Dark, and Gorgeous showing up there, I physically shiver. I look down to see my nipples protruding underneath my white tank top and quickly cover them with my hair. Never before has my body reacted like this over a guy. A ridiculous grin crosses my face and I shake my head as I make my way through the check out.

Walking outside, I take a deep breath, trying to restore my composure, after my encounter with the only guy who's ever affected me like that. I take another cleansing deep breath, smelling the pine trees and clean mountain air as I walk through the parking lot and that's when I feel that delicious tingle again, so I automatically look around feeling like someone's watching me. I don't see anyone, so I open the back of my Journey and put my groceries in, and then head over to Mr. and Mrs. Fisher's house, which is down from the grocery store.

It's a weekly ritual I took over from my mom. She'd take milk, bread, eggs, their favourite cookies and whatever else was on the list for the week for them. Since Mrs. Fisher's been in a wheelchair, it's too hard for her to get around. I think I took over because they're the cutest old couple I've ever seen. They remind me of my parents and they keep me grounded, thinking maybe I could have a relationship like theirs someday. I know it's cliché to say, but every girl dreams of finding their true love, only I want more. I want a relationship that's filled with so much passion and heat that it could set the world on fire. A relationship where we grow old together and can't imagine ever being apart. Like Mr. and Mrs. Fisher. Like my parents had.

I place the groceries in the cupboard, with the help of Mr. Fisher who always collects a cookie and glass of milk for me.

"Sit, dear, have a cookie." Mrs. Fisher motions for me to sit beside her and we talk about things that happen around town, or the weather, and I ask if they need me to bring anything else during the week. Mr. Fisher gives me the weekly list and then I give them both a kiss on my way out.

Usually when I'm leaving, Mrs. Fisher always says something nice. Today it's, "What a beautiful woman you've turned into. Rachelle and James are smiling down upon you right now. I bet they're so proud."

"Thank you very much Mrs. Fisher. I think about them constantly. And I know they're watching over me. K, I'll see you next week. Bye!"

When I get home, I grab my groceries out of my Journey and

look around again. That feeling of someone watching creeps up on me again, along with the same tingle I felt in the grocery store.

A black pick-up two doors down catches my eye, but I dismiss it almost immediately and think of the task at hand. I go inside and start making dinner. While I'm eating in front of the TV, I hear a noise outside.

I get up and go outside to search my wrap around front porch, but I don't see anything, so I go back in and watch TV again.

Before bed, I put some more wood on the fire and take a shower then climb beneath the sheets trying to stay warm. It feels like I've just fallen asleep, when suddenly I wake to another loud noise. What the hell was that? I stay as still as possible glancing around frantically, making sure no one is in my room with me. I slowly get out of bed and reach under my mattress for the fairly large knife I placed there a couple months ago when I first noticed my stalker watching me. With my mind racing, thinking of every possibility, I tiptoe over to the door and slowly inch it open a crack. I peer out into the hallway and after seeing that no one is there, I open my door fully and make my way into the kitchen. With the knife ready to strike, I search the rest of the house cautiously.

After finding nothing unusual and making sure the doors are locked, I lie back in bed with scattered thoughts. My stalker enters my mind and then it quickly switches to the gorgeous guy I saw in the grocery store. I finally fall back asleep around two.

When I wake in the morning, I can't stop yawning from my restless night. Clumsily, I shuffle out of bed and walk to the kitchen to fill my kettle to make a tea and then saunter to my closet to find something sexy to wear for later tonight. Somewhere along the way, my mind shifts to Mr. Tall, Dark, and Gorgeous and I can't erase the ridiculous grin on my face. My God! I've never seen anyone so hot. Why haven't I seen him before? He can't be from around here. Can he?

Looking down, I find my bra and thong on the floor outside my walk in closet. What the frick! I pick them up and stare down at them confused, trying to figure out how they got here. I don't remember leaving these here. Did they fall out of the basket of clothes and I didn't notice? Maybe. I decide to wear them, anyway.

I hold up my little red dress that has a low neck line and shows some major cleavage. It clings to my every curve. It'll work. It's mid-thigh so it'll show a lot of leg and these shoes will do the trick, matching perfectly with it.

To keep myself busy, I bring in some more wood, exercise and clean the house. While I'm cleaning up, I notice my keys on the counter. It's strange, but I quickly dismiss it and hang them back up. Later I throw my hair up in a messy bun and head out to the nearest store to find red nail polish that matches the dress. When I get back to my house, I quickly paint my nails.

The day has flown by, so I hop in the shower to get ready for our night at the bar. As I'm washing my body, I replay in my mind the way Mr. Tall, Dark, and Gorgeous was staring at me in the store. Instantly, I get that tingle down my spine and that ridiculous grin stretches across my face again.

I fantasize about him standing in front of me, placing his big strong hands all over my body. His touch. Would I feel that tingle every time he touched me? His kiss. How would those lips feel on mine? I'm surprised to see how aroused I am thinking about him, but then my mind flips and I think, who are you kidding? Could you actually go through with him touching you or would you push him away like the couple of guys who have tried to get close and failed. Christ, I'll be single and lonely my whole life if I don't let someone in.

Why do I keep thinking about him? I should stop. I'll never see him again. He most likely doesn't live around here. The thought saddens me.

After rinsing the conditioner out of my hair, I slide the door to the side to get out. Opening the pantry, I grab a towel and when I turn, I see a towel on the closed toilet seat. What the…? I. Did. Not. Put that there! Who's been in my house? Oh my god! While I was in the frickin' shower. Holy shit! Okay, now I'm freaking out. I hurry to wrap the towel around me and then cautiously walk out of the bathroom and into the kitchen. I grab another trusty knife and search every room in the whole house again, but find nothing.

Am I losing my mind? I swear to god, I think I've lost it.

When I calm down, I comb out my hair, dry it, curl it, get dressed, put a little make-up on and I'm out the door, ready to meet the girls.

The Lodge is the place to be. It's always busy. It's Leena's favourite bar because of the huge wrap-around porch which we use quite extensively during the summer months. The exterior looks like an old saloon from a western movie. The interior walls are filled with memorabilia like snow shoes, trapping gear, stuffed deer, bear, moose, and every other animal that you can find in the Northern Ontario town of Huntsville. The bar itself, is the length of the building, and the music can be heard outside before you reach the door.

Leena and Katie are waiting for me in the parking lot when I arrive and we go right in together, straight to the bar to get a drink. We're talking above the music, swaying to the beat, scoping out the place to see if there is anyone we know.

"Jeez did you even taste that one?" I clink my beer bottle against Leena's drink teasing her.

"Going down good tonight." She bumps her hip against mine.

Katie turns to clink both our drinks. "To the good times."

"To good times." Both Leena and I say at the same time.

A table becomes available when a group of people get up to leave and we claim the table as ours, getting comfortable on the high back bar stools, hanging our purses on the chairs. The waitress saunters over and we order another round.

Another good song comes on and we get up to dance. We try to talk and dance at the same time, but the music is too loud, so we give up talking.

With having a little booze in us, we are feeling fine and are having a great time. We head back to the table when the waitress brings our second drink, chugging another sip, and then head back to the dance floor. Sweat beads start to form down my back and my nape as we dance our butts off, making sure we get a good workout.

"Time to hit the john, girls!" Katie says. So we grab our purses and dance our way to the washroom. When the door closes, we finally get a chance to talk without yelling.

We slip into the stalls, not skipping a beat with our gabbing. Katie's been travelling from home to university, but now that winters coming she's going to live on campus, leaving us until Christmas, and then Leena drops the bomb on me that she's going to see her father in Aruba for a week, leaving me alone.

What am I going to do without them? I don't have anyone else except my grandfather who lives a little more than an hour away. I guess I can go visit him or he can come see me.

Both my parents died in a car accident when I was eighteen. It was a very sad time in my life. The doctors told me I was going through depression, but I still refuse to believe it. I was devastated and I went through hell. Anyone else at such a young age would've acted the same, if not worse. The big settlement from the trucking company helped pay the bills once I received it, easing the stress of learning to be independent all of a sudden, so I could take care of a household. My parents were my life and I think about them all the time. My grandfather and grandmother and both my friends helped me get through the grief. My grandparents came to live with me after the accident for a few months until my grandmother got sick. She died a few months after that, which devastated my Gramps and I've been on my own ever since. It teaches you to grow up in a hell of a hurry. I'm improving greatly as the days go by. But I still need my two best friends.

As we're coming out of the washroom my step falters suddenly, when my eyes catch sight of Mr. Tall, Dark, and Gorgeous confidently leaning against the bar.

Acting on pure instinct, I stop dead in my tracks.

Leena and Katie pile up behind me. "What the hell, Keera?"

We all laugh and then I quickly recover, risking a peek, visually devouring his gorgeous body as we make our way back to our table.

My face turns beet red. I'm irritated with myself for being a complete klutz. And why? What is it about him that makes me lose my cool? Jeez, if he didn't know I wanted him before, he sure knows it now. My stomach quivers and I'm almost shaking. I can't believe how excited I am to see him again. A little part of me was hoping he'd be here.

I tell the girls about my encounter with Mr. Tall, Dark, and Gorgeous in the grocery store and how he's all I can think about. I urge them to peek over nonchalantly.

He could do a jeans commercial with the jeans he's wearing. They fit perfectly. He has his back to the bar and his legs crossed, a position that accentuates his impressive package. His elbows rest on the bar as he leans back, very relaxed.

As I'm looking at him standing there in that sexy pose, I can feel a tingle between my legs. I look periodically trying not to gawk at him. But I am. His T-shirt is skin tight and it has a fire department logo on it, which sends my mind into overdrive wondering if he's really a fireman.

His muscles bulge, straining his skin tight T-shirt and I can see the outline of every muscle through it, giving me a great view of his eight pack abs. His silky black hair is styled to perfection and falls a couple inches from his shoulder. That face and those mysterious eyes. He's perfect. I glance again checking out his luscious lips.

I shiver. Goddamn, he's gorgeous!

The girls grab my arm, pulling me up off my seat. "Come on. Let's dance." I try not to look at him, but I can feel him staring again, so every now and then, I look his way. His intense gaze sears my skin making me feel a bit uncomfortable.

The sexy little waitress walks over to talk to Mr. Tall Dark and Gorgeous, but he waves his hand like he's saying no. He talks to his friend, the same one that was in the grocery store with him, and now that I've gotten a better look at them together, I think maybe they're brothers. They sure do look alike. Every time I look over at him, I see that he's still staring and my stomach quivers.

I wait patiently for him to come and talk to me, but as the night winds down, my hopes fade.

It's late and Leena and Katie have to get up early, so we say our goodbyes.

"I have to run to the washroom again, you go ahead, love you guys, you have fun at university, and you have fun in Aruba. I'll miss you two!" We kiss and hug each other and then they disappear out the door.

Taking my last sip of beer, I collect my purse and stagger to the washroom. Feeling a little dizzy, I push through the door and then the stall to quickly sit. I only had two beers. What's wrong with me?

When I make it to the sink, I'm feeling warm and sweaty, so I splash a little water on my face. I look in the mirror fixing my makeup quickly. I want to get out of here. I head for the door and when I get outside and haven't fallen like I thought I might have, I am quite proud that I didn't make a fool of myself. The cool breeze hits my face as I walk toward my car. My vision is blurry and I stumble, but I feel someone pick me up and into their strong arms.

He's warm and very muscular. My head's spinning so I rest it on his chest. I hear a conversation, but I can't lift my head to see who is talking.

"Now what are you going to do with her?"

"I'm taking her home with us."

"No way! Are you nuts? Fuck, I knew you were losing it, but…"

"I'm not arguing with you. Here's her keys, drive in front of me."

He places me on what I think is the front seat.

I'm confused, my ears are now ringing, and I feel faint, like I'm going to pass out.

I can hear more talking in the distance.

"Bryce, think about this. Someone's going to be looking for her. Like maybe a big fucking husband. You're not thinking straight. Use your head. Not that head!"

"I've been thinking about her for two days now. She lives alone and I'll deal with the consequences."

"How do you know that?"

"I was in her house. No husband, no boyfriend, just a psycho stalker."

"Aw Christ, breaking and entering. Kidnapping…you're not listening! You have to take her home."

"I am. To our home."

"Fucking bull head. You can't! Just take her home!"

"No! I've got less than two weeks."

"To do what?"

"To make her fall in love with me."

2

WHEN I WAKE, I have something over my eyes, blinding me. My mind tells me to take it off my face, but I can't, I feel my hands are tied. I wiggle trying to remove my restraints, I yank and pull, but they won't budge. My ankles are also tied with my legs spread wide open. I no longer feel the constricting tightness of my dress and my feet are bare, but at least I have a blanket covering my body, keeping me warm.

I feel the bed dip on one side of me and I jump. My eyes darting rapidly from side to side to see any kind of light, but there's none. The first thing that enters my mind is my stalkers face. Was he at the bar and I didn't see him? Adrenaline curses through my veins immediately and my natural instinct is to pull harder on the ropes, to loosen them so I can slip my hands out, but they seem to tighten more around my wrists, biting into my skin.

"Stop!" I hear a deep male voice and then his hand covers my wrist. "It's digging into you."

My heart beat quickens, my pulse leaps and when he touches me, I feel an electric current shoot straight up my arm to the hairs on my nape.

He lowers his voice to a whisper beside my ear. "I'm not going to hurt you." Flashbacks of Jake almost raping me when I was fifteen enters my mind and I relive those terrible moments again. Sweat starts to form at my temple and a lone tear seeps from my eye. Do not cry Keera. Be tough. And you'll get through this.

There are so many things racing through my mind right now. Where am I? Who is he? How did I get here? Why am I tied up? How am I going to get out of this? I remember the dizziness I felt walking out of the bar. Did my stalker slip something in my drink so he could kidnap me? Who knows I'm missing? No one. Leena might text me in a few days? Maybe, if she's not too busy in Aruba. Gramps will call if I haven't checked in with him by the end of the week. Oh god, I could be held captive for a week or two before anyone even realizes I'm missing. What am I going to do? Think. Think of something fast. I just want to go home.

His fingers gently glide down my cheek, and I flinch bringing me back to the here and now. My breathing hitches. I've never been so scared in all my life. Except, of course, the ordeal with Jake. He continues along my jaw line and to my neck caressing my skin. I pull on my restraints again, harder this time. The pain is intense, but I can deal with it if it helps me get out of this situation.

The weight of his body lays half on me and his hands touch both my wrists. "Stop. Please. I don't want you hurt." He kisses my cheek softly. I stop moving, paying attention to what he's doing. He continues kissing me so gently, like he's trying to convince me that no harm will come to me. A shiver travels down my spine, but it's not because I'm cold. I feel warm.

I feel him get off the bed, on the left. A few seconds pass and then I feel the blanket is lifted slightly, and the bed dips on the right side of me. His warm body is plastered against mine. I flinch and then my body starts to shake. Oh God what is he going to do? Why is this happening to me?

Something really hard rests against my thigh, and when I

realize what it is, I tense and freeze. Not moving an inch, not moving a muscle. What the frick? That cannot be his cock! That thing is huge!

He whispers in my ear. "I need you to relax. I need you to trust me. I won't hurt you, I promise." I can't see where I am from whatever's covering my eyes, but I can hear his breathing and I can smell his cologne and a hint of wood burning. If this is my stalker, I have no experiences with him to compare. He watches me from afar. I've never heard his voice and he's never got close enough that I could smell his cologne.

I think my senses are returning now that the grogginess is subsiding.

His arm lays across my chest. I flinch again. "I'm going to untie you. Do not take that blind fold off your eyes. I'm letting you go to the washroom. This will tell me if I can trust you, or if I have to tie you up again."

He's going to untie me. If I do what he tells me to do, I can win his trust and the moment he lets his guard down, I think I can escape.

Feeling his warm breath gusting against my ear when he whispers does strange things to me. Something I've never felt before. He whispers again. "Can I trust you?"

I shake my head yes.

He gets off the bed, and I feel his fingers rubbing gently along my ankle as he unties it. He then moves to the headboard, untying my hand, and then he waits. I want to take the blindfold off. But I don't.

Be smart about this Keera, you need to win his trust. Do exactly what he says.

I hear his feet on the floor coming around to the other side of the bed. He slowly unties my ankle, skimming his fingers along my skin, gently touching me. I shiver at his touch. Why am I shivering? I'm warm. Is my body showing fear differently?

He moves to the headboard once again and I feel the rope

loosen. The bed dips beside me as he removes my last restraint on my wrist. He raises my arm and gently kisses my wrist. "You've left welts on your beautiful skin. I didn't want you hurting yourself."

Is that regret in his voice? Does he care? I might be able to use this to my advantage.

Taking my legs off the bed to the side, he gently lifts me up under my arms until I'm standing. "Are you okay to stand?" I nod yes, even though my knees are ready to buckle from me shaking and I'm still a little light headed and groggy from whatever was slipped into my beer or is this feeling from fright? I don't know. Too many emotions, my mind is a scrambled mess.

He helps me toward the bathroom and my blanket falls to the floor. I feel naked as I stand there with my white lace bra and matching thong on.

I hear his sharp intake of breath as he stops for a few seconds, so I stop with him. I can feel his hot burning gaze searing my skin. I can't see him, but I can feel him and after a few moments we continue to the toilet.

"If you take the blind fold off, you'd better have it back on before you come out. Do you understand?"

I nod yes.

He closes the door behind me. "I'll be right here." I hear him say behind the door.

I take the blind fold off and frantically search for a way out. I desperately tug at the window, but it doesn't budge. There's no way out. I'm being held captive in a log cabin, and a nice one at that. It seems fairly new. I run my finger along the window sill. There's no dust anywhere. It must be new or someone's cleaning skills are fabulous. Focus Keera. I check out my surroundings. The very large bathroom is light stained cedar. In one corner of the room is an extra-large triangular shaped Jacuzzi tub, a large shower with glass and brass doors, in the other corner, along the one wall is a large rustic bench. On the wall above the vanity is a huge mirror with rustic cedar wood all the way around it, matching the bench. Black granite double sinks, and heated black granite floors. Whoever owns this place is certainly not hurting for money.

"I don't hear you going yet." I hear him say from behind the door. "What's taking so long? Do I have to come in there?"

Thinking quickly, I finally break my silence toward him. "No! I'll be out in a couple of minutes." Think Keera. You've been taken against your will. Kidnapped from the bar by your stalker. He's going to be waiting outside that door when you open it. Weapon. Search for a weapon. I open both drawers, rummaging through it quietly, hoping to find a pair of scissors, but there's nothing sharp. Okay now what are you going to do? First I need clothes, but I'd better hurry before he comes in here.

I go pee and then yell to him. "Can I have my dress? I'm cold."

"No, I'll put some more wood on the fire."

I think about how Gramps taught me to protect myself by punching my intruder in the throat and to kick him in the balls. That's the only chance I have of getting out of this and then I can make a beeline for the door.

Waiting patiently until I hear the door of the wood stove open, I then come charging out the bathroom door. Except his large muscular body is right there holding the door frame. My hand reaches up so I can hit him in the throat, but he quickly grabs my hand. I try to knee him in the groin, but he stops me with his arm. I try to go to the right and then to the left. He's laughing, which makes me even more furious. I look up and see…HIM. Mr. Gorgeous.

"YOU!" I shout. He spins me around and picks me up while he wraps his arm around my waist, holding me there. My back is against his front and I'm swearing. "Put me down, you fucking asshole! Who the fuck do you think you are? You think you can go around kidnapping anyone you fucking please? I'm going to chop your balls off."

He pissed me off by laughing, so I let loose on him. My legs and arms flailing in different directions, trying desperately to get out of his grasp. I'm furious and I'm not giving in without a fight.

"I told you to keep the blind fold on! You bad girl!" Then he smacks my left ass cheek.

My whole body stiffens. "What the fuck?"

"Every time you're bad, I get to punish you."

"Are you fucking insane?" Then I really let loose on him again, swearing, throwing my arms and legs all over trying to wiggle out of his grasp.

"Calm down." He grabs both my arms to restrain me and then whispers in my ear. "You need to calm down, I won't hurt you, believe me." His big strong arms hold me tight, in a bear hug.

Not going to hurt me, eh? He slapped my ass! Keep the blind fold on? I'm a bad girl? He'll punish me? All this runs through my mind. What kind of freaky shit is Tall, Dark and Gorgeous planning on doing with me?

He carries me into the bedroom and sits down on the side of the bed, placing me in a comfortable position on his lap. He holds me close for quite a long time, rubbing my back, rocking me like a baby and I start to calm down.

I look at him and he's staring deep in my eyes. "Why are you doing this? Why can't I go home?"

"Let's start over." His hand reaches out for me to shake. "My name is Bryce. And you are?"

I keep my hands in my lap. "I'm not telling you."

"That's fine. In time you will tell me." He places me back on the bed and ties my right hand. When he grasps for my left wrist, I wiggle it loose and he quickly grabs it again, tying it to the bed post.

"Please don't tie me up again."

He ignores my plea and ties my legs.

He stares down at me for a few moments with dark lust filled eyes. His hesitation has me wondering what he's thinking and has me feeling very uncomfortable again.

"I have to. Until I know you won't run." He gently places the blanket back on, tucks me in and leaves the room. He leaves the blindfold off.

Looking around the bedroom I can see I'm lying on a four post cedar log bed, with dressers to match. The light fixture above my head and the lamp beside the bed has deer antlers on it. At the other end of the room is a rustic tall wardrobe with a lock. The bedding and curtains are camouflage. This is definitely a man's room.

He's gone for quite a while. Maybe half an hour, I'm not sure, but I listen intently for any sound from the other room and there's nothing.

All of a sudden, I hear a door closing in the other room. "Honey, I'm home." It isn't Bryce's voice, it's another male voice.

I hear faded voices in a deep conversation. I try to listen but they're whispering and all I can hear are muffled sounds.

The door opens and Bryce saunters in carrying a plate with a sandwich and a drink. He sits on the side of the bed so he's facing me. "I've decided I'm going to call you Angel or would you rather Tiger, since you almost scratched my eyes out." The corner of his mouth curls into a smile. "Now, Angel, I want you to eat. You're going to need your strength. I'm going to prop you up."

Strength for what?

He leans over to place the plate and drink on the nightstand and then he unties my legs. He reaches over me for a few pillows from the side of the bed and I inhale sharply. He then gently lifts me up underneath my arms so I'm in a sitting position. He pushes me forward a bit and places the pillows behind me. My arms are still tied.

When he leans over me again, I inhale his masculine scent and his cologne. Did he put more cologne on? God, he smells so good. Jesus Keera, get a grip!

Taking a piece of the sandwich, Bryce raises it up to my mouth and I take a bite. "That's a good girl."

Jesus, he's talking to me like I'm two.

If I do what he tells me to do, I think I can win his trust. Then the moment he lets his guard down, I'm escaping.

Whenever he brings a piece of sandwich toward my mouth, I watch as his muscles bulge. I check out every feature on his face and I watch every expression, every move he makes. He does the same, studying me.

Bryce raises the glass of water to my mouth and I take a sip with his eyes staring intently at my lips. He places the glass of water back on the nightstand and then he takes the ropes off my wrists.

I rub at my wrists. He takes one in his hand and kisses it. Then he picks the other one up and slowly kisses it, while looking deep in my eyes, holding his stare like he's going to say something, but then it's gone.

After what seems like an eternity, he finally speaks. "Let's get you to the bathroom."

He helps me up and my blanket falls to the floor again, except this time I can see the expression on his face. He stops dead again, looks all the way down, then back up again, focusing mostly on my breasts and the apex of my thighs. He's burning that hole through me again, staring, and the expression on his face is priceless. I can see the corner of his mouth curl up into a wicked smile. He finally comes out of his daze and shakes his head.

He wraps the blanket around my body and he guides me to the bathroom. "I'll be right here waiting."

"I'm sure you will."

Bryce closes the door and I hurry to look in the vanity drawers again for something. Anything that can help me get out of this situation. All I find is a brush, a new toothbrush, toothpaste and a face cloth. Think Keera. What can I do? Nothing comes to mind and I think I'd better hurry or he'll be in here in a few seconds so I brush my teeth, wash up and brush my hair. I feel so much better after cleaning up.

"Are you done yet?"

"Shit!" I say under my breath. He's still there. I quickly wrap the blanket around me again.

When I go to step out of the bathroom, Bryce guides me back in with him. I frown at him as he shuts the door behind us. He saunters to the toilet, unzips and drops his pants. He's going to the washroom right in front of me. I quickly spin around and stare in the shower.

He chuckles. He thinks this is funny. "It's okay, Angel, you're not going to be shy in a few days."

A few days? He's going to keep me here for a few days?

I hear the water running so I peek over my shoulder to see what he's doing. He washes his hands and gets a clean face cloth out of the linen closet. He comes up from behind me, wrapping those strong arms around my waist. I can feel how warm he is and I almost melt, but quickly realize he's distracting me. I move out of his grasp and turn around to face him. "Why am I staying here for a few days? Why can't I go home?"

"I want to get to know you."

"Don't you see how wrong this is? You can't go around kidnapping…" Bryce places his finger over my mouth shutting me up.

He steps so close, invading my space, pulling me into his body at my lower back. His other hand snakes through my hair and he holds me there, staring deep in my eyes, like he's going to kiss me. His lips are half an inch away from mine. Oh God, is he going to kiss me? I hold my breath waiting, staring at those luscious lips forever it seems.

Awareness of him standing so close has goose bumps covering my skin and my heart racing uncontrollably.

He hesitates for quite a while and then he finally speaks. "Let's take it one day at a time."

Holy crap! I'm flustered and I can't think straight. My mind spinning. He guides me to the door.

When he opens the door I search around for his friend, but no one's in sight. He guides me back to the bedroom and closes the door. "Austin. Lock us in." I hear a lock slide into place on the outside of the door.

"You're staying here with me tonight. Don't try to escape. I can't even get out. Were locked in here, together. So you might as well relax."

I'm standing in the middle of the room shaking, even though I've got the blanket wrapped around me. From fright? I don't know.

"Do you want to get under the covers to stay warm?"

"Who is Austin?"

"You tell me your name and I'll tell you who Austin is."

He starts undressing, pulling his shirt off, unzipping his fly, taking down his pants and then he picks them up and hangs them on the foot board of the bed.

The whole time I watch. I'm mesmerized by his gorgeous body. I can't turn away.

"Like what you see?" He says in a husky, sexy voice that seduces every part of my body.

As I realize I'm still staring, he drops his underwear revealing his massive cock. I sure do turn away then, quickly looking toward the wall. I close my eyes, replaying his cock springing out of his boxers.

I feel Bryce approaching by the electricity crackling before he even touches me. He quickly pulls my security blanket away. Totally naked, he picks me up in his arms. He's so muscular and warm. He looks deep in my eyes. "You're turning red. You shouldn't feel embarrassed." His dazzling, drop dead, perfect, blinding, white teeth smile sends me into a lust filled trip. God, he's gorgeous!

He places me on the bed. I'm cold, wearing only my bra and thong, so I cover myself with my arms.

I feel naked as his eyes do a slow inspection of my body, but I'm doing that with his.

"Push over, Angel, unless you want me to lie on top of you."

I scoot over, quickly.

He climbs in bed beside me. "You've got to relax. You're too tense. Everything's going to be fine." He turns on his side with his elbow extended as he props his head up on his hand and looks deep in my eyes. "I won't hurt you. I promise."

My heart's racing. My whole body's tense and my stomach quivers. "I don't know what the hell you're thinking, but this is not happening." I point from me to him.

"What are you talking about?"

"You know damn well what I'm talking about." I can hardly spit the words out, I'm a nervous wreck. "You and me. In this bed. It's not happening."

He grins at me and then his eyes quickly change to puppy dog eyes. "I have nowhere else to sleep. You don't want me to sleep on the floor, do you?"

Aw Christ. I'm screwed. He's so adorable.

I think about it for a bit. I can't let him sleep on the floor. This is his bed. "Fine! You stay on your side of the bed and I'll stay on mine. Got that?"

"Okay, if that's the way you want it?"

He's staring, examining my face. "Do you know how beautiful you are?"

"Will you quit doing that?"

"What? What am I doing?"

"The way you're looking at me. It's making me feel uncomfortable."

Oh, what the intensity of his stare does to me. I can't tell him he's making me hot and wet.

"So, I can't look at you now."

"Not like that."

"I'm confused. Was I looking at you in some strange way?"

"Yes. You know what you're doing."

He can see I'm getting flustered. Bryce throws back the covers, gracefully rising out of bed and saunters across the room totally naked. He stands in front of the mirror with his back to me and takes a sip of water.

I swear to God my mouth almost drops open. He has broad shoulders, long legs, honed muscle everywhere and that ass. How it flexes when he moves. Everything about him makes my mouth water. I can't take my eyes off of him. He watches me in the mirror.

What a tease!

He turns around with the glass of water in his hand and walks closer to the bed so that his hard cock is only inches away from me. "Would you like some?"

Oh God, is he talking about the water or himself? I reposition myself so I'm sitting up. I hold out my hand, pointing my finger, making sure I don't touch it. I turn my head. "You need to cover that thing up."

I can hear him smile. "Cover what up?"

"You think this is funny, don't you? Will you quit doing this? Yes, I'll have some water please." I'm trying not to smile as I take a sip. My eyes wander back to his sexy abs and then down to his overly large endowments and I realize I'm looking again so I quickly look back into his eyes. "Thank you."

"You're welcome."

Lying back down under the covers, I close my eyes.

I feel the bed dip as he gets back in beside me. His cock presses hard against my hip. My eyes fly open and I slide over quickly. "You, on your side. Remember?"

He chuckles. "Jeez, you really do need to relax. You've got to understand. I'm like a kid in a candy store right now. This is killing me."

I roll over on my stomach with a slight smirk on my face, quite happy with the effect I have on him, but I quickly pretend like I'm going to sleep, unaffected by his charm. My arms slide under the pillow and I rest my head on top.

He lifts the covers.

"What are you doing?"

"I'm checking out that fine ass of yours. Do you know how perfect that ass is?"

I lay my head back down on the pillow, trying not to show any emotion. Not saying a word.

I hear it in his grumbles that he's frustrated. He gets out of bed and fumbles around in his top drawer for something. He walks over to the tall wardrobe against the far wall and starts to move it.

He moves the whole wardrobe over to the other wall. I watch his totally naked body in action. His muscles contract everywhere. He looks like a Greek God pushing a bolder around. His arms and everything else for that matter shows so much definition. I can even see the indents on both sides of his ass cheeks when they flex. What a view!

He opens the wardrobe with the key. I can't see what's in it because it's facing away from me.

Obviously, he doesn't want me to see what's in there.

As he's busy, banging and rattling things around in the wardrobe, I know that this is my only chance to get out of here.

To escape.

3

THROWING BACK THE covers, I bolt for the door, thinking maybe I can get out. I frantically turn and pull on the door knob, but the door doesn't budge. "Let me go."

After tugging for a few more seconds, I finally give up. I position my hands at my forehead against the door and close my eyes, surrendering in defeat.

I feel a cocoon of warmth surrounding me, a force field and then I realize that Bryce has come up from behind me.

His palms press on each side of my head, caging me in. He doesn't touch me, but I feel the energy, the electricity crackling all around me.

I see him in my peripheral vision.

"Hey, look at me." He says in a soft concerned voice.

His forearm leans on the door frame beside me, pulling him closer. He looks down trying to see the expression on my face. He rubs my lower back to calm me, I presume. His touch makes me shiver, but I want more. My body strains toward his to feel more. Sexual tension radiates off the both of us. Its an edgy restless feeling, making my body hyper aware. Were like two magnets straining toward each other.

Resisting him has taken every ounce of energy out of me. Draining me, until there's nothing left.

Picking me up in his arms, he plasters me up against his muscular body. He spins around to walk toward the bed and I catch a glimpse of what's inside the wardrobe.

What the fuck is this guy into? Fur handcuffs?

He gently places me on the bed and climbs in beside me. We lay there staring at each other, not saying a word, trying to read each other.

Facing me, he props his head up with his hand. His rock hard cock rubs against my hip. He rubs my arm and then his fingers run gently across my stomach and then they go lower. Our feet intertwine. When he gets to the top of my thong, he opens my legs with his and slips one finger underneath the material. Before I realize it, his whole hand is inside my thong.

I grab his hand. "Oh, no you don't. What do you think you're doing?"

Bryce arrogantly smirks at me and before I can pull his hand out, he slips his finger between my lips down there. I pull so hard at his hand to get it out, but it doesn't budge. He takes his time exploring parts of my body that have never been touched. He stares deep in my eyes with the biggest grin and then he slides his finger into his mouth. He's licking it like it's a lollipop and then he sucks on it with deep seductive sucks.

Holy crap! My eyes widen with surprise.

"I've been dying to know how you taste and my god, you taste so good. Sweet and delicious. Someone's wet for me."

I can't believe he did that, but somehow I feel it all the way down there. My muscles clenched when he sucked on his finger and now I'm having this feeling of emptiness, almost like I want him to put his fingers back where they were.

"I know you like me, I can tell by the way your body's responding to me."

"Maybe I'm not interested. Have you ever thought about that?"

He arrogantly smiles at me. "Somehow I don't think you're telling me the truth."

"Oh, really. You don't know anything!"

"You'll be surprised how much I know. I'm going to teach you everything about your body and mine."

He grabs my hand and places it on his cock.

I pull it away quickly. "What the hell do you think you're doing?"

"That's the first time you've ever touched a cock isn't it?"

"Y-ya…No!"

"Yes it is. Don't lie to me Angel. In this relationship we will never lie to each other."

Relationship! What is he talking about?

Bryce holds my face in his hands. "We have to have trust." He stares deep in my eyes like he's going to kiss me, hesitating for a while, staring at my lips. Then his eyes search mine again, and he lowers his mouth, slowly, gently parting my lips. Sliding his tongue deep inside my mouth. Taking what he wants with long leisure licks. His kiss is confident and skilled with the perfect amount of aggression to make me beg for more. His tongue thrusts deeper and his groans reverberate in my mouth. His cock is rock hard grinding against my leg making me aware that he's getting hot, and so am I.

My resistance melts away and I kiss him back with the same ferocity, sticking my tongue in his mouth. He latches onto it and begins sucking. Seductive sucks that make me squirm, as it travels all the way down to my warm achy spot inside. I run my fingers through his jet black silky hair, grabbing a handful at the back of his neck. I like how it feels. I've wanted to run my fingers through his hair from the first time I saw him.

Rising above me, his legs force mine apart. He lowers his cock onto my lacy little thong, as he holds my hands above my head. He kisses me ferociously again. His other hand fondles my breasts, his fingers slip inside my bra to feel my puckered nipples.

"Look how hard these fucking things are." He says appreciatively as he rolls them between his finger and thumb.

He moves down my body, knelling between my legs. He pulls my thong down off my butt as he lifts my legs in the air, sliding it all the way to the tips of my toes and then it's gone. Flung across the room.

I stare at him with shock and surprise on my face. He spreads me open wider and then he dives for it. He licks the right side of my juicy folds and then the left, shoving his long hardened tongue deep inside me. Deep thrusts in and out. I'm pushing at his head, to get him to stop, but he won't. He's ignoring me. He doesn't stop. Licking upward he finds my enlarged clit, his softened tongue circles around it making my pelvis jerk from sensitivity.

No one's ever touched me like this and drove me wild with the simplest of touches.

I know it's wrong! I can't give in to him. I'm shaking my head no, because I'm torn between morality and how good it feels.

My body isn't cooperating with my mind; it's deceiving me. My hips start to move ever so slightly and then I let out a whimper. He peeks up at me while he's still feasting, but doesn't stop.

His enlarged index finger swirls around the entrance of my pussy and gently pushes in, deeper and deeper until he can't give me anymore. Slowly he thrusts in and out, while his expert tongue swirls around my clit. His fingers reach for the cup of my bra and he pulls the material down exposing my hardened nipple. He pinches and tugs and the sensation travels directly down there.

I'm struggling with myself not to give in to him, but my body is overwhelmed with intense sensations and its making my mind spin. I grab his head with my hands. I'm protesting, shaking my head. "No, you can't do this!" I finally blurt out.

He stops and looks up at me. "Do you want me to stop?"

He can see it in my eyes that if he stops I'll self-combust.

I hesitate. My mind's a scrambled mess not really knowing

what I want, but my body's telling him not to stop. My fingers grip tighter onto his head forcing him down again.

"That's what I thought!" Bryce dives back in driving me insane. He flicks my clit for a few seconds and then slides his tongue between my lips, separating them. He licks up each side, with long slow strokes. His hardened tongue spears deep inside my pussy. His nose bumps and teases my clit. There are so many sensations that I'm overwhelmed with. That I've never felt before. It's hard to wrap my head around it.

He gently inserts his finger back inside me, deep, with long unhurried strokes. He pulls it back out and licks his finger. His eyes turn dark and seductive and his voice is slow and sexy as hell. "You're so tight. Your pussy's sucking on my finger." Bryce thrusts deep inside me, his finger exploring the sensitive tissues inside. My muscles instinctively clench around it. "I will learn what pleases you and you will learn what pleases me. You will take whatever I give you and you'll want more. We will fuck like wild animals, but there will be so much passion and fire, you'll never be able to extinguish the flames."

"Oh God!"

Bryce lowers his mouth again continuing his torturous assault swirling his tongue on my clit, while he plunges his finger deep inside me with confident thrusts at a steady pace. I can't take much more. My breathing has slowed and I feel warm, almost feverish. The vision of his dark hair between my thighs giving me complete pleasure is an erotic image that arouses me and will be embedded in my brain forever.

Every part of my body tensing, has me wondering why. "I'm not sure what's happening to my body? But oh, oh…oh my god."

"That's it. Let your body take you higher and higher until it can't take anymore and then let go, Angel. Come for me." He lowers his mouth once more, continuing his assault with lashes of his tongue.

Grabbing his head, I hold it steady with both hands, thinking maybe I might be hurting him. My legs start shaking. My back is arched.

I try to be quiet knowing Austin will hear. I whimper, but I'm too loud. My vision blurs and my whole body shakes. I claw at the sheets and buck my hips into his delicious mouth.

I've never felt so good in my whole life. Wave after wave, my body shakes and quivers, taking me under for another ride.

Bryce doesn't stop. He laps and licks, every last drop until my body is limp and I'm pushing him away from the sensitivity.

When I can finally breathe, tears seep from the corners of my eyes and I laugh. "That's what the girls were talking about."

He crawls up my body licking his way up, alternating with gentle butterfly kisses. I feel his hot breath on my stomach. "What do you mean?"

"They told me it's amazing. Sensations I've never felt before. It's mind blowing!"

"Is that the first time you've had an orgasm?"

I smile a sheepish smile, almost embarrassed. "Yes."

Bryce holds my face in his hands and looks deep in my eyes. "Do you have any idea what you do to me?" His hard cock grinds against my upper thigh and hip.

I look down to see him grinding against me. "I think I know."

He rolls me on top of him and I straddle his hips. My pussy lips are wide open, slick and wet on both sides of his cock. He pulls me down onto his chest and says, "Let me see these beautiful tits!" Bryce unclasps my bra at the back, he pulls the straps off each shoulder and flings it across the room.

Bryce urges me to sit up. "Let me see you. You're so beautiful!"

My hands instantly and instinctively want to cover up.

He quickly takes hold of my wrists and holds them to my side.

My nipples are so hard. They stick out at least half an inch. With both of his extremely large hands he cups me from underneath. "They fit perfectly in my hands." He says with his husky purr and a hint of satisfaction in his voice.

He pinches and tugs on my nipples between his forefinger and thumb. He twists and pulls on them until the tingling sensation goes straight to my pussy and I shiver. He holds onto my hips, pulling and pushing me, helping me glide up and down the length of his massive cock. My sensitive lips slide along every plump vein. Long strides, I take to the tip of his cock, feeling every sensitive sensation along the way until my clit bumps on the swollen head, making me shiver with pleasure.

"That's it Angel, ride me. I want to make you come again."

Pulling my upper body down, he lowers my breasts to his mouth and then he alternates between sucking, flicking and biting the right, then the left. I've never felt anything like it before. I pick up the pace, gliding faster, up and down the length of his cock.

"You like this, don't you, Angel?" The sexy purr in his voice is enough to make me lose control.

The pressure's building and I inhale sharply. "Yes!" I breathe savouring every sensation between my lips and my clit. My breathing accelerates as I stare down into his dark intense eyes. The look of pure satisfaction surfaces across his face.

"That's it Angel, come for me." Pleasure spirals all around me as I increase the pressure, grinding harder against his cock, thinking how hot he looks beneath me and how good he makes me feel.

All of a sudden another orgasm rips through me, taking me by surprise. I burst into a million pieces as my body starts convulsing.

His fingers grip my hips still guiding me along his stiff shaft, making sure my orgasm lasts, sending me into oblivion.

My back arches and my head tilts back, chest heaving outward, nipples rock hard. My hair tickles his thighs as I let out a whimper of ecstasy. My body shakes as he watches with such pleasure and happiness, observing my every move.

When I start to go limp, he pulls me down onto his chest, wrapping his large muscular arms around me. Hugging me tightly, where it's almost too much and I can't breathe, but then he eases up.

I feel so safe and warm in his arms, I don't want him to let go.

I pop my head up and look at him with my mega-watt smile. "My name is Keera."

He smiles back and extends his hand out for me to shake. "Nice to meet you. My name is Bryce."

He rolls me onto my side and then slides out of bed gracefully. He stands only inches away from my face with his rock hard cock in his hand. "Now that we've had our introductions, what are we going to do about this?"

I stare at his hard cock, which is way too close to my mouth and I think about my friends when they'd talk about giving a blowjob, but I don't think I'm ready to do that yet.

Bryce starts stroking his cock. I can't believe he's doing that in front of me, but my eyes dance with amazement, watching, and learning, taking it all in. I can't take my eyes off of him. I've never seen anyone masturbate before. A tingle shoots straight to my pussy, making me ache for him. He's so frickin' hot!

His eyes darken and bore into mine and I watch mesmerized as he strokes himself. He's staring like he wants to eat me alive, a sight that has me shivering from head to toe.

Stroking rhythmically up and down, his other hand fondles my breast pinching, pulling, and tugging. "Touch your pussy!"

I hesitate. Not knowing if I can do this in front of him and he senses it.

"Look at me, Angel." His hand moves from my breasts to his tight abs. He splays his fingers across each hard slab of muscle, massaging upward across his hard pecs where he pinches his own nipple between his fingers.

My eyes widen with desire. He's showing me how to touch myself. To masturbate.

"You like what you see?"

"Yes."

"I love what I see, too." His tongue slides along the seam of his lower lip, as if he tastes me and he eyes me up and down with his dark hazel eyes burning into my skin. "I want you with me, Angel. I want you to come with me."

Jeez, what the intensity of his stare does to me.

He lifts my hand and places it on top of my breast with his hand, teaching me how to do it. "Show me how you can touch yourself."

My fingers brush against my nipple and it puckers and hardens instantly.

"That's it show me how hard these beauties can get." He says coaxing me.

His deep sexy voice spurs me on to continue. My other hand slowly slides across my abs up to my aching breasts, I cup them both, trying to release the ache I feel.

"Ah fuck, you don't know how fucking sexy that is. Look what you're doing to me."

I want to be sexy and seductive, giving him ultimate pleasure like he's given to me. My hands caress back down my belly.

"That's it, Angel, go lower. I want to see you touch that sweet pussy."

I do what he tells me to do by letting my legs fall open wide. My hand caresses to my lower abs until my fingers find and explore in between my lips, massaging down one side then the other. I'm surprised at how wet I am. My fingertips move upward finding my clit. I circle and massage it rapidly, enlarging it.

"Jesus!" His eyes turn to a fiery red watching me play with myself. "You're so sexy." He says appreciatively with a husky purr. His stroking quickens and I watch as his balls lift and tighten. "Grab my balls."

I reach underneath getting a handful. Feeling them is another new experience for me and as soon as I touch him, they tighten immediately, he can't hold back.

"Fuck, I'm gonna come." He groans and I watch intently as he inhales, then exhales, letting the air out a little at a time.

I stare fiercely at the expressions on his face. His whole body stiffens and his muscles bulge. His eyes close and then open again. His jaw and neck strain and I watch as he falls apart.

He spurts his warm come all over my breasts and stomach and I watch with amazement.

When he starts breathing again at a normal pace, he looks at me with the biggest smile. "Do you see what you do to me? I swear I've been hard since the first day I saw you."

His eyes gleam appreciatively as they inspect the droplets of come scattered across my breasts and belly. "I've marked you. YOU ARE MINE!"

What? Holy shit. Where'd that come from? Slow down, your making my head spin. What is he thinking? That I'm his now?

4

REACHING FOR THE face cloth on the side table, he gently wipes the come off my tits and stomach. I'm amazed at how gentle he is as he cleans me up with such care, but I'm still thrown off balance by his comment. I gaze intently as he wipes the come off the head of his still swollen cock.

He lies back down on the bed next to me, turning on his side with his head propped up on his hand. "You didn't come, did you?"

"Well yeah, twice."

"I wanted you to come three times for me. We'll work on that tomorrow. I promise."

He lifts my body so I'm facing him and kisses my lips gently, then his tongue parts them. Deepening the kiss with long leisure licks. When he pulls away he looks deep in my eyes. "You don't know how much this means to me. I know you've never done this before. And for you to give yourself to me? It's the biggest gift you could ever give me. I don't even know how to describe what I'm feeling right now, except that you make me so happy." He hugs and kisses me again.

"I want to break you in gently, because I know you're a virgin. We're going to take it slow. And before you know it, this…" Bryce grabs his hard cock and strokes it again. "Is going to fit in that tight little pussy of yours." He bumps the head of his cock against my clit.

What the hell? He went from sincere and sweet to blunt rudeness in a millisecond.

How is that monster going to fit?

His hands touch my cheeks and his thumbs caress slowly as he looks deep in my eyes. "Don't worry, the first time I stick this in, we'll go slow, let you adjust." Christ, it's almost like he can read my mind.

Bryce pushes me down and then flips me on my side, so my back is facing his front and I can feel that monster of a cock on the crack of my butt.

His large arms wrap around me. I'm in a cocoon of warmth, feeling his muscles flex to hold me tight.

At this moment I realize there's nowhere else I'd rather be and I'd almost do anything he wants me to do. I sigh contently and melt into him.

"Austin's my brother." His breath gusts against my ear. "He keeps telling me to leave him out of this. That he wants nothing to do with this. He's been flipping out ever since I brought you home with me."

I lean into him, turning my head so I can see his reaction. "You mean, because you kidnapped me."

A hint of a smile forms on his beautiful mouth. "No, I didn't kidnap you. I was keeping you safe. You passed out in the parking lot. Don't you remember?"

"I remember bits and pieces. Did someone put something in my drink? Is that why I passed out?"

"I didn't see anyone go near your table, but then I came in late. You and your friends were coming out of the washroom when I saw you."

His mouth gets close to my ear and he whispers. "I remember the first time I saw you in the grocery store. I couldn't keep my eyes off of you. I had this feeling in me. I don't know how to explain it. I've never felt that way before. I knew I had to meet you. I had to have you."

I have the urge to tell him how he makes me feel, but something is telling me I need to hold back.

"What if I'm married?"

He looks deep in my eyes with an intense searing gaze. "You aren't." He says confidently.

"Oh yeah, how do you know?"

"You wouldn't have given in to me so easily. But there is one thing I need to know. Any boyfriends that are going to get in the way?"

"In the way of what?" I ask.

"Me and you. Together."

"No. Any girlfriends or wives I should know about?"

"No. Good now that that's settled." Bryce says concluding his business.

We're both smiling at each other with goofy grins.

His big strong arms hold me and my arms hold his. Our bodies intertwine and silence fills the room.

I am sated. Any tension that's been built up is now gone. We hold each other, enjoying the silence, feeling exquisite pleasure rushing through our bodies. I don't want this feeling to end, but I have to ask, "Where does Austin go all day?"

"He's been setting up our hunting camp, because I'm a little preoccupied."

"What do you hunt? Besides women, obviously."

He ignores my last comment. "Rabbit, bear, moose, deer mostly.

I let out a big yawn, I can't help myself. I'm exhausted.

Lying on my back, I close my eyes, but I can feel him staring and when I open them again, he's studying every feature on my face.

"I want to kiss your lips again. I want to kiss your cheek, your neck. I want to kiss you from head to toe. I can't believe that you're actually lying right beside me. In my bed. I'm lying here torturing myself, thinking of all the things I can do to you and I'm getting hard again."

"So kiss me." I say softly.

He lowers his mouth onto mine giving me a gentle lush wet kiss. I'm getting hot and needy almost immediately. Suddenly he pulls away and I hear the regret in his voice. "I should stop. I'll let you sleep now."

Lying his head down, he twitches and then falls asleep.

Sunlight's shining through the outer edge of the curtains in the morning and I can feel Bryce's hard on, rubbing up against my hip.

He kisses my lips. "Good-morning beautiful."

"Good-morning to you, too. I think that's the best I've slept since my parents died."

Bryce looks at me with such pain in his eyes. Almost like if he could take the pain away from me, he would. "How did your parents die?"

"A head on collision with a logging truck, around a bend in the road. Neither one saw it coming. They died instantly."

He holds me tight and I hear sympathy in his voice. "I'm so sorry."

"Thank you. It's been a rough four years for me, but every day gets a little bit easier. My late grandmother, grandfather, Leena and Katie have always been there for me. My rocks to lean on. If it wasn't for them, I don't know what I would've done."

"I can't wait to meet them."

Taking in the view, I watch as Bryce pulls on some black pajama bottoms, then he turns to the closet and pulls out a black three quarter length velour house coat.

He holds it up in the air as he walks back to the bed. "I would much rather you didn't wear anything, but it's cold in here."

I stand and his eyes are on me in an instant. Scanning my naked body up and down.

He opens it and slips it over my shoulders. And before I can do it up, his arms slide inside and wrap around me. Holding me tight, he looks deep in my eyes. "You make me so happy, I've been dreaming about you and you finally came true."

My heart skips a beat and I smile. A wave of emotions crash down on me. My mind spins and before I have time to think and recover, he's grabbing my hand and pulling me toward the door.

He stops suddenly and looks down at me. "You're not going to bolt again, are you?"

I smile at him. "No, I'm hoping you'll make me breakfast and I can take a shower."

In the kitchen, I sit on the bar stool and watch quietly as Bryce goes to work, making his coffee. "Would you like coffee, tea, or hot chocolate?"

"Tea, please."

I look around noticing the oak cabinets are a medium to dark stain, with a high gloss finish. The counter tops are a U-shaped navy blue granite, so rich looking with the dark wood. The bar stools are on one side of the large raised island, in the middle of the kitchen. The light fixture over the island counter has three lights, navy blue marble glass goblets with brass accents.

And then my eyes focus on Bryce. He has his back to me with no shirt on and I can see every well-defined muscle. His back is magnificently sculptured and narrows down extensively to his waist line. I check out how every muscle contracts and then my eyes slide down to his ass cheeks flexing when he moves. When he turns to face me I can see his beautiful chest with a smattering of hair between those perfect pecs, strong shoulders, large muscular arms and eight pack abs. Oh God, how I desperately want to run my hands all over him right now. I lick my lips because my mouth has gone dry as a desert in the summertime heat.

His black pajama bottoms hang on his hip bones and I can see that tight muscle on each side of his hips, that sexy V and the happy trail that I'd love to run my tongue down to see where it goes. I'm really enjoying the view and that tingle, that tingle that doesn't stop; it travels all the way down there.

"Damn!" I whisper and shift on my bar stool. Fuck me. God, he's irresistible.

He flashes me a smile.

I watch Bryce's large talented confident hands and forearms with the thick veins running through them as he works on breakfast and it stirs dirty thoughts and memories of them touching every inch of my body. I then focus on his lips, those perfectly shaped luscious lips and remember that sinful mouth all over me. And that black silky hair that falls into place, looking fabulous. I picture that dark hair between my legs and how I was yanking on it to stop him. And then how I was pushing his head back down for him to keep going. Christ, it's a wonder I'm not having another orgasm just looking at him like this.

Bryce does a double take.

"Sorry, can't help myself." I shrug my shoulder and smile.

He chuckles and slides the plate in front of me.

"A woman could get used to this. I'm starving. Thank you." I take a bite of my toast with bacon, scrambled eggs and home fries on the side. "Mmm, this is good."

"My pleasure and you're welcome."

So polite, too.

Bryce saunters around the counter with his plate in his hand and sits on the bar stool next to me. His hand gently grasps my knee and then slides to my thigh where it stays there the whole time we're eating. His foot gently rubs against mine periodically and I wonder if he needs my touch or does he think I'm going to disappear on him. I savour every second of his touch and the thought sends butterflies fluttering around my stomach.

As we're doing the dishes, I feel a force field surrounding me, like electricity crackling. I feel tingling down my spine and I wonder why he has this effect on me.

I sense Bryce behind me before he touches me. His big strong arms wrap around my belly and he holds me tight. I can feel every rock hard inch of his cock against my ass. He pulls my hair to the side, exposing my neck, running his lips gently down, alternating with kisses. My senses are so intensely heightened, I don't know how to explain this, but I want him again.

Backing up, I put pressure on his cock and squirm suggestively with my ass. By his satisfying moan, I see how it affects him. His hand slips into my robe grabbing a handful of my breast. He fondles my nipples, pinching and tugging on them between his fingers.

The heat and desire consumes and engulfs us both. He spins me around and his mouth is instantly on mine.

His tongue dips deep inside my mouth and his hands make their way to the back of my head holding me in place. My hands reach up grasping his hair and I pull gently, loving how silky his jet black hair feels between my fingers.

We're going wild like animals. Our bodies shaking and trembling, seeking more. I've never lost my head like this before in my whole life. I've always had control, but with him, I don't. What is he doing to me?

He devours my mouth as he picks me up in his massive arms and starts to carry me to the bedroom.

I finally come back down to earth when I realize what his intension is. "Wait! If you want to continue this, I'm going to need a shower."

Bryce switches direction and struts to the bathroom. He can't get me there fast enough. "I get to wash you."

"What? We're taking a shower together?" Bryce gives me his devilish smile. And I take that as a yes.

Bryce closes the bathroom door behind us and reaches in the shower turning the water on. Showering with a man is going to be another new experience for me. He drops his pajama bottoms and is over to me instantly taking the robe gently off my shoulders until it falls on the floor, pooling at my feet.

Every time Bryce sees my naked body, he smiles.

I'm feeling a little shy, so I cover my breasts with my arm and hide my private bits below with my other hand.

Bryce gently removes my arm and hand. "You shouldn't be embarrassed. You have a beautiful body. It's perfect. If I looked like you, I'd be running around naked all day."

He makes me smile.

Wrapping his hand around his stiff cock, Bryce pokes my pussy lips with it. "Don't you see what you do to me?"

I look down, watching his every move, watching his beautiful cock rub and poke me. That thing is huge. Holy hell!

He opens the door and leads me inside, pulling me out of my strange thoughts and into a tight embrace, shielding me as he adjusts the water.

I'm enjoying the warm water, while Bryce lathers up a wash cloth. He starts washing me from my neck and moves downward. He stops at my breasts and glides his hands over my skin and my nipples pucker to tight peaks.

I observe as his touch is so gentle. He washes my belly, then he bends down making his way south to my pussy, focusing as he gently washes. I love the way my heart skips a beat when his fingers lightly feather across my skin. It sends tingles all over my body awakening every nerve ending.

Bryce cups and tugs at my pussy with his oversized hands. "Were going to take care of this."

What does he mean by that?

He spins me around, pulling my arms up over my head and

places my hands on the glass enclosure so I face away from him. "Don't move your hands." I don't, but his deep, sexy, controlling voice makes me want to.

As I'm looking down, I watch as he uses his feet to spread my legs and then I move my ass ever so slightly, squirming suggestively.

He leans into me and I feel him smile against my neck at my attempt to tease. "I know what you're trying to do." He smacks my ass.

"Ouch!" I say with a frown and then a smile.

I know my seduction skills aren't the best, but I will learn. He stays focused, starting with my arms and moves downward. When he gets to my butt, he takes his time. I feel his body lean against me once more as he whispers in my ear. "God, how I love this ass. I love everything about you." He crouches down finishing with my legs and feet.

He loves my body. He loves everything about me? He doesn't know me yet.

"My turn." I say grabbing the cloth from him.

I start at the top and make my way down. When I get to his large muscular chest my hands caress his skin, massaging the soap over his beautiful pecs. I glance up at him through my lashes. The expression on his face is priceless, he can't stop smirking. He loves every second of my touch. His mega-watt smile lights up the shower.

Next I wash his arms. "Arms up." I command and he obliges. I wash his arm pits, his eight pack abs and I can't help myself, I have to run my hands across them, too. I grab hold of his massive cock, wash it first, and then intimately massage the soap up and down his shaft.

His head drops back against the glass with a thud. "Fuck! You make me feel so good!" His body jerks.

Giving him a mischievous smile, I examine his face. I reach under his balls and get a handful, thinking to myself, is this normal for them to be this large? I skim the wash cloth over and around, spending way too much time focusing my attention on the gift he's given me. Complete satisfaction surfaces across my face. This is my new toy and I can't get enough.

Motioning for him to turn around, he listens to me and I place his hands on the glass enclosure above his head. I spread his legs with mine, and with a little help from him.

"Don't move!" Then I smack his ass. I can see his side profile and how his cheeks move up into a smile. I'm thoroughly enjoying this, feeling a rush of adrenaline and I want to smack his ass again.

With the position he's in, I stand back visually devouring his beautiful body. His muscles bulge and flex everywhere. I shake my head, smiling and physically shiver. Focus, Keera.

I continue washing, his powerful back and shoulders, feeling his impressive muscles along the way. My hands move down to his perfect butt. He has the indents on the sides of his ass cheeks. I'm envious. I run my hands up and down each cheek, feeling how perfectly sculptured they are.

Suddenly, I'm overwhelmed by my emotions. I pounce, wrapping my arms around his chest, leaning into his back, my nipples poke his skin.

He groans and spins himself around to face me. "I can't take this anymore."

Bryce pushes the taps off to conserve water. Then his mouth is on mine in an instant, kissing me fiercely, savagely. I'm as excited as he is, kissing him back with the same intensity, the same ferocity. Our tongues dip deep, with long swirling motions.

He growls into my mouth. "I want you. I need to be deep inside your sweet pussy!"

Holy crap, like right now? Am I really going to do this?

Give up my virginity?

5

"DON'T WORRY, WE get tested every six months with my job. I was tested last month. I'm clean and I don't have to worry about you, do I?"

I shake my head no. Am I really going to do this? Bryce is the only guy who has ever had me this aroused and excited. If I don't let him take my virginity than who will I ever trust? Leena's words break through my mind again. "You have to get Jake almost raping you, out of your head and move on. You have to trust someone Keera, or you'll end up being a forty year old virgin. Come on. It's time. We need to get you laid."

His hand strokes up and down his cock making sure it's wet. He presses the head into my clit. An electric current jolts me and I immediately want more. My virginity is something that I've always cherished and wanted to keep until I was married, but the way he looks at me and how he makes me feel, has me weak and I want to give up the fight. You can do this Keera. You know you want him more than anything you've ever wanted before. He's the one. Do not stop him. Let him fuck you, even if it hurts.

"Put your foot on the glass." He says in that deep commanding voice.

I spread my legs wide open.

"Are you sure you want to do this?" He asks.

"Yes," escapes from my mouth without hesitation.

"Are you sure? There's no turning back, once I stick this in."

"I know, I'm ready. I've been thinking about this for a while now. Please Bryce, fuck me!"

He pushes his cock in to the opening. Stretching me.

I let out a pained gasp. "Holy fuck!" I'm feeling pleasure and pain at the same time. He pulls it back out. He can see it's physically painful by the look on my face. His finger slips between my pussy lips. Testing me, making sure I'm wet enough.

He lubricates me with his finger pushing in as far as he can go. In and out, and I pant softly as we stare deep in each other's eyes.

I've never wanted anything so much. I've always fantasized as I lay in bed at night, wondering what it would be like. Wondering if I'd ever let my guard down long enough to have any one get close to me and to experience a real relationship like my parents had. I moan and then whisper in his ear. "Please, try again." I want him so bad.

He drops to his knees and holds on to my thighs, dipping his tongue deep inside me. "You're so wet for me." He says appreciatively.

Seeing him on his knees in front of me, devouring my pussy is pushing me over the edge.

Bryce glides up my body and aggressively slaps a lush wet kiss on my mouth. His tongue slips deep inside, and I taste the juices from my arousal.

"Can you taste how sweet your pussy is?"

"Yes."

The way he speaks to me with that sexy tone fills me with crazed desire.

Bryce pushes his cock inside me again, going a little deeper than before.

"Oh Angel, you're so tight." He hesitates, trying to be gentle. "I'll stay right where I am, to let you adjust. You tell me when you want me to continue."

I tense. What? There is no way, that that monster is not all the way in yet? It's incomprehensible. "I'm fine. Keep going."

"It's going to hurt for a bit, but if you relax, you'll feel nothing but pleasure. I promise."

I love how tender and caring he is, but I think he's prolonging the inevitable.

Holding onto his shoulders, I yell out. "Fuck me. Push it in, all the way!" My body's pressed hard against the glass. His cock inches its way in and I inhale sharply, letting out a fierce cry. "Holy fuck!"

He tenses and stops moving totally.

I look deep in his eyes. "It's okay, don't stop."

"You feel so fucking good right now. Your pussy is so tight. It's sucking my cock, milking me, but I don't want to hurt you."

I circle my hips. "We'll go slow."

"Do you know how hard it is for me not to bang the shit out of you right now? I'm dying! But I'm not going to until I know for sure that you're fine."

I smile, delighted that I have such an intense effect on him and that he's worried that he'll hurt me. He's such a gentleman.

Bryce pulls his thick cock out and gently pushes back inside me, inching further up. "Let me know if you need me to stop."

"I'm good, keep going."

Kissing me with long leisure licks, he strokes his hardened tongue along mine and intimately sucks on my tongue. I know he's trying to keep my mind off the intense pain I'm feeling and it's working.

He holds me up against the glass enclosure with his massive arm under my butt while pinching and tugging at my nipples, making them pulse with pleasure and then he leans down to nibble and bite on them, making sure his cock stays firmly in place, sending an exquisite sensation throughout my whole body.

I relax my muscles briefly and realize it doesn't hurt as much if I'm not so tense.

Relax Keera, relax. I repeat in my head.

To ease the discomfort, Bryce circles my clit, massaging it with his thumb. Slowly, he pulls his cock out, a fraction, then he inserts it deeper. It's pleasure and discomfort now, instead of pain.

Never in my wildest dreams did I think that this could be so painful, but yet beautiful and amazing all at the same time. A lump in my throat forms and tears threaten, but I hold them at bay not wanting Bryce to think he's hurting me. I concentrate on the feeling of him inside me. How it stretches my walls and when he pulls back out, how I feel the head of his cock scraping inside. My movements are sensual; I'm surrendering and letting go, enjoying and releasing my inner goddess. My head tilts back and I moan softly to spur him on so he'll stop worrying how he's hurting me and give me what I need. I look deep in his eyes and run my tongue along my lower lip.

He grasps my ass tighter and shoves me hard into the glass, penetrating me deeper. I inhale sharply.

He pulls his cock out to the tip. "Again?"

"Yes." I say breathless.

He slams into me again. Pushing me harder against the glass this time. He's as deep as he can go. I can feel my body warming with beads of sweat. I concentrate on how he feels inside me and how warm it is where we're connected. His movements are slow and methodical, in and out slowly. All the way out, to the head, then slamming all the way back in as far as he can go.

"Play with your clit." His voice commanding.

Reaching down, I massage it frantically in circular motions. Our orgasms build like a thunderous storm, leaving us breathless.

"Bryce, please." My nails almost pierce the skin on his back.

"Come for me, Angel."

That's all I need to hear. My back arches. The back of my head thuds against the glass enclosure and I yell out, "Holy fuck!"

An unexpected muscle contraction has me clamping down on his cock. My legs start to shake and my whole body tenses. Watching me fall apart, right in his arms, destroys any self-control he has left.

"Fuck, fuck, fuck. You feel so good." He shoves hard into me, once, twice, and then he loses his breath. I focus on every facial expression, how he closes his eyes, then looks at me, how he takes in slow laboured breaths. His muscles flex, then release and tighten again. He's pouring his warm come deep inside me, and what a feeling it is. His body shakes and convulses with complete pleasure. Then his body goes limp.

We hold each other tightly and we both laugh, our voices hoarse from our explosive orgasms.

"Wow that was unbelievable." I say breathless.

We both wear a perma-smile as Bryce makes his way down my neck kissing me softly.

"I've never felt this way before. I don't know what you're doing to me!" Slowly he slides his cock out and I wince with discomfort as we watch a few droplets of blood fall to the shower floor.

"Did I hurt you?" His voice is caring and concerned.

"No, that was amazing!"

"Are you sure?"

"Yes, I feel phenomenal!" I put my head down, thoroughly embarrassed that I'm crying. I don't want him to notice.

It's cold now, chilling us to the bone since the water is off and our workout has ceased, so Bryce quickly remedies that by turning the water back on and cranking it to hot for a few seconds, shielding me as he adjusts to warm.

We let out a sigh of relief when the warm water rains down upon us. We wash up again very quickly.

When we get out of the shower, Bryce wraps a plush towel

around me and then gets one for himself. He turns to look at me and sees the tears flowing. He's over to me in an instant. "What's wrong Angel? Did I hurt you? Tell me, please." His pleading voice has me thinking about why I'm crying.

He brings me over to the bench and sits down beside me. I can see it in his eyes that it kills him to see me this way. His finger lifts my chin so I'll look in his eyes and he waits patiently for me to speak.

I don't know what to say, so I blurt it out. "I'm not a virgin anymore!" I'm laughing and crying at the same time.

"Oh, Angel." He wipes the tears off my face with his thumbs and looks at me, like he's at a loss for words.

"I was saving it until I got married." I can't control my emotions. My chest heaving for my next breath as I try to calm down. He holds me tight not letting me go.

"I want to marry you."

I give him a half-hearted smile.

I'm pissed off at myself for giving in so easily. I've been such a good girl all these years. My virginity was important to me to keep until I was married. Was I afraid of still being a virgin later in life? Did I want to see if I could trust someone enough to actually go through with it?

I look up to see Bryce is sitting right next to me, silent, still, with his arm wrapped around me.

My face turns red. Embarrassed that I'm crying over this.

Bryce lifts my chin and wipes the tears off my face with his thumb, once again. Then he kisses my left cheek.

I study the sculptured muscle tone on his face and his gorgeous hazel eyes. Every time he looks deep in my eyes, it sends a delicious shiver down my spine, and an ache between my legs.

Bryce pads across the bathroom floor with bare feet to the vanity drawer. His towel drops and what an eyeful I get. His beautiful body has hard slabs of muscle everywhere. I focus on his ass. There's no way it could be any more perfect than it is. He pulls a wide tooth comb out of the drawer, and when he turns, I can see his massive chest. My eyes scan his eight pack abs, his happy trail to his hips and yes, his abundant package at his groin.

I shift on the bench because staring at that body does me in, every time.

That's when it strikes me and I realize, it's him! How sexy he is. That face, his muscular body, those eyes, his jet black hair that falls perfectly into place, every large defined muscles in his back and chest, his abs, that sexy V at his hips, that ass, oh God, that ass! It's him, it's all his fault that I gave up my virginity, and partially mine, I guess. If he wasn't so goddamn gorgeous, this would've never happened. I've always had control when it came to men getting close to me.

His lips curl up to one side of his mouth to reveal his sexy dimple. God, that smile, he's so mischievous and adorable at the same time.

"You want this?" His cock is hard again. He's teasing me by making it jump up and down.

I can't help but laugh, he's too adorable.

Bryce reaches for the dial of the timer on the wall, illuminating the heat lamp on the ceiling, in the middle of the room. It's our only source of heat other than the heated floors and wood stove in the living room. Now that the temperature had plummeted, Indian summer is over and winter is coming.

He takes the velour house coat off the hook and lifts me by my hand. My towel drops revealing my naked body and he stops dead in his tracks. He stands back admiring the view as my nipples jet out to rock hard peaks. I shiver and he can see how cold I am. He drapes the house coat around me, tying the belt to secure it and then he wraps his massive arms around me, warming me up and we sway back and forth, lost in a tight embrace for quite a while.

What is he doing to me? I'm breaking all my rules. I've never lost my head over any guy like this.

Bryce lets out a regretful groan releasing me to pull me over to the vanity mirror. He slides his pajama bottoms on and I let out a disappointed sigh. I love seeing him naked and feeling him plastered against me. I'm craving his touch again, like a drug surging through my veins. I want more. Already. Will I ever get enough?

I comb out my hair and watch observantly while he shaves. We both brush our teeth. Him in one sink, me in the other. It's such a normal domesticated thing to do and yet we both enjoy it immensely, standing back observing each other. The smiles plastered across our faces are proof of our enjoyment. Standing next to this man getting ready to take on the day, feels so comfortable and normal, like I've been doing it for years.

Bryce takes a black bottle of cologne out of the cabinet, returning my thoughts to the here and now and sprays some on.

"What cologne is that?" My curiosity has me asking.

"It's 'Unforgivable' by Sean John."

"You smell so good!" I could eat you up.

"Thank you."

I gasp as a horrific thought enters my mind. "Oh my god! I don't have my birth control pills." Worry sets across my face.

"Everything's going to be fine." Bryce says in that deep voice of his.

I glare at him with a frown and a look that says, have you lost your mind? "No, it's not."

"Why are you taking them, anyway?"

"If you must know? To regulate my periods. Bad cramps."

"Oh, I gave you one this morning in your eggs and I watched you eat it."

I frown again. Hesitating for a moment, while it registers. "How did you get my pills?"

"Well, it's a long story."

"I've got nothing but time. Spill it!" My voice sounds a little angry even for my ears.

"I followed you home from the grocery store and sat a few

doors down watching you go in the house. Then I saw that asshole that was staring at you in the grocery store pull up and get out of his car. I don't like the way he looks at you."

"He was there at the grocery store? I didn't see him."

"Who is he?"

"I don't know his name. He follows me around town, watching. He's never approached me. He's harmless."

"He's not harmless!" Bryce raises his voice a fraction and when he realizes he lowers it back down. "He was looking in your window, so I drove by slow and scared the shit out of him then he took off. I had to drive my pain in the ass brother back to the cabin, because he's a little impatient and when I made it back to your place, that asshole was looking in your window again."

"And?"

"I'm getting to that part. So I parked down the street again and snuck up on him. This time I really scared the shit out of him. He knocked over your planter that was on the window sill and fell to the ground. He got back up, bolted and then he was gone!"

"So?"

"So then I thought I would look around. I went to your back door and it was unlocked. Do you have any idea what that asshole could have done to you?"

"Yeah, he could have kidnapped me."

"Are you being a smart ass?"

"Me? Noooo!" I say sarcastically.

Bryce hugs and kisses me.

I push him back to look at him. "You're distracting me. Are you going to answer me? How did you get my pills?"

"But I like to distract you." He smirks at me and releases me. "I was looking around."

"You were inside my house?" My voice raises a few notches.

"I had to make sure there wasn't someone else and I had to see if you were safe. I heard the shower running, so I looked in to see if you were okay and, oh boy, you were doing fine. I couldn't keep my eyes off of you."

"You stood there and watched me?"

"Yeah." Bryce is lost in deep thought for a few seconds and then he recovers, shaking his head. "Then I had to make sure the house was secure."

It struck me then, that every delicious tingle I'd felt was my body instinctively reacting to his presence, unaware that he was near.

Oh god! He watched me in the shower when I was fantasizing that he was standing in front of me with his lips and hands all over me.

"Bet you got an eyeful?"

"Yeah, I wanted to climb right in there and seduce you, but you probably would've screamed."

"So that's why that towel was laid out for me?"

"That was the next day."

"You were in my house two days in a row?" A little obsessive don't you think? I can't believe this. To do what? To watch me in the shower again? "Why?"

"When I came back the second day, your stalker was circling your house, looking in your windows again. He was acting crazy, trying to get inside through the window, because I'd locked the doors, but I scared him off. You're welcome, by the way." He says pausing, waiting for an answer. "Do you always leave your doors unlocked?"

"Just during the day. I've never had to worry about it."

"Not anymore, you don't." Bryce lifts my chin so I'll look at him. "Do you hear me?"

"Yes." Control freak.

"I mean it!"

"Okay, jeez, I won't leave my doors unlocked anymore."

"Good." Bryce says satisfied with my answer.

"You moved my keys and you checked out my bra and thong, which you left on the floor."

"I touched your keys, but your bra and thong were on the floor already. So in my travels, I found your pills in the kitchen and thought I'd bring them because I had a feeling you'd be with me and need them."

I pace across the bathroom floor shaking my head while my arms fly up in the air. "I can't fucking believe this! You planned to kidnap me!" My face turns red like I'm going to blow steam from the top of my head.

"You've got a red headed temper, don't you?" Bryce laughs and smiles down at me, which infuriates me even more.

Irritated, I shake my head and point my finger at him. "Don't even go there right now."

Bryce stops me from pacing by standing in front of me while he holds my wrists at my side. "Angel, look at me." He bends down to look deep in my eyes. "I didn't kidnap you. I was keeping you safe."

I got my Irish temper from my grandfather. It takes a lot to get me riled up, but when I do, and finally blow, people know about it.

"Your stalker was in your house. Think about that."

6

THE ROOM SPINS, so I quickly walk over to the bench and sit in silence, thinking as a series of images flashes in my mind of all the encounters I've had with the stalker.

Bryce comes to sit beside me, but doesn't say a word. He sees my wheels turning, so he waits letting it sink in, I presume.

"Well, I thought he was harmless, but if he's getting bold enough to look in my windows and come in my house." I look down at my hands still lost in deep thought. "Holy shit! I heard a big bang that woke me up out of a dead sleep that night. I wonder if that was him. Oh my god! What if he was watching me sleep?" I shiver at the thought.

Bryce takes my hand in his. "That's why I was following you around. I need to keep you safe." His intense gaze sears into my eyes. "How many beers did you have at the bar?"

"Two. Why?"

"Because when you left the bar you were staggering and before that you were fine. I'm trying to figure out why you lost consciousness?"

"The thought crossed my mind when I was in the washroom that someone slipped some kind of drug in my beer."

"That would explain why you were fine most of the night and then it hit you suddenly." Bryce is in deep thought. "Who would do that? Other than your stalker?"

"I don't know. But the next question is, why would someone want to drug me?"

"Date rape. Or maybe your stalker was planning on kidnapping you that night."

Lost in thought, I think hard about anyone else that would want to drug me. Then my mind flips to my stalker. What if he was planning all along to kidnap me that night and Bryce ruined his plans?

"I can see the worry on your face. I don't want you stressing over this. I'll keep you safe."

I have no doubt in my mind that he can keep me safe when I'm with him, but what about when he can't be with me every day.

"Where do you live?"

"Barrie."

"Do you work in Barrie?"

"Yes, I'm a firefighter. I'm on a two week vacation right now."

"How far away is Barrie?"

"Just a little over an hour. I can see your wheels turning. Don't worry, we'll figure something out. You can stay with your grandfather or your friends. Hell, you can come with me if you want. I'll be working, but you can stay at my place."

"I'll be fine. I'll stay at my grandfather's. He'd love to see me."

"When I return to work after my vacation, I have to work for four days, and then I'm coming back. Okay?"

Bryce lifts me from the bench and holds me close in his arms. His finger tilts my chin up so I'll look at him. "Let's do the dishes, then we're going to your house to get you some clothes." He kisses my forehead and I smile.

My head is still spinning from the news of my stalker entering my house.

Bryce holds me steady. "You okay?"

"Yeah. If you wouldn't have followed me home that day…" I hesitate, deep in thought. "What would've happened? Where would I be right now?" I shiver and Bryce holds me tighter.

"Try not to think about it. He's not getting anywhere near you. I'll keep you safe."

"I need to get my journey from the bar."

"It's in the garage. Austin drove it here."

"Boy, you thought of everything didn't you?"

"I didn't plan this, if that's what you're thinking."

"Mmm hmm." I lift one eyebrow and shake my head in disbelief.

He holds me tighter in his big strong arms and kisses my forehead. "Seriously, all I thought about was keeping you safe. You didn't see the way he was acting when he couldn't enter your house, because I'd locked the doors. I'm telling you he's unstable."

"So, if you were trying to keep me safe, why was I tied to your bed? You didn't want me to hurt myself?" I try to be serious, but fail miserably.

He chuckles. "That was a little fantasy of mine and I didn't want you taking off, while I was preoccupied."

"Aww, the truth is finally revealed."

"Come, let's get dressed."

I sit in the passenger seat of Bryce's black dodge pickup truck, with my little red dress that I wore to the bar. It's the only thing I have to wear other than his coat over top to keep me warm. I watch every move he makes and study every feature on his beautiful face. Watching him drive is turning me on and I don't know why. I can't take my eyes off of him.

Too fast. I have to admit, I'm falling too fast.

Bryce looks over at me. He must feel me staring. He smiles

and I smile back moving right beside him. He wraps his arm around my shoulder.

We pull up to my house and we go in. "Stay behind me." His eyes darken like he's on a mission. The expression on his face is serious and determined. His stance and whole demeanor changes before my eyes. He's tense and rigid, almost like he's a different person and I find myself hoping there's no one here for their sake, because he's ready to beat the hell out of anyone that crosses his path. He locks the door behind us and we search from one room to another, scoping it out.

"Let me know if you see anything out of place." His voice is deep and he's focused.

"Okay."

He physically relaxes when he sees my house is vacant and everything is fine. His expression softens instantly.

His hand rubs the kitchen table and he scoops me up in his arms holding me tight and whispers in my ear. "I'm going to fuck you on this table one day."

What? That is too weird. Two different personalities? "Oh yeah? Is that a promise?"

"A promise, I can't wait to keep." Bryce tickles me and I squirm out of his arms running and giggling toward my bedroom. Bryce is hot on my heels, chasing after me. He swoops me up in his arms, tackling and rolling me, so I'm on top when we land on the bed. "You can't run from me. I'll chase you to the ends of the earth and I'll always catch you. Look how fucking hard you make me doing that." He pulls me down and kisses me ferociously.

"Go get your things together." Bryce smacks my ass and then helps me get up. Walking into my closet, I gather some clothes and a suit case, lying them on the bed, and I pack quickly.

Bryce flops back down onto my bed with his feet crossed and one hand behind his head, the other rubs across my duvet cover. "I'm going to fuck you here, too." I see the determined expression on his face and how cute he looks with his naughty smile and it makes me giggle again.

"I love hearing you giggle." He gracefully gets up to hold me again and whispers in my ear. "I'm going to fuck you in every room of this house." His large hands reach down to grab both cheeks of my ass and he pulls me up as I wrap my legs around his waist. He tugs me hard against his impressive erection.

"Oh my!" I say.

"See what you do to me. You make me so fucking horny. I can't wait to bury my cock deep inside you again." He slaps a wet lush kiss on my mouth and as I start to deepen the kiss he pulls away. "We can't start this now, but I'll make good on my promise."

I sigh as my legs slide down his.

"Shit, we have to go." Bryce says quickly.

I rush to my walk-in closet. "Wait, I have to get changed." I throw on a pair of jeans and a t-shirt as Bryce peeks in to watch.

At the back door, Bryce picks up my snowsuit and boots. "You might need these if it gets cold."

Locking up the house, we head to the truck. Bryce looks up the north side of the street and then down the south looking for any signs of my stalker. As we drive down the road, Bryce looks in the rear view mirror quite often. "I want you to feel safe at the cabin."

"I do feel safe when I'm with you."

He slides his arm around my waist and pulls me across the seat, close to him. His arm wraps around my shoulder and he leans over and kisses my hair. "Good."

I look up at him. "Your cabin is nice. Was it built recently?"

"We had it built last year. This is our first year that we get to use it. The exterior we had a contractor do, the interior, we mostly did ourselves. It took us a bit longer than expected, but only because we have full-time jobs and we could only come when we had time off."

"That's why I haven't seen you around town before."

"Yeah, we've been busy with the cabin."

Driving down the dirt road, I see that the leaves on the trees have changed to autumn colours. The scent of pine trees wafts up through the truck as we climb through our hilly and mountainous region. I have no idea where I am out here as we travel the back roads of town, but it is very scenic and I'm enjoying every moment of it sitting next to Bryce.

We pull up in the driveway next to the cabin and Bryce squeezes my knee. "Stay right there." He runs around the truck to open the door and holds out his hand for me to take. "Let me take you for a tour."

"Okay." Such a gentleman.

Looking from the outside view of the cabin, I can see large triangular shaped windows in front with a huge peek, and a forest green metal roof.

The rest of the cabin sprawls out on each side of the peak. The huge logs are a light to medium stain. There's a winding stamped concrete sidewalk leading to the front door. The front yard is landscaped beautifully with white crushed stone and huge rocks strategically placed.

"This is beautiful!"

"Thank you, we had a vision and I think we succeeded." Bryce guides me to the backyard on the asphalt driveway with his hand on my lower back leading me toward the fairly large garage that matches the log cabin.

Looking around inside the garage, I see my Journey, and two large doors at each end of the garage.

"Why do you have two large garage doors?"

"We had it built like this so we can take our toys out the back and be right on the trail."

I glance around the garage eyeing two snowmobiles and a four wheeler.

"Austin has his ATV."

"Oh." I say softly.

My eyes scan around the garage taking in a large metal work bench with a vise bolted to the side of it. A large tool box stands beside a large saw for woodworking, I'm guessing, and a huge gun safe with a combination lock that stands beside them. There are numerous tools suspended on the wall with hooks and a metal cabinet with labels of various sized nuts and bolts hangs beside them. Very clean and organized.

When we walk outside we pass by a huge wood archway with a concrete pad at the bottom. The inscription carved in the wood at the top reads, The Hamilton's. Underneath the inscription are three large chains with hooks.

"What's that for?" I ask.

"We hang the deer on the hooks to gut and clean them."

"Oh." My eyes glance over to the huge wood pile with a log splitter next to it. "Wow, you guys have all the toys."

"Have you ever shot a rifle before?"

"No, I haven't."

"I'm going to teach you that."

We walk back to the truck to get my bag out and suddenly Bryce picks me up in his arms, surprising me.

"What are you doing?"

"Anything I want. Just lie back and enjoy the ride."

Bryce bends down retrieving the suitcase with his fingers and I melt into his warm strong chest as he walks up the winding sidewalk to the front door.

He places the suitcase inside the door. "We're going to do this right. The last time I carried you through the doorway, you were passed out."

"Jeez, with this kind of treatment, I'm never going to want to leave."

"That's what I hope. You're so light, like a feather." He lifts me up and down in his arms. I giggle.

Making dinner together was a true test in surviving acute sexual tension. It radiated between the both of us so much that it got to be unbearable. We started out standing close to each other, but not quite touching. We'd gaze into each other's eyes and smile. Occasionally we'd bump into each other while we tried to focus on the task at hand, but after the slight grazing of a simple touch on the hip or a rub against my butt, our focus diverted to each other. Feeling that familiar energy pulsing that I love, and have become accustomed to in the couple days of knowing him, surrounds us.

Suddenly Bryce's powerful frame traps me against the counter. Hunger and desire radiates off of him in waves. Holding the back of my neck, he leans down slowly, kissing me and I relish the feel of his lips fused to mine.

His large hands slide down and cup my ass cheeks with a firm hold, while he grinds his cock into me hard. He deepens the kiss swirling his tongue around mine, as I run my hands through his hair and tug gently. Bryce moans and it reverberates in my mouth, working me up into a frenzy. My pulse quickens and my hearts racing. I'm getting really warm and I feel Bryce's temperature rise. I try hard to control my breathing, but fail miserably.

Bryce pulls away, flustered and panting, too. "Holy fuck, I can't catch my breath. I can't even concentrate around you. What are you doing to me?"

Warmth fills my heart and complete joy and happiness flows through me as I pant and smile. "What are you doing to *me*?"

"Christ, that body of yours."

My eyes scan appreciatively up and down his body. "That's what your body does to me."

Bryce shakes his head and grabs my hand. "Come, let's eat."

"Oh." I say disappointed and sigh.

Bryce chuckles.

We calm our hormones down for a bit while we sit at the breakfast bar and eat. After dinner we clean up and save a plate for Austin.

"Come. I've been thinking about this all damn day." Bryce tugs my hand leading me to the bathroom. "Were taking a bath together."

"Oh, okay."

Why am I so willing to do what he wants? I don't know, maybe I'm tired of being independent and need someone else to lean on? Or am I sitting back observing, taking notes for future reference. Or am I so hot for him, that he distracts me and I lose my mind when he's so close. I think it's my last thought.

I follow his every movement. He takes shave gel, razors and new wash cloths out of the linen closet, while the tub fills with warm water, and places them on the shelf that surrounds the edge of the Jacuzzi. He takes a lighter out of the vanity drawer and lights the candles on the counter and surrounding the tub.

Then he closes the gap, prowling towards me, attacking my clothing. First my shirt, then he unbuttons my tight faded jeans with holes strategically placed throughout the thighs and knees.

"I love these jeans on you." He runs his hand down the curve of my butt. "And these holes have been teasing the hell out of me all day. I want to rip them off of you." His fingers find their way inside the hole and he caresses my skin gently. "I've been rock hard watching you prance around in them, but I would much rather see you naked." He yanks at the zipper and slides them down, then helps me step out of them.

Standing in front of him, I'm wearing my baby blue lacy bra and thong. "And I like these. I mean, I really like these." His finger runs along the lace at my breasts. "But for now, they've got to go." He skims his fingers along my sensitive skin while he takes them off of me, sending a shiver jetting through my body.

I watch him strip off his cloths in no time. His hard cock springs out of his boxers and he kicks them away as they hit the floor. I scan appreciatively up and down his naked hard body and shiver. That body of his gives me an agonizing ache between my legs every time.

"I want you to get in the tub and sit on the edge." I do what I'm told. He climbs in the tub and grabs the razor. "I'm going to shave you and then you'll shave me."

"Shave what?" Somehow I already know the answer before he stares at my pussy with that cute corner of the mouth grin, showing me his adorable dimple. Leena once said to me, 'You need to trim Chewbacca, or shave it right off. Guys think it's hot'. I've wanted to shave it off for years now, but had no one in my life to see it, so what would be the point?

"Spread your legs wide." Bryce doesn't hesitate. He quickly gets to work. He squirts the shave gel in his hand, kneels in the water and wipes gently on my pubic hair.

I can't believe he's doing this. He focuses, shaving in gentle long strokes. He rinses between each stroke, while I hold my breath.

"Trust me." He says.

I relax after a bit and decide that I'm really enjoying this. His fingers graze my sensitive skin as he opens up my lips and shaves with his other hand. His touch is gentle and really focused. Occasionally he'd look up to meet my gaze then lower and focus again. He's making sure he doesn't nick me. He looks up at me and does a double-take, smiling. "You can breathe, you know."

Exhaling, I didn't notice I wasn't breathing until he brought it to my attention. I can't take my eyes off of him. His touch is so intimate and erotic at the same time.

A terrible thought crosses my mind and I wonder if he's ever done this before? I wonder how many other women there were and what they look like. Now, is not the time to ask!

"You like this, Angel?"

"Yes." I squirm with a needy ache.

"Keep still." He warns.

I try to stay still, but it's difficult. His touch always makes my skin so sensitive and I always want more.

"Scoot down in the water, rinse and come back out. I want to make sure I've got it all." He says as he finishes.

I do as I'm told, rinsing thoroughly.

His fingers open all my silky folds as he does another close inspection. I'm spread wide open, looking down, watching his every move as he takes his time touching and caressing every single spot of my sensitive flesh. His confident touch makes me hot and I think if he doesn't do something to me soon, I'm going to spontaneously combust.

He peeks up at me and sees exactly what he's doing to me, almost like he can read my mind. He licks up each side of my folds, like he's licking a lollipop, with slow leisurely licks.

His touch fires every cell in my body and I shamelessly spread my legs wider. With my arms extended outward, behind me, I lean on my hands and my head falls back enjoying the pleasure of his magical tongue. My movements are sensual and seductive. My hips circle around his tongue and just as I'm really starting to move and enjoy it. He stops licking me.

I let out a sigh. "What the… why'd you stop?"

He gives me his wicked smile. "You have to wait." He palms my pussy. "This is so fucking sexy. I love you bald." He stands up in the water, stroking his cock with his overly large hand. "Your turn to do me!"

His statement arrows straight down to my pussy. I can't believe the effect he has on me. I've never felt this way before.

I switch spots with him and kneel in the water with the razor in my hand. "Spread 'em."

He listens to me, giving me the most adorable smile I've ever seen.

I squirt the shave gel in my hand, lathering it up as I softly rub it on his jet black pubic hair. I make sure I cover the whole surface and Bryce groans. "Here we go?" I start at the top with long gentle strokes, trying to be very careful. Biting my lip helps me focus and I don't even realize I'm doing it until it almost hurts. I hold my breath and rinse between each stroke, making sure it's clean.

"Open wider." I command and he does what he's told.

I lift his balls and shave underneath. I hold onto his cock

moving it from one side to the other. My face and lips are so close to his cock. I peek up to see his reaction. His gaze is dark and intense and I wonder if he's envisioning me opening my mouth and wrapping my lips around the head.

Seductively, I lick my lips and he actually squirms as I'm shaving him. "Yeah, you might not want to move. This is my first time doing this."

"Oh fuck, you're driving me insane."

"Keep still!" I warn him. "I'm not done yet."

"Getting me back. Aren't you? Little tease."

A mischievous smile forms at the corner of my mouth while holding onto his balls moving them from one side to the other making sure I give him a smooth shave and to drive him crazy. They tighten immediately.

I shave over the whole area again, gently caressing and touching as I do my final inspection. I concentrate hard making sure I haven't forgot anything. I look up at him and he has such an intense, burning, sexy stare that I do a double take.

Looking back down, I rub the whole area with my fingers, feeling for any stubble. I lift his tight balls and slide my finger on the soft spot between his ass and balls.

He shivers and groans. "Do you have any idea what you're doing me? This is so fucking erotic!" Unexpectedly, he takes the razor from my hand and drops it on the shelf. "I can't take this. I want you now." He rinses off the shave gel, and takes my hand.

"Come with me."

7

WE'RE WALKING THROUGH the cabin totally naked, hand in hand. We make it just inside the bedroom door, he spins me, caging me against the wall. He kicks the door closed, then his mouth is on mine with a wet lush kiss. Our tongues dip deep inside with swirling motions.

He shoves me aggressively against the wall with his hard body, while he holds my hands above my head. His knees are bent, so he can place his big swollen cock against my clit and he teases me with the right amount of pressure to drive me mad. I moan in his mouth from the sensation. I can almost hear my heart thumping right out of my chest.

I think about Leena and Katie and how they instructed how to give the perfect blowjob. I think to myself, yeah, I can do this. I want to give him as much sweet pleasure as he's given me.

Bryce notices I want to switch positions when I push myself off the wall, so he doesn't resist. I hold onto his arms, spin him around, and push him hard against the wall.

Dropping to my knees, I look up to see his reaction. His surprised look is priceless. I hold his hard cock with both hands and take him in my mouth. His eyes darken with lust and desire as he gazes down at me. "That's it, Angel, take my cock in that pretty little mouth of yours."

His voice is deep and seductive, sending a pulse of pleasure right to where I want it. His cock is rock hard, but it surprises me that his skin is soft against my tongue and lips.

I pull his cock out and lick my lips, hesitating for a second while I gaze up at him and he stares down at me with wild hungry eyes. I feel him grow hard in my hand. My mouth opens wide and I take his cock to the back of my throat. My head bobs up and down the length of his shaft as I simultaneously give him the right amount of suction while I stroke his wet shaft knowing that my performance is a damn good one because of his moans.

"Christ! Angel, that mouth." I try to take him further. "Fuck, how far can you go?" I pull it all the way out, getting it wet with my saliva. "That's it Angel, get me wet. I feel it dripping down my balls." I suck harder, and faster, trying to relax my throat muscles, so I can take him deeper.

I wipe the dripping saliva around his shaved balls and they tighten immediately.

My pussy is wet and tingling. I had no idea giving him such, sweet pleasure could turn me on this much. My hand strokes up and down his shaft from root to tip, milking him as my head bobs up and down while I suck.

My index finger runs along the soft skin between his balls and ass and I am rewarded with a drop of pre-cum and his deep pleasurable moans.

I feel his fingers snake through my hair while he holds onto my head with both hands securing me in place. He thrusts his hips aggressively to the same rhythm, fucking my mouth. "Fuck, I can't take anymore. You'd better stop or I'm going to come in your mouth."

I don't stop. I grab onto his balls fondling and squeezing

slightly. His thighs tighten, his eyes close, and his breathing is shallow and laboured.

"Fuck, Angel, I'm coming!" I feel a spurt of warm come at the back of my throat.

I try to take it all, swallowing, quickly. He empties every last drop, into my mouth, but there's so much it spills out and down my chin.

When he's finished and his aftershocks fade, he opens his eyes. "Fuck, I'm supposed to make you come first. I'm sorry, Angel, it won't happen again!"

I can't understand what his problem is? "I wanted this, I wanted to give you pleasure like you gave me." I wipe the rest of the come off my chin with the back of my hand.

"You did Angel, but it's written in the book of great lovers that the male always satisfies the female first." He lifts me up by my arms, from my kneeling position and holds me tight, kissing me passionately. With the immense gratification he's showing me, I know I've done a good job and I'd definitely do it again because he appreciates it so much. "That was unbelievable. Are you sure that was your first time? That was so good, I mean, really… really…good."

"Yes, that's my first blowjob." I say proudly. I give him my biggest, blinding, full white teeth smile.

"You're amazing, do you know that? Now it's my turn… any idea, what I'm going to do to you?"

Oh, his delicious promise makes me melt.

He gently places me on the bed, and lowers himself on top of me, giving me gentle kisses on my neck. He whispers in my ear. "I would love to stick my hard cock in that tight sweet little pussy, but I'm not going to…"

What? Why not?

"Because I know it's tender from this morning." Bryce finishes my silent question.

Oh. Okay.

It turns me on when he talks so bluntly about sex.

He kisses all the way down to my left breast, nibbling, tugging, biting and swirling his tongue on my nipple while he pinches the right. He switches to the right with his tongue and pinches the left, sending a torturous tingle south. He licks from the middle of my breasts, straight down to my navel. "You're killing me!"

"I know, Angel. I'm getting there."

He grazes his lips over my left hip and then kisses and licks. Then over to my belly button, circling it with his tongue. Then he moves to my right hip and slowly licks and kisses it.

My breathing is so erratic sounding and then a whimper escapes. "Please." I try to push his head between my legs, but he lifts his head and smiles with his teasing half smile, "Oh no, Angel, not yet."

I'm so frustrated and the craving to get some relief is so acute, it makes me want to scream.

Okay, two can play this game. I stop moving completely.

Bryce's eyes meet mine. They've changed drastically, they're dangerously dark now as he purrs with his sexy as hell voice. "What do you want me to do to you?"

"I want...I want what you did before."

"And what was that? I want you to say it." He commands with his forceful voice.

"I want to feel your mouth on me." I blurt out.

"Tell me. Tell me you want me to eat your pussy."

I hesitate. Is he for real? He wants me to say that?

"Tell me!" He repeats.

My blood races through my veins and I'm frustrated with this intense sexual tension that's been building like a hurricane in my body, so much that I feel like I'm going to unravel and explode. I pant softly, and then I finally blurt out. "I want you to eat my pussy!"

"That's my girl." His mouth lowers to my clit with expert

swirling motions, round and round as I feel it grow larger against his tongue. My legs shamelessly spread wider than before. His hardened tongue dives in between my sopping pussy lips and he licks up one side then the other. "You taste so sweet. I might make you wait more often." I yank his head back down. He lifts his head again and smiles with that crooked half smile then he chuckles. "You're so impatient."

"And you're such a tease!" I push his head back down between my legs.

His mouth returns to feasting on me. His tongue swirling around my clit, while his finger dances around my entrance. He glances up at me again with his wickedly teasing smile. "Do you want my finger?"

"GOD, YES!"

His finger slides right in with confident thrusts, in and out, while his tongue circles my swollen clit.

I can't take much more of this erotic torment that he's putting me through. My hearts beating so fast, it's almost physically painful. My hips rotate and grind into his tongue. My breathing has almost ceased.

Threading my hands through his tousled jet black hair, I hold him in place, clamping my slick walls around his finger, while my back arches. "Bryce!"

My head thrashes from side to side. My legs shake uncontrollably. I fall apart all around him, clawing at the sheets and bucking my hips to meet his mouth. Somehow his mouth stays on me, and he laps up every drop of my juices.

The jolting spasms seem to last forever, leaving me breathless.

I vaguely feel Bryce crawling up my body to whisper in my ear. "How was that Angel?"

When I finally get my vision and senses back and the energy to speak, I say, "My God, that was amazing."

"See what happens when you prolong an orgasm?"

"Please, don't do that to me again." I say yawning.

Exhaustion takes over and I close my eyes.

Bryce caresses my hair and kisses my cheek. "That's it Angel, go to sleep." He covers me with the comforter and leans up on one elbow. I feel him staring.

I open one eye and see that he's studying every feature on my face. "What are you thinking about?" I say as I yawn again.

"How beautiful you are."

He thinks I'm beautiful.

"Oh yeah? What else?"

"The thought of leaving you alone when I go back to work is going to be driving me crazy. Just the thought of that jackass getting anywhere near you, makes my blood boil. I won't be here to protect you."

"I'll be fine. I'll go visit my grandfather. I won't be anywhere near this town."

I hear the roar of the engine from Austin's ATV as it pulls into the back yard and I feel Bryce get out of bed. He caresses my cheek and gives me another kiss. "Sleep now beautiful."

Bryce walks from the bedroom, to the kitchen, leaving the door open a crack.

I hear the back door close and a voice come from the kitchen.

"Honey, I'm home!"

"Shhh, she's sleeping." Bryce whispers.

I'm not asleep yet. I want to be nosey and listen to their conversation.

"What's for chow? I'm starving." Austin asks. "What'd you do, wear her out?"

"Yeah she's tired."

"What's wrong with you? You look a little worried."

"How am I going to protect her from that jackass stalker?"

"Holy fuck, look at you. I can't believe this, she's got you by the balls already, doesn't she?"

"I do not!" I whisper.

"Nobody falls this fast. You've only known her three days."

I can't hold back my excitement. He's falling for me?

"Keera said she only had two beers at the bar. She mentioned that someone slipped something in her beer, and I'm starting to think that her stalker was there and was planning on kidnapping her that night."

"Keera?"

"Yeah the little blonde that was passed out in my arms, and you were having a shit-fit over."

"Yeah jackass, I know. Her name is Keera?"

"Yes her name is Keera. Can we focus here? Can you help me figure out a plan to keep her safe?" Bryce complains.

"We can take her out in the bush and teach her to shoot." Austin's voice sounds like he's excited.

"We can lend her one of our shot guns to put beside her bed, to scare the asshole or if she really needed to use it, at least she'd know how. Then we can teach her self-defense, in case she can't get to the shot gun." Bryce's chuckles. "Although she is a feisty one when she gets mad. She almost kicked me in the balls and I had to restrain her, because she was losing it."

"You're shittin' me. That little thing?"

I smile, quite proud of myself.

"I'm telling you. She's a wild one when she gets mad."

"Can't wait to see that. Hey we'll teach her tomorrow, check out the camp." Austin says excitedly. "You've got to see it."

"Sounds good. What time do you want to leave?" Bryce asks.

"Say around nine? So she's got no problem with you kidnapping her?"

"Fuck! Why do you two keep saying that? You've got it all wrong, I was keeping her safe from her stalker. You didn't see the way he was circling her house, looking through every window. He was pissed that I locked the doors so he was searching for another way in. I thought I got rid of him, but the jackass keeps coming back."

"So you think he's going to be a problem?"

"Do you ever listen to me? I would've never brought her here if I wasn't worried that something was going to happen to her. He's unstable. I can see it by the way he moves. He's obsessed with her."

"Well then, we teach her to shoot."

"She's warming up to me. We went to her house to get her some clothes and she wanted to come back with me."

"That's a good sign. Not that she had any choice, right?" Austin teases.

I hear Bryce yawning.

"It looks like she's wearing you out, too. Stamina brother, stamina.

The next morning I roll onto my back, stretch with my arms over my head and squeak like a little mouse. I feel him staring at me again and when I peek up with one eye open, he's propped up smiling down at me. "I love watching you sleep."

"How long were you watching me?"

"Oh, about half an hour now."

I roll toward him, curling my leg over his and blink up at him and smile, "Good morning."

"Good morning to you, too, beautiful."

My smile gets bigger. He thinks I'm beautiful.

"Waking up next to you, seeing your beautiful face, smelling your hair, feeling your body, your warm silky skin next to mine. I couldn't ask for a better morning, but we should really get out of this bed or I'm going to make love to you all damn day."

"And what would be so wrong with that?"

"I'm already hard for you." Bryce places my hand on top of his cock. "See? Come with me, we're going to teach you to shoot."

Bryce rolls out of bed, totally naked. What a glorious sight to see. I can't take my eyes off of him. The intense sexual attraction that I feel for him travels straight to the achy spot between my legs every time my gaze rakes over his body.

"Do you have any idea what you're doing to me right now? The way you're looking at me? Looks like I'm going to be walking around with this hard on all day. Come with me." He holds out his hand and I take it. "And quit licking that lip. Every time you do that, I envision you getting ready to suck my cock."

When I stand up with nothing on, he smiles, shakes his head and says, "We've got to get the hell out of this room."

It makes me feel so good knowing that my body's affecting him like this. I grin from one ear to the other. I throw my bra and a t-shirt on and some tight yoga pants commando, while Bryce throws on his boxers, faded Levi's and a tight black t-shirt. His eyes almost pop out of his head when he sees I'm not wearing a thong.

"Oh, that's really going to help this." His fingers wrap around his impressive erection through his jeans. "Thinking you're panty-less all day."

I can't help but smile at him.

Austin's up making breakfast already. "Good morning, my name is Austin. It's a pleasure to meet you." He extends his hand out and we shake.

"Good morning to you too, I'm Keera, It's a pleasure to meet you."

Austin places our plates in front of us, as we sit at the breakfast bar. "Dig in, before it gets cold."

"Thank you." I say softly.

"I found some empty cans. We can use them for target practice." Austin mutters as he maneuvers gracefully around the kitchen while I watch and eat my breakfast, not saying a word.

Austin's as tall as Bryce with the same silky jet black hair, only it's a little shorter. He has broad shoulders with huge muscles. Seeing them together, I compare features on both their faces. Same eyes, same nose, the only difference is the shape of their faces. "Are you two twins?" Oh crap. Did I say that out loud? I cover my lips, surprised that it slipped out.

Austin and Bryce chuckle, obviously amused by my outburst.

"No, we get that all the time." Austin complains. "But I'm the older, good looking one."

"Fuck you." Bryce shoots back.

"Both you guys are excellent cooks." I say trying to defuse the looks flying back and forth between the two of them.

8

THE ATV'S ARE loaded with supplies and pulled outside of the garage, I've noticed as I walk toward them and Austin waits patiently for us to climb aboard. Bryce slips a helmet on my head making sure my long hair is inside my snowsuit and it's done up properly. He protectively fusses, making sure I have all my safety gear on. When he's close, I feel butterflies in my stomach and the smell of him and his cologne is intoxicating. I observe his every move and stare lovingly in his eyes. I love the way he pampers and takes care of me. I haven't felt this in a while.

Bryce lifts my face shield and gently touches my nose. "You keep looking at me like that and we're not leaving. We'll be going back in that cabin."

My eyes squint and he knows I'm smiling.

Austin stands on the floor boards of his ATV, shaking his head, oozing impatience now, dying to get moving.

I hop on the ATV behind Bryce and wrap my arms around his waist. My body's plastered against his and it feels so good. He squeezes my hand and yells above the roar of the engine "You ready, hang on tight."

He guns it, spinning the back tires and I let out a squeal of delight and giggle. We speed through the trails, dodging tree branches, puddles, streams, and rocks. I take in all the beautiful scenery as we climb up a mountain, until we reach a clearing in the trees.

Bryce pulls up to the ledge of the mountain and shuts the engine off. I follow Bryce's lead, taking my helmet off to see the landscape below us. All the leaves are changing to a bright yellow, red and orange and some have already fallen. We look out over the mountains edge, viewing the taller mountain to the right with thousands of trees changing colour.

I'm in awe at how magnificent my surrounding area is. Riding on this ATV, through the trails brings me to places I've never seen before. My town is pretty impressive too, but I've lived here all my life, so I'm used to it. This is all new unexplored territory for me.

I look at Bryce with the biggest smile. "My god, this is beautiful!"

"You're beautiful and your smile, I can't get enough of it."

"I love seeing your beautiful smile too." I say softly and rub against him.

Austin spins around, parking in front of us and shuts the engine off. He lifts his face shield and looks at us with a hint of a smile as he shakes his head. "Are you done, trying to impress her now? Can we go?"

We smile at him replacing our helmets on our heads and quickly fasten the strap. The engines roar to life and we speed down the trails once again for a few miles.

Austin slows to a stop, and shuts the engine down. Bryce does the same. Looking down the trail, we can see three deer. Austin can't get his helmet off fast enough. He grabs for his rifle, opens it up, loads it, and quickly slams it closed, just as the deer scurry off the trail. They're gone and out of sight. "Fuck!" Austin shouts.

Austin places the rifle back on the side of the ATV, starts the engine and drives to where he last saw the deer, while he holds onto his helmet so it doesn't fall. Bryce follows him. We search in the trees and we can see them running and jumping in the distance. They're too far away to get a shot.

"Fuck, do you believe that, so close." Austin says to Bryce.

This is very exciting to me. My heart is racing, while adrenaline curses through my veins. My life was lonely and boring before Bryce came along, but now, I've never felt more alive.

Austin places his helmet back on his head and they start their engines. We drive a few more miles until we come to a clearing in the trees.

There we see an old decrepit shack and an old rusty flatbed truck that someone's abandoned.

We get off the ATV's, stretch our legs and take our helmets off.

Bryce sets up the tin cans on the back of the truck, while Austin loads the rifle, then he hands it over to Bryce.

"You think you remember how to do this? You've been a little preoccupied lately." Austin glances over to me and smiles.

"Fuck you, give me the gun." Bryce says annoyed.

Bryce gives me some pointers of how to safely shoot a rifle. He aims and fires, and the can flies in the air.

"Wow, I guess you do remember." Austin says as he sets up the next can.

Bryce pulls me over and stands very close, showing me how to place the rifle right against my shoulder so it doesn't kick back and tear my shoulder off. He helps me with my other hand showing me how to hold my arm straight out. While he explains he plasters his hard body against mine and whispers in my ear. "I know you don't have any panties on." He rubs his hard cock on my hip and nips on my ear lobe and I giggle.

Austin smiles, shaking his head. "Why don't you get away from her so she can concentrate and shoot?"

"Wait! You're going to need these." Bryce places hearing protection on my ears. "Okay, you're ready to go."

I point the rifle, looking straight down the barrel and I concentrate really hard. I spread my legs, so my stance is a little wider preparing myself for the kickback.

I look in the scope, focusing really hard and then I pull the trigger. "Holy crap!" I shout as one of the cans disappears. I lower the rifle and rub my shoulder. "That was fun!" I smile from one ear to the other.

"Good job, Angel." Bryce congratulates me by smacking my butt as he takes the rifle from me.

Austin runs to the truck, yelling out. "You got one!"

I rub my shoulder and Bryce notices.

He rubs it for me. "Are you okay? Are you hurt?"

"No, I'm fine." I laugh. "I don't think that was the one I was aiming for, but that's okay."

Bryce scoops me up in his arms, dips me backwards and kisses me fiercely.

Austin's groans are heard loud and clear. "Will you let her up so she can focus?" Austin places only one can on the back of the truck this time. "Let's see if you can hit this?"

Bryce pulls me back up, returning me into the here and now and it only takes half a minute to gather my wits and focus again. I set the rifle up, like I did the time before. Focusing really hard, looking in the scope, placing the butt of the rifle hard against my shoulder, preparing myself for the kickback.

"You don't know how hot you look holding that rifle. Christ, I'm getting hard just looking at you." Bryce's warm breath gusts against my ear.

"Quit trying to distract me." I smile, but stay focused.

"But I like to distract you."

I shoot. "I got it!"

Bryce takes the rifle from me and places it on the ATV. He scoops me up in his arms and slaps a wet lush kiss on my lips in congratulations. When he pulls away he looks in my eyes. "I want to take you deep in the woods where no one can find us and make love to you on this ATV."

He places me back on the ground and I giggle. His overly large hands hold both sides of my face. "I love that sound. You should giggle more often."

Austin glares at us. "You guys are almost sickening to watch."

"You're jealous!" Bryce states.

"You're right. Keera, do you have any good looking friends?"

I smile and think of Leena.

Bryce quickly launches into detailed instruction. "This is a Remington thirty odd six. You pull up and back to open the chamber. Put your magazine in, and then push forward and down to close. Then you're ready to take the shot." I study his beautiful face as he explains, trying to pay attention, but he's so god damn gorgeous, I could stare all day.

Bryce chuckles. "Did you hear me?"

I shake my head, trying to focus on what he's saying instead of his beautiful face. "Yes, yes I did."

He laughs. "You've got to quit looking at me like that. You know what happens when you do."

I blush as my thoughts change to his gorgeous hard body making love to me. I soon dismiss my thoughts.

Pulling the trigger, the can flies into the air. I shoot a few more times hitting the target with expertise.

"I think our job is done here." Austin mutters.

When we get back on the ATV's, we race through the trails and Austin points off to his right. We slow to a crawl and turn our heads to see a bear climbing a hill. We drive a couple more miles, until we reach their hunting camp.

As we pull up to the camp, I see pieces of wood nailed from the bottom of the tree trunk, leading all the way up to the top where Austin's tree blind sprawls between two trees and is covered with thick branches to disguise it.

"Wow, great job."

Austin flashes his beautiful smile. "Thanks, I've been busy."

Over in another tree, down a little further is a metal tree stand, high in the tree, with steel foot pegs leading up the tree trunk.

"This is why you haven't been at the cabin much." I say observantly.

"Yup." Austin says proudly.

"Come with me." Bryce pulls me to the steps and I climb in front of him. He wants to make sure I don't fall, I'm assuming. Once up top, I look through the doorway of the tree blind, and see that it's a good size. It has a roof and walls and a porch with a railing. Inside is a small table with a lantern on it.

All three of us sit on a large bench that Austin made, on the porch, high up in the trees, studying our surroundings.

"Who wants a sandwich?" Austin says as he reaches in the cooler.

Bryce holds out his hand. "Hell yeah, I'm getting hungry, so is Keera."

I guess he assumes that. But he always makes sure I eat with him. I don't really have a choice, he's pushy that way.

Austin tosses two sandwiches to Bryce and he catches them. We eat lunch in the tree blind enjoying the view.

"You can see for quite a ways." I pipe up.

"Yeah and if you can't get a shot, maybe I'll be able to in the other stand." Bryce says between bites of his sandwich.

Austin grins.

I can see he's quite proud of himself. My gaze floats between the two of them; they make me smile. They're so happy and excited.

We stay up there for quite a while, eating and looking around, admiring Austin's hard work. I spot something on the tree.

"What's that?" I ask pointing toward it.

"Come on, I'll show you." Bryce takes my hand. "I'll go first; I don't want you to fall." We carefully climb down from the tree fort.

I smile, liking the way he fusses and tries to protect me.

"See, it's a camera, we've got three. There's one way down at that tree and the other one…should be around here somewhere?"

"I set it up down the trail a bit, I'll show you." Austin grabs his rifle off the ATV and carries it with us. "We can't leave without this. Bears out here."

We walk down the trail until we reach the other camera. Bryce explains how it takes pictures of any movement and stores it on a memory card inside.

As we make our way back to the tree stands, Austin mutters, "If you two want to head back, I'm going to stay here and work on this for a bit." He takes some supplies off of the ATV, stopping mid-stride. "Oh, and it would be nice if you had dinner ready for me again."

"Since when am I your bitch?" Bryce complains.

"Since you're not out here helping me. Yeah, I can see how you're dying to get her back to the cabin. I'm not an idiot."

"Look how cute she is when she blushes." Austin points out. "She's shy and quiet. I like this one. She's not a psycho bitch like the other one."

Who is Austin talking about? The other one…psycho bitch, I play that over in my head.

"Hey, remember? Dinner." Austin reminds Bryce again.

"Yeah, yeah, I'll remember." Bryce slaps Austin on his back. "Be careful, man."

"Yeah, both you guys, too."

We say our goodbyes, hopping on the ATV and we speed down the trails again.

My mind plays back what Austin said, "Psycho bitch." I've got to ask Bryce who Austin's talking about. Is this a girlfriend I should worry about?

I tap Bryce on the shoulder and he slows right down to a crawl, then stops and shuts the engine off. "I've got to go pee."

"That's fine, so do I. Come over here and we'll go."

"Out here in the woods?"

Bryce laughs out loud. "Yeah, we still have at least five more miles to get back to the cabin. You won't make it, Angel." His voice is soft and considerate. "Come over here, pull everything down and squat. Try not to pee on your pants."

Bryce is already whipping it out and peeing against the tree with the biggest smile on his face.

Clumsily I pull my pants down and squat with Bryce watching me. He's enjoying this, he can't stop smiling.

"Don't watch me!"

"Okay, okay."

I sit there waiting, patiently for the waterworks to start. "Hey, who was Austin talking about?"

"What do you mean?"

I can tell he doesn't want to tell me; he's avoiding the question, obviously.

"The psycho bitch?"

"My ex-girlfriend."

I almost fall over when he clarifies the psycho bitch is his ex-girlfriend. Bryce rushes over to help me. "I'm okay." I hold up my hand, to shoo him away so he'd go back to where he came from.

"So how long have you been broken up for?"

"About two months now."

I swallow hard. Did you actually think he's had no girlfriends before you? Don't be an idiot Keera.

"How long did you go out for?"

"About six months."

"Oh." I say softly and finally start to pee. Crap six months is a fair amount of time to get attached. "Why'd you break up if you don't mind me asking?"

"She was very controlling and it didn't end well. Did you want to ask me anything else?"

"I'll think of something." Controlling hun? I wipe with the

Kleenex Bryce gave me. I then pull up my snow pants and adjust my straps and head out of the tree line.

"Austin didn't like her too much?"

"No, they couldn't stand each other."

"Oh." Is all I can say as I put my helmet back on.

Climbing back onto the ATV, we drive for miles and I have no idea where we are and don't see anything that looks familiar. I place my complete trust in Bryce that he knows where we are and he knows his way back to the cabin. When we get closer to the cabin, I notice a few things that look familiar, like the huge rock face and a massive tree that's fallen and they've made a trail around it.

After we drive for about half a mile, I see Bryce reach down to his key fob and push a button. We park and Bryce opens the gun safe to store his rifle away.

"I had such a good time today. It was fun!"

"I'm glad you had fun, next time we'll take a camera and you can take some pictures."

Bryce stares at me with dark, wanting eyes, almost like he flips a switch. His mysterious wicked smile makes me giggle. He looks like a predator stalking his prey, ready to pounce.

"Do you have any idea, how you've been torturing me all day? Knowing, you're not wearing any panties."

He pulls me by the hand to the cabin. My mind is all over the map thinking about his ex. Is she a blond, like me? Or does he prefer brunettes or auburn hair? Austin said she's a psycho bitch. Nut house crazy? Or just when she gets mad like me.

Is she a problem I'll have to deal with in the future?

9

TAKING OUR BOOTS off, we get undressed out of our winter clothing. I hang them up while Bryce adds more wood to the fire. Then he walks gracefully to the bathroom and fills the Jacuzzi tub. A moment later he's standing in front of me dragging me to the bathroom by my hand and I follow.

His lips curl into a wicked half smile. "I've got a million idea's running through my mind of all the things I want to do to you."

He can see the effect his words have on me. I bite my lip, envisioning in my mind all the erotic things he can do to me too.

His hand snakes through my hair and he holds the back of my neck, while his other hand and finger runs down my cheek and across my lower lip, releasing it. "You, biting that lip, drives me wild!" His mouth claims mine in a firm demanding kiss. Our tongues dance in circles as we deepen the kiss. Suddenly he pulls away saying, "Let's take a bath."

What? Alright, change of pace. I stand there breathless and panting.

I lift the hem of Bryce's shirt and pull it over his head in one swift motion with the help of Bryce lifting his arms and bending.

He does the same with my shirt. It's up and over my head in a split second and tossed across the room.

I reach for a hair clip in the vanity drawer, twisting and clasping my hair up and off of my shoulders.

The distance between us shrinks as he stealthily closes the gap with that look on his face. His tongue runs along the seam of his lip as if he tastes me. And I swear to God, I feel a zap right between my legs.

Bryce gently runs his fingers along my neck and in a low sexy drawl he says, "I like this look on you."

"Thank you."

He drops to his knees and my attention is one hundred percent focused on him pulling down the waist band of my yoga pants to reveal my hips. He gently nips his way to my left hipbone and then trails his lips across to my belly button. The butterflies release inside my belly. He slowly circles my button with his expert tongue, then moves to the right with his lips feathering my skin. He gently kisses and then softly nips. "Your skin is so soft, I could eat you alive."

How does he do that with words? In an instant, I'm a hot liquid mess.

He pulls my yoga pants down and off of me, revealing my moist stain on the inside of my crotch. Oh, God, how embarrassing.

His eyes follow to my sopping bald pussy and then he brings my yoga pants up to his nose and inhales sharply.

My eyes widen. I can't believe he did that.

He gracefully raises in front of me and gazes deep in my eyes. "You've been wet for me all day. You smell delicious, so sweet!" His voice sounds appreciative.

I study his facial expressions while I undo the button and unzip his jeans revealing his sexy happy trail. Slowly, I run my thumb down his trail.

He gives me his crooked half smile with his dimple showing. "You know where that leads to."

"Yes, it's my happy trail too."

We both hold on to the waist band and swiftly, his boxers and jeans are down to his feet then kicked to the side. Bryce unclasps my bra slowly and seductively he pulls it off my shoulders, one by one, his fingers run along my skin, leaving trails of fire as he gazes deep in my eyes, my bra is off and dropping to the floor.

Bryce takes hold of my hand and guides me to the hot bath. We simultaneously lower into the water with my back to his front. "That's it Angel. Lean back." I can feel his stiff cock on my lower back and my head lies on his muscular chest, while his hands caress my stomach.

Silence fills the room for quite a while, both of us lost in our own thoughts.

My thoughts are scattered, my mind thinking about his ex-girlfriend. What she looks like and what if he doesn't come back? I lost my parents. I don't want to lose him. This week and every moment spent with him has been the best days of my life. All I know is, I don't want this feeling to end between us.

Bryce switches to pouring water over my breasts watching how it separates, flowing across my nipples and then he breaks the silence. "What's going on in that pretty little head of yours?" Bryce asks in a concerned voice.

"What if you don't come back?" I say so soft that I swear there is no way he could've heard me.

He pulls me up onto his lap, holding me in a tight embrace. "I'm coming back! That's a promise."

I wrap my arms around his neck and hug him tight. My fingers run through his jet black hair. We kiss each other like our life depends on it. With our mouths still sealed on each other, I shift my body so my legs wrap around his hips and my arms around his neck, so I'm in his lap and we're facing. The water almost sloshes over the edge. His hands grasp my ass and he pulls me close so I can feel his hard cock. We stare lovingly into one another's eyes. Bryce's hands move to my hips and he glides me effortlessly along his hard shaft. My nipples graze his chest, forming tight hard peaks.

"You believe me. Don't you?"

"Yes."

He lets out a regretful groan. "I wanted this bath to last a bit longer, but I can't wait. I need you." He takes my hand and we make our way to his bedroom. He closes the door with his foot and pulls back the covers. "I've been dying to make love to you all day." He stands beside the bed, staring down at my body. "Look at you, I could stare at you all damn day. You're so beautiful!"

"So are you!" My eyes start at his face and follow all the way down and back up again. I physically shiver.

After he climbs onto the bed, his body hovers over me. His massive muscular arms hold all his upper body weight and his rock hard cock lays heavy on my swollen clit. He rocks his hips and I can feel how aroused he is. His warm breath caresses my ear. "Do you see what you do to me? I can't give you up. I'll be back. I promise."

How I want that statement to be true. I hope he isn't one of those guys that promises you the moon and uses you for a piece of ass. Disappearing when their heart strings get tugged on, fearing when it gets too intense and intimate. It would break my heart if he did that. At this moment, all I know is that I'd do anything for him. I don't think I could give him up either.

Leaning down he kisses the corner of my mouth, my neck, gently nipping at my ear, his lips run along my jaw line, and then he tugs on my bottom lip. He presses his mouth to mine, slipping his tongue inside. We deepen the kiss and moan into one another's mouths.

As he kisses down my chest to my breasts, I can feel his cock rub along my leg and his warm lips surround my puckered nipple. He gently bites and licks each nipple, giving them his undivided attention and then he flutters his tongue over the tips making them pucker even more. He licks his way down the middle of my stomach while he opens my legs with his large thigh.

He pulls my knees up giving him access to my damp pussy. I am open wide. "Hold your knees." He commands. He slips one finger in carefully exploring as he gazes up at me. His other hand pinches and tugs on my nipples. His voice lowers to a slow sexy purr. "You're tight and wet for me. I've got to taste you!"

Yes, please do.

His fluttering tongue circles my clit, while his finger slides in and out. All of a sudden his finger pulls out and he spears me with his hardened tongue, in and out as deep as he can go. Seeing his black silky hair tickling between my thighs and his nose bumping against my swollen clit is such a turn-on and it's a vision I never want to forget.

My breathing accelerates. I'm fisting his hair and my hips rotate in a circular motion.

His tongue makes its way back to my clit, flicking wildly, as his skilled finger plunges in and out.

He keeps up this torturous rhythm and I beg. "Bryce, please." He can see I'm close.

My legs start to shake. Every muscle in my body tightens, clenching around his finger. He doesn't stop, he keeps flicking my clit. He tastes my sweet arousal.

"Bryce!" That's all I can take. I'm unravelling! "Oh my God!" I scream and buck my hips into his face. I hold on with both hands grasping his hair in an almost painful tug as my orgasm rips through me, exploding and I fall apart. He laps up every last drop.

With my vision still blurred, Bryce kneels up and yanks me down with rough hands to the center of the bed by my legs. My grip loosens from the sheets and I place both hands on his pectoral muscles and squeeze as he settles between my thighs.

The tip of his cock probes and enters my pussy. "I can't wait any longer, I need to fuck you!"

"Slow!" I grimace in pain as he inches his way into me. He pulls back out, letting me adjust, then slowly inserts it back in, a little at a time.

All his weight comes down on me, and he stops moving. "You're tight. I'm fighting the urge to slam my cock deep inside you, but I don't want to hurt you."

After I tell myself to relax, my muscles immediately loosen and I say, "Do it, fuck me now!"

As Bryce hovers above me, he pulls out to the tip, and then shoves his cock back in. I gasp, but the feel of his thick cock stretching me and the fullness deep inside me is mind blowing.

I crave the feeling of him when he's inside me, like a drug surging through my veins. I need him and there's no way I could go without sex ever again.

I circle my hips while he keeps the pace going with his expert thrusts inside me. Bryce collapses on top of me, once more, freezing, not moving a muscle. "Wait, don't move. I don't want to come yet."

His cock pulls out and I sigh wanting it back inside me. He kneels up straddling my legs and blurts out, "doggy style."

My eyes widen. "I…I don't know what that is?"

His big hands man-handle me, lifting me into position. "Hands and knees."

My ass is up in the air and very exposed.

"I love this ass." He rubs me gently, like he's shining a crystal ball. He leans down running his lips across my butt, giving me slow feather like kisses. I turn my head around to see what he's doing. "Oh no, Angel, eyes straight ahead." He continues kissing and caressing for a bit. Then he lifts and slaps my right ass cheek.

"Ouch." I feel his weight shift as he gets off the bed.

I wonder what he's doing.

"Eyes straight ahead." He repeats in a stern voice and I do as I'm told.

The mattress dips as he gets back on the bed. His warm heavy muscular body drapes over me as he wraps the black velour robe tie around my eyes. "Can you see?"

"No."

"Good, don't take it off!"

I have no idea what he's going to do to me. He's kneeling at my back entrance and all of my senses are heightened. My heart beats so fast and I feel like it's going to jump right out of my chest. I can't believe how aroused and excited I am.

Caressing my ass cheek that he slapped, Bryce leans down to kiss it, mouthing his words against me. "Oh the things I could do to you." He slides his thumb deep inside me while fondling my clit with his middle finger.

I moan and tilt my head back. I wiggle my ass around in circles. "Yes! This is what I want." I squirm with a needy achy discomfort.

He pulls his thumb out. "Not yet Angel." Bryce kneels behind me and I feel the big crown of his cock rub along my butt, skimming softly over the sensitive tissues.

I feel it positioned at my entrance now and he gently sinks into me. "Oh my god!"

"Your pussy just clamped down around my cock, Fuck, you're melting me." His full weight collapses on my back. "Don't move!" We both freeze, not moving a muscle. "I want to fuck you for a while, but you're making me lose control."

I am? I'm doing this, my bodies doing this?

Reaching underneath me, he gently squeezes and kneads my breasts, then he tugs and pinches my tight nipples.

His big hard body lifts off of me and he stirs his cock round and around, while holding my hips in place.

I like the exquisite feel and start moving my hips in a circular motion.

Bryce pulls out with one smooth stroke, and then thrusts deep inside, again and again, keeping up the same torturous rhythm, in and out. To the tip, all the way back in until I feel his balls slapping against my clit.

Our orgasms build as he reaches around to fondle my swollen clit with his finger. I'm breathless and begging, "Bryce, please!"

"I know, Angel, come for me!"

I fall apart and then he follows. One last hard thrust and he freezes, every muscle in his body tightens.

"Fuck!" He blurts out. I feel his warm come pouring deep inside me. When he finishes I feel the weight of his body fall down on me. I'm so weak that I tumble to my side breathless, immobile and spooning him.

Bryce whispers in my ear with his cock securely planted deep, as he pulsates inside me and I feel it. "I love watching you come. I love hearing the sounds you make. The whimpers and that little sound of pleasure deep in your throat, it sends me over the edge. The way your body responds to my touch, your sensual movements and when you surrender and fall apart, quivering. I've done that to you. I made it happen. I don't think I'm ever going to get enough of you. I'm always going to want more. You're like a drug to me."

My heart melts at his words. I don't think I'll ever get enough of him either. Ever.

Bryce pulls the robe tie off of my eyes and I turn to look at him. "I feel the same way you do." We lay tangled in each other's arms.

He kisses my cheek.

"I can't move," I say. "My whole body's tingling."

"So is mine." Bryce kisses my cheek again. "After making love to you, all I think about is getting you beneath me again. I think I'm obsessed."

"That's good, because so am I." I melt into his strong arms that are holding me and he squeezes me tighter.

We lay there for a bit catching our breath feeling sated and completely satisfied. Then he breaks the silence. "Come, we'll go take a shower then make some dinner."

After washing each other's bodies, I pour the shampoo in my hands. "I want to wash your hair."

Bryce smiles and says, "Go for it."

He bends down so I can reach. I squirt the shampoo in my hand and massage it in with the tips of my fingers and nails. He distracts me by pinching and pulling on my nipples. "Look how big these fucking things get. I want them in my mouth."

"Don't distract me."

"But I like to distract you."

I lift his head and smile. "Pay attention!"

"I am paying attention, to your nipples." He flashes me his adorable smile.

I massage harder, which makes him immobile. He can't move. When I'm done I slap his ass. "Rinse." And he does what he's told.

Bryce opens one eye while rinsing and see's that I'm reaching for the shampoo. "Oh no! I'm washing your hair." He squirts a large amount into his palm and massages it into my scalp then follows down my long strands, collecting it all together on top of my head, like I do. Bryce massages my scalp with enough pressure that it sends tingles all the way down to my toes. I freeze and then he stops, looking down in my eyes with a smirk on his face. "Are you enjoying this?"

"Yes, I am."

We decide on a sweet and sour chicken stir-fry, quick and easy. We're running out of time, Austin will be home soon.

I chop the veggies while Bryce cooks the chicken. We move around the kitchen, slightly grazing, bumping into each other. A touch here and there and a look or two has me thinking I want him again.

When he finishes his task, he undresses me with his seductive eyes. A delicious shiver runs through me, feeling his eyes upon me. I'm wearing my light pink tank top with matching tight little shorts. I'm quite happy that I brought them, knowing that when Bryce stokes the fire it gets really hot in here, not to mention the heat I feel from his intense heated stare.

I keep eyeing Bryce's low hanging black pajama bottoms and his wash board abs and when he turns toward the stove away from me, I can see hard slabs of muscle, his sculptured back and his perfect ass flexing when he moves a certain way. I fight back the urge to run my fingers through his silky, jet black hair.

The acute sexual tension that radiates between us creates a rush of adrenaline through my veins.

I can't help myself any longer. I pounce on his back, wrapping my arms around him, splaying my fingers on his meaty pecs.

Bryce spins around in my arms and holds the back of my neck. His other arm crosses my back and holds me firmly in place. He kisses me, with slow savouring licks, tasting me.

Closing my eyes, I deepen the kiss and run my fingers through the silk strands of his hair, grabbing a handful. I moan into his mouth. He squeezes as he lifts me up by my butt and I'm vaguely aware that we're moving until I'm shoved hard against the kitchen wall and he grinds his cock into that perfect spot.

Bryce's other hand confidently slides up my shirt and under my bra, fondling my breasts. Wild for him too, from his forcefulness and greed for me, I don't hold back, we go at each other like feral animals. The heat and passion consuming us both.

"Christ, you can't keep your hands off each other. Is that all you two do all day?" Austin's voice startles me.

We break away from our kiss and Bryce slides me down off the wall.

10

*M*ORTIFIED BY THE intrusion, I hurry to adjust my bra, shirt, and shorts. Flustered, as my face turns red from embarrassment. Austin's arrival wasn't heard when he came in the back door, probably because of the heavy breathing and panting.

"I didn't think you'd be home so soon." Bryce grumbles.

"Well, that's obvious!" Austin grins at me as I adjust my clothing. "I finished the tree fort, as Keera calls it, and I'm starving." Austin finishes hanging up his winter clothes at the back door and saunters into the kitchen and leans against the counter waiting patiently for his food.

I scurry over and dish out dinner onto three plates, thoroughly embarrassed, waiting for the redness in my face and my hormones to subside.

After placing the plates on the breakfast bar, I maneuver around to the other side, quickly sitting, but wince at the tenderness of my private parts.

Bryce whispers in my ear. "That's how I like you, remembering what beautiful love we made, that my lips and hands touched every part of you and how tender you are from being thoroughly fucked."

His wicked smile and delicious words send a tingle, straight between my legs. I shift restlessly on the bar stool.

Austin turns to see Bryce whispering in my ear. "Can you two keep that shit down to a minimum when I'm around?"

I turn beet red again.

"You're jealous, you don't have a girlfriend." Bryce blurts out.

Austin teases me again. "Look how red she turns, and yeah, I am jealous, I'll admit it. Are you coming with me tomorrow, hunting?"

Bryce looks at me searching my face for an answer.

I don't think he wants to leave me alone. I can see it in his face.

"Go enjoy yourselves. I'll work out and have dinner ready for you guys when you get back. "

Austin slaps Bryce on the back. "See, she wants you to go and have fun."

Bryce holds my hand gazing deep in my eyes "Are you sure?"

"Holy fuck! Are you ever pussy whipped?"

We both ignore Austin's outburst.

"I want you to go. You're supposed to be up here hunting and I stole you away from your brother. I really do want you to go and have fun."

"See? It's settled." Austin slaps Bryce on the back again.

"After dinner I'll show you the workout room."

"You have a workout room?"

Austin shakes his head in disgust. "She hasn't seen the place yet? What the hell have you two been doing? Forget I asked that question. I'm an idiot."

Bryce shrugs his shoulders and smiles at Austin. "We've got a Bow Flex, treadmill and weights. There's also a big screen T.V. and Blue Ray if you want to use that."

The living room has medium stained hardwood floors, a black leather sectional that faces the huge triangular windows at the front of the cabin. A big screen T.V. with an impressive amount of DVD's in the cabinet below. The light fixture above has six lights with camouflage glass goblets and deer antlers criss-crossing strategically throughout. The décor is hunting oriented, like the stuffed deer head on the wall and stuffed bear sitting in the corner playing with his foot. The etched glass face wood stove is in the other corner, which is surrounded with black marble tile. A brass container holding logs of wood sits beside it.

We make our way down the hall. "This is Austin's room."

"How many years apart are you and your brother?"

Peering in, I can see he has the same bed and dressers as Bryce.

"He's one and a half years older."

"How old are you?"

"I'm twenty-seven. And you are?"

"I'm twenty-two."

Bryce hugs me tightly from behind and whispers in my ear. "I'm cradle robbing. I love it!"

"Boy, we don't really know much about each other, do we?"

"We will. What do you want to know?"

"Any other siblings?"

"Ciara. She's twenty-one. How about you Angel, any brothers or sisters?"

"No just me. Only child." I shrug my shoulders. "Where do your parents live?"

"In Barrie. Not far from my house. What's your last name?"

"Johnson."

"Keera Johnson. Pleased to meet you. I'm Bryce Hamilton." Bryce seals his mouth to mine and I sigh as his tongue explores deep inside. He bends me backwards, holding my head and lower back, giving me slow savouring licks. My hair dangles down and hits the floor.

Grinding his cock against me, he lifts me back up. "See we're getting to know each other." Bryce surprises me by hauling me up by my butt, cradling me in his arms and I wrap my legs around his waist.

He carries me to another room down the hall. "This is the workout room."

Bryce gently places me back on the floor so he can show me how to use the bow flex, wearing only his pajama bottoms that hang on his pelvis showing his sexy V of muscle at his hips. He pulls down on the overhead bar, giving me quite the show.

His muscles flex everywhere. His arms are huge and his washboard abs tighten even more showing slabs of honed muscle.

Slightly drooling, I stand there shaking my head. He's everything that I've ever wished for and fantasized about in a man. From the way his body moves with grace to the way his hard body feels beneath my hands when I caress his magnificent body.

I can't explain it, I have a sudden urge to pounce on him, but I restrain myself. I'm still holding back for some reason. Why am I holding back? Trust issues still? He's everything you've ever wished for, so what's the problem? I don't know.

Bryce brings me back from my internal struggle. "This is how you change the weight. I'll set it so it's light. Sit down, try it."

Straddling the seat, I reach up to grab the bar, pulling it down slightly. I push my butt into position and pull down the rest of the way. Bryce's eyes darken and his lip curls up with his half wicked smile. He leans down close to my ear. "One day I'm going to fuck you on this." He likes talking dirty to me knowing the effect it has on me.

I smile at his comment and watch him as he sits on the total gym.

He glides up and down with his abs contracting and his muscles bulging everywhere. He shows me all the different positions.

"Get on, you try it." He motions for me to take over.

Bryce watches me with hungry eyes and a wicked grin and before I have a chance to try it, he comes over and quickly straddles me, climbing on top, flexing his hips with that expert roll, grinding into me. "I'm going to fuck you on this one too, in every position possible."

I love seeing him so playful.

"Will you get off that poor girl? I told you to keep that shit to a minimum when I'm around." Austin complains.

"What? We still have our clothes on."

"I love how red she gets. Hey you two want to watch a movie?" Austin asks.

Bryce gracefully lifts himself off of me and extends his hand. I take it and he helps me up and hugs me from behind. I can tell Bryce doesn't really want to watch a movie, he's got other things on in his mind like the python trying to escape out of his pajama bottoms, but I think he has to make his brother happy.

Guiding me into the living room, Bryce gently holds my lower back, and with that simple touch he turns me on to no end and I want him right here and now. Jeez, what's wrong with me? Control yourself Keera.

"Hey, let's watch *Battleship*." Austin opens the Blue Ray player and pops it in.

We sit on the sectional together and while Austin has his back to us, Bryce runs his hand up my thigh almost reaching my moist spot. My eyes open wide and I hold his hand from going up any further. I'm shaking my head no, but I know I'd cave if he were persistent enough. I glance at Austin to make sure he's not watching us.

He grabs my hand and positions it on his hard cock. My eyes open wider and he smirks at me with his wicked smile. I feel his warm breath on my ear as he whispers. "See I'm always hard. I can't get enough of you! I want to take you in that room and make love to you right now."

I squirm on the leather couch, clenching my legs together in delicious anticipation.

We try to keep our playful touching to a minimum, with Austin around. Or at least I do. Bryce wants this movie to end, so he can get me back in his bed.

When the movie finishes Bryce stands, yawns and stretches like he's tired. He holds his hand out to me. "Time for bed."

Bryce tugs me to the bedroom holding my hand, undressing me with his eyes. He closes the door behind us and captures me against the wall, while he runs his hand under my tank top, skimming his fingers along my skin to unfasten my bra. "I want you to trust me. I've wanted to do something to you, from the first time I had you tied up in my bed, which was one of my all-time favourite fantasies, by the way."

He undoes my bra and pulls it out of my pink tank top and he stands back with an intense searing gaze. "Look at you!" Bryce shakes his head and his smile blinds me. "You're every young boy's wet dream and every man's fantasy!"

My nipples pucker and stick out half an inch under my shirt. Bryce grips both breasts from underneath while running his thumbs across each nipple. "Holy fuck, I want those in my mouth." He lowers and gently bites each nipple through the fabric.

I watch as he lifts my shirt off, he leans down and sucks on each nipple, giving his undivided attention to both. He looks up at me through his long black eye lashes. "Can I tie you up and blindfold you?"

My heart is pounding so hard in my chest, I think I can almost hear it. "Yes." My response is instantaneous.

"You know what to say if you don't want this."

"Yes."

"And you know what to say if I'm too rough."

Oh my, the sweet anticipation. "Yes."

He slowly skims his hands along the curve of my waist, slipping his thumbs into my waistband, as he slides my thong and shorts down in one smooth motion. "I want you in the middle of the bed."

I'm so excited, I jump on the bed and hurry to get into position.

I watch him undress. I can't take my eyes off of him.

He finds the keys in the drawer and then he struts over to the tall wardrobe in the corner. He opens it and pulls some rope out. He makes his way around the side of the bed. He skims his fingers across my arm, sending goose bumps everywhere as he wraps the rope around my wrist, tying it to the bed. "How's that feel?"

"Good."

He runs his fingers all the way down my thigh to my ankle, sending shivers throughout its wake. He grasps my calf and pulls my legs apart, then wraps the noose around my right ankle and he tightens it, securing it to the bed post.

"I'm going to make you beg." He analyzes my facial expressions as he struts around to the right side of the bed, with his half wicked smile.

"Beg huh?" I lick my bottom lip and I stare at his cock.

"You like what you see?"

"Oh yes. I do."

Bryce sits on the bed and feathers his fingers across my pussy lips. Just that slight touch sends a jolt deep inside and I arch my back wanting more. His fingers feather my sensitive skin all the way down my thigh to my ankle.

Spreading my legs wider, Bryce places the last noose around my left ankle. By the time he's done tying me up, I'm so hot, moist and needy for him and I can't wait for what's next.

He gracefully saunters back over to the tall wardrobe and pulls something else out. It's a deep dark purple, silky blindfold. He sits on the side of the bed and holds it up so I can see. "I'm going to put this over your eyes, okay?"

"Yes."

I feel his finger run down my cheek and across my lower lip. "You biting that lip makes me want to fuck you. Hard!"

Oh, well, in that case, I'll keep doing it.

He releases my lip and slides the blindfold over my eyes securing it in place. "Can you see anything?" Bryce asks.

"No."

"Good." He kisses my lips and I feel his tongue dart out to separate my lips, but it's quick to tease me with what's next.

The bed shifts and I hear his feet walk across the floor, away from the bed, the door opens and he's gone.

Lying there in silence, I'm left wondering where he went. What's he doing? Is he coming back? I pull on my restraints maneuvering my wrists around, but they just pull tighter.

I hear him walk back in the room and I feel his warm breath against my ear startling me. "You can't get loose. Remember? I'm a fireman, trained extensively to tie excellent knots."

He's close, I feel the heat from his body, so I arch my body farther to his touch. I'm on fire waiting for him to touch me, but he doesn't yet. I take a deep breath and inhale the smell of him and his cologne. He's so intoxicating. I could drink him up all day.

"Do you know how beautiful you look right now, tied up in my bed?"

I smile.

I hear him walk back to the wardrobe moving things around in the cabinet. Then I hear him walk back and he places something on the table next to my head. I feel the bed dip beside me, as something tickles my forehead, my cheek, across my neck, around each breast. Both nipples pucker when he spends time taunting each of them. It tickles across my stomach, my hips, my belly button, down each leg, my inner thighs, until he reaches my sweet spot. "When I tied you up the first time and took your dress off, I stood there, staring at you. I couldn't take my eyes off of you. You were so beautiful! You made me so fucking horny, I had to go beat off three times."

I can't stop smiling. His admission has me shocked and delighted at the same time.

He shakes something and I feel the bed dip in another spot. I think he's kneeling over top of me. I hear something squirt and

I feel cold on my left nipple, followed by warmth. His mouth devours me. Finally! What a sensation, cold then warm.

I pull uselessly against my restraints, I want to pull the blindfold off, I want to see what he's doing, but then another part of me is really enjoying the erotic anticipation and suspense.

"Oh no, Angel, you are mine, all of you, every inch of this beautiful body, mine to do with whatever I please."

Oh my. Really? I hear a squirt again and then I feel cold on my right nipple, then warmth. I start to squirm.

"Patience, Angel. Patience!"

I hear a long squirt and feel a trail of cold in between my breasts all the way down to my belly button. I feel him shift on the mattress, then a tickling on the inside of my thighs. He's now settled in between my legs, lapping all the way up with his warm tongue. He covers the whole area again with long strokes, slowly licking.

He circles my belly button then slides his tongue down where my pubic hair used to be. I lift my butt off of the mattress to meet his tongue, hoping and praying he'll go lower, but he doesn't.

"Bryce, please!"

"I like it when you beg. It sends a tingle to the tip of my cock."

I wonder why being tied up and blindfolded gets me so aroused. I remember when he had me tied up the first time and all the emotions I felt. I remember how scared I was, because I didn't know who had me tied up. I remember that I was nervous, anxious, aroused and adrenaline laced fear ran through my veins like a freight train.

Squirt. The sound and the cold sensation has me arching my back, yanking on my restraints and inhaling deeply. The cold liquid runs down my pussy lips exactly where I want it. I can't take anymore. I thrust my hips into his tongue to feel more. "Stay still or I'm going to stop."

"Please, you said you wouldn't do this to me again."

I feel him smile against my pussy.

"Oh no, I never said such a thing."

I let out a heavy sigh.

He starts licking with more pressure up each side, until all the liquid is gone. His finger circles around my opening. "Is this what you want Angel?"

"Yes."

Blood races through my veins and my breathing escalates.

I'm panting and I circle my hips to feel some sensation.

He slowly inserts his finger, as far as he can go. "What else do you want?" Slowly, lazily he pulls it back out, then slowly, he pushes it back in.

"I want your mouth on me."

"Where?"

I can't point, but I also can't take much more I'm going to explode. "I want you to eat my pussy!"

"Good girl, that's what I want to hear."

His tongue circles my clit, round and round, while his finger slides in me with expert thrusts, in-out, as he picks up the pace. It doesn't take long for my building orgasm.

All the erotic torment, all the sensations, this is what I want. My pulse quickens, my breathing slows and my back arches as I hold the ropes and pull. My legs start to shake.

He doesn't stop, pumping his finger faster, as he flicks, sucks and circles on my enlarged clit.

"Bryce!" I want to scream it feels so good.

My body quivers uncontrollably beneath his mouth.

I vaguely feel the bed shift and then I feel him untie me while I lay there as the aftershocks rip through me. He bends down, and softly whispers in my ear, "I love watching you come. I want to make you come over and over again until you can't take anymore and you beg me to stop."

11

THE BED DIPS and I feel the warmth of his body sitting on the bed next to me. He gently takes my blindfold off. "Welcome back, beautiful."

I give him a satisfied grin as he lifts my wrist to his lips and kisses them.

"Did I hurt you?"

I smile. "No, not at all."

He hauls me up in his arms and holds me so tight. "You're amazing! Do you know that?"

I grab hold of his cock. He moans at my touch as I look deep in his eyes and stroke up and down the length of his cock. "I want this!"

"Oh, you can have it." Bryce positions himself in the middle of the mattress, with his hands clasped behind his head, and his legs spread, showing every fine line of his muscles. His eyes darken with desire and rake up and down my body as I kneel, straddling one of his legs.

My eyes can't look away from him. I shake my head and smile. "Bryce, you're so hot."

"I am eh? So I take it you like?" Bryce gives me his corner of the mouth smirk.

"Oh yes, I like very much."

I can't help myself, I have to touch him. Kneeling over him, I place my hands near his head, on his wrists and run them all the way down with a light touch until I reach his underarms. "This is so sexy!"

His adorable dimple shows with his half smile. "I'm glad you approve."

Running my hands across his chest, I feel his hard nipples between my fingers, the slight smattering of chest hair and his meaty pecs. I squeeze slightly to get a feel of each one in my hands. Then my hands follow down to his hard washboard abs and they tighten further with my touch. His skin feels so good under my hands. I run my finger across the sexy V at his hips as I move to the end of the bed. Leaning over I run my hands down each leg, starting at his thighs, gently grazing my fingers across his balls. And I'm rewarded with his body jerking.

"Angel you're sending a chill through my whole body." His eyes darken as he watches my every move.

It's a good thing I don't open my mouth because I'll drool all over him. My eyes follow every muscle, until they reach his massive cock and then I pounce.

I take him in my mouth as far as I can.

Bryce hisses through his teeth. "Your mouth feels so good on my cock!"

My mouth opens wider to accommodate for his huge circumference, inching my way down. I relax my throat muscles so I can take more of his length making it little more than half way down. Then I ease him out to the tip then go as far down as I can again, licking and sucking, wetting with my saliva.

My head bobs up and down as I stroke his cock. When I flutter my tongue across the tip, I taste a bead of pre-cum. So turned on by this, I moan with pleasure.

"I love that sound. Mmm, oh yeah, that's it Angel, lick me clean. I love fucking your mouth." The rawness of his words sends a shiver through me. "Oh yeah, like that, get me wet. I can feel it dripping down my balls."

He's getting close. I sense this because he's more aggressive as he holds my head tightening his grip with both his hands while pumping his cock into my mouth.

I see his balls tighten and I know it's payback time. I lift my mouth off his cock, look up into his eyes, and smile mischievously. I hold up my index finger and wave it in the air, "Oh no, baby, not yet!"

Suddenly, I'm tackled to the bed and flipped on my back.

I giggle.

He's on top of me, pinning my hands to the mattress and I'm smiling so hard my dimples are showing and my cheeks hurt. I'm so proud of myself.

Bryce looks down at me with his half wicked smile. "What do you think you're doing?"

"Back at ya, babe."

"So you're teasing me?" Bryce asks.

"Frustrating, isn't it?"

"You tease the hell out of me all damn day, every time I see you. I only have to look at you and I could blow my load. So you don't get to play this game. I'm always hard for you!"

Bryce opens my legs with his large thigh, settling between my legs and impales me with his cock. I gasp at the sudden shock.

Oh yes! Is this supposed to be punishment? Hardly. I love it.

He freezes, not moving a muscle. His large arms hold himself up as he stares down at me. "Did I hurt you? Are you okay to fuck me?"

"No, you didn't hurt me. And yes, you can fuck me. Fuck me hard!"

He pulls out and then plunges hard into me, spearing me as far and as deep as he can go. His cock pulls all the way out to the tip and then slams back in. "See how fucking hard I am for you? I can't get enough of your sweet tight pussy. This is where I want to be, deep inside you, always!"

Picking up the pace, Bryce moves faster, in and out, slapping his balls on my ass.

I reach down, grabbing and squeezing his ass cheek with one hand, while holding his left peck muscle, and pinching his nipple with the other.

Bryce collects my wrists together holding them to the mattress. Restraining me, possessing me. He takes my mouth moaning, as he kisses me. "You're going to make me come, already."

Were both breathless, gasping for air, as our hearts pound. Sweat mists our skin as my muscles clench around him. "You're so tight!"

He reaches down, cupping my ass cheek, tilting me, aiming for that sweet spot deep inside. "Play with your clit." He orders.

I frantically run my finger in circles around my enlarged clit.

"I want you to come for me!" I hear him say as pleasure ripples through me.

He pounds into me a few more times and his whole body tightens as I fall apart underneath him, shaking violently.

"Keera!" He hisses through his teeth as he empties his warm come deep inside me. He Jerks then releases then tightens again, making sure I get every last drop.

Bryce wrestles me, pulling me on top of him with his cock still jerking inside. He cradles me in his big strong arms, as the aftershocks fade and then speaks against my ear. "Holy fuck you're going to kill me!"

My whole body pulsates and tingles. I smile against his neck, still breathless. "That was amazing!"

Lying there wrapped in each other's arms for quite a while, we listen to our hearts beating, trying to regulate our breathing.

We gaze deep in each other's eyes.

"I don't think I can move." He lets out a satisfied breath of air.

"Me neither." We relax, totally exhausted. "Wow! You wear me out." I finally blurt out.

He lifts my chin and looks deep in my eyes "Tell me something, I've been curious. I don't get this. You're twenty-two years old and gorgeous. Why are you still a virgin? You must have had guys lining up? They must have been all over you in high school?"

"I had boyfriends, but when it started to get intense, I always pulled away. It didn't feel right. Not like I feel with you."

I still don't want to share that I'm damaged from the incident with Jake almost raping me.

"Jesus, I'm the luckiest man alive. And do you have any idea how much it means to me that I'm your first. Your one and only?"

"You're too sweet. Thank you, but I think I'm the lucky one."

"I mean it, Angel, I'll never forget what you've given me."

I kiss his cheek and let out a satisfied sigh.

"You should get ready for round two!" Bryce smiles mischievously.

"What! You've got to be kidding, you can go again?"

His cock jerks inside me, making it pulse. "Feel that?"

"Yes, I feel that." I smile. "But you won't get up to go hunting with your brother."

"Yeah, you're right. I'll let you off this time."

When I wake up, I'm way too hot and realize why. Bryce has me wrapped up in his massive arms and his legs are tangled in mine. I don't want to wake him; he's sound asleep. I move my head so I can look at him, study every feature on his beautiful face. God, he's gorgeous! I lay there thinking that this is exactly where I want to be, in his arms forever. I feel safe and warm. But my life never seems to go as planned. There is always some kind of obstruction to keep me from what I want in life. What I want is to have a relationship like my parents had, how they hardly ever fought and how intense and passionate they were together. They were best friends and lovers. I want that in a relationship. I stare at Bryce thinking, could he be the one? The one I could spend the rest of my life with? He's been great, the perfect boyfriend. Considerate, protective, responsible, a great lover, oh God, and that body and face, he's got everything I've ever wanted in a man. I decide I'm going to take this as far as I can go.

Bryce wakes and sees tears seeping down the corner of my eyes.

"What's wrong?" He wipes them away, with his thumbs and kisses my forehead.

"I was thinking about my parents and how much they loved each other and how perfect their relationship was."

"I'm so sorry! Angel If I could take your pain away, I would." He holds me tight and kisses me again. "That's what we have. I can feel it already. I'm telling you. I've never felt like this before. In any other relationship that I've had."

My eyes stop leaking and I sniffle. "How many have you had?"

"Umm, seven."

"How long did they last?"

"Anywhere from three to six months."

I smile. "So if we make it to a year, we're doing something right."

"We'll make it there!" He kisses my forehead again. "I hate seeing you like this, it rips me wide open. I don't want to leave you alone today."

"I want you to go. I'm going to exercise and call my grandfather. I need to check in with him at least once a week. I'll let him know I'm coming to see him."

"Are you sure?"

"Yes. I want you to go."

The alarm sounds and Bryce reaches to shut it off. "I'm going to take a quick shower, would you like to join me?"

"Thank you for the offer, but I'll take a shower after I've worked out. I'll go make you guys some breakfast and some sandwiches."

Bryce gracefully rises out of bed and stands there holding onto his hard cock, swinging it around, grinning from ear to ear.

"Are you sure? We could have some fun with this."

I smile. I love it when he's playful.

Bryce jumps in the shower, while I get busy in the kitchen.

"Good morning." I hear from behind me.

"Good morning, Austin, you're up early."

"I took my shower and got everything ready outside, I have to make some sandwiches and wait for his ass to get out of the shower."

"Oh, I can do that."

"We can do it together if you want." Austin offers.

"Sure."

While we make the sandwiches, I think this'll be the perfect time to pick Austin's brain.

"So what happened with Bryce's last relationship, if you don't mind me asking? I was curious because you said she was a psycho bitch."

"She's psycho all right. She would go nuts on him, throw a complete fit. Hysterical, didn't matter if they were out in public. They'd break up and then he'd get sucked back in every time."

"How many times did they break up?"

"Fuck, it seemed like every week. The final straw was when she went to the fire department and flipped out right in front of everyone. She slapped him across the face, accused him of cheating on her, swore and spit like a nut job. He had to carry her out of there kicking and screaming. That's when he knew it was finally done. She's still stalking him."

"Oh." I say quietly. "Was he cheating on her?"

"Bryce would never do that. He's a one woman man, but somehow she always got that shit in her sick brain that he was cheating."

"So she's still stalking him?"

"Yeah, but don't worry, he's never going back to that. This is the happiest I've ever seen him. He can't get enough of you."

I hear the shower shut off.

"Thanks Austin."

"No problem Blondie, you can ask me anything."

I smile. "Is that my new nickname?"

"Yup, you like it?"

"Yeah, I do."

Austin bumps my shoulder.

Bryce comes out of the bathroom with just a towel wrapped low on his hips and I can't take my eyes off of him.

"And what are you two doing out here? Looks like you're having way too much fun without me."

"I've been waiting for you to get out of the damn shower, you making a career out of it. Were supposed to conserve water remember?"

"Are you done bitching at me?" Bryce asks.

"Depends, are you going to haul ass?"

"I'm hurrying. You need to take a chill pill." Bryce saunters toward the bedroom to get dressed and drops his towel right at the door giving me a perfect view of his fine ass.

"Man! Shut the damn door." Austin yells.

My cheeks hurt from my full, white teeth, face splitting smile. What a glorious view. I don't mind one bit, but it's too hard, taking every ounce of energy out of me, not to follow him in there.

Austin and I make Canadian bacon, egg, cheese and ketchup on an English muffin with home fries for a side dish. Quick and easy, grab and go food.

Bryce comes out of the bedroom looking amazing in his tight jeans that accentuate his large package, tight black t-shirt, which shows every hard ripple of his washboard abs, his large pecks and his hard nipples. His hair is still wet and he looks sexy as hell.

I look him up and down, with my corner of the mouth smile.

Bryce saunters over to me, coming up from behind me and

I feel the warmth from his body cocooning mine as he wraps his arm around my belly, pulling me closer to his semi-erect cock.

He bends and whispers in my ear. "I'm nice and smooth for you now."

I turn my head and look up at him as he smirks down at me with a gleam in his eye and I realize what he means.

"Are you sure you want me to go?"

"I'll be fine. I'm going to make our stroganoff for tonight and then I'm going to exercise. You go have fun with your brother."

Bryce comes to sit next to me on the bar stool and Austin stands at the breakfast bar, both inhaling their English muffins. "Mmm, these are good!"

Austin quickly finishes his breakfast and is standing at the back door, waiting impatiently for Bryce. "Holy fuck, are you in slow motion today or what?"

Bryce gracefully lifts off the bar stool and saunters around to the other side of me. "Okay, relax, I won't be long." He gives me a heart stopping kiss. "Bye."

"Bye, be careful!"

We hear Austin mumbling in the background. "I've never seen anyone so pussy whipped." Austin pulls Bryce by his shirt collar. "Fuck, we're never going to get out of here. I hope you don't take this long responding to fire calls."

"Screw you! I'm on vacation!" Bryce moseys to the back door and dresses in his winter gear.

Bryce is taking his time just to piss Austin off, I think. I smile at their playful antics of teasing and wave good-bye.

Since meeting Bryce, I've been a little preoccupied, slacking from my workouts. While I'm punching and kicking, to my DVD of Turbo Jam, my mind wonders about what Austin said.

I picture how Bryce's ex-girlfriend went to the fire station and slapped him across the face. How she spit and swore at him in front of everyone there and how he carried her out kicking and screaming. I shake my head. I wonder what her name is and what she looks like and how she got him to go back to her every time.

How would I feel being Bryce's girlfriend for six months and him breaking up with me? Would I go a little psycho, too? No, I wouldn't do that. It's not in my nature. I'm not that type of person. Or would I?

What if she convinces him to go back to her again? Already I can't stand the thought of not being with him. With all that's happened in the last five days with him, I couldn't stand to lose it. I've never felt more alive than what I do right now, being with Bryce.

I finish working out and get in the shower. After washing my body down, I put shave gel on my pubic area, pits and legs. "Well here goes nothing."

Finishing up my shower, I wrap a towel around me and play some music on my phone, while I dance and comb out my hair.

"Shit, I have to call Gramps."

When I walk into Bryce's room to get dressed, I glance at the tall wardrobe in the corner.

"I wonder what's in there."

Absent mindedly, I fish the keys out from his dresser, place the key in the lock, turn it and open the door.

I get a quick glance of what's inside and then I slam the door closed. "What the fuck!" My hearts racing, ready to pop out of my chest. I shake my head as I lean my arm on the door above my head.

My mind is a cluttered mess as I turn and slide my back down the length of the cabinet until I reach the floor. I hesitate for a minute thinking.

"Do I really want to see what's in there?"

12

I STAND BACK UP and open the door again. Inside are the fur handcuffs, the ones I got a glimpse of earlier. I pull out a whip with feathers on the end of it and run it along my arm. "I wonder if this is what he used on me?"

Then the unbidden thought enters my mind. Has he used these on psycho? That's when I see vibrators still in the package.

"Hmm, maybe not."

Coloured glass dildos? "These are pretty." Jeez you could use these as a centerpiece on your kitchen table, they're so pretty. Just think of the hilarious conversations you'd have with your friends.

I rummage through everything, exploring. "Ben Wa balls? What do you do with these?"

Taking a paddle out, I smack my hand. "Ouch!" Then a riding crop. I turn and smack my ass, just to see if it hurts. Nipple clamps, butt plug? Oh Bryce, you're scaring me. What the hell are you into? I shake my head.

Something else that's hanging up catches my eye. "What the heck is this thing? A ball with a leather strap? Strange."

I pull open the drawer below, inside are silk ties, silk masks, lubricants, scented oils, bras, thongs, silk lace top panty hose and garter belts.

This is all too overwhelming. I don't even know what to do with half of this crap. Jesus, this is moving way too fast. I was a virgin a few days ago and you want to introduce me to all this kinky shit already?

"Well now that we've let the cat out of the bag. What else are you into? How can I tell him I was snooping? Maybe I won't say a word. He's going to see it on your face dumb ass!"

Placing everything back where it was, I close the door, lock it and replace the keys back in the drawer where they were.

I keep talking to myself. "I knew this was too good to be true. I was wondering when I'd see the other side of him. Mom always told me to stay away from guys like this. Why aren't you listening? Maybe I should make a bee line for the door, get the hell out of here and never look back. How could you do that to him? You can't. You were saying a couple minutes ago that you couldn't live without him. Jesus, I'm getting a headache."

Rubbing my fingers between my eyes, I try to suppress the sudden ache coming on. I need to stop thinking about it.

Searching around, I find my phone. I've got to call Gramps before I forget with all this shit on my mind. What does he plan on doing to me? Will he hurt me? Will he take it too far and I'll eventually have to leave him?

I dial it three times before I finally get it right. Shit, maybe calling right now isn't such a good idea. Get it together Keera. It's only kinky paraphernalia. No big deal, get over it.

"Hi, Gramps, how are you doing?"

"Do' in good. How've you been Giggles?"

"Good, I'm coming to visit you Sunday."

"That's good to hear. I haven't seen you in a while."

"Can I stay for the week?"

"A week? You sure you're okay?"

I chuckle. "Yeah, I'm fine. I'm missing you Gramps."

"Missing you too."

"Friday morning I'll head back home."

"Sure you can stay for as long as you want. Honey."

"Would you like me to bring anything?"

"A case of blue."

"Sure, no problem. I'll call before I start driving to your place. Okay I'll see you then. Bye love you Gramps."

"Love you too, Giggles. Drive safe."

Good he didn't ask me what I was doing. Oh, ya no, I've been kidnapped, tied up, blindfolded, oh and now he's my boyfriend and he's quite the kinky fucker.

I put some more wood on the fire and start boiling the water for the noodles and then I get dressed.

Since I was just introduced to sex and have no experience at all, I don't know how to handle this. I knew I should have never opened that. Damn it!

The unwelcome thought of him using his kinky toys on his other girlfriends pops into my head again. He's obviously got a few more years' experience than I do. I have no knowledge at all, so I've got to learn and catch up fast. I've got to be the great lover he expects me to be and the sex goddess that he deserves. So far everything that he's done to me hasn't been that bad. Did I enjoy it? Hell yeah! So what's the problem? Is it the mystery of the unknown? I don't know, but I decide I'm going to take it one day at a time and enjoy every minute of his kink. If it doesn't hurt, than it can't be that bad. Right?

As I'm rinsing the noodles for the stroganoff, I hear a four wheeler pull into the back yard. I look outside, to see that it's Bryce. Austin isn't with him. Oh shit! What do I tell him? Nothing! I quickly go back to what I was doing. You say nothing. Okay I can do this.

Bryce walks in the door. "Well hello there beautiful!" He strips out of his boots, insulated cover all's and coat, hanging them up on the hooks at the back door.

I stand at the kitchen island in front of the sink and feel the atmosphere in the room change instantly. Like an electric charge sparking all around us.

"Hello, to you, too, gorgeous." We both smile at each other. "How come you're back so early? Not that I mind, I'm glad you're here."

"Austin said something about me fidgeting too much, and that I'm useless because I've got pussy on my mind. He said I'm scaring the deer. He told me to go, and shoved a grocery list at me."

"Is he mad at you?"

"He'll get over it."

He prowls toward the wrap around counter facing me and gazes deep into my eyes. Then his eyes slide down to my cleavage, which is popping out from my buttons being undone. He saunters closer, coming around to the opening of the counter and sees that I'm wearing a short sun dress. He circles me like a predator, ready to pounce, eyeing me up and down. "You're trying to kill me aren't you? All the blood's going to be rushing to my cock and I won't be able to think straight."

His hand slips through my hair holding the back of my neck, the other hand rests on my lower back, holding me close. He seals his mouth to mine giving me a slow lush kiss and he moans. "I've missed you!" He deepens the kiss, as our tongues dance in circles. He grips me aggressively tighter and grinds into me. Just as we're getting hot, he pulls away quickly. "Fuck, see what you do to me? I can't concentrate when I'm around you. Austin's going to be pissed if I don't get my ass to the grocery store. We better leave before I have you sprawled out on this counter." He rubs down the surface like he's rubbing my skin and it does strange things to me.

"Okay we'll go, I have to get my boots and coat." I say as I dart to the bedroom.

Bryce's deep voice carries from the kitchen to the bedroom.

"We're going to the other grocery store so we don't see your stalker. And I also want to pick up a phone so I can text you when we're not together. I need to know your safe."

I come out of the bedroom with my short cowboy boots and a short jean jacket over top of my sun dress.

"Holy fuck, do you look hot! You really are trying to kill me aren't you?"

I smile. "Thank-you!"

"No! Thank you!"

It takes us longer than usual going through the back roads, to the North end of town to the mobile phone store. But along the way, we see a mother bear and her cubs, scurrying to get back into the trees when they hear the sound of Bryce's engine.

When we arrive, Bryce comes around the truck to help me down, but hesitates lifting my dress to see what's underneath.

I look around cautiously to see if anyone's watching us. I don't see anyone, so I let him continue.

"White lacy thong, one of my favourites, but underneath this dress you should have nothing on, so I have easy access." He runs his finger behind the fabric, until he reaches my clit. "Nice and smooth. I love this. Something's popping out for me." I smile at him and he pulls my dress back down and then helps me out of the truck. Bryce holds the door open for me, gently placing his hand on my lower back as we walk into the cellular store.

The two saleswomen behind the counter almost fall over themselves to help Bryce. They quickly launch into detailed instruction after he tells them which phone he wants. I stand back and watch the fiasco unfold of how they touch and flirt and lean into his personal space. Bryce doesn't even pay attention to the way they're falling all over him. They blush when they touch his hand, or rub up against him and when it comes time to explain the features on the phone, I finally get pissed and say, "I'll show him, I have an iPhone." I've had enough. "I'll be in the truck."

Bryce turns to see me walking out the door. "Angel."

Fuming, I keep walking to the truck and climb in. Why am I so pissed? Am I jealous? Is this what I'm feeling? Jeez, Keera calm down. Relax.

Bryce stands at the glass door with his hand on it ready to leave, but he's still talking to the over exuberant saleswoman. He finally comes walking toward the truck and gets in. "Why did you leave?"

"I don't know." I spit out.

Bryce looks at me trying to figure me out. "Are you mad?" He's smirking slightly.

"Are you laughing at me?"

"No I'd never do that." He touches my knee. "Are you okay now?"

"No. Jeez they couldn't keep their hands off of you."

Now he's really smiling. "All I was doing was asking questions."

"I know. It's not your fault you're too damn gorgeous."

He slides me across the seat, plastering me against him, hugging and kissing my hair.

I look over to see the saleswoman at Bryce's door. "There she is again."

Bryce turns and rolls down his window.

"Here's what you asked for Bryce. I added it to your bill. If you need anything, come in and see us again."

Bryce takes the bag from her. "Thank you."

She leaves to go back in the store, but her and her friend stare at us through the window.

Bryce starts the truck and we head over to the grocery store.

In the parking lot, Bryce opens the bag and hands me a box wrapped in colourful paper. "Open it."

I hold it and look up at him.

"What's this?"

"Open it and you'll find out."

Opening the iPad, I stare down at it then look at Bryce. "Thank you, but…"

Bryce gives me a scorching kiss shutting me up and all train of thought is gone.

"Since you love music, I thought we'd put a playlist on there for you."

Boy, do I feel like an idiot. "You're so sweet thank you. I love it." I hold it to my chest hugging it. And just like that my jealous tantrum is forgotten about.

"Here's the list Austin gave me." We push the cart down the aisles in the grocery store, crossing off the items when they're found. Bryce stops in the middle of the aisle and stares at me with that hungry I want to fuck you now, stare. He prowls close and holds me tight as he whispers in my ear. "I'm so happy I went to the other grocery store that day. You know what that is? It's fate. We're meant to be together." He holds me against the shelf, running his hands down my butt. "I can feel the outline of your pretty little thong." He looks down both ends of the aisle and then lifts the back of my dress up so he can rub my ass cheeks. "I'm glad you wore this dress today, I like it. I mean, I really like it. Look, you're making me hard already."

I reach back retrieving his hands. "Then quit doing that!"

He's so fast, his finger quickly slips down my cleavage and I playfully swat his hand.

"I want to do you right now, in this grocery store. Fuck, you make me so horny!" He runs his hand up my inner thigh, and then realizes someone's coming down the aisle.

"Bryce!" I smack his arm, thoroughly embarrassed. "Talk about being molested in the grocery store." I giggle.

He quickly fixes my dress and straightens up, like he's not up to something.

Bryce laughs. "God, I love it when you giggle. That's the

sweetest sound." He tugs me down the aisle and we smile ridiculously all the way to the end.

We head for the seafood counter and Bryce looks over the fish, while I find the relish and mayo. When I come back, I hear a commotion in the next aisle. I peek around to see three women, approximately my age, giggling, laughing and pushing each other to go speak to Bryce and he's clueless with his back to them, paying attention to his fish.

Hesitating a moment, I watch them.

Bryce Hamilton is the kind of man that catches the eye of women. Their attention diverts to him immediately. Not only for his stunning good looks, but also because of the way he moves. His walk is a sexy strut and when he stands stock-still anyone that looks at him, male or female can see the power in his stance. His face is beyond beautiful and that body of his makes women think of extraordinary, adrenaline fueled, explosive, mind numbing sex. I know, because I've been on a lust filled trip from the moment I've met him.

This is something I'm not used to. Women throwing themselves at him. I shake my head. "Forget it bitches, he's mine." I mumble under my breath. Walking over to the cart, I place the items in it. I stand beside him feeling that familiar tingle down my spine and he wraps his arm around my waist and kisses my forehead. I reach into his back pocket and grab his ass cheek. He tightens his grip letting me know he likes it.

I hear. "See, I told you he's taken."

"Lucky little bitch."

Seeing how these women react around Bryce makes me jealous. This is something new, some foreign emotion I've never felt before. I don't like the way it makes me feel and I wonder when I'll quit with the jealousy and stop caring how women are affected by my boyfriend. Probably never, but it does make me appreciate what I have, and I'm not about to let it go.

We find the remaining items on the list, and cash out.

While we drive through town, I put my phone number and my Grandfathers, into Bryce's contact list.

"What about Leena and Katie?"

"Oh, okay." I put them in too.

"I'll probably never use their numbers, but in case I need to find you, say, if your phone is dead, or you're mad at me."

"You think I wouldn't answer my phone if I was mad?"

"I don't want to see you mad at me. I like you just the way you are."

As we drive down the back roads, Bryce constantly looks in the rear view mirror, making sure were not followed, I presume.

When he finally relaxes, he runs his hand up my thigh, sliding his finger underneath my thong and separates my moist silky folds.

"You're wet for me again! Take your thong off!"

What? Is he kidding? I hesitate. Obviously he's not, by the intense look on his face. All righty then, I guess I'll lose these.

His eyes stay glued to me as I slip them down my legs. "Hand 'em over." His finger motions for me to give them up.

Bryce looks up at the road for a second, then looks back at me while he takes them in his hand. He reveals the wet spot, sticking his nose in them and takes a long exaggerated sniff. "You smell so sweet!"

I can't believe he did that. I shake my head and smile.

Stuffing them in his back pocket, Bryce resumes caressing the soft skin on the inside of my thigh. "Your skins so soft." His fingers gently flutter over my pussy lips. He smiles and watches my reaction as he separates my moist folds.

"Right here too."

He sticks his finger in as far as he can go, palming my enlarged clit in circles.

I moan and my head falls back against the seat. I'm so hot for him. I want him right now!

Desperately, I want to give him beautiful memories of our

time together, knowing it's coming to an end soon. I want to make sure he comes back for more.

He pulls his finger out and my head flies back up and I let out a heavy sigh.

"Look what you do to me!" He grips the outline of his hard cock through his jeans.

I lick my lips, visualizing myself sucking his cock, while he's driving. "I want your cock!"

"What are you going to do with it, if I give it to you?"

"I'm going to take you deep in my mouth and suck it."

"Fuck, I love hearing you talk nasty."

I watch him undo his pants and shimmy them down to his knees. He takes out his bulging cock from his boxers and pulls them down. I wrap my hand around his shaft and take him deep in my mouth.

"Keera! Fuck. Your mouth feels so warm on my cock."

He adjusts the seat further back so my head doesn't hit the steering wheel. My head bobs up and down taking him as far as I can go, stroking and sucking simultaneously.

The truck accelerates as he moans. "You suck me so good. That's it, Angel, keep sucking me like that."

He lets off the gas and we coast now. I reach down to fondle his balls and they tighten immediately. "Woman, that mouth of yours, fuck, you're so good at that." His cock grows hard as steel in the palm of my hand and I run my tongue all the way up feeling his plump veins. "Keera, you've got to stop! I'm going to come in your mouth!" I don't stop. I keep up the same relentless rhythm. "Angel." Bryce taps my hip. "I want to come inside you."

Lifting my head, I wipe my mouth.

He pulls onto a laneway going through big muddy puddles, dodging large boulders, branches and trees.

"Where are we going?" I ask curiously.

"I want to show you something." He stops, puts it in four wheel drive and we continue to climb. A tree lying across the laneway blocks our way through the trail. Bryce stops, puts it in park and pulls his pants back up. He sets the parking brake because of the incline we're on and then gets out without his coat on. I watch as his muscles flex under his T-shirt when he bends to lift the tree up and out of the way.

He gets back in and proceeds to drive again. It's a rough laneway and I'm bouncing all over the cab of the truck. "Better put your seat belt on, Angel."

Now we're driving on a decline. I hold on to the dash with my hands as we bounce up and down.

I take my boots off and press my feet against the dashboard to steady myself. I look over at Bryce and his face lights up like a little boy with a new toy, he's having such a good time four wheeling through the rough terrain. Mud flies everywhere, plastering the sides of the truck.

When we reach our destination Bryce stops the truck and comes around to my side, opening the door. He undoes my seatbelt, scoops me up in his arms and spins me around. We're in awe standing in front of a mountain with a stream running along the side of it and a waterfall cascades down the rock face into the stream.

"So what do you think?"

"Bryce, it's beautiful!"

"Just like you."

"Thank you."

He holds me in his arms as we take in all the beauty.

I start to shiver, so he places me back on the seat in the truck.

"I want to make love to you, in this truck, right here. Right now."

He runs around to the driver's side. With the door open, he strips out of his clothes. He throws everything in the back seat of the cab and looks at me. "You're still dressed. Get naked, like now!"

"Sorry, I was enjoying the view."

I can't get my clothes off fast enough.

He shimmies over to my side and I straddle his legs, rubbing my clit along his length as I hold his face with my hands.

"I want you," I say. "I want you inside me."

Our mouths slide over each other's and our tongues dance as he holds onto my ass, pulling me closer into him. We kiss frantically, desperately.

I suck on his tongue knowing that he likes it and so do I. It sends a sweet tingling sensation straight to my insides. We both moan. "I need you inside me, Bryce!"

"I know, I need you too, Angel."

Holding onto his shoulder with one hand, I shift onto one knee, rising to gain the height I need to feel his length beneath me as I hover. Wrapping my fingers around his long shaft, I position it at my entrance.

Garbled sounds escape from deep within Bryce's throat, as I lower myself down onto the swollen head of his cock. "Damn, you're so tight."

I relish the exquisite fullness of his cock stretching me. Then I lift up slowly, tilting my hips slightly and I feel the plump veins when I descend, letting him slide deeper inside me.

I inhale sharply, "Oh God, Bryce, you feel so good."

"So do you. I've been thinking about this all damn day."

I slide all the way down as I gaze into his beautiful eyes. We hold our stare as he holds my hips and guides me up and down faster. Being so close, face to face out in the wilderness is so damn intimate and erotic at the same time.

"I can't think of anything else. You're like a drug to me, Angel. I'm dying until I get my next fix. This is where I love to be—with you, inside you, always!"

Cupping his beautiful face in my hands. "You're doing the same to me. I'm getting greedy and I don't know how to handle it."

"I think we're handling it fine."

"Umm yes." I lift and lower.

He looks so frickin' hot underneath me. His washboard abs, his huge arms, sculpted to perfection like a Greek god and his large forearms, thick with veins cursing through them and I have to run my hands down them. His thighs are large and muscular. His cock is hard as steel and every time I think about it, I want it inside me. The impact of his face, the chiseled distinct outline of his jaw, his adorable eyes and how he affects me, he melts me with every glance. I can't stop looking at him even if I tried. I won't ever get enough.

Were hot and breathless and we're fogging up the windows.

"That's it Angel, ride me, ride me hard."

He cups my breasts, squeezing my nipples together as he sucks on both, sending a shiver of ecstasy through my whole body.

We reposition ourselves. Bryce slides his butt closer to the dash and I place my feet on the seat next to his thighs so I can ride him hard. His hands grip my hips tighter, guiding me up and down on his rock hard shaft. He flexes his hips, so his cock tilts slightly and hits my sweet spot inside me. Slapping flesh, moans and whimpering sounds resonate throughout the cab of the truck as he meets me with every expert thrust. "Fuck, your milking my cock."

I focus on the intense feeling of where we're connected and I tighten my slick walls around him, never breaking eye contact.

"Angel, I can't hold out much longer!" He reaches down and circles my wet swollen clit with his finger, shocking me with the unexpected muscle contraction around his massive cock and it sends me over the edge.

"Bryce!"

"That's it Angel, let go. I'm right here with you." We fall apart together, staring deep in each other's eyes. I let out a fierce loud cry and he groans holding his breath, shaking and tensing underneath me as he squirts his warm come deep inside me.

I fall limp on his chest, pressing him into the seat, as he wraps his arms around my back, holding me tight against his heated body. We hold one another for a bit, until our breathing calms.

He pulls my chin up to look at him and he kisses my lips gently. "I love the sound of you whimpering."

"I love watching the expressions on your face and how your muscles tighten up and when we're done, you hold me tight and kiss me." I caress his cheek intimately.

"You do, eh?" He kisses me again. "What we have together. It's almost scary."

"What do you mean?"

"I mean, I don't think either one of us could stop this feeling if we tried."

"I know. I've never felt this way before."

Bryce holds my face in his hands and looks deep in my eyes like he's going to say something. He hesitates, gathering his thoughts I presume. He shakes his head and then finally speaks. "I'm a changed man, but then I knew that the moment I saw you that I'd never be the same. You grabbed my heart, soul and mind in that instant and now I'm royally fucked. Don't get me wrong, that's a good thing. I'm not explaining this well, am I?"

I can't close my mouth from the huge grin that's plastered across my face. "Yes you're explaining it fine." I love how he starts out caring and vulnerable, but when he sounds too mushy his tough guy image kicks in to offset the vulnerability.

Bryce reaches into the glove box for some napkins. He lifts me up, pulls out and runs the napkin gently between my legs. The way he takes care of me before he focuses on himself makes me smile every time. When we're all cleaned up, he wrestles me down against the seat. I'm lying down, staring up into his beautiful eyes, waiting for him to continue what he wanted to say earlier.

"Do you know what you do to me? How much you mean to me?"

"You do the same to me, Bryce."

"How am I going to leave you for four days?"

"I know I've been thinking about it and I hate the thought."

"I'll text you every day, in the morning and at night."

"You're going to be working. If you don't have time, that's fine." I say it, even though I really do want him to text.

"I'm texting! I'll find the time. I'll be going out of my mind, crazy without you."

"Same here, I'm going to miss you so bad it hurts." I can't help myself, the tears start to flow.

"I know Angel, please don't cry. It kills me, seeing you like this." He wipes my tears with his thumbs. "We've got to quit thinking about it and enjoy every second that we have together." Bryce tries desperately to stop me from crying. "You know what keeps running through my mind?"

"What?" I try to stop the waterworks.

"The first time I got inside you, when you told me, I'm not a virgin anymore! It broke my heart seeing you cry, but those words. God, those words will be stuck in my head for the rest of my life. Do you have any idea what that means to me? What you gave me? I'll always be thankful! Thank you Angel."

He slaps a wet lush kiss on my lips and I stop crying. "Look you're making me hard again."

I smile and laugh. "You're always hard."

"Yes, it's all your fault. I want to fuck you again, but it's getting dark, we better get out of here. If we get stuck we'll be sleeping in this truck. We'll finish this when we get home."

I smile. "Thank you Bryce, this was nice, very romantic."

"You're welcome Angel."

Bryce lifts up and off of me. He holds his hand out helping me up and then he hands me my clothes.

My gaze slides over his amazing face and body with love and lust filled eyes as he dresses.

I'm falling under his spell and there's no turning back now.

13

I CHECK THE WEATHER on my phone during the ride back to the cabin. "Bryce, the temperatures are going to dip below freezing in the next few days, I have to go back to my house to shut the water off, since I won't be there for a while and I also need to bring Mr. and Mrs. Fisher their groceries."

"No problem, we'll go tomorrow."

When we get back to the cabin, Bryce holds his hand out to help me down from the truck. I slide down his body while he runs his hands underneath my dress, feeling my behind. "You've got one fine ass Angel, do you know that?"

"Thank you." I say lowering my lips to his, giving him a lush wet kiss.

Turning to grab my phone and purse, I notice a white stain that I left on his charcoal leather seat without my thong. "Oh my god." I climb on the running board and bend over reaching across the seat, desperately trying to wipe it off with the sleeve of my coat, but it's dry and it's not coming off.

My attention turns to Bryce because I hear him laughing. His lips curve into his half wicked smile and his eyes light up. "Look how wet you are." He holds my lower back with one hand and reaches under my dress with the other and sticks his finger in between my pussy lips. "That's fucking beautiful. I like you bent over like this." He lifts my dress and kisses my ass. "I want to fuck you like this."

"Bryce, concentrate! We need a wet cloth to get this off so Austin doesn't see it."

"Nope, we're leaving it right there, I love it!"

"You can't."

"Yes I can, this is my truck and I can do whatever I want. We're leaving it there, and every time I get in my truck I'm going to think of today and you and every moment we've spent together." He picks me up by my waist and shuts the door. He walks to the back of the truck and puts me down to get the groceries out.

"But Bryce…"

"No buts, it's staying!"

The cabin's filled with the aroma of a hearty home cooked meal as we enter, and the smell has me rushing over to lower the temperature of the crock pot. "Almost forgot about this. See how you distract me."

"Smells good." Bryce rubs against me. "I like distracting you."

"Didn't you get enough in the truck?"

Bryce pulls my hair to the side and kisses down my neck. "Yeah, but I always want more."

Austin comes through the back door and sees Bryce seducing me. "Christ, you guys are at it again?" He grumbles and then retrieves a few plates out of the cupboard. "Smells good. I'm starving."

"It'll be ready in two minutes."

"What have you two been up to? Forget I asked that question." Austin shakes his head in disgust.

"We went grocery shopping, got a new phone and showed Keera the waterfall down the laneway."

"Trying to impress her again, eh? And did it work?" Austin directs his question to me with a grin and then lines up to dish out his food.

"Oh yeah, it was beautiful! I loved it."

"We came across the waterfall by chance." Austin says proudly between bites. "We were out four wheeling."

"We were lost." Bryce teases. "Austin was leading the way."

"I got a deer. It's on the ATV, we've got to go hang it." Austin can't contain his excitement.

Bryce rushes over and looks out the window. "Damn, that's a good size, look at the rack on that! You'll have to get that mounted." Bryce can't contain his excitement for his brother.

I walk over to the window to see. "Wow! That's big."

"Let's celebrate! Turn the flood lights on! We'll get some beer, start a fire, and we'll clean it. We'll marinade some steaks from it, for tomorrow's dinner."

I watch Austin explode with excitement and I smile. I love seeing this side to him. He's always trying to be Mr. Calm, cool and collected.

As I sit around the fire, keeping warm, I set up Bryce's phone, while the boys prepare to lift the deer onto the large hooks.

"Is there anything I can do to help?" I ask.

"You can jump on the ATV and pull it away to lift this."

I'm excited that I have something to do.

I sit on the ATV and start it as Bryce and Austin hook up the chain. "Give it a little, nice and slow." I gently push on the throttle and ease forward slowly until I hear, "Whoa!"

They secure the deer to the hook at the top of the archway. Then they tell me to, "Back up." I do as I'm told and they unhook the chain. Everything goes smoothly.

Taking pictures with Bryce's phone, I watch the whole process of skinning and gutting a deer. It's a little gross but I'm still curious. I run into the cabin to get freezer bags and hold them open, assisting as they place the meat in.

When the boys finish cleaning up we sit around the fire drinking beer. Austin tells us in full detail how he took the deer down. The excitement in their voices and the brotherly love makes me appreciate this special moment. I feel bad for stealing Bryce's attention away but mostly because he missed his opportunity to get a deer with Austin.

"Hey what are you two doing tomorrow?" Austin asks.

"We have to go shut the water off at Keera's."

"Well since I already bagged my deer, I'll come with you."

As Bryce plays with his new phone, trying to learn a few things, he gets a text. *You have to clean off the seat in your truck before Austin gets in.*

Bryce looks at me with his wicked smile. *I told you Angel, it's staying.*

Bryce you can't!

Do you know how beautiful you are by the fire?

Quit changing the subject!

He gets close and takes a picture of me, then sits beside me and whispers in my ear. "Since you liked being tied up, I thought we'd try something new."

"Oh yeah, what did you have in mind?" I'm distracted that easily. I'm ready and willing to do anything he wants the instant he whispers dirty thoughts in my ear. My greed for him is intensifying with every moment that passes, and it's hard to wrap my head around it. Where did my control over men go? I have no willpower with him. He's like decadent chocolate, but the craving is more intense.

"It's a surprise!"

I smile.

"Come." He holds out his hand for me to take. "Let's go in. You look like you're freezing to death."

"You two going in?" Austin asks.

"Keera's cold. I'll get her warmed up." We walk arm in arm toward the cabin. "I've been dying to get my hands on you all night." He says in that sexy tone.

As soon as we get into the cabin, we undress from our winter gear. He leads me into the bathroom and starts ripping his clothes off and then he corners me against the wall, pulling at my clothes, trying to take them off and I smack his hand. "Bryce, your brothers out there, you have to wait until we get in the bedroom."

"I can't wait. I want you now!"

Anxiety and impatience consumes him. He kisses me desperately, ferociously, like he's been starved for years. He runs his hand up the back of my shirt unclasping my bra.

I pull away. "Bryce, you have to wait! I thought you had something planned?"

"I do. I love it when you deny me though."

I smile and shake my head.

I finish brushing my teeth with Bryce still trying to molest and undress me. He finally gives up and concentrates on brushing his own teeth.

He peeks out of the bathroom to see if Austin's in the kitchen and then quickly pulls me into the bedroom, totally naked and cages me against the wall. He kicks the door closed and locks it. His mouth is on me in an instant, giving me gentle savouring kisses while he undresses me. Every time he takes an article of clothing off, he kisses me. "I want to try something different. I think you'll like it since you liked being tied up." Bryce swats my butt. "Middle of the bed."

I do as I'm told. I can barely contain my excitement. My nipples are proof of my arousal; they're rock hard and puckered for what he has planned.

Bryce retrieves the keys out of the drawer and gracefully walks over to the tall wardrobe, opening it. Bryce searches for something, rattling things around in there and it has my curiosity peaked.

"Ah, here they are." He says.

Sitting on the bed beside me, Bryce drapes the dark purple silk tie over my nipples. His fingers slide underneath pinching and pulling on them making them harder.

He stands and lifts one knee placing it on the bed beside my hip so he's leaning over as he lifts my arms above my head, clasping my wrists with the dark purple, fuzzy handcuffs.

"Look at you, you're so sexy. Can I take a picture of you?"

I roll my hips to give him a sexier pose and so I don't reveal too much. I mean seriously, I hardly know Bryce. "You're not going to show anyone, right?"

"I would never do that. This is for my eyes only, no one else, I promise you!"

"Sure."

Bryce takes a picture with his phone. "My God, look how beautiful you are." He shows me.

I watch his gorgeous hard body saunter over to the wardrobe. He looks so happy and excited. I can't take my eyes off of him. I hear him clanging things around in there again. "Stand on the bed!"

Eagerly I stand, waiting for my next instruction. He climbs on the bed and stands in front of me with a chain and he hooks it to the carabiner on the ceiling.

I was wondering what the four hooks on the ceiling were for. I should really ask more questions.

I'm staring at his beautiful body while he's busy and I can't help myself, I run the back of my hand down his chest and across his nipple, then his rock hard abs, leading downward.

His eyes darken and he restrains my hand. "Oh no, Angel, you don't get to touch me."

Somehow with him telling me I can't touch him, it makes me want to more.

"But you're so hot!"

He tries to be serious but I see a ghost of a smile.

I watch him hook another carabiner to the end of the chain, and then he lifts my arms above my head and clasps my handcuffs. "Hold onto the chain, don't let go. Do you hear me?"

"Yes."

"I think you've seen enough." He slips the dark purple silk blindfold over my eyes.

I'm standing on the bed with my legs spread, my wrists handcuffed above my head and I'm holding onto a chain to give me support so I don't fall over and I'm blindfolded.

My senses are going wild, wondering what he's going to do next.

"THIS…IS…SO…FUCKING…EROTIC!!" He accentuates every word slowly in his deep sexy voice.

I feel him shift on the bed, then he's back.

Awareness of him standing in front of me from the warmth of his body has goose bumps covering my skin, he hesitates for a couple seconds and then I hear him take a picture. "Do you know how fucking hot you are and how bad I want you? Fuck, what you do to me."

Shifting on the bed again, I feel his finger slide inside me. His body is plastered against mine from behind me, his other arm is wrapped around my shoulder, and his hand is holding the front of my throat, almost like a choke hold, but he's gentle.

He whispers in my ear. "You're wet for me. I love it!" He inserts his finger slowly, then withdraws slowly, in and out, lazily.

I start to squirm, meeting his finger as he inserts way too slow with his torturous rhythm.

"Bryce. Please!"

"I know Angel." His big warm body moves in front of me now and he kisses me, sliding his tongue deep in my mouth, fucking me with his tongue and finger, using the same torturous rhythm.

I moan in his mouth.

He drops to his knees, still fucking me with his finger, and his mouth flutters my clit.

God, I hope Austin doesn't come in this room right now. He'd get one hell of a surprise seeing us being so naughty, but it's kinky as hell and I'm loving every minute of it.

My blood feels like it's on fire, my chest is heaving, I'm so close, its building.

"Bryce! It feels so good." I clamp down on his finger, clenching and squeezing my muscles. My whole body quivers and I hold onto the chain for support or my knees will buckle. The feeling is so intense as my orgasm rips through me and Bryce doesn't stop, he laps up every last drop, making sure I have an explosive orgasm.

Bryce climbs up my body and holds me tight as my body goes limp against his chest. He kisses my lips, so soft and so gentle. He lifts my handcuffs off of the chain and we slide down together onto the bed. He holds me in his arms on his lap, until my breathing settles.

"You're amazing, thank you for fulfilling one of my fantasies."

"You're welcome! That was so erotic."

"Sex with you is always erotic, Angel."

"What are you going to do to me now?"

"Always so eager to learn, I like that."

Bryce lays on the bed in that sexy pose with his fingers clasped behind his head and his legs spread. "Straddle my legs backwards and lower yourself down onto my cock. I want to see this sexy little ass going up and down."

I straddle his legs, holding onto his sexy large muscular thighs for support and slowly lower onto his stiff shaft.

"Oh my, I like this position, it makes it so sensitive."

"I'm glad you like. That's it Angel, up and down on my cock. I love being inside you."

He guides me up and down and every time I lower, my clit bumps against his balls, making it hypersensitive and large. I have every inch of him inside me and I can feel him growing harder and thicker. My breathing quickens as the feeling intensifies. He thrusts his hips up to meet every plunge I take.

"That tight sweet pussy is sucking my cock. You're milking me, Angel." The rawness of his words and the sensation unravels me.

All of a sudden I feel his thumb. I think it's his thumb, circling the entrance of my butt. What the hell! But I'm quivering and shaking already. I can't stop. "Bryce!"

"I know Angel, touching your ass is going to make me come."

His thighs tighten beneath me and I hear his breathing change. His skin is damp like mine and I hear. "Fuck, you feel so good!"

He falls apart underneath me and I fall limp hugging his legs. I lay like that while the aftershocks roll over me.

When we both stop shaking and we can finally breathe, I roll over, off of Bryce onto my side and his cock slips out.

He spins around and climbs up my body, trailing sweet tender kisses all the way up. "How was that for my Angel?"

"It was very nice. Except for the invasion near my backside." I say annoyed.

"You know you loved it. You came right away as soon as I touched you. So did I. Touching that sexy little ass of yours gets me off every time. I can't hold back."

I didn't have the heart to tell him otherwise; he seemed to enjoy himself.

We lay there basking in the afterglow of our kinky "sexcapade", kissing one another's neck, sliding our lips across each other's skin. I don't know how long we stay like that, but it's quite a while.

"I'd really like to work out tomorrow, before we go to my house, if we have time?"

"Sounds good, I haven't worked out for a few days, since you've been distracting me, making me have sex all the time." He gives me his mischievous smile.

I bite his neck. "Aren't you cute?"

"Ow! I like it when you bite me."

"You do eh? You're a sick puppy."

He laughs and I giggle.

We lay there holding each other with our legs entwined and we fall asleep.

14

WE WAKE TO the smell of bacon. Austin's cooking us breakfast already.

"Mmm, that smells good." I say as the smell of the bacon wafts up through the door.

Bryce sticks his nose in the crook of my neck. "Mmm, you smell good. You smell like me and sex, I love it. Look you're getting me hard again."

"You're always hard! And you used to call it Mr. Wiggly?"

"I am when I'm around you. Maybe I should call him Mr. Stiffy now."

"Oh Bryce, you're adorable, way too cute. What am I going to do with you?"

He rolls on top, pinning me to the mattress, threading his fingers with mine, above my head, then he kisses my neck and licks up the side of my cheek. "Well, you can play with Mr. Stiffy if you want." He grinds into me and we both laugh. "Let's go eat, we'll workout, take a shower and go to your place."

I get dressed in my yoga pants and matching top.

"What are you wearing?"

"Clothes. Why?"

"You can't go out there like that! Austin's going to get a chubby looking at you. That top looks like you're wearing a bra."

"Oh Bryce come on, let's go have some breakfast." I pull him by the hand into the kitchen and Bryce reluctantly follows.

"Austin I could have helped you."

"No that's okay I like…" when he turns to look at me, he hesitates mid-sentence and his eyes almost pop out of his head and then he continues saying, "to cook." He swallows hard and then turns back around, shaking his head.

"Do you need any help?" I ask.

Austin doesn't turn to look at me when he answers my question. "Umm, maybe some ketchup, plates, and silverware."

Bryce and I set it up and we eat at the breakfast bar.

"Austin this is good!"

"Thank you. What time did you two finally go to bed?"

I can feel my face getting warm.

"She's so cute when she blushes. Yeah, I heard you guys getting all wild and crazy. Let's just say my hand still works. I've been neglecting my buddy."

I almost choke.

"Aww. Too much information." Bryce blurts out.

"What! I need a girlfriend. Hook me up with your friend. She's hot."

"Which one?"

"The one with brown hair."

"Oh that's Leena. I forgot you saw her at the bar. She went to visit her dad in Aruba, I'll call her and see if she's home."

Austin looks me up and down. "So, by the looks of you, you're working out first before we go to your place?"

"Is that okay?"

"Yeah, I need a good workout. It'll help me get rid of some stress and anxiety and sexual tension and whatever else I can think of."

I smile at Austin's honesty.

We clean the kitchen then go into the workout room. I get on the treadmill, Bryce uses the Bow flex and Austin lifts the weights. Every fifteen minutes we switch.

Austin's body is perfect like Bryce and he's wearing just his shorts that hang low on his hips.

Damn, I'm one lucky girl having both of them in my sight. Talk about eye candy? Wow! I admire their muscles flexing, their tight abs, tight butts and strong sexy legs. I don't want Bryce catching me taking a peek of Austin, so I try to focus on Bryce, but I'd look every once in a while. I am human.

After our workout, Bryce and I take a shower together to conserve water, but we get a warning from Austin, "No hanky panky. Haul ass!"

We finish getting ready and on the way out to the truck I remember the white stain on the seat, so I hurry past Bryce to get into the truck before Austin gets in.

"Wow, you're eager to get to your house." Bryce teases.

My eyes widen and I smirk at him then nudge him in the ribs in passing.

"What? You can smack my ass later."

"Bryce!" I shake my head and flop down onto the seat of the truck.

I shift restlessly on the seat, trying to rub out the white stain periodically during the ride to town, without detection from either one of them.

First thing on the to-do list is to get the truck washed. I can tell it's bothering Bryce that his beautiful truck is plastered with mud. Bryce pulls into a stall and grabs my knee. "Stay right here."

Austin kicks the hanging mud and then throws the clumps into the forest behind the car wash.

Bryce holds the high pressure wand and I watch the material on his jacket tighten when his muscles flex. I watch how he focuses intently on the task at hand, but every now and then, he looks up at me and notices I'm staring back. It doesn't matter what Bryce is doing. The man is awe inspiring to watch. I squirm restlessly on the seat.

When he's finished washing the truck, Bryce hops back in grabbing my knee giving me a knowing smirk. He knows how hot and horny I get from watching him. He backs the truck up and exits to thoroughly clean the bay for the next person. It makes me smile how responsible he is.

We stop by the grocery store to pick up a few things for Mr. and Mrs. Fisher. Bryce and I quickly run in to see them and to deliver they're weekly groceries while Austin waits in the truck. Mrs. Fisher lets out a, "oh my," when Bryce takes her hand while I introduce them. Mr. Fisher and Bryce immediately strike up a conversation about trucks because he noticed Bryce's truck when we pulled up. We only stay for a couple of minutes and when we say our goodbyes Mrs. Fisher makes a comment on how handsome my boyfriend is. She's so cute.

When Bryce and I walk down the steps Bryce says, "That's how cute we're going to be when we get old and grey." It makes my heart skip a beat.

As soon as we turn down my road, Bryce gets that look on his face and he scans around suspiciously.

We walk up the back deck to the door and notice that someone's taped a note there. All three of us stand back and read it.

Where are you?

I've been looking everywhere for you!

Remember you're mine!!!

I reach to pull it down and Austin grabs my hand. "Don't touch it, we're taking this to the police. This guy is fucked up!"

Bryce paces on the deck, running his hands through his hair. "See I told you, this fucker's unstable!"

The raising of his voice, getting angry and the running his fingers through his hair is a coping mechanism, no doubt.

Austin grabs my arm to get my attention because I'm watching Bryce lose it. "Can you find me a Ziploc bag, big enough to fit this in?"

"Sure." I fumble for my keys in my purse and when I look up, Bryce has his keys in my door unlocking it. I hesitate looking at him confused. "How'd you get the key for my house?"

"Aww, long story."

"Spill it!" I feel the blood rising to my face and ears.

"Calm down. Relax." Bryce rubs my arms.

"Jesus, look at her. I've never seen you so mad." Austin is smiling from one ear to the other.

"How Bryce?" I ask again.

"That day I was in your house, when your keys were moved, that was me."

"You had a key made?"

"Oh this is so fucking entertaining." Austin laughs out loud.

Bryce tries to wrap me in a hug, but I back up. He holds his hands in the air. "Okay I won't touch you, but Angel I was worried about you. That lunatic came back the second day and I knew I had to protect you. Can you see that he's fucked in the head?"

I look at the note still hanging on the door.

"He's got a point. This guy is fucked up." Austin says with a smirk on his face as he tilts his head toward the note.

"Un-fricking-believable!" Furious, I shove the door open a little harder than what I normally do entering my house.

"Christ, you pissed her off." Austin chuckles.

When I come out of the house with the bag, I've calmed down, knowing it's pointless to stay mad. Bryce has calmed too.

I hand the bag to Austin. "How's this?"

"Perfect, thanks."

Bryce scoops me up in his arms and holds me tight against his body and gazes deep in my eyes. "That fucker isn't getting anywhere near you!" He realizes his tone is still angry so he takes it down a notch. "Do you know how much you mean to me? If anything were to ever happen to you…" He closes his eyes as if he's in pain. He doesn't finish his sentence.

"I'll be fine, we'll be fine."

"You don't worry too much, do you Angel?"

"Why, you'll stress yourself out for nothing. Like my Grandmother used to say, it'll all come out in the wash, no worries."

"But I do worry Angel, I worry about you."

"I'm okay, I'm not worried. I've got you guys to protect me."

We watch Austin take his pocket knife out to lift the corners of the tape and then he uses his sleeve to lift the remaining paper and then he slides it into the bag, careful not to touch it.

"Let's go shut your water off." Bryce says.

"Then we'll go to the cop shop." Austin replies.

Austin takes control of the situation as soon as we get to the police station. "Hi, who can we talk to about a stalker?"

"One moment, I'll get you a Constable."

After a few minutes a police officer returns with her.

"Constable Grant. This way please." He ushers us into his office.

Austin explains the whole situation and hands him the note. He tells him that he's been caught looking in my window and we think he's been in my house because of the things that have been misplaced.

Constable Grant takes some of his own notes and then directs a question at Austin "You on the job?"

Austin replies. "Not at the moment. I'm on vacation from the Barrie OPP."

I look at Austin and Bryce and wonder why they didn't tell me he was a cop.

"So have you had any other encounters with this guy?"

"At the grocery store, The Lodge and around town. He stares, but he hasn't approached me."

"Any other locations?"

"Not that I've noticed."

"I don't recommend that you stay at your house. Is there somewhere else you can stay until we catch this guy?"

"I've been staying with Bryce and Austin at their cabin."

"Good. Stay there. I'm going to need your phone numbers and addresses. I'll keep a car going by your house and see if we can get some information on this guy. We'll keep you informed."

We stand and shake hands. "Thank you." I say.

As soon as we exit the building, I blurt out. "Why didn't you tell me Austin's a cop?"

Bryce turns his head to gaze at me. "I guess it never came up."

Austin looks down at me. "I don't like to brag."

"Thank you for helping me with this problem."

"You know how you can help me, Blondie?" Austin asks. "You can call Leena for me."

"I'll see if she's back from Aruba. Let me take you guys out for lunch."

"Yeah, we can go for lunch, but you're not buying, I am."

"Bryce, please I want to."

"No! I'm buying, Angel."

"Yeah, listen to him he's buying." Austin teases.

He's so stubborn.

I call Leena. "Hey, girlfriend. Your home. Could you meet me at Grandma's country cookin'? I want you to meet someone."

"Okay. I'm on my way."

Austin looks a little nervous after I tell him Leena's meeting us, but he's still Mr. Calm cool and collected.

We wait to order until Leena arrives. She has a golden tan

and is wearing tight black jeans, leather boots, and a double breasted trench coat, also a tight fitted white blouse that shows a lot of cleavage.

Austin stands eagerly and pulls the chair next to him. He extends his hand out introducing himself before I have a chance to. "My name is Austin."

I smile. "Leena, this is Bryce, my boyfriend."

Bryce rubs the inside of my thigh. I think he approves of my introduction. He stands to shake her hand. "Nice to finally meet you, Keera talks about you and Katie a lot."

"Nice to meet you."

After ordering, we talk about her trip, my stalker, the note he left, and how we went to the cop shop. The conversation flows easily.

I notice Austin and Leena talking together. I smile at Bryce and whisper in his ear. "I think their getting along fine. Look at Leena; she's blushing. She doesn't do that too often."

We watch them entering each other's phone numbers into their phones. Bryce pulls my chair closer to him. He wraps his arm around me and rubs my leg.

I can tell something's bothering him; he isn't himself.

"Are you okay?" I ask.

"Yeah, I'm fine." He says.

I don't want to push, so I let it go.

Austin invites Leena over for dinner tonight.

"I'd love to. I have to take care of a few things before I can come to your place. Would you like me to bring anything?" She asks.

Austin looks at her with seductive eyes. "Just you baby! But I'll come pick you up, because you'll never find the cabin. Text me when you're done."

"Okay sounds good. I'll bring wine coolers and dessert."

Austin tells Leena we'll follow her home so he knows where she lives.

We say our goodbyes and I tell her I can't wait to hear more about her trip.

Austin kisses Leena on the cheek. "I'll see you tonight."

While following Leena back to her house, Austin asks me a hundred questions about her.

I watch Bryce looking in the rear view mirror periodically. He's so serious and quiet, like he's deep in thought. He finally relaxes when we're out of town and down the back roads.

Back at the cabin, we prepare creamy dill and garlic scalloped potatoes. Our venison steaks have been marinating for almost twenty four hours now, so they'll be nice and tender. We cut up some veggies to steam and top our garlic bread with cheddar cheese.

Austin cleans up the cabin and I'm surprised that he even dusts. Not that it's that dirty anyway.

Pulling Bryce down, I whisper in his ear. "I think he's trying to impress her."

Bryce notices, too. We smile at one another then back at Austin cleaning. Bryce bends to whisper in my ear. "I've never seen him this nervous. Watch this! Hey! Trying to impress her?" I nudge Bryce in the ribs, but he quickly recovers to tease again. "Look who's pussy whipped now." He says as he holds his ribs and laughs.

"Fuck you!"

"Back at ya Bro!"

"Yeah, Yeah. Hey instead of staring at me, why don't you go get some more wood?"

"Fine, I'm on it."

As soon as Bryce goes outside Austin comes to ask me some questions.

"What does Leena like in a guy?"

"Austin, be yourself. You have a great personality. She's going to love you."

"But what does she like, flowers, chocolate, jewelry?"

"You can buy her that stuff and she'd like it, but she's a simple girl like me. We're not into material things. If you treat her good, she'll love you forever."

"I can't stop thinking about her."

Just then I get a text from Leena. *I can't stop thinking about him.*

I show him. "See, she feels the same way."

Austin receives a text from Leena. *I'm done all my running around; you can pick me up if you want.*

I'm on my way. He replies.

"Thank you Blondie."

"Anytime, Austin."

Austin disappears down the hall to his bedroom and when he emerges and passes by me to put his shoes on at the back door, I smell his cologne and see that he's wearing jeans that fit perfectly with a tight black T-shirt that reads OPP in white across his left pec muscle. He looks good.

He makes me smile. "Mmm, you smell good and you look good too."

"Thanks Blondie."

It's too cute how nervous he is.

Bryce comes back in with a box full of wood. "You leaving? Guess you'll need these." Bryce tosses Austin the keys to his truck.

"Be back in a bit." Austin heads out the door to go pick Leena up.

Bryce and I are finally alone. He has this lost look on his face when he comes over to me and holds me in his arms. I slip my hands underneath his shirt and rub his back. It feels so good, holding each other. I look up at him. "Are you sure you're okay?"

"Oh yeah, I'm fine."

I don't want to pry and be pushy so I leave it like that. He'll tell me when he wants to, so I enjoy holding him and being held by his strong arms.

Later, when I hear a vehicle pull in the driveway, I look out the back window to see Leena's car pull in first with Austin following as he stores Bryce's truck in the garage.

When Austin and Leena come through the door, I notice she's changed into a different outfit. I think she's trying to impress him, too. I take the pie and drinks from them placing everything in the fridge and then we give Leena a tour of the cabin.

"This is beautiful!" She says.

"Thank you." Austin is as proud as Bryce when it comes to the cabin. They worked hard on it and it paid off. It's perfect.

We sit around the breakfast bar drinking and talking.

Leena shows us her pictures and tells us about her dad's resort in Aruba, how he started with a couple bungalows and now has two luxurious hotels, with five pools, and thirty deluxe suite bungalows.

"Wow, that's beautiful! Look how blue the water is." I comment.

"We should all go." Leena says animatedly. "It'll be free. We can book it in the middle of winter. We'll need a vacation by then. The only thing we'll have to pay for is our flights."

"Sounds great." Austin says.

"Talk to your dad and see when's the best time for him. We can let Bryce and Austin know, so they can try to book the time off."

Bryce goes outside to start the barbeque and I hand him the marinated venison steaks. We dress warm, get a drink and keep Bryce company while he cooks the steaks to perfection. Our whole dinner is excellent. We finish with the homemade apple pie that Leena brought.

"You made this pie?" Austin asks as he devours the first piece.

"Yes."

"A woman with many talents. I like that. This is delicious."

Leena smiles. "Would you like another piece?"

"Yes. Definitely." Austin holds out his plate and Leena slides on a piece of apple pie.

I want some time alone with her to catch up on things, but I don't think Austin is going to let her out of his sight. That's okay, I can wait.

We play a few games and laugh a lot. My favourite is twister when Bryce falls on top of me, pinning my hands to the floor. He gives me one of his wet lush kisses, setting me off, leaving me wanting more.

Austin and Leena sit on the couch hand in hand with her leg across his, watching us. At the same time they say, "Get a room!" They both look at each other and laugh.

Bryce picks me up off the floor. "We have a room and we're going to use it."

I tell Leena I'll text her in the morning. "We'll leave you two alone to get better acquainted."

She mouths. "Thank you."

"It's about time." Austin blurts out.

Bryce pulls me to the bedroom. He shuts the door with his foot and pushes me against the wall aggressively. He kisses me hard, almost bruising my lips. Grinding his cock into me. He pulls away lifting my shirt up and off in a split second.

Impatience and vibrating anxiety rolls off him in waves. "I need to be inside you. Right now!"

What the hell is up with you?

15

His fingers go to work on my button and zipper and then hook into the waist band of my jeans and thong. He pulls them down fast and then helps me step out of them. He strips instantly, kicking his clothes out of the way. His movements are fast and aggressive.

He then drops to his knees in front of me, spreading my legs, lifting one over his shoulder for better access.

Looking down at him with his dark hair between my legs, licking me aggressively, has me hot and mindless instantaneously. He looks up at me with those beautiful eyes and I see the evidence of my arousal covering his slick lips. "This sweet pussy is mine."

His mouth continues sucking and licking for a while, then he climbs up my body caging me against the wall, grasping my hands above my head. He lifts my left leg up and hooks it on his hip and I hold it there while he guides his cock to my opening. He shoves his cock deep inside me.

I gasp as he stretches me. "Bryce, I love having your cock inside me."

He pulls out slowly, then rams into me again.

His silence and aggressiveness from the moment we entered this bedroom has me a little worried that something's still bothering him.

He sticks his tongue deep in my mouth swirling it around, like the stirring motion he's doing with his cock. He's so talented when it comes to sex and probably everything else. Round and round, then he rams me into the wall again. He changes it up by pulling all the way out to the tip, teasing me, then he slowly inserts it back in as far as he can go, then he picks up the pace. The feeling is exquisite. Our breathing escalates quickly and our skin is misted with sweat. He doesn't stop. Ramming me harder, tunnelling deeper and deeper with every push, but it feels so good.

My muscles tighten down on his cock as he slams me once, twice, three more times, and then he quickly pulls out.

He turns me toward the wall, roughly, placing my hands above my head. "Use your hands for support. I'm going to fuck you hard."

Oh my. But you were doing that. Am I missing something here? If I ask him what's wrong I'll get a vague answer or he'll tell me he's fine. So I let it go, for now.

Bryce bends his knees and I lift with my toes, arching my back, with my butt up to give him better access. He slides his cock deep inside me, stretching me. He reaches down capturing my nipple between his finger and thumb and tugs on it. He pulls back out to the tip and when he pushes back in he almost lifts me off my toes. He holds onto my hips, guiding me down onto his cock, in and out. He picks up the pace, slamming into me harder, faster. His balls slapping my pussy deliciously.

Breathing hard, I reposition my hands, knowing this is going to get rough. My orgasm builds like a wild storm again and as soon as I squeeze my muscles around his cock he pulls out, spins me roughly, and lifts me up with one arm shoving my back against the wall.

"Wrap your legs around my hips." He commands.

I do and I grasp onto his shoulders for support.

He positions his cock at my entrance and plunges deep inside me, pushing me hard into the wall. I love this position, face to face.

Possessed by him, in this intimate moment, I feel as if I'm under his spell. We stare deeply into each other's eyes and something in his tells me he's worried and hurting.

He penetrates me deep. He's definitely fucking me hard. Like he has a stronger need to, trying to go deeper than the thrust before.

"Feel me! Feel my cock. This is the only cock that will ever be in this sweet pussy. This pussy is mine and mine only! You. Are. Mine!!"

I knew it! I knew something was bothering him. It strikes me then that it's probably the note my stalker left on my door. Is this jealousy or is he being possessive? Does he feel threatened by the note he left? Or does he have a need to remind me that I'm his?

"Yes, and you are mine, Bryce."

I run my fingers through his hair, grabbing a handful at the back of his neck.

He kisses me ferociously like he needs to, like I'm the air he breathes. He moans into my mouth still flexing his hips into me, ramming me hard into the wall, sinking balls deep and I'm loving every second of it.

He always knows exactly what I need.

Our chests heave for air, our orgasms build wildly.

"Bryce!"

"Angel, you're mine."

"Yes. Yours." I tug harder on his silky jet black hair.

He slams into me three more times and we both fall apart, trembling and convulsing.

I feel his cock jerking, and then I feel warm come, squirting inside me. We've both come standing up. Well, he's standing, I'm lifted onto his cock and against the wall.

I'm vaguely aware that we're moving, then I feel us fall onto the bed and I'm on top of him with his cock securely lodged inside me. We lay there catching our breath, absorbing the aftershocks. I wait for him to speak. I wait quite a while.

"Are you going to tell me what's bothering you or are you going to lie to me again and say your fine? I thought we don't lie in this relationship?"

I feel his chest heave and then he lets out a heavy sigh. "Knowing there's a psycho out there that wants my girlfriend… It's driving me insane. I can't think straight. Rage is consuming me." He shakes his head. Disgusted.

"I knew I should have killed that fucker when I had the chance."

Girlfriend! He thinks of me as his girlfriend? He wouldn't actually kill him? He's just saying that. Right?

I lift my upper body and gaze deep in his eyes. "Bryce, you can't let this bother you. I'll stay out of sight when you're gone and maybe the cops will catch him at my house again. We only have two more days together. Let's enjoy every minute of it."

"Promise me you'll stay at your grandfather's."

"I promise." I think he's happy that I agree to stay put.

I feel his cock twitching inside me and he's getting hard again. I try to lighten the mood. "Oh, by the way, I like being fucked hard up against the wall."

"You do, eh? I like it, too."

Hovering over him, I lean down to kiss him softly, my hair falls all around us, blanketing our faces. His tongue slips into my mouth and we deepen the kiss swirling our tongues around. I can feel his cock grow thick and hard as I lift and lower onto his stiff shaft.

"Feel that? That's my come inside you. I'm going to rock your world and give you more." He's back! My vocal lover is back. It turns me on listening to him purr his crude words in my ear. I love it and I can't do without it.

"Come here." He says.

I lean forward and he takes a hold of my breasts, squeezing them together and then he sucks on both my nipples at the same time.

What a sensation, I moan.

"You like this, don't you, Angel? Look how fucking hard they get."

Glancing down, I watch him continue the assault as I lift and lower onto his steely erection.

He thrusts his hips up to meet mine. "I love watching how your body reacts to the things I do to you."

He resumes sucking until I can't take anymore.

"Bryce!"

"I know, Angel, I bet I could make you come like this, but before you get too excited, I need to get a few things out the cabinet."

I let out a heavy sigh and roll off of him. I smack his ass before he walks away. "You mean the kinky cabinet?"

I watch his gorgeous, gloriously naked body saunter over to get the keys out of his dresser. His smile can't be missed. I don't think I'll ever tire of this view. God, looking at him naked does the strangest things to my body; I always want more. I'm getting so greedy. I couldn't stop this if I tried. I've become addicted.

"Is that what you call it? I like the name of it and yes, you've got the right idea."

He struts back to the bed with the dark purple silk tie. "Stand next to the bed."

I get up eagerly and stand. "I don't like it when you're in a mood. I like it when you're playful and happy and when you talk dirty in my ear."

"You do, eh?" He stands in front of me, lifting his arms to put the silk tie over my eyes, but stops abruptly when I run my hand down his washboard abs.

He grabs my hand quickly and his eyes darken, almost like he flips a switch. "No! You don't get to touch." He places my hands at my side.

Oh Bryce, I think you have a dark side, but I think I'm going to see how far I can push you.

He lifts his arms again to put the silk tie over my eyes.

I touch him again and he quickly grabs both my hands and ties them in front of me with the silk tie that was supposed to go over my eyes.

"But you're just so yummy!"

Bryce is trying to be serious again. "I am, eh?" He turns to go back to the kinky cabinet and I see his cheeks lift into a smile.

He's searching, "You know what happens when you're bad?"

"What? I was bad?"

He gets another purple silk tie and prowls toward me, while I look him up and down, licking my lips, and then I bite my lower lip.

"You know what biting that lip does to me, and you're still taunting me?"

Yeah, I know exactly what I'm doing to you.

He stands in front of me again, while he puts the silk tie over my eyes.

"Can you see anything?"

"Nope."

"Good."

I run the back of my hand down his abs and across his hard cock.

He backs away. "Oh, you're asking for it, aren't you?"

"Asking for what?"

"You'll see. Open your mouth."

I do and it tastes like strawberry. It's a ball in my mouth and I feel him clasping the strap at the back of my head.

The thrill and excitement I can't contain as it runs through me. My heart is pounding so hard I can almost hear it.

I hear his bare feet walking across the hardwood floor away

from me. He's moving things around in the kinky cabinet again and then he's back. Before I know it, I'm flattened across his knees and he's gently rubbing my butt cheeks. Oh, I like this.

I hear smack.

"Argh!" Escapes from deep within me and then my butt cheek is on fire.

He squirts something cold on the same cheek and he rubs it gently again. He keeps doing this, smack with the paddle, squirt and a rub. Smack, squirt, rub. A total of three times alternating with his hand on each cheek.

"There, I think that's enough punishment."

Silence fills the room as he rubs and I realize my butt is not stinging as much now. What a strange feeling. It feels good now. I feel him bend down and he gently kisses my butt cheeks in several spots making it feel even better.

He stands me up. "Look how beautiful you are." He unties my hands and goes to work unclasping the leather strap at the back of my head and then takes the strawberry ball out of my mouth.

"Now you can touch me. I think you've earned it."

I've earned it? Oh Bryce, you're so strange.

He hugs me tight. I wrap my arms around his strong back and he kisses my forehead. "You did well for your first punishment."

My eyes widen under the blindfold. What the hell, there's going to be more?

"I like spanking you. It gets me so hot and hard. You liked it too." He grinds into me. "Didn't you?"

I hesitate answering, so he lifts my chin in an attempt to get me to talk. My hand instinctively wants to lift the blindfold off so I can see him when I speak.

Bryce's hand stops me. "Leave it on." He says in that deep commanding voice.

"You don't think that's a little strange that you want to spank me?"

"I'm going to introduce you to quite a few strange and kinky things, testing your limits, and you'll take it all and want more. Now, I need you to sit on the side of the bed with your legs open." He guides me to the bed because I'm blindfolded and lowers me down, I wince at the tenderness of my butt as I sit. "Lean back on your hands."

I hear him rip a package open, and then I hear something vibrating.

Wow! What the heck!

Bryce is vibrating my clit with it and what a feeling this is.

I moan and circle my hips.

"Look at you, you're so beautiful. I didn't know if you'd like this, but as usual you blow me away with your eagerness to learn and to try new fantasies."

He caresses all the way up my left leg and then lifts it so it's on the edge of the bed. He does the same to my right. When his fingers skim my sensitive skin, his touch fires every cell in my body, sending shivers down my spine.

He vibrates down the left side of my juicy folds and then the right, holding it upright so I feel it on my clit at the same time.

I moan. God, it feels so good, I'm so close.

He inserts it inside me.

Oh my! I circle my hips.

He's going in and out, and then I feel his mouth on my clit sucking and flicking simultaneously.

Flopping down on my back, I can't take much more. My breathing is erratic, all these sensations are driving me wild. All of a sudden my legs start to shake uncontrollably and I let out a muffled cry. My head thrashes from one side to the other. I'm grasping the sheets, bucking my hips into his face.

He doesn't stop. He keeps flicking and sucking, lapping up every drop.

My pussy's so sensitive. I have to get him to stop.

It's almost like he reads my mind.

He climbs up my body and I feel him hovering over top of me. "I love it when your whole body shakes for me."

Straddling me, Bryce lifts my upper body to his and kisses me tenderly. "How was that?"

I fall back down onto the bed. "Wow! Holy shit. That was incredible!"

He leans down, reaching to undo the silk tie, whispering in my ear. "Round two for me, round three for you. I could make you come all night if you'd let me. Lift your head."

Bryce pulls the silk tie off my eyes. I can see again. I can see his gorgeous rock hard body again.

He hovers over me with one arm supporting his upper body and grasps his hard cock. He inserts it deep inside me and bangs the hell out of me. "YOU. MAKE. ME. SO. FUCKING. HORNY." With every slam he says a word. "I. CAN'T. GET. ENOUGH…YOU. ARE. MINE."

Bryce passes me the vibrator. "Put this on your clit."

I do. "This feels so good."

"Come with me, Angel!" Bryce groans.

I tighten my slick walls around him. I can feel sweat misting his skin, like mine. We're breathless and panting. My hearts going to pound right out of my chest.

"Fuck, you're milking me, Angel."

"Here it comes, Baby!" I'm coming undone, underneath him and it takes me by surprise that it's happening so fast again.

Two more punishing lunges Bryce takes, tunnelling deeper inside me and his whole body tightens and convulses. "You're mine!" He comes long and hard emptying himself and then I feel all of his weight collapsing onto me.

We lie there trying to catch our breath for I don't know how long and then he rolls to the side of me, pulling out. He props up his right arm and leans his head on it. I do the same with my left, so I'm facing him.

I automatically run my hand across his chest and down to his abs. "You're not going to spank me again, are you?"

He rubs my left butt cheek and chuckles, "No, only when you're bad."

"I'm confused."

"I'll let you know when I'm going to punish you."

I let out a big yawn. "You wear me out."

He kisses me. "I love to wear you out and I also love hearing you call me baby when you're coming."

"Maybe I'll call you that for now on."

"I'd like that." He kisses me again. "Sleep now, Angel."

When I awaken the sun is shining through the crack in the dark camouflage curtains, blinding me and Bryce is wrapped around me like a vine.

I don't want to wake him, so I lie there very still, checking out his beautiful face. I'm staring at his long black eye lashes thinking that I'd love to put mascara on them to see how much longer and thicker they'd get. He has perfect features and his jaw line is tight and sculptured. I can stare at him forever. I can't resist lifting the covers to take a peek at his chest, abs, happy trail, and oh yes… his beautiful cock! I can't get enough. I want this visual forever.

"What do you think you're doing? Can't get enough of my cock, can you?"

I drop the covers and giggle. "Oh shit! You caught me."

He hugs me tight and I can feel him smile against my cheek. "We better get out of this bed or you won't walk for a week."

We peek out of the bedroom and see that Austin isn't in the kitchen, so we scurry with our clothes in hand, totally naked, to the bathroom. Bryce pauses at the doorway teasing me, getting me flustered and anxious. He reaches down pinching my nipple. "Look how hard these fuckers get when you're excited."

"No time to stop and smell the roses." I try to push his large muscular body inside. "Get your ass in there!"

He chuckles loudly because I haven't moved him an inch.

"I love this shade of red on you." He runs his thumb down my cheek slowly and then he takes his sweet ass time moving out of the way.

I smile and smack his ass. "Brat!"

We brush our teeth and then get into the warm shower. We wash each other as I watch Bryce's cock grow. I drop to my knees, licking my lips and open my mouth wide. I take him as far as I can to the back of my throat and then gently ease out getting it wet with my saliva.

He moans.

"Damn, woman, you're so good at this."

I love pleasing him, love having his cock in my mouth. I get his shaft slick and wet, then wrap my hand around it jerking and sucking at the same time. I pick up the pace going in and out faster, cupping his balls with my other hand.

He groans with pleasure, a rumbling throughout the bathroom.

"I love fucking your mouth."

I look up to see him gazing down at me with dark lust-filled eyes.

Sliding my finger below his balls, I caress the soft skin. His balls lift and tighten immediately and I taste a drop of pre-cum on my tongue.

"Angel, you've got to stop. You're going to make me come." I keep going, letting him know that I love sucking him, love giving him as much pleasure as he gives me.

He grabs my arms and lifts me up. "Come here, Angel, I want to be inside you." He lifts my left leg holding it with his arm, opening me wide. He positions his cock, rubbing it back and forth, getting it slick and wet at my entrance. "Sucking my cock turns you on, gets you wet, doesn't it?"

"Yes."

He slides his cock deep inside me.

I gasp and moan against his ear. "Babe, you're so hard, you're stretching my pussy."

"Fuck." He pulls out then he slams me against the glass, shoving his cock deep inside me. "I love when you talk dirty to me."

I hold onto his shoulders for support.

"Play with your clit. I won't last much longer."

The pressure builds, bringing me higher and higher. He slams me against the shower enclosure. Capturing me. An unexpected muscle contraction has my pussy clenching down on his cock.

I drape my arm around his shoulders as he lifts me up by my ass, and I wrap my legs around his hips.

"Fuck me hard, Babe, give it to me." I circle my clit, vibrating it with my finger. I start to shake feeling Bryce grip my butt tighter as he tilts his hips expertly hitting the right spot, nailing me harder than the thrust before.

Every muscle in his body stiffens. He slams into me four more times with every word "You. Feel. So. Good."

I feel his cock jerk as he spurts warm come deep inside me. He presses his whole body against mine as our muscles go limp. I lower my legs so I can stand and he slips out of me. My legs feel like jelly, but I have his strong arms to hold me up and they feel amazing.

He kisses me. "Well, this wasn't supposed to happen. You never cease to amaze me. Thank you."

"You're welcome and thank you. Hey, remind me to take my pill."

"Yes, as soon as we get out of this shower, we wouldn't want any little kiddies running around just yet."

"Yeah, that can wait." So someday he'd like to have children? I feel giddiness flowing through me.

16

WE DON'T HEAR Austin, which is unusual because he's always up before us making breakfast. He must be sleeping in.

Getting dressed, Bryce wears his black pajama bottoms that hang low and a tight white t-shirt. I wear my tight yoga pants and a pink t-shirt. Bryce can't keep his hands off of me when I'm wearing this. Come to think of it, he can't keep his hands off of me anytime, it doesn't matter what I'm wearing, but I love it.

We walk into the kitchen and start breakfast right away. As I'm moving around I notice Leena's shoes by the door. "Babe, look!"

Bryce comes over to hold me. "I like it when you call me that." He doesn't look as surprised as I am.

"I can't believe she slept with him on their first date. She's always preaching to me like my mother. Never, ever sleep with them on your first date. Get to know them first. Unbelievable!" I shake my head. Disgusted.

Bryce looks at me sideways, but doesn't say a word.

"I'm pissed that she doesn't practice what she preaches." I

shake my head, pretending that I'm angry. "Wait until she gets out here. But it is cute, don't you think?"

Bryce wraps me in his big strong arms. "I love this feisty side to you. You're the cute one."

"Thanks." I reach up to pull him down for a quick kiss.

We cook a big breakfast, bacon, eggs, home fries, waffles and sausages. They must have smelled it, because Austin and Leena come walking down the hall hand in hand moments later. Her eyes glance at me and my eyes get really wide. She shrugs her shoulders and blushes a little. I don't say a word. I don't have to. She knows I'll talk to her later when we have time alone.

Bryce and I smile at them.

Austin pipes up. "What's your problem?"

"No problem." Bryce says, still smiling.

Leena and Austin sit at the breakfast bar and we serve them breakfast, but of course Bryce can't leave it alone, he has to tease Austin. "What the hell! Sleep in much? Think you're on vacation? I hope you don't take that long to respond to calls. She wear you out? Stamina brother, stamina."

"Yeah, yeah, I know, you're getting me back for teasing Blondie aren't you?"

I sit next to Leena and bump her shoulder with the biggest grin on my face.

"You two want to go on the ATV's today? We can show Leena the camp and go out for dinner." Austin asks excitedly.

"Yeah, sure." Bryce says. "Were up for it."

Leena takes a bite. "Good breakfast, thank you." She says around a mouthful.

"You're welcome." Bryce and I say at the same time.

"We'll get the dishes done while you guys get the ATV's ready." I want some alone time with Leena so I try a diversion.

When were done our breakfast and the guys go outside, I glare at Leena. "What the hell were you thinking?"

"I know exactly what you're going to say. It kept running

through my mind while I was trying to resist him, but he's so hot. My mind was telling me no, but my body was telling me to fuck his brains out…so I did."

"But you're always preaching to me." And then she cuts me off like she always does.

"Okay, little miss perfect! How many days was it before Bryce got into your pants?"

I start blushing, remembering our first day together.

"Oh, just what I thought." She gives me a hug. "Thank you for introducing us." She grabs my arms and spins me around in a circle. "I'm so happy." Then she stops dead. "Why didn't you tell me he's a cop?"

"I only found out myself before we met you at the restaurant."

"He's so hot, and that body. My god, I'm getting wet thinking about him."

Leena's always so talkative and expressive when it comes to her sexual partners. She tells me things like their size, the kinky toys they use, different positions, how to give a good blow job, which I don't even want to know. But she tells me anyway, almost like she needs to teach me because of my inexperience.

"Austin's coming back with Bryce in four days, so I'll get to see him again." Leena can't contain her excitement. She claps her hands together like she usually does when she's happy and excited.

"I don't think I've ever seen you this happy."

"I know. You and Bryce look very happy, too. You two make such a cute couple."

I smile. "Yeah, I really like him. I don't want him to leave."

"I know but they'll be back."

Austin comes in the back door, takes his coat and boots off and then grabs Leena by her hand. "Come with me beautiful, were taking a shower."

Austin guides her through the kitchen and her smile lights up the room. She spins her head and winks at me as they disappear into the bathroom.

"Boy, if the walls could talk in that bathroom." I say out loud.

I quickly pack us a lunch and some drinks because we'll be on the trail all day.

Bryce comes in the back door and over to me, "I don't know how I'm going to leave you. I can't stand to be away from you for more than ten minutes." He leans down and gives me a soft kiss.

He holds me in his arms and I grab his tight ass cheeks, squeezing them hard. We hear the water shut off then some banging, giggling and moaning. We stare at each other and smile.

"I'm getting a chubby listening to them."

"How did I know you were going to say that? You've always got a chubby."

"Yeah, it's probably because you're holding my ass cheeks. Oh, by the way when we were in the shower and you called me babe and talked dirty in my ear? It sent me over the edge instantly. I love it when you talk dirty to me."

Holding my hands behind my back, Bryce corners me against the counter and grinds his hard cock into me just as Austin comes out of the bathroom smiling, looking very refreshed and satisfied. "Will you let that poor girl go for a second?" Austin blurts out.

Bryce lets me out of his embrace and backs away. Austin saunters over and stands in front of me. He opens his arms to give me a big hug.

"Thank you Blondie, you're the best."

"You're welcome, but all I did was give her a call."

Austin walks away saying, "You've made me a very happy man."

This is our last day together so when we're on the ATV, racing through the trails, I hold Bryce tight whenever I can. Bryce shows me the same affection by caressing my arms that are wrapped around his waist.

I know that our limited time left together is bothering him, too. I can see it in his eyes, when we stop to see a waterfall. He holds me in his arms and squeezes me tight. I melt against him.

When we reach the camp, I sit on Bryce's lap as we eat lunch in Austin's tree blind and Leena expresses how impressed she is that Austin made this himself. She asks about the camera on the tree like I did and Austin explains how they work. After about ten minutes, we get a chill running through us so we venture back down the tree and collect wood to make a fire.

The conversation flows easily and is filled with laughter as we sit around the fire, drinking beer.

Later, we drive for miles blazing through the trails, finding wildlife, rock formations and another waterfall. It's beautiful, bigger than the other one. The water cascades down over large boulders leaving a white spray mist in the air. This time we have our cell phones with us and snap some amazing pictures.

Leena whispers in my ear. "Were not making it back anytime soon. Where do we go pee?"

"Pick a tree. Any tree."

"Are you serious? You've gone out here?"

"Yup, pull your snow pants down, lean on the tree and try not to pee on yourself." I say amused.

"Are you serious? You've gone out here?"

Austin yells out. "Leena, honey, would you like me to hold you up?"

"No, I think I can manage it on my own, but thanks for the offer."

"Anytime."

We walk for a bit until we find the perfect spot, gabbing all the way there.

"So how did you and Bryce meet? Other than the grocery store."

"Well, that night at The Lodge, after you left, I went to the washroom and almost passed out."

"What?"

"Yeah, I think someone put something in my drink. Anyway, I managed to make it out into the parking lot and when I almost passed out, I fell into two strong arms."

"How romantic is that?"

"I'm not done yet."

"There's more?"

"When I woke up, I was tied to his bed in my bra and thong. Oh, and I had a blanket."

"What? Get the hell out of here. Why were you tied up? Did he kidnap you?"

"Tying me up was a fantasy of his that I found out about later. As for the kidnapping, he was keeping me safe from my stalker because he caught him looking in my window."

"See I told you he was a stalker by the way he was looking at you. Was I right? Of course, I'm always right."

"Yes, you were right about my stalker."

"You're changing the subject again, back to Bryce. Did he rape you?"

"No, he got me so hot and aroused, I couldn't resist him. I tried."

"See, I told you. I know what that's like. They're so frickin' hot."

"I know, eh."

"So did you lose your virginity while being tied up?"

"No not that time, he said he wanted to break me in gently, because he assumed I was a virgin. I guess he didn't want to hurt me."

"That would be so erotic, don't you think?" I giggle at her curiosity.

"So did you fuck his brains out or not?"

"Yes."

"Details. I need details. When and where were you when you lost it?"

I hesitate telling her. I like keeping things private.

"Come on, Keera, I tell you everything. Spill it!"

"The first time we had oral sex."

"And?"

"The third time, he took my virginity in the shower."

"The same shower I was in this morning?" Leena's face is priceless.

"Yup."

"No shit. So did it hurt?"

"Yeah, for a bit, but he took it easy on me."

"So who do you think drugged you and why?"

"Bryce thinks it was my stalker and that he was planning to kidnap me that night, but Bryce ruined his plans."

"Oh Keera, this is getting weird. Aren't you scared?"

"Now that I'm learning more, yeah, I'm getting scared."

The guys start to walk toward us. "We thought we'd better come check on you two, make sure you're okay. Big bad bears out here."

"Shit!" Leena says. "I want to ask you more questions."

"We're fine." I holler from behind the tree. "Were gabbing. You know, girl talk." We pull up our snow pants and head back to the guys.

Good, I'm saved from Leena's interrogation.

Back on the ATV's and blazing through the trails, the four of us climb up the mountain, stopping for the occasional downed tree, which the guys lift up and off the trail. When we get to a clearing that overlooks the side of the mountain, the sun is setting behind giving us, an awe inspiring view. Twin waterfalls cascade down the rock face and the leaves on the trees have changed to the most vibrant colours.

As soon as we take our helmets off, Leena says, "Wow, this is unbelievable. We don't get to see anything like this in town."

Bryce and I lean against the ATV, me in his lap. We're holding each other, staring out at the beauty of it all.

After we take some pictures Bryce says, "Let's go find a restaurant and get you girls warmed up. I saw a sign on a tree down the trail about a mile back." He can tell I'm getting cold.

His awareness to my needs has me smiling.

Outside the restaurant, Austin takes Leena in his arms and I hear him say, "You're going to sleep over again, right?"

"I thought you'd never ask."

The restaurant has a very cozy feeling about it from the moment we walk in. There are shelves and hooks to hang your helmets and snow gear, obviously catering to snowmobilers and ATV'ers. We grab a booth across from the fireplace, settling in, warming up. The waitress appears taking our drink order, leaving us the menus to look over. We talk, eat and enjoy each other's company.

Leena calls her mom to let her know that she's having a great time and she won't be home tonight.

When she's done talking I ask, "How's Mom doing?"

"She's great. She has a new boyfriend and she's so happy. She was asking about you. Instead of going to your grandfather's, why don't you stay with us?"

Bryce interrupts. "I want her out of this town until this psycho's caught."

"Next time I will. I've already called Gramps and made plans. He can't wait to see me." I try to smooth over Bryce's outburst. Jeez, he really is touchy when it comes to my stalker.

Bryce noticeably relaxes after I say I'm leaving town to see Gramps.

I like riding the ATV's at night. Everything looks different, frightening almost. It gets my adrenaline pumping because it's much more difficult to find your way back, but Bryce and Austin navigate fine. We stop and they discuss which way to go, then we're back on the trail, blazing down it again. We make it back to the cabin and pull into the garage a couple hours after dark.

As soon as we take our helmets off, Leena grabs my hand. "We're going to make a snack, we'll be inside." She pulls me toward the cabin. "So what was it like, your first time?"

"Great, Bryce is really amazing."

"How do you know? You have no one to compare him to."

I want to blow her mind so she's speechless, but I don't think it's possible. "He's quite kinky, I mean, KINK…Y."

"Really? Oh, I'm looking at him differently now."

She wants me to spill more, but the guys save me by coming in the back door. Bryce takes his boots and insulated coveralls off and comes right to me and holds me tight.

I look up at him. "Thank you. Today was fun. I had a great time."

He whispers in my ear, "I would have rather been in that bedroom all day with you."

I smile.

Leena and Austin hold each other, and I hear her say, "This was a perfect day, thank you so much."

He kisses her. "You're welcome."

"So what did you make us?" Bryce is hungry again.

"Chili cheese. It'll be out of the oven in ten minutes." I say.

In the living room, we sit and eat our munchies watching a movie, covered with blankets because it's still a little cold from letting the fire go out since we've been gone all day.

Bryce and I sit at one end of the sectional; Austin and Leena sit at the other end.

While the introduction is on, I'm deep in thought.

So much has happened in the past two weeks. It's like a flashback in my mind. How he kidnapped me or like Bryce says, he was keeping me safe. Which I'm really starting to believe now that I've seen the evidence of the note my stalker left. Bryce must have seen the crazy obsession in my stalkers face and knew that he had to act now or it would've been too late. He saved me. I look up at him and smile, he squeezes my thigh and then his attention goes back to the TV. My mind flips and I think about when I was tied up and seduced, our first night together having oral sex. I observed how he started out gentle, touching me with tenderness, then he'd grow aggressively rougher as lust and desire for me consumed his self-control. I think about when we shaved each other, when I lost my virginity, and all the beautiful lovemaking and kinky sex from beginning to end. I squirm in my seat.

Bryce bends to whisper in my ear. "I'd give anything to know what you're thinking about right now." Then he releases my bottom lip from my teeth with his thumb gently gliding it across, sending a chill through me. His intense gaze into my eyes makes me feel cherished, like I'm his whole world.

"You've got to quit doing that. You know what that does to me."

"What am I doing?" I say in my seductive voice.

"The way you're looking at me? Angel, I want you right now."

His touch sets my blood on fire and right now he's running his hand up my thigh, until he reaches my clit. He massages it gently underneath the blanket so no one can see. Oh God! It feels so good. He's such a tease. I'm trying not to pant. He bends down and whispers again. "If you were wearing a dress, my finger would be deep inside you right now."

How does he do that? He's hardly touched me and yet I'm almost shaking with want, need, and desire.

Reaching underneath the blanket, I wrap my fingers around his impressive erection, running them along the whole length. He's so hard. I peek at Leena and Austin, who are still staring at each other, lost in conversation. Then I look back up at Bryce with a mischievous smile, not saying a word, touching him.

"See what you do to me?" He whispers. "Oh yeah, you're going to get it, every inch."

I clench my legs together. He knows the effect he has on me.

I'm trying to control my breathing, and doing a really bad job at it. We're being so naughty underneath the blanket, I have to stop because I'm so excited already.

Bryce glances down at me with his knowing wicked smile. I swear he already knows my body better than I know it myself.

I try to calm my breathing; I don't want to bring any attention to myself.

Bryce hugs me and kisses my forehead. "You can breathe now." Then he chuckles lightly.

Bugger, he's enjoying this. He likes getting me all worked up. I can't wait for this movie to end.

We keep our touching to a minimum because we get engrossed in Contraband, with Mark Wahlberg.

I blurt out. "He's so hot."

Bryce looks at me with one eyebrow up, "You know who's hot? Kate Beckinsale. She gives me a chubby."

"Everything gives you a chubby." I slap his chest.

Austin and Leena join us laughing.

I think he's trying to get me jealous and It's actually cute.

This is our last night together. I can't wait to experience what he has in mind.

When the movie ends Bryce starts to yawn. We're trying not to make it look obvious that we want to rush into the bedroom, but we do. I think they do too.

Austin yawns, "Yeah, time for bed. Good night you two."

Men! They're so predictable.

"Night, see you in the morning." I say

"Come with me." Bryce holds out his hand for me. "Put that pretty little hand in mine."

17

I PLACE MY HAND in his. His other hand snakes around my lower back and I feel that familiar electricity running through my body. He then leads me to the bedroom.

Bryce goes straight for the keys to the kinky cabinet. He pulls out a light pink lace bra, thong, garter belt and pale pink lacy silk stockings. "Can you put this on for me? And I'll be right back."

"Sure." I say taking them out of his hand.

I see him carrying something in his hand as he leaves and I smile because I think he's trying to surprise me.

Quickly undressing from my clothes, I shimmy into this sexy lingerie as my thoughts shift and I wonder if he gets embarrassed walking around the kinky store, shopping for all this stuff.

Looking in the full length mirror on the back of the door, my gaze floats inspecting my body. "Wow! This is pretty…pretty sexy." I spin. "Nice!"

I don't quite get the stockings hooked up to the garter belt when Bryce comes back in. He looks me up and down with those dark seductive eyes, while I do the same, stopping at the dark purple thong he's wearing for me and his impressive package, which is bulging everywhere.

"Look at you, you're so sexy."

"Thank you," I say. "And look how hot you are? Hotter than Mark Wahlberg."

He smacks my ass.

"Ouch!" I rub my butt cheek, even though it's a love tap.

He drops down onto his knees in front of me and his fingers gently skim along my sensitive skin clasping my garter belt to the silk stockings.

Seeing Bryce knelt down in front of me, helping me dress with his gentle touch and tenderness of his fingers gliding over my thighs is too erotic.

Bryce runs his hand up the back of my thigh to the curve of my butt. He spins me so I can see my butt in the mirror. "Look how sexy this is." He's caresses both my butt cheeks again gliding his hand down until he reaches my thigh and then he clasps one garter, then the other to the silk stocking. My head is turned so I can see what he's doing. He gently kisses one cheek, then the other.

He spins me again so I'm facing the mirror now. "Look at these. I love the butterfly. So sexy!" He runs his finger behind the lace butterfly pattern on my thong, setting my blood on fire. "So smooth, I love it that we both shave."

Bryce continues running his finger up my pussy lips until my clit pops out of its hood. "Look how big this is? So nice." He runs his finger past my clit a few more times.

"Babe, please!"

"I know Angel, but I'm just getting started."

He stands in front of me and when I look down I see that his cock is too large now to fit into his dark purple, almost black thong. The head is peeking out.

I drop to my knees holding his tight butt cheeks and I lick the head. With one hand I unclasp the plastic clip on the side of his thong and his huge hard as stone cock springs out. I unclasp the other side and it falls to the floor. I wrap my fingers around his shaft and his pelvis jerks at my touch. I run my tongue along my lips and then bite my lower lip as I look up at him with wanting eyes.

His eyes darken immediately.

I lick my lips again and then take him in my mouth.

He groans. "Fuck, that feels so good!"

Taking him deeper, I watch in the mirror how I'm sucking him off. I pull him out of my mouth to the head of his cock and wet my lips with saliva and then I take the rest of him to the back of my throat.

"How deep can you go, Angel?"

I pull out then go deeper. "Fuck, you keep this up and I'm going to come in your mouth."

He pulls out of my mouth and I sigh. I was just getting started.

Bryce lifts me up by my arms and then picks me up cradling me in his strong arms. He looks deep in my eyes, "This is our last night together. I want to make love to you." He places me on the bed and climbs in beside me. His warm lips encase mine. Kissing me slowly, gently. "I don't know how I'm going to live without you." He resumes kissing me again. I can hear and feel the pain in his voice. I'm going through the same emotions, trying desperately to fight them off. His kisses are slow and passionate as his hand moves across my cheek and then his thumb takes over caressing. "Our time together has been the best days of my life."

"Yes, for me, too, but why does it sound like this is the end?"

"Oh no, Angel, it will never be the end. We will be together forever, even when we're apart, I'll rush back to you as soon as I can. You've got to understand I'm really struggling. Leaving you for four days has got to be the hardest obstacle I've ever had to face."

"I know, we've got to tell ourselves it's only four days."

Bryce is staring deep in my eyes, hesitating like he's going to say something and after a few moments he finally speaks. "I'm going to miss you so much."

"I'm going to miss you, more."

He kisses me passionately again, sending a tingle straight down there. How does he do that with a kiss?

Snaking my fingers through his hair, I grasp a handful at the back of his neck and a pained moan vibrates in my mouth from his. He hovers over me and I open my legs wide to accommodate him. He then gently lowers himself down on top.

I feel how hard he is. "Babe, I want you inside me, please."

"I love it when you beg."

He kisses me, stopping at my breasts to pull down the cups of my bra, exposing my nipples as he sucks and pinches, leaving trails of fire throughout my body.

"You crave my cock more and more every day, don't you?"

"Yes."

"You need it deep inside you."

"Yes."

"Filling you. Stretching you."

"Oh God, yes. I need you right now!"

"You need to come don't you Angel?"

"Yes. Please."

"I'm…Almost…There." He says between kisses as he's heading south. "Is… This…what…you…want? Right…here?"

"God, yes!"

"I love these, but they've got to go!" In one swift movement he rips my thong off and tosses them across the room.

"Wow!" I feel his lips kissing my lips down there, gently, one side then the other.

He slides his hard long, magical tongue inside me and I moan. He's fucking me with his tongue and his nose bumps and teases my clit. He keeps doing this to me, driving me crazy.

"Babe, please!"

"I know Angel. I'm going to make you come." He inserts his finger deep inside me and his mouth is on my enlarged clit, sucking and flicking it.

He knows my body so well, already. He pays attention to what I like and what my dislikes are. He knows when and where I need to be touched, how much pressure to exert and exactly when to hit my G spot. He's my perfect lover.

He picks up the pace with his finger and tongue. The feeling is absolutely breathtaking. My orgasm builds taking me higher and higher, until I can't take anymore.

"That's it, Babe. Oh…oh Babe, I'm coming!"

I can't catch my breath, my whole body is convulsing, my back is arched off the bed, and I'm clawing the sheets, bucking my hips up to meet every flick of his tongue. He doesn't stop until my body goes limp.

Looking down, I see that he's gazing up at me watching my every move. "Holy frick. That was so strong."

"How I love to make you come. You're so beautiful." He gives me a kiss, fluttering his lips across my pussy. "You taste so sweet. I love eating you."

Bryce is prowling up my body, like a panther now, until he reaches my mouth. He swirls his tongue in my mouth. "See how sweet you taste. Now I'm going to make you come again."

He positions his cock at my entrance and gently slides in. "More?"

"Yes."

"More?"

"Yes." He gives me every inch. I moan into his passionate kiss while he stirs his cock round and round, then in and out.

He pins my hands, linking our fingers together. My knees are up at my chest. My hips are curled so I can feel him penetrate deeper. He starts out gently, but his aggression takes over as he loses control and I love it.

"It's so deep this way."

"Yes, I want you to have every inch. I want you to know tomorrow that I've marked and claimed your body. When you sit you'll remember that my cock was deep inside and you'll remember all the beautiful love we've made and that you are mine! And only mine!"

"Yes."

"Every inch of your body is mine, Angel."

"Yes."

He's fucking me so hard now. All the way out to the tip, and then he slams back into me. I'm pushing my hips up to meet his every thrust and we're in perfect rhythm. Our skin is misted with sweat as my heart pounds. "Come with me, Angel."

I do. Falling apart underneath him while he slams into me two more times. His muscles tighten and his cock jerks inside me, rewarding me with his warm come. I look at the expression on his face. A shield forms over his beautiful features, but he doesn't fool me, I see pleasure and pain in a split second before I feel the full weight of his body falling on top of me. His lips flutter across my skin. He buries his face in my neck, kissing me.

He lifts his head and looks deep in my eyes, "Come with me." He says again and then I realize what he means.

"Next time, I will, I promise."

"Promise me then you'll stay at your grandfather's until I call you to tell you I'm on my way." He pulls out and lies beside me.

"I promise."

"This is driving me insane, that I won't be with you to protect you."

"He won't find me, I'm going to be an hour away. I'll be fine, Babe. You've got to stop worrying, you'll worry yourself to death."

Bryce kisses me and I see a gleam in his eye as his lips curl into a wicked half smile. "When we get back I'm taking you out for a night of dancing on Saturday."

"What?" Talk about a three hundred and sixty degree mood swing. "I thought you wanted me to stay out of sight?"

"I do when you're not with me."

"I'm confused."

"I'm not waiting for the police to catch this lunatic. I'll lure him out and catch him, myself."

"Babe, I don't think that's a good idea. What if you get hurt?"

Bryce raises his voice a fraction and his face shows anger. "He's the only one that's going to be hurting after I get a hold of him."

Oh no, he's getting mad. How can I get him in a good mood again? A thought enters my mind to distract him.

I clamber on top, straddling his hips and place his cock between my pussy lips. I lean forward, splaying my fingers between his, capturing him against the mattress. My hair falls, blanketing both our faces. My breasts hover close to his lips. "I remember the first time I saw you in the grocery store. I couldn't take my eyes off of you." I slide up and down the length of his cock grinding into him.

He's growing hard again.

"I thought, holy shit, is this guy gorgeous. I nicknamed you Mr. Tall, Dark, and Gorgeous."

"You did, eh?"

"Yeah, you made me so hot that day. My thong was wet instantly."

"Look what you're doing to me, talkin' like this?" He grinds back.

I'm staring seductively at him, licking my lower lip, not taking my eyes off of him.

"You, talking dirty to me and licking that lip is going to get you fucked. Hard!"

"Promises. Promises."

He smiles, "You're going to get it now." He rolls me so I'm pinned underneath him and he tickles me.

I giggle, grabbing for his hands, "Stop! No. Please."

"Please, you want me to keep going?"

"No. No. I can't breathe."

"That's just how I like you, giggling and breathless. Now look what you've done." His hard as stone cock bounces up and down. "Tickling you gets me hard."

"We've come to the conclusion that everything gets you hard."

"Yes, when it comes to you. Remember when I told you I was Mr. Wiggly before."

"I find that hard to believe."

"No one's ever affected me like you. The way I feel when I'm around you. Angel, you make my head spin."

I do that to him? "Not even your last girlfriend?"

"Definitely not."

"Umm, how do I say this?"

"Just say it Angel, you can ask or tell me anything."

"Okay, umm…Austin told me your ex keeps sucking you back in and you keep going back to her."

"He did, eh?"

"Don't be angry with him. I was prying the information out of him."

"So all this time, you've been thinking I'm going back to her?"

My voice is soft. "Yes."

He rolls so I'm on top of him again and my hair falls to my left side as he pulls me down to hug me tight. "I'm so sorry to put you through that. Believe me I'm never going back to that."

I press my lips to his giving him featherlike kisses. "How did she get you to go back to her?"

"It's hard to explain. I guess my self-esteem was low. She'd fuck with my head and play mind games. We fought all the time. Austin brought me here because I was pretty fucked up, but since I've met you I'm back to normal, at least that's what Dr. Austin says. He also says he loves everything about you and if I screw this up, he's the first one standing in line for you, but that was before Leena, of course."

"So why would he think you'd screw this up?"

"I'm very possessive. I get insanely jealous. Didn't you notice how I always sit between you and Austin?"

"Yeah."

"That's because he said he'd be first in line. He likes fucking with me. He knows what I'm like. And since we're on the subject, when we were working out, I saw you looking at Austin. I don't want you looking at anyone but me."

Oh shit, he saw me. Here we go. He's showing me his true colours. "I won't look at anyone but you. You know I can't take my eyes off of you."

"And that's the way I like it. If that sparkle in your eyes was ever gone, it would rip me apart."

"So tell me. What does she look like?"

"You really want to know?"

"I wouldn't be asking, if I wasn't curious."

"She's got long straight brown hair, maybe three inches taller than you, thin."

"What's her name?"

"Lindsay."

"Did your mom and dad like her?"

"They did at first until they got to know her better. They hated seeing the change in me. I wasn't happy. She keeps coming back. I don't understand why she won't move on with her life."

"I do. Bryce, look at you." I'm running my hands down his muscular chest to his washboard abs. "It would kill me to give you up. I'd have a huge hole where my heart used to be."

"You're never going to find out. We'll be together forever, like Mr. and Mrs. Fisher. We're going to grow old together."

He knows exactly how to melt my heart.

"You are too sweet, you know that?"

"Thanks." He hesitates like he's deep in thought. "Angel, I need you like the air I breathe. I need to make love to you over and over again. I'm addicted to you and this gorgeous body of yours."

He pulls me down and my lips meet his, we kiss passionately and when we pull away we're hot and breathless again and ready for more. We make love over and over. His hands, roaming every inch of my body; his cock, finger, or tongue was inside me constantly. I touched and caressed him with possessive need. We didn't stop until we were totally exhausted and our bodies gave out. I remembered seeing 3:25 on the alarm clock.

We wake up to sleet hitting the metal roof of the cabin. Bryce has his arm wrapped around me and I'm lying half on him, half on the mattress with my leg and arm slung across him.

I glance up at him to see if he's awake. "Good morning, Mr. Tall, Dark, and Gorgeous." I purr in his ear as he looks lovingly into my eyes.

"Good morning to you too, beautiful."

I tell myself I'm going to keep him in a good mood and I. Will. Not. Cry, because I know leaving me will make it that much harder for him.

"So you'll come with me next time? I want you to meet my mom, dad, and sister."

"Yes you mentioned a sister and I wanted to ask you about her, but somehow I got side-tracked with you molesting me in the workout room."

"I like molesting you." His eyes turn dark and seductive.

"I know you do. So why is it I never hear you and Austin talking about her?"

"She's the pain in the butt in the family."

"What's her name, other than Pain in the Butt?"

"Ciara, with a C…can you see what my parents were thinking? ABC. Austin, Bryce, Ciara."

"Yeah, I see that. So she's younger?"

"She just turned twenty one."

"Big age difference."

"Yeah, we tell her she was a mistake all the time."

"Oh, you guys are cruel."

"Yeah, we like to get under her skin, but you know what?"

"What?"

"She told me Lindsay was crazy from the beginning, but I didn't believe her. I'm seeing it now that my mind is clear."

I run my hand gently down his hard abs not being able to resist. I need to touch him.

He notices my need and tugs me closer to him.

"You know, you can text me anytime, I might not answer right away if I'm out on a fire call, but as soon as I get back to the station, I'll check my phone and I'll text back, okay?"

"Okay."

"No texting and driving. I want you safe. I've seen too many accidents over the years from texting."

"Yes, sir!" I put my hand up to my forehead and salute him.

"Are you being a smart ass? You want me to tickle you again?" He rolls on top, before I have a chance to answer him and he straddles me, tickling my ribs.

"No. No." I'm giggling. "No, please stop!"

He rolls off and out of bed, then holds his hand out for me to take. I wince at the discomfort of my crotch as I rise up out of bed to stand in front of him.

"A little tender?"

"That's an understatement." I roll my eyes.

"Do you want me to kiss it and make it better?"

"You do that and you know where that'll lead. And then I won't walk for a week."

He pulls me close, holding me in his arms. "Yeah, I know where that leads. With your legs over your head and my cock buried deep inside you. Just the thought is getting me hard."

"Hey?" I run my fingers along his length as I bend down and talk to his cock. "Mr. Wiggly, where'd you go?"

Bryce laughs while he tugs me back up, then he hugs and kisses my forehead.

"God, I'm going to miss you so much."

"I'm going to miss you."

He runs his hand along my jaw line, tipping my chin up so I'll look up at him and gently grazes my bottom lip. "So, you didn't answer me?"

I stare at him, confused.

"You'll come home with me next Sunday?"

"Won't you be working all the time?"

"I'll be on days so I'll get to see you at night and I'll take whichever day off you want me to. Maybe mid-week. We'll get to spend the whole day together. I'll show you around Barrie, we can do some sightseeing. We'll come back to the cabin or your place for the weekend."

"Yes, I'll come with you."

He hugs me. "You've made me the happiest man alive. Thank you, Angel." He hugs and kisses me again, then he runs his fingers down my spine, grabbing two handfuls of my butt and hauls me tight up against his hard cock. "Come on we better get out of here, or you'll be on your back in two seconds."

"You're such a romantic."

"I know eh?"

In the shower, we can't keep our hands off of each other while we wash. The atmosphere changing instantly as our eyes meet. Bryce's hand grips my nape, his other arm pulling me into him. "Kiss me." Our lips fusing together in a slow sensual kiss. "Let me make you come."

"Yes, God, yes."

Bryce drops to his knees in front of me. I lift my leg and drape it over his shoulder. I push the dial to shut the water off as Bryce inserts his finger deep inside me. He looks up at me. "You're so tight and you taste so sweet. A mixture of you and me."

His tongue assaults my clit as he alternates flicking, sucking and biting simultaneously. His finger slides in and out of me at a very fast pace.

I run my fingers through his wet hair holding his head in place. My breathing is shallow and ragged. I've learned that when I breathe like this, my orgasms explode and linger on. My head falls back against the shower door as every sensation in my body intensifies. He finds the perfect rhythm, driving me closer to orgasm as my hunger builds and when I look down and see his black silky hair between my thighs, I clench down on his finger and start to shake.

"Oh, that's it. Right there Babe. I want to scream. It's so good. Oh God, Babe, I'm coming." I climax, biting my lip to hold in the scream that wants to escape. His talented tongue and finger relentless in their pursuit to make me come hard.

I shake uncontrollably and my leg wants to buckle, but Bryce holds me up with one arm. He doesn't stop until he sees I've gone limp.

When I finally catch my breath, I lift his chin so he'll see my appreciation. "Holy crap, Babe that tongue of yours is amazing."

"I aim to please." He climbs up my body, leaving strategically placed kisses en route, until he gets to my mouth.

When he shoves his tongue hard and deep inside my mouth his growl vibrates me. "I love making you come."

"Now it's my turn." I say seductively.

I kiss his neck moving downward to his nipples. I gently nip and pull with my lips. As I move south, I kiss and run my lips down every hard ridge on his tight abs.

"Angel you're amazing!"

I drop to my knees licking my lips and take his cock to the back of my throat.

"Christ!" He groans.

I feel his fingers in my hair. He's holding the back of my head, guiding his cock into my mouth.

"I love fucking your mouth."

He bucks his hips to meet my mouth with every thrust. I reach down to cup his balls and they tighten immediately. "If you don't want me to come in your mouth, you'd better stop now."

I don't stop, I suck harder and slide my finger under his balls. His grip tightens even more on my head as he guides my mouth up and down his shaft aggressively. I know he's close. I sense it.

Peeking up at him, to see his reaction, I touch the soft spot, waiting momentarily for when it sends him over the edge. I'm so proud of myself. I'm learning what drives him wild too.

"Here it comes, Angel." His body tightens and his cock jerks. I feel warmth on my tongue. I look up to watch his every move. I feel him grasp the back of my head tighter and when I glance up again, I see his eyes close then open again.

He gasps for air and every feature on his beautiful face tightens then relaxes.

I swallow and he hauls me up in his strong arms. He kisses me and holds me tight.

"Angel, I want to try something, it's always been a fantasy of mine."

"Right now?" I'm so excited.

"I wish! If we only had more time. You're always so eager to learn. I like that. We'll have to wait until I get back though."

"So what's your fantasy?"

"I have a lot of fantasies. You'll have to wait and see."

"Oh sure, leave me hanging."

"By the way, I want your pink lace thong that you wore on the ATV yesterday."

"What? Why? I have to wash them."

"No, I want to smell your sweet pussy juices on them while I'm searching through my spank bank of all the beautiful and kinky things we've done while I envision your beautiful body."

Bryce is still holding me, so he steps back and eyes me up and down. "It's all right here." He points to his temple. "And then I'm going to jack off thinking about you." I laugh and we exit the shower and towel off.

"You can't be serious?" I say as we're getting dressed.

"Look at my face. I'm dead serious."

I smile and shake my head. "What am I going to do with you?"

He grins wickedly at me. "Love me and give up your panties."

18

WE FINISH GETTING ready and then saunter into the kitchen.

Austin and Leena are eating a quick breakfast. "It's about time you two get moving. We've got to be on the road in fifteen minutes."

"See Angel, I told you he's a pain in my ass. Relax, buttercup. Keep your pants on. We'll be ready."

I pop the bread into the toaster and Bryce pours us some cereal. We eat and make it to Austin's deadline.

Bryce pulls my Journey out of the garage and I place my bag inside on the back seat. When I turn, Bryce is standing right there and he runs his fingers through my hair holding the back of my neck firmly in place. He gives me such a passionate kiss, it almost makes me cry, but I hold it together telling myself not to. When he kisses me like this, all sound disappears and it's just me and him, lost in the moment.

Then I hear Austin at the end of the driveway with his husky voice. "Are we leaving today?"

Bryce mumbles. "Impatient asshole."

I smile and pull my Journey up to Leena's car and Bryce's truck. I get out and give everyone a hug, but I make it quick. I don't want to give Austin a coronary.

Bryce gives me another long kiss. "Bye, I'll text you," He says. When he turns, he pulls my florescent pink thong out of his back pocket, just a fraction so I'll see it.

I look at him and he gives me that mischievous smile. My eyes widen with surprise and I reach to grab it.

He laughs, spins, and pulls his butt away sidestepping me at lightning speed, tucking it back in his pocket. "Oh no, Angel, it's mine. Like you. I'm really going to miss you." He says as he gets in the truck.

I shake my head. "Brat!"

Lowering into the driver's seat of my Journey, I can't stop smiling and my cheeks hurt. "God, he's irresistible." I love it when he's playful. I wonder if I'll ever get my thong back. I look up to the truck and he's smiling back at me. "You have no idea how much I'm going to miss you."

Leena and I follow the guys from the cabin in our own vehicles until we get to town. That wasn't so difficult. I think I'd be able to find my way back to the cabin by myself?

The guys and Leena wave and I wave back. We all go our separate ways. Leena to her house, and the guy's head to Highway 11 for their hour long trip back to Barrie.

Instantly, I have a few emotions flowing through me that I've never felt before. I feel sad, like a part of me is missing and I have an ache in my heart. Is this love that I feel? I don't know, but I also feel fear, thinking, that he might not come back. I dismiss my thoughts.

I pull up to the drive through at the bank to get some money and then head to the beer store to get Gramps a case of Labatt's Blue. I get back into my Journey and I hear that I have a text.

It's from Bryce. *I miss you already.*

I miss you too.

You're not texting and driving are you?

No, I'm in the parking lot of the beer store.

You're not texting and driving are you?

No, we stopped at the Tim Horton's. Austin went in to get us a coffee. Guess he can't live without his Timmy's.

Yeah, it's addictive.

Do you know what I'm doing right now?

No, what are you doing?

I'm smelling your pink thong and my God, do you ever smell sweet! I'm getting hard!

A tingle instantly travels straight down to my pussy and I clench my thighs together. How does he do that through a text? We're not even together.

Stop that! Do you know what you're doing to me? Your making me wet.

I love making you wet. Look at you talking dirty to me.

I guess this is sexting.

Shit! Here comes Austin, got to put your thong away. No more texting until you get there and I know you're safe.

No more smelling my thong in parking lots.

I'll smell your sweet juices for the next four days.

You're so bad. But I like you being a bad boy.

The faster you get out of town, away from psycho the happier I'll be.

Oh shit, he's back to Mr. serious.

Okay I'm leaving now, be careful.

Text me when you get to Gramps place and I'll text you when I get to Barrie. Bye.

Bye.

I have to make a quick call to my Gramps.

"Hi Gramps I'm on my way. I'll see you in about an hour and a half."

"Be safe. I'll see you when you get here. Bye Giggles."

I get onto Highway 11 and head for North Bay.

I think about Bryce and all the wonderful, lovemaking and kinky sex we've shared and how great we get along. My mind wonders back thinking about how mad he got when he saw the note and how he gets in a mood every time he thinks about my stalker.

Remind me not to ever piss him off.

I love it when he's playful; he's so cute. I think about him smelling my thong in the parking lot and it makes me smile. It also gets me aroused.

Listening to the radio, I quickly flip through the stations when I hear the sad songs, avoiding the emotional stress and try to find something upbeat.

My mind drifts to my Gramps and I wonder if he's found a girlfriend. Gramps is a very handsome man, very muscular. He reminds me of Denis Leary, but with white hair. He even styles it the same way. His choice for clothing is a white tank top that shows his muscles and work pants because he's always working in the wood shop. I have to admit, I've got a cool Grandpa.

Before I know it I'm already pulling into the driveway. I text Bryce.

I'm here.

It takes him a while to answer.

This is Austin, Bryce is driving. He wants to know if you were speeding.

A girls got to have some fun you know.

He says you know what happens when you're bad.

Tell him to relax. What can I say? I've got a lead foot. Sorry Bryce, no changing me now. So you might as well get used to it.

I'd love to see his reaction. I bet Austin's teasing him right now.

He sure is taking a long time to text back.

This is Bryce we pulled over, Austin is driving.

Oh, shit I'm in trouble now.

I want you to drive the speed limit. I don't want anything to happen to you.

Okay, okay. Jeez you're going to give yourself a heart attack.

If I was only with you right now.

I know what would happen if you were.

Yes, just wait and see.

I want to say promises, promises, but I shouldn't get him wound up. I'm trying to be a good girl.

Got to go, Gramps is coming out to see me.

I'll text you when we get home. Bye Angel.

Bye.

I get out of my Journey and give Gramps a hug and a kiss. "Hi, Gramps."

"Well, hello there, Giggles, what took you so long to get out?"

"Oh, I was texting."

"What the heck is texting? Let me see that thing."

Frantically, I switch my text to Leena's conversation. Gramps would have a coronary if he saw what I text Bryce. I'm so nervous while he holds it and I thank God he doesn't have a clue of how to use it. Our conversation about smelling thongs isn't what you want your grandfather to see.

"I brought you some beer." I try desperately to distract him. He hands my phone back to me and I pop the back door of my Journey open.

"I'll get that, Giggles."

Boy, I can't get away from that nickname. They say when I was about two or three, I'd have giggling outbursts. I've seen it on video and I have to admit, the sound is cute with my little voice.

I grab my bag out of the back and we walk into the house.

"I took some chicken out for dinner. I told Mary you'd be cooking for me this week."

"Who's Mary, your girlfriend?"

"You know my only love is your grandmother."

"But Gramps, Grams been gone for almost four years now."

"I know, but I'll get to see her soon."

"Gramps, don't say that."

"I don't mean right now, but in due time, I know she's watching me. She's watching out for you, too."

Sadness and grief overwhelms me and I find myself getting emotional again. "Let's change the subject. What do you say we put some of these beers in the freezer, and get them cold?"

"Sure."

"So, Mary cooks you dinner all the time?"

"A few days a week. You'll meet her tonight. She wants me to bring you for our nightly Tim Horton's coffee. Now, let's talk about you. I see you have a new car."

"Yeah I bought that and paid off the mortgage on Mom and Dad's house."

"That's good. So your dept. free?"

"Yup. So let me buy you a new truck."

"Honey we've been through this before. I like all my old stuff. That truck out there is a classic."

"Okay I'll buy you one and when I bring it home, hopefully you'll like it. My boyfriend has a two thousand and twelve, black dodge diesel pick-up, he loves it and so do I."

"You have a boyfriend? What's his name?"

"Bryce Hamilton."

"Where'd you meet him?"

Shit. Think fast.

"At the grocery store. He's really nice."

"Well I want to meet this young man."

"You will. He had to go back to work. He's a fireman."

"Well he sounds like a responsible young man."

"I hope so."

Listening to myself tell my Grandfather about Bryce almost sounds too good to be true.

I can still hear my Mom warning me. Keera baby, boys and

men will tell you anything to get into your pants. Don't believe them. Don't be naïve.

Jesus I still have trust issues. What if he's bullshitting me?

My mind wonders to Bryce and why it's taking him so long to text me. They should be in Barrie by now.

"Let's have a beer Gramps. They should be nice and cold by now." Maybe this will help me take my mind off of Bryce until he texts me back.

"Gramps, I've got some dirty laundry, would you like me to throw anything else in?"

"No honey, did it yesterday, but go ahead and use it."

After drinking our beers, Gramps goes into his wood shop and I get to work doing laundry. While I'm in there loading the clothes, I remember that I need to call a security company in Huntsville. When I'm finished speaking with a security specialist, my fears and concerns have diminished greatly, knowing they will install one of the best quality security systems to keep my stalker from ever entering my house again.

As soon as I end the call with the security company, I get a text from Bryce.

Sorry it took so long to text, we came upon an accident, must have just happened, so I had Austin call 911. We helped a Mom and her two kids out of their car.

Is everyone okay?

They should be. Just a little blood, cuts and bruises. Ambulance took them to the hospital. I've got to get my butt to work. They called in extra people, because of the roads. I'll text you later. Thinking about you always and miss you.

Are you and Austin okay? Constantly thinking of you, miss you Babe.

Oh yeah, we're fine. I'll text later, bye.

Bye.

What a text from Bryce can do to me. I'm so happy. I have a three hundred and sixty degree mood change.

Flipping through my text messages, I read the ones that Bryce has sent me again.

If I absent mindedly leave my phone lying around and Gramps picks it up and by some small miracle figures out how to use it…Let's just say it wouldn't be good.

I search through my phone for some type of locking system. I tap settings, general, pass code lock and punch in four numbers. I'll have to do this for Bryce's phone.

I'm in such a good mood now that I know Bryce and Austin are home safely, so I put some music on and start dancing in the laundry room and then out to the kitchen to prepare dinner.

I'm multi-tasking keeping my mind busy, but of course it wanders to Bryce and Austin coming up on the accident. I'd love to see him in action, or would I?

Maybe I'd be a nervous wreck watching him?

I hope the mom and kids are okay.

Making my way through Gramps wood shop to turn the barbeque on, I stop to check out all his hard work. "Wow, Gramps look at all this stuff, you've been working hard."

"Oh I like to keep busy."

"Are you still selling it on weekends?"

"Yeah, I just finished putting it away when you pulled up." Scooting around the table, I give him a kiss on the cheek. "You're so talented. I love my kitchen table and the hope chest you made for me. I've got all the things I cherish from Mom, Dad, and Gram in there."

"I'm making you something right now."

"Oh yeah, what is it?"

"It's a surprise, you'll have to wait."

"Okay. Hey, I thought I'd make barbeque chicken breast. What do you think?"

"That's perfect, honey. I haven't had that in a long time."

Every time I go through the wood shop, he rushes to cover it up so he can keep it a surprise.

My Gramps. He's too cute! I'm so happy I came to see him.

After dinner, I get the laundry and dishes done quickly and then get ready to go for coffee at Tim Horton's.

The drive over to Tim Horton's is a trip down memory lane. I picture my dad with his arm around my mom's neck with me across dad's lap and Gramps driving with grandma tucked in his side, all crammed into the old single cab truck and it puts a smile on my face.

There's a beautiful older lady sitting by herself in the middle of Timmy's and I follow Gramps over to her.

Gramps introduces us. "Mary, this is my Granddaughter, Keera. This is Mary."

I extend my hand for her to shake. "Nice to meet you."

"Nice to meet you dear." She rubs my hand gently. "James you didn't tell me she's beautiful."

"Yeah, I guess I left that part out."

"I've heard so much about you." She says in the sweetest voice and I like her immediately.

"Giggles, what would you like?" Gramps asks.

"I'll have a French vanilla, please."

Both Mary and I sit while Gramps leaves us to go up to the counter.

"Giggles?" Mary asks with her eyebrows up.

"Yeah, it's my nickname. I used to have giggling outbursts when I was two and it's stuck with me, I've been called Giggles ever since."

"Oh, that is precious."

"Yeah, it's embarrassing."

I watch Mary's eyes float over to where Gramps is standing and then her features change drastically. So much that it has me looking over to see what she's scowling at. Another older lady is talking to Gramps and something in Mary's eyes tells me she doesn't like her very much.

Gramps returns. "I brought you ladies a cookie too."

Both Mary and I say thank you at the same time.

The conversation flows easily as we enjoy each other's company and throughout the evening I notice how Mary cannot hide the love in her eyes for my gramps.

Mary has flawless beautiful skin, short white hair that is styled to perfection. She's small like me with a smile that can light up the room. She has a great personality and she's gorgeous. Why isn't Gramps going for it? I don't understand it.

When we get back home to Gramps' place, I head for my bedroom that he still keeps for me. I had washed the bedding earlier and as I'm making the bed, I get a text from Bryce.

Hi Angel, I miss you so much. All I do is think about you. The guys at the station are ripping on me because I'm off my game. I can't concentrate like I usually do. They keep saying it's a woman isn't it? Boy, do they know me.

I miss you too. I was so happy to hear from you. When you didn't text, I was worried something happened to you. But after you text me, my mood changed instantly.

I'm glad to hear that. What are you wearing right now? Tell me you're naked.

Oh Babe, you're so cute, you make me smile. I love your one track mind. Well I'm sure as hell not wearing my pink thong. LoL

No you're not. It's in my pillow case.

You brought it to the fire station with you?

Yeah I can smell how sweet you are right now. Fuck I'm getting hard.

I'm shaking my head. Oh Babe, what am I going to do with you?

Oh the possibilities are endless. So are the things I want to do to you.

My pervert. Don't ever change.

Never! Shit Angel, got to go, got a fire call, I'll text tomorrow bye miss you.

Bye, I miss you.

I climb into bed thinking about Bryce, my pink thong in his

pillow case, and the pictures of me on his phone, unprotected. I hope no one touches his phone.

I need to put a password into it.

The next morning I wake to the sound of a saw cutting wood.

I lie there and the first thing that pops into my head is Bryce. I wonder what he's doing right now. I get a text.

Hello beautiful I wish I was waking up with you naked beside me.

Yes so do I. I can almost feel you rubbing up against me.

That's the best wake up call, don't you think? Feeling my hard cock grinding into you.

You're doing that to me again.

Are you getting wet for me?

Yes.

Say it.

I'm getting wet for you.

Fuck, now its rock hard. I love it when you talk dirty to me. Well I'd love to talk dirty all day long to you, but I have to get up and get to work. I'll text you tonight. Bye, miss you.

Bye, miss you so much.

Why is it after talking to Bryce I'm in such a good mood?

I get the phone book out and look for the closest Chrysler dealership and give them a call.

"Who could I talk to about the specs on your Dodge pick-up trucks?" They transfer my call to a salesperson. "Yes, I'd like to know if this Longhorn is fully loaded and if it has leather seats. It's white? Yes, if you could give me a price. So for that price you'll throw in the tinted windows, chrome running boards and line X the bed of the truck? So this thing has all the bells and whistles? Okay, can you deliver it say Tuesday? The address is one two five lakeside drive. I'll have my bank transfer the funds. Oh, I forgot, it should be put in my grandfather's name, James Johnson. If you need any other information don't hesitate to call me. Thank you, Bye."

Can't wait to surprise him, I hope he likes it, or I guess I'll be driving a new pick-up.

I make breakfast then go find Gramps in the wood shop. I'm surprised to see Mary in there talking to him.

"Good morning dear." Mary says.

"Good morning, I have breakfast ready if you two would like to join me?"

"Oh no, I should get going."

"Please I'd like you to stay." Gramps takes her hand and we walk into the kitchen. We eat, talk and laugh. I love this woman, she's great. And the way she looks at my Gramps, is the way I look at Bryce.

Gramps goes back into the wood shop and Mary and I do the dishes.

"What was your grandmother like?" Mary asks in a soft voice.

"She was so sweet, always happy and would try to make everyone else happy. She'd say 'oh, everything will be fine, it'll all come out in the wash'. She was a fantastic cook and she'd do anything for you. I miss her so much. I have a picture, would you like to see it?"

"Oh yes, your grandfather is a closed book. He doesn't like to talk about certain things. I thought if I could be more like her? I might…" She hesitates for a moment. "Someday win his love."

"Mary, you shouldn't change. Just be yourself. He'll come around."

"You're very wise. I think you may be right."

"Thank you." I show her the picture of Gram and Gramps.

"Oh, she's beautiful!"

"And so are you, Mary."

"Thank you, dear."

"I'll tell Gramps again that it's okay to move on with his life now that Gram is gone and maybe I'll get through to him. He does have a thick head."

"Oh, yes he does." We both laugh.

I want to tell her about my big surprise, but I don't know how he's going to react. So it'd be best if it were just me and him here when it arrives.

"Well, dear this was very nice, thank you for breakfast and the girl talk, but I've got to get to the hospital."

"What? Why?" I ask.

"Oh, I volunteer there, dear."

"Oh, okay. We should do this again. I like our girl talk."

"Me, too. Maybe I'll learn more about Lily." Mary takes my hand and rubs it. "I don't want to replace her, you know that, don't you, dear?"

"Yes, I can see how much you love him."

"Yes, I do."

She pats my hand and then saunters into the wood shop to see Gramps.

I take a shower and get ready to go shopping. My mission is to find a perfume that Bryce will like. I say goodbye to Gramps and then head for the store.

When I get there, I make my way directly to the fragrance counter first and ask the saleswoman, "What's your best-selling perfume that smells really good."

"Well our Adam Levine woman's cologne is selling very well. We can't keep it on the shelf. It's selling like hot cakes."

"Could I get a sample please?"

The saleswoman sprays it on a piece of paper, waves it in the air to dry it and then hands it to me.

"Mmm, this smells nice. Thank you."

As I'm walking around the store, looking for sale items, I get a text from Leena.

What are you up to?

I'm at shoppers getting some perfume and other stuff. What about you?

I'm getting wet thinking about Austin. We've been sexting. Getting pretty steamy. I can't wait until he gets back to have a sexfest.

You're something else.

Yeah and you love me. Hey Austin was blown away by Bryce at that accident eh?

What do you mean?

He didn't tell you? Bryce broke the back window, climbed into the car and handed the baby and two year old out to Austin. The Mom's leg was trapped and Bryce had just released it when the other car caught fire. Everyone was out of that one. Austin was telling Bryce to hurry up, the other car is on fire and there's gas everywhere. Bryce finally dislodged the mom's foot and handed her out to Austin. Bryce had just got out himself and it went up in flames.

Oh my god why didn't he tell me?

He probably didn't want to worry you.

Not that he had time to tell me, he's been so busy. It's been crazy at the fire department. Holy shit eh?

Yeah Austin gave Bryce a kiss and a hug right there in the middle of the street. He didn't care who was around. He said I love you man.

I'm getting pretty emotional myself, you had to tell me this when I'm in shoppers? Out in public?

Sorry I didn't think you'd cry. You wanted to know didn't you?

Yes.

Austin said Bryce just sprang into action as soon as they came upon the accident. He said he has a lot more respect for his Bro. Okay I'll let you finish you're shopping. You're okay. Right?

Yes I'm fine.

Okay I'll text if I find out anything else from Austin. TTYL

Bye, TTYL

19

DESPERATELY, I TRY to get my mind off of the accident and think of something else. I've come to the conclusion that I really like the Adam Levine perfume and I want to be irresistible and smell as good as Bryce does. So I buy it.

I pick up some groceries to stock up for Gramps' house. He doesn't have a lot of food. It's a good thing Mary's been feeding him.

When I get back, I walk into the wood shop with two beers and tell Gramps about the accident.

"I bet that mother is counting her lucky stars. Well, I want you to bring that brave young man here so I can meet him. And he did the right thing not telling you. He didn't want you to worry. That's what I would have done."

We eat dinner and then make our way to Timmy's for our nightly coffee.

I tell Mary the story.

"Oh, my! Somebody's watching over that family. Thank heavens they were there at the right time. Your boyfriend is a hero. I would love to meet him."

"Oh, you will." I say.

"Hello James, how are you doing tonight?" A different voice has us looking over to an older lady with her hand on Gramps' shoulder.

I look at Mary and she has a smile on her face, but I think it's fake. This is the same older lady he was talking to at the counter last night.

"Hello ladies." Gramps says.

"Well, who is this beautiful young woman you have with you?"

"Ladies this is my granddaughter, Keera."

"Pleased to meet you." I say.

"Oh James, why didn't you tell us you had a granddaughter?" Now she has both her hands on his shoulders and Mary's eyes follow her hands.

"Never came up I guess."

The one with her hand on his shoulder is now rubbing Gramps' back. "We'll let you get back to your visit with your granddaughter. Take care, James."

Jeez, what is it with all these women wanting my Gramps.

Mary relaxes after the two women sit down at their own table in the corner.

When we get into the truck, I have to say it. "Gramps, what are you a chick magnet?"

"A what?" He laughs.

"You know, all the women want you."

"Yeah, yeah." He says with a smile and shakes his hand, dismissing my thoughts.

I think he's speechless because I notice.

When we get back to Gramps' house, I climb into bed waiting for a text from Bryce. Not five minutes later I get a call.

The picture I took of Bryce, pops up on my phone. "Hi Angel, How are you?"

"I'm good, how are you?"

"I'm good, but I miss you."

"I'm glad you called."

"I couldn't go another minute without hearing your voice. I miss you so much it hurts."

"I told my Gramps I have a boyfriend who is a fireman and I told him about the accident. He wants to meet you."

"He does, eh?"

"It doesn't have to be right away. I know you're busy. Leena text me the details of the accident."

"Damn it! I wanted to tell you. I wanted to hold you in my arms when I told you so you'd know that everything's fine. I didn't want you to worry. I'm sorry Angel."

"That's okay, you saved their lives. You're amazing. I pictured it in my head. And holy crap weren't you scared?"

"When Austin told me to hurry, that the other car was on fire, I could hear the panic in his voice and I knew we didn't have much time. But you're so pumped up from the adrenaline rush it helps you focus on what you're doing. I have to admit sometimes I get scared, but I love my job. I couldn't do anything else."

"I wish I was with you right now, holding you."

"So do I, Angel."

I'm bombarded with all these feelings. I have an overwhelming urge to tell him I love him, but I can't. I don't want to scare him away.

"You know what I was doing earlier?"

"No. What?"

"I was lying in bed, flipping through my phone, looking at your pictures and smelling your pink thong."

"Babe, what if someone sees you?"

"They're all sleeping. I was thinking I like this one. And, oh, this is my favourite. You standing on the bed, tied to the ceiling and blindfolded. You look so sexy, I got so hard I had to go into the washroom and rub one off."

He makes me laugh how he can be so vulnerable one second,

be a romantic the other, than his blunt truthful boyish charm comes out the next.

"Oh, Babe, you're too cute."

"What? I had to get rid of the poison. You wouldn't want me to get blocked up, would you?"

"No, I wouldn't want that." I say with a smile.

"You can touch yourself, but I don't want you coming."

"What? So let me get this straight. You're saying that it's okay for you to have an orgasm, but I can't?"

"I want you climbing the walls when I see you."

"Oh, I'm already climbing the walls."

"Good, that's how I like you. Hot and wet and climbing the walls."

"Just talking to you turns me on."

"Good, hold onto that thought Angel." I hear a loud noise in the background.

"Shit, the tones are going off, got a fire call, I'll text tomorrow, sleep well. Bye Angel, miss you."

"Bye, I miss you and be careful."

"I will, Bye."

Lying there thinking about our conversation, I wonder why I have a hard time talking about our kinky sex life. I blush and squirm and I shouldn't feel so shy, I should be bolder, I should be the sex goddess he deserves. I've learned so much in the last couple weeks we've been together. I vow that from now on, I'm going to be more dominate and aggressive, I'm not going to be that shy little virgin anymore. I find myself touching down there.

I can touch myself, but can't come. Boy, he's got a lot of nerve. Maybe I should go buy myself a battery operated boyfriend for when he's not around.

Finally, I fall asleep and when I wake I remember dreaming about Bryce and vibrators. I smile. "Yeah, I've got to get one of those."

The truck was being delivered in an hour, so I had to get

up and take a shower. I hope his reaction is a good one. I'm so excited.

I make a quick breakfast, scrambled eggs, ham and cheese on an English muffin, with home fries.

"Mmm, this is good." Gramps groans appreciatively. "I haven't had this in a long time. It's nice to change it up every once in a while."

"Yes, a change is very good, Gramps."

We hear a knock at the door.

"Who is that? Mary usually comes in, so it's not her."

"Aww, Gramps." I hesitate speaking. "I've got something to show you. Get your shoes on."

I walk to the door and tell the salesman, "We'll be out in a second, I have to break it to him gently."

I close the door. "Gramps, you know how you said change is good."

"Y…essss? What have you done, Keera?" His voice is stern, angry.

Jeez, no, honey, no giggles? Uh ooh, I'm sensing a little hostility here.

"Come with me, Gramps." I take his hand. That usually turns him to jelly. We get outside and he stops dead. He looks down at me.

"You didn't. I told you my old truck is just fine."

"I know, but I want you to have a new one, you can store the other one in the garage. Keep it in mint condition for special occasions. It's a classic. You want to keep it that way don't you?" Damn, I'm good.

He lets go of my hand and walks over to the salesman, and asks, "What size engine we got in here?"

The salesman hands Gramps the key fob.

Gramps looks down in his hand, and sees there is no key attached to it, and then he looks back to the salesman, confused. "Where's the key?"

"You don't need a key. It's a keyless entry. It has a push button start. See?"

Pulling the latch for the hood, the salesman walks around to the front grill lifting the hood, then launches into detailed information. "It has a 5.7L Hemi V8w/ Fuel saver technology."

The salesman reads off the build sheet while Gramps looks over the engine for quite a while.

Gramps climbs in the driver's side, the salesman in the passenger seat, and me in the back. The salesman shows Gramps how to use the U-connect radio that controls the whole truck inside, including climate control, heated and cool air flow seats, satellite radio, and navigation. The whole process is overwhelming--he's quiet.

"I'll teach you how to use it. I've got one in my Journey. You'll get the hang of it in no time." I reassure Gramps.

"One last thing this is how you put it in four wheel drive, say, if it's heavy rain or snow. It has a 5 year/100,000 mile power train, limited warranty. If you have any problems, just bring it in. We'll fix it, no charge." He gives us his business card. "Thank you for your purchase and enjoy your new truck."

We shake hands with him.

"I thought this was a test drive?"

"Nope, I bought it for you, Gramps."

"Oh, no, you don't; I'm making payments."

"You're so stubborn. Can't you accept gifts?"

"Not like this." He says.

I take his hand in mine again. "Let's go for a ride. If you don't like it, then I'll send it back."

He grumbles, but gets in the driver's seat.

Driving around North Bay, Gramps points out some of the features in the truck, and I show him the same features that are in my Journey. I think he's trying to contain his excitement, but that's okay, I'm excited enough for both of us. What is it about men? They can't show too much emotion. I guess it's just not cool. Although he did say they've come a long way since his classic, so I think he likes it.

"Gramps, lets swing by Mary's and see if she wants to go out for dinner with us."

"Sure, but I'm buying. Don't even think about it."

When we walk to the truck from Mary's house Gramps says, "Look what giggles bought me." And it makes me smile.

We end up at a quiet restaurant on the outskirts of town. I'm assuming so Gramps can drive the truck longer. In our travels, I see a naughty store, so I put the name of the street in my phone to remember the vicinity, so I can find it again. Can't really go shopping for vibrators with your grandfather.

Bryce text me while we drive around, saying he wishes he had more time, but he is obviously busy. I tell him that's fine, I know you're busy. He says he'll call me tonight.

We drive over for our nightly Timmy's run for coffee and then Mary comes back to the house to hang out with us. I tell them I'm tired, so I can give them some time alone. Gramps hugs and kisses me and tells me he loves the truck.

Oh sure, leave me hanging all day.

I give Mary a hug and say good night.

Retrieving my laptop, I fire it up and research vibrators. This way I know before I get into the store what I want, and spare myself the embarrassment of staying in there longer. I research for half an hour and then Bryce calls me.

"Hi, Angel."

"Hi, how was your day?"

"Busy, how was yours?"

"Good, I bought my Gramps a Dodge Longhorn truck; they delivered it today. We drove around town and went for dinner then did our usual Timmy's run."

"I can't wait to see it. That's my next truck, right there."

"Yeah it's nice. So you were busy?"

"We had a house fire, grass fire along the highway and an accident."

I picture Bryce hard at work in my head and it makes me proud. "Wow, you were busy."

"Hearing your voice is the best part of my day."

"Babe, you say the sweetest things. I sit by the phone waiting for your call. I love hearing your voice, too. I get so happy."

"Listen to you saying the sweetest things. Are you trying to sweet talk me?"

"Yes I am."

"You're trying to get me hard. Aren't you Angel? Well, it's working."

He goes from sweet and romantic to his blunt boyish charm in a Nanosecond. Seriously, who could resist him?

"Babe, I can't wait for Friday to see you."

"I know, it can't come fast enough, I can't breathe without you. If we leave at eight O clock, then we should be there by nine-thirty."

"Okay I'll leave at eight-thirty."

"No, you should leave at eight O clock. No speeding."

"Jeez, you're so bossy. I was kidding. I just wanted to see your reaction. I'll leave at eight."

"I think you need a spanking when I see you."

"Promises, promises."

"Oh you're just asking for it, aren't you Angel?"

"Yes. Yes I am."

"You sure are bold when you're on the other end of the phone. You were so shy and quiet when we were together. Another side to my Angel. I like it."

Why is it I'm getting excited about being spanked? Oh, how I'd love to have his hands on me right now.

"Well, I'd better get to bed, I'll text you tomorrow."

"Okay, bye. Be careful, I miss you."

"Bye Angel, I miss you. Can't wait for Friday."
There's silence on the phone.
"Hang up, Angel."
"You hang up."
"Okay, we'll both do it, on the count of three. One, two, three."

On Wednesday, I go to the naughty shop, to get a vibrator and some sexy lingerie that will drive Bryce insane. And yes it is embarrassing at first, until the girls help me feel comfortable.

Walking through the parking lot, I get a text from Bryce, so I hurry to throw the bags in my Journey.

Sorry Angel, I haven't been able to text, it's been crazy around here again. I get to go home for eight hours. I'll call you when I get home.

That's okay don't feel obligated to text. I'm keeping busy too, I'm at the naughty shop.

Oh yeah what'd you buy?

It's a surprise.

Can't wait. I'll call you tonight, Bye. Miss you.

Bye. Be careful and miss you too.

As soon as I get to Gramps' I hide my stuff from the naughty shop. I keep busy all day, cleaning Gramps' house, and before I know it Bryce is calling me.

"Hi, Angel."

"Hi, Babe. How are you? You sound tired."

"Yeah, we've been so busy, it's been non-stop, but I'm at home now, and then I go back at eight, work all day and night, then I get to see you."

"I know. I'm so excited."

"Me, too, Angel, more than you know. I'm going to do my

laundry then I get to sleep in my own bed. I wish you were here with me."

"Yes, so do I."

"So you'll come home with me on Sunday? You haven't changed your mind. Right?"

"No I haven't changed my mind."

"I wouldn't let you. This week I'll be on days, so I'll get to come home to you at night and I'll get to sleep with you."

"Wouldn't let me eh? Sounds like a controlling personality to me."

"Not controlling, just persistent. I'd keep bugging you until you said yes. Which you still haven't answered yet."

"Yes, I'll come with you."

"Good. Get some sleep Angel, I'll text you tomorrow."

"Okay, bye. And you get some sleep too."

"I will. Bye Angel."

In the morning, I wake to the sound of the saw ripping through some wood. I get up, look outside and there's a dusting of snow on the ground. "What the heck, it's mid-October. It's not supposed to snow yet."

Hopefully it won't snow tomorrow. I don't want to drive in this crap.

I get a text from Bryce.

You fucking whore!! Stay away from my boyfriend!!

I look again to see who sent it.

It's Bryce's phone. Holy fuck! It must be Lindsay. She must be with Bryce.

My heart drops out of my chest.

Aren't you going to answer me? You fucking bitch!!!

He can't know that she's texting me. He wouldn't let her talk to me like this would he?

Ten different scenarios are going through my head. Did she spend the night with him? Did she get him to go back to her?

Well, think about this bitch, I just fucked his brains out all night. That was the best make up sex ever!!! He's mine stay away from him!!!

Oh, God, I feel sick. I run to the bathroom, pull my hair back as I kneel in front of the toilet and hurl, until there's nothing left in my stomach. After a couple minutes, I force myself to get up, I look in the mirror and tears are streaming down my face. This is déjà vu all over again. I feel the same as I did four years ago when my parents died. It feels like someone's ripped my heart out and kicked me in the gut.

I need to get a grip. Gramps can't see me like this.

A shower might help me stop crying. I've got to get this psycho bitch out of my head. Once I get out and dressed, I pull myself together and check my phone. Nothing. I hope she's given up.

I head out to the kitchen to make breakfast and put a happy face on for Gramps.

He notices right away. "What's wrong, honey?"

I feel bad that I have to lie to him. "Oh I must have caught something. I don't feel too good."

"Well you take it easy today. Don't worry about dinner. I'll take care of that."

"I'm going to take your advice. I'll take it easy, play on my laptop today."

"If you need me, I'll be in the wood shop."

I hurry back into the bedroom to see if she's sent another text.

I can see that you're reading my text. Answer me bitch.

Yup, I think I'm pissing her off even more by not answering her.

I just saw the pictures. You fucking cunt!!! That's how you lured Bryce. You're into that S&M shit aren't you?

Ooh the C word! She's pissed. I think I can have some fun with this. I'm done taking this shit from her.

I text back.

If you would have treated Bryce with respect and you weren't such a psycho bitch, you might have been able to keep him. And yes, thanks to Bryce I am into that S&M shit…It's soooo erotic!! He loves my touch and all the kinky things I do to him.

Oh, God, this is really going to get her going, I press send.

Lindsay texts back. *You're a sick fucking bitch.*

I can't help myself I have to text back. *Oh he hasn't tried any kinky shit on you? Aww, that's too bad. You don't know what you're missing. When I see him again I'm going to tie him up like he did to me and do all kinds of freaky shit to him. Would you like me to send you a picture?*

Her head is probably spinning around three times, I'm sure.

You better hope I never find you, because I'll rip every strand of that bleach blond hair out of your head.

I text her right away. *Oh it's natural blond. Ask Bryce, he shaved me.*

I think she's going to lose it now.

Lindsay texts back. *I'm going to fucking kill you CUNT!!*

Well we could chit chat like this all day long, but I've got better things to be doing. DON'T TEXT ME AGAIN!! I hit send.

That was almost too much fun.

Gramps knocks on the door.

"Come in."

"Honey, I've got your present done. Come see it." When we walk into the wood shop, I see a cedar bench with a K&B beautifully carved in the middle of a heart. It also has carved leaves and vines running through the back rest.

I wrap my arms around him and give him the biggest hug. "Thank you so much, it's beautiful!"

"You think it'll fit in your Journey? If not, I can take it to your place with my new truck."

"Oh yeah, should fit." I run my fingers over the initials and then give him another hug and kiss. "I love it! Thank you so much."

"You're welcome honey."

I go back into the bedroom and check to see if another text was sent. Leena had text me.

Austin called me. He said Bryce needs your phone number. Why does Bryce need your number when you put it in his phone?

I don't get a chance to text her back; I get a phone call. I look at my phone, it says Barrie fire department.

"Hello."

"Hi, Angel, it's me. I couldn't call because my phone disappeared. I had to get your number from Austin. I didn't memorize it yet."

"Well, I know who has it? Lindsay. She text me and said she just finished fucking your brains out, all night."

"Don't believe her, Angel. I'm so sorry you had to put up with her. She still has a key to my house, obviously."

"She told me it was the best make-up sex ever."

"Please don't believe her. I fell asleep with my phone on the table next to me and when I woke up it was gone. That's it."

"So you didn't have sex with her?"

"No, Angel, you're the only one I want to have sex with. You believe me, don't you? Remember, we don't lie and we have to have trust."

There's a pause.

"Angel? Are you going to answer me?"

"I'm thinking."

"How can I make you believe me?"

"I believe you." I say with a soft voice.

"It doesn't sound like it."

"You wouldn't be calling me if you did have sex with her. I believe you."

"You can't listen to anything she says, Angel."

"I won't."

"Are you okay?"

"Yes, I'm fine."

"Are you sure? I'm not hanging up until I know that you're okay. That we're okay."

"Yes, we're okay."

"I'll see you tomorrow. We'll meet at your house, say around nine-thirty."

"Okay, I'll see you then."

I text Leena back. *Yeah his crazy ex-girlfriend broke into his house while he was sleeping and stole his phone.*

What?

Yeah and then she text me and said she just finished fucking his brains out.

No! Holy shit, what did you do?

I let her rant for a while. Not answering her just pissed her off even more. But then I was tired of her shit and let her have it. Oh yeah, I tried to piss her off and I think I succeeded.

I can't really tell Leena the details of our conversation, it gets a little explicit and I like to keep my relationship private.

Yeah at the end of the conversation she was so pissed at me, she told me she's going to kill me and used the C word.

No! Not the C word. Leena says sarcastically. *I can't wait to see your phone.*

Leena loves drama, and I hate it.

So I'll see you tomorrow. I'm clapping my hands I'm so excited. I get to see you and Austin. Oh and Bryce too.

Bryce wants to meet at my house, nine-thirty. I'll see you then. Ttyl.

See you have a safe trip back. Bye.

Boy, this has been a fun filled morning. Not! But I'm feeling much better since I talked to Bryce.

The day came and went, but not as fast as I wanted it to.

Friday morning when I wake, the sun is shining and I can't contain my excitement. In a couple of hours I'll be seeing Bryce.

I take a shower and get dressed in my favourite jeans, and

Bryce's, with a black, form fitted satin and lace bustier, that buttons all along the front and ties at the back with a satin ribbon. I look in the mirror. "Oh he's going to like this." I spray some perfume on, then put my little black leather boots and jacket on. I place all my bags in my Journey and pull the back seat down so we can get the bench in there.

We eat breakfast then we attempt to put the bench in. "See, Gramps, it just fits. You made it the perfect size."

"I guess I did."

I give him a kiss and a hug, "Thank you so much for everything."

"You're welcome. Thank you for the truck, I'll call you for your account number and I'll put money into it monthly and I don't want any argument."

I get into my Journey.

"Okay, okay. You know, Gramps, Mary is an amazing woman. Gram would want you to have a happy life. You can have two loves of your life. Just think about it, okay?"

"I will. Bye, honey. Be safe."

"Bye, love you Gramps."

I wave to him as I pull out of the driveway.

20

WHEN I MAKE it back to Huntsville, as I'm driving by Mr. and Mrs. Fishers house I see smoke coming across the road and some people trying to wave me down. I pull my Journey into the driveway next door, grab my cell and call 911.

"911, what's your emergency?"

"There's a house fire at 102 Main street east, please hurry, Mr. and Mrs. Fisher are in that house."

"We've already received a call for this location, fire and ambulance have been dispatched."

"Thank you."

Running to the front of the house, I climb the stairs and just as I'm getting to the top step, the door opens, smoke billows out and Bryce emerges with Mrs. Fisher in his arms.

My breath leaves me.

"Bryce!"

So many emotions flow through me and tears swell in my eyes, but I have to concentrate with all of this sudden commotion.

"Come with me Angel, I'll go back in to get Mr. Fisher once we get Mrs. Fisher to the ambulance." Bryce commands.

"Can you go get my foolish husband?" Mrs. Fisher Grabs Bryce's hand after he places her on the gurney. "He's probably collecting our pictures."

"Angel, you stay here with Mrs. Fisher."

The fire department arrives and within a couple of minutes they've got water on the fire.

Bryce still isn't out yet. I keep looking over toward the house and I worry that something's happened to them. Different scenarios are going through my head at the moment and I can't just stand here and wait. The ambulance attendants are taking care of Mrs. Fisher, so I give her hand a squeeze before darting back up the stairs.

Mr. Fisher and Bryce are coming out with boxes in their hands, just as I reach the top step. "I wasn't about to leave our memories in that house." Mr. Fisher says.

Grabbing Mr. Fisher's arm, I help guide him down the stairs.

"I have to go get Mrs. Fisher's wheelchair." Bryce runs back up.

Once I get Mr. Fisher to the ambulance, I notice a fairly large crowd of people forming to see the spectacle.

I feel Bryce approaching before I even turn around and when I do, Bryce is staring deep in my eyes.

"Do you feel that?" Bryce asks.

"Yes, I feel it."

That same intense sexual attraction is still there in both our eyes. The electricity crackles, but more intense now because I haven't seen him from our four days of separation.

He holds me in a tight embrace and kisses me passionately. It's just me and Bryce, alone, in our own little bubble. Everything outside it ceases to exist, all sight and sound disappears, while inside it, my body fires to life, straining toward his. I don't know how long we hold that kiss for, but WOW! Desire unfolds deep within my pelvis and a tingle quickly travels straight there. We're lost in each other, reconnecting. Claiming and possessing. My knees are weak and I want him right now. He takes my breath away.

Distantly, I register the chief of the fire department approaching us from the corner of my eye and some people clapping loud. We break our intimate contact. I don't think I've ever turned this red before in my whole life.

I look up at the chief who's introducing himself to us and when he starts asking Bryce questions, that uneasy feeling creeps up on me and I tense. Glancing around, I see some of the people in the crowd staring at us. My eyes quickly scan and then abruptly stop.

Amongst the people in the crowd is my stalker, and he's scowling, looking very angry. I look at Bryce, who is still talking to the chief. When I look back at the crowd, my stalker's disappeared.

Bryce is still holding on to me when a firefighter approaches the chief with a gas can. "We found this thrown in the woods."

"You had your gloves on?" The chief asks.

"Yes."

"Good, I'll call for an investigation." He turns back to look at Bryce. "I want to thank you again." The chief shakes Bryce's hand.

Austin and Leena walk toward us, arm in arm. "What's going on?" Austin asks.

"Someone torched Mr. and Mrs. Fisher's wheelchair ramp. Bryce got them out of the house."

"How do you know it's arson?" Austin asks.

Bryce replies. "They found a gas can in the woods."

"Who would torch Mr. and Mrs. Fisher's ramp? Everybody in this town knows them and knows they're always home." Leena states.

"Some sick fuck." Austin grumbles.

"Oh, that reminds me. My stalker was in the crowd. He didn't look too happy."

"Why didn't you tell me?" Bryce asks.

"You were talking to the chief. I didn't want to interrupt and when I looked back, he was gone."

"So he saw me holding you?"

"Oh yeah, he saw more than that."

"Good. We're going to catch this lunatic. Let me know if you see him again."

We walk to the back of the house to assess the damage of the burnt ramp.

"Well, the house is fine." Bryce says.

"I can remember when my parents built that ramp for Mr. and Mrs. Fisher. I'd help every once in a while, but mostly I just fed the chipmunks. I was twelve."

"Their insurance company will take care of that." Austin says.

I grab Leena's hand. "Come with me. I want to show you the bench Gramps made for me and Bryce."

Walking to my Journey, I open the back hatch. Bryce runs his fingers over the engraving. "Wow, he does good work."

"Gramps suggested putting it outside, but I think it's too nice to get all weathered outside."

Austin takes a quick look at the bench and then he walks to the front of my Journey, clearly distracted by something.

"What the hell? Bryce come look at this." Austin says.

Leena and I walk around to the front of my Journey, curious to see what they're looking at.

Gathering around, we all focus on reading the note stuck behind my wiper blade on my windshield.

You've been with him! Not me.

You are mine!!!!

Dump him, or he will die!

This is the result of my anger.

Get rid of him and we can be happy together, forever.

Mine! Remember that.

WE WILL be together. That's a promise!

"This guy's delusional!" Leena says when she's done reading it.

Bryce is running his hands through his hair and pacing. "That's it! We're catching this fucker tonight."

He comes over to me and holds me. "Angel, can we stay at your place tonight?"

"Sure."

"Blondie, do you have something I can put this in?" Austin says lifting the wiper blade carefully.

"Yeah, I have a bag, I'll dump my makeup out."

Austin says, "Don't look, but you do know, he's probably watching us right now."

"Most likely." Bryce says.

When I come back around to the front of my Journey, Bryce holds me tighter this time. I hand Austin the bag.

"Were taking this to the cops." Austin says in that deep voice of his.

"You and Leena drive a bit down the road, then hang back to see if anyone follows me and Keera when we leave. Text if you see anything. If not, then you two take off to the cop shop. At Keera's, if you see anything suspicious, let us know. You'll have to text Keera's phone, since I don't have one anymore."

"Aren't you going to get your phone back from her?" I ask.

"No, it's easier this way. I'll buy a new one."

"He's scared of her." Austin teases.

"No." Bryce gives Austin a disgusted look. "My life is so much better with her out of it. Oh, and I took care of her breaking and entering." Bryce looks directly at Austin and I wonder if there's a hidden meaning about that look. "I sent my buddy to my house to change the locks."

"We should hook my stalker and her up."

"Yeah, no shit." Bryce counters.

I give Austin and Leena a hug like we were saying goodbye to put on a good show, in case my stalkers watching.

Sinking down into the seat of my Journey, I reach up as Bryce bends down to give me a kiss before he shuts my door.

Bryce climbs into his truck and I follow him out onto the road, glancing around suspiciously all the way back to my place.

I get a text from Leena when I pull into my driveway.

No one followed you.

Thanks.

We take in our bags then go back to get the bench.

"I can get this." I watch Bryce as he lifts it out of the back of my Journey by himself.

"Ooh! Look at those muscles."

"Wow, this thing is heavy." Bryce groans.

"Yeah, I know. Gramps and I loaded it in there."

I open the back door and Bryce walks through the kitchen to put the bench down in the living room, then he prowls like a panther toward me. He inches his way closer until I'm up against my kitchen table. Bryce has that hungry stare. The stare that tightens every muscle from the waist down. The intensity of his dark gaze makes my heart skip a beat and my nipples stand at attention. He's not saying a word; he just eyes me up and down and licks his lips like I'm his next meal. He holds my lower back with one hand; the other is splayed in my hair at the back of my neck, holding me in place. He's staring at my lips and then he runs his finger along my bottom lip like he cherishes everything about me. I think he's trying to melt my panties off. I look at his lips and then he lunges, his mouth melds to mine.

We kiss passionately for quite a while and when we pull apart we're hot and breathless. Wow! What a kiss. He doesn't have to say he missed me; his kiss says it all. I watch Bryce take the candle and a few other items off the middle of the table and put it on the counter, then he struts back over to me, unzips my pants and slides them down with graceful expertise. I lean against my table wearing my bustier and black lace thong and he stands back, inspecting my body, slowly.

"You look so hot! And this…" He runs his fingers inside the cup of my bustier. "…is so sexy."

I can't hide the shiver that runs through me.

He stands back admiring with lust and appreciation in his eyes. "My god, look at you."

"You like it?"

"Oh yeah, I love it."

He likes it. I mean, he really likes it. I'm so hot for him right now. It feels like I'm going to explode already and he's hardly touched me. I'm shaking with wild anticipation.

Lifting me up so I'm sitting on my table, Bryce slowly pushes my legs apart. He skims his hand along the inside of my thigh. "So soft. I've been thinking about me touching every single inch of your body." His finger finds its way behind my thong and skims gently over my clit. I watch his every move as he takes his time caressing. "You should breathe. I don't want you passing out on me."

He lifts one leg then the other.

"My Angel needs to come, don't you?"

"Yes." My voice is soft. "I want you so bad."

"I know."

He hooks his thumbs in my thong pulling it down both legs slowly, teasing as he skims my sensitive skin, driving me mad. He places my heels on the edge of the table again and spreads my legs wide settling between my thighs. Then his mouth is on me…

finally! Bryce slides his skilled finger in me, thrusting at a very fast pace. His magical tongue flicks my clit wildly.

This has been the longest four days of my life. I was fine before I met him. Now I crave his touch, his body, everything about him. I can't get enough. I never will. I would do absolutely anything for this man.

I lean back on my elbows and my head falls back, savouring this unbelievable feeling. God! He's so good at this. I flop down on my back and hold his head. My hips circle shamelessly and my breathing slows. I hold his head tighter in place with both hands now. I'm bucking my hips up to meet his finger and tongue, as he flicks my clit relentlessly. This is what I've been waiting for to take away the irritable edgy feeling I've felt for four days now.

"Babe!" My sudden orgasm takes me by surprise.

My legs shake uncontrollably. The aftershocks continue and I'm vaguely aware of Bryce unzipping his pants, then he climbs on the table, on top of me.

I open my eyes. "Holy shit, what you do to me. That was so strong and fast." Cupping his beautiful face in my hands, I wipe the evidence of my arousal off his lower lip. "How I've missed you."

"I've missed you. Anytime you need me, Angel, I'm here."

He slides his cock all the way in and I gasp as it stretches me. "You're so wet for me."

"Yes, you do that to me."

"I told you I'd fuck you on this table."

"Yes, I didn't doubt you for a second."

He pulls out then gently pushes back in.

"I'll have to thank Gramps for making such a sturdy table."

He holds himself up with one arm and his chest muscles bulge everywhere. He tugs down my bustier with little difficulty, so it sits below my breasts and he pinches my nipples. I lift my knees to give him better access and he inches all the way in. He picks up the pace thrusting harder in and out. His skin radiates so much heat against me that I'm warming to the point where a sheer mist of perspiration layers my skin. Our breathing escalates to a pant as we stare lovingly in each other's eyes.

"You smell and feel so good; you're going to make me come already." He stops moving. "I've got to stop. Don't move!"

"Please Babe, it feels so good. I'm begging you." I move my hips in a circular motion.

"You can't move."

"Please, I need you."

I touch my clit and clench my muscles around him, milking him.

"Aw, fuck!" And he starts to move, fucking me hard. "Come for me, Angel."

I do. Reaching out, hanging onto the sides of the table, as my whole body quivers. "Babe!"

He slams into me two more times and I feel him tense. "You. Feel. So. Good." He says in between breaths.

I feel his cock jerk inside me and I feel warm come filling my insides. I watch him intently. I love to study every feature on his face as he's coming because I'm giving him this ultimate pleasure…me…me and my body.

The full weight of his body falls down on top of me and he buries his face in my neck, neither one of us saying a word. I rub his back calming him after his explosive orgasm.

I listen to his breathing return to normal and feel his heart pound and I watch every expression on his beautiful face.

"How I've missed you." I kiss the corner of his mouth, then down his neck giving him gentle tender kisses.

"I know, I've been dying a slow death without you, that's how much I've missed you. This is where I want to be for the rest of my life, with you and inside you."

He wants to be with me for the rest of his life?

I feel his cock jerk inside me as we stay so intimately connected.

"I've been dying without you, Babe. It's like a part of me was missing and I had a constant pain in my heart."

"I know Angel, but I'm here now."

We hug in a tight embrace, then I slide my hands down his back feeling every tight muscle until I reach his tight butt cheeks and squeeze, pulling him into me.

"You want more?"

"Yes please, I can't get enough of you."

"I feel the same way, Angel."

"God, I've missed you."

"I've missed you. When I came out of that house and saw you, I got a semi right away. And when I got to hold you, I was rock hard. I couldn't get the fucker to go down."

I flash him a full white teeth smile. "I know, I felt it."

"I wanted to fuck you right there."

"Well, I'm glad I still have that effect on you."

"Angel, it's more severe now, I think."

"I had all these emotions running through me, I was anxious and scared, thinking you weren't going to come out of the house, but when you did and you held me, a rush of other emotions flowed through me. I wanted *you* right then and there."

"I could tell by the look on your face you were scared for me. But don't worry, Angel, I do this every day."

"I think it's going to take some time to get used to. Your mom and dad, do they worry about you?"

"Oh yeah, my mom used to have bad dreams, but she's relaxed now."

I look down and realize that I'm still wearing my bustier.

His finger gently grazes my nipple as he touches the satin on the ribbon. "This is so sexy, I love it. Oh, by the way, you smell fantastic."

"Thank you, so do you. You've got a mixture of cologne and smoke."

He gives me the biggest full white teeth smile, "Yeah, don't you love that smell?" Bryce says sarcastically.

I shake my head and smile as I look lovingly in his eyes.

We hear a car door slam.

"Oh shit!" Bryce pulls out of me and rolls off of the table.

Gathering my pants quickly, I hold myself and scramble to the bathroom to get cleaned up and dressed.

When I come out Bryce is dressed and he's replacing my candle to disguise our playful antics on my kitchen table.

Closing the gap, he comes to me wrapping his arm around my waist. "That'll hold us off until we can continue this tonight." He gives me a lush kiss. "At least now I'll be able to think straight, so I can catch this psycho." Bryce sticks his finger down my cleavage. "You're all I've been thinking about for the last four days."

Austin and Leena come through the back door, holding hands and gazing deep in each other's eyes. Jeez they've got it bad…like us. They make such a cute couple. I'm so happy for them. Austin is perfect for her. They both have loud uninhibited personalities, but it seems to work for them as one will always cave in, submitting to the other.

"Did you see anything suspicious out there?" Bryce asks. "Or were you looking?"

They don't see anything except themselves, they're lost in each other.

"We went up and down the street twice and we didn't see anything. It's pretty quiet." Austin says.

"So what did Constable Grant say?"

"He thinks Blondie's stalker is progressing and we shouldn't take his threat lightly. He wants me to watch your back. I told him we'd be staying here and he said he'd keep a car driving by."

"You can stay in my spare room. I'll strip the bed and wash everything. We should also go get some groceries. I haven't been here for three weeks. The cupboards are a little bare."

"Yeah, but we all go." Austin says protectively.

21

AT THE GROCERY store, Leena notices how women react around Bryce and Austin, how they blush and get flustered when they talk to them. There are very few women that aren't affected by their stunning good looks.

"You haven't seen anything yet." I tell her. "Just pay attention. It's unbelievable."

I notice Bryce is a lot more touchy feely than usual. He can't keep his hands off of me. He's either holding my hand, sticking his hand in my back pocket, has his arm around my waist, or on my lower back. Or he's standing behind me, rubbing his cock against my butt. I don't mind one bit. I love it and the fact is, he's turning me on again.

Bryce observes people in the grocery store and when we leave he studies every vehicle around him and down the road, but my stalker is nowhere to be found.

"Where the hell is this asshole hiding?" Bryce asks as we unload the groceries.

Austin pats Bryce on the shoulder as we carry the groceries in the back door. "Don't worry. He's going to screw up. Then we'll catch him."

"I thought we'd see him by now." Bryce complains.

Leena gets a rush of energy. "Well, since your stalker isn't around, let's go find a new dress for tomorrow night."

Leena's excited about going to dance at the local bar. It's formal night, she loves to dance and so do I. I wonder if I'll get Bryce up on the dance floor with me.

"I want him to come out in the open." Bryce says as he helps me put away the groceries in the pantry. "I think we need to be seen around town, which might draw him out of hiding."

Leena claps her hands together, "Good I know the perfect store to get a dress."

Our bodyguards sit on the couch playing bass pro fishing on my phone, while we try on dresses. Every time one of us comes out with a dress on, they look up.

Leena finds a sexy light blue dress that shows a lot of cleavage and hugs every curve she has that Austin approves of. And when I come out of the dressing room with a light pink chiffon dress that criss-crosses at the waist, showing some major cleavage, Bryce's priceless expression tells me this is the one.

Bryce comes over and stands in front of me, staring with his hungry eyes. He slips his finger in between my breasts and whispers in my ear. "You're only going to wear this with me around. Right?"

"Yes, you'll be right beside me."

Bryce looks me up and down with lust and approval in his eyes. "I won't let you out of my sight."

I give him my seductive smile. "That's exactly what I want."

"Okay you two, break it up. You're a little embarrassing. You're out in public." Austin teases.

We both turn and smile.

When Leena and I come out of the dressing room to pay, the saleswoman behind the counter informs us Bryce and Austin have already paid. We argue until we're blue in the face, but it gets us nowhere.

"Thank you for the dresses and being our bodyguards." I say.

"No problem, thanks for being quick and not torturing us too much." Bryce teases.

I smack his ass for that comment.

Bryce bends and whispers in my ear. "I love it when you smack my ass."

"You want me to smack it tonight?"

Bryce threads his fingers through my hair, taking hold of my neck as he pulls me in for a kiss.

"Cut that shit out! You're in public." Austin complains and heads out the door with Leena in tow.

Bryce wants us to be seen around town to draw my stalker out of hiding, but I'm very concerned because he threatened Bryce. I mean really, you don't know what an unstable person is capable of. I'm relieved Austin is here shadowing his brother.

I'd be in a mental institution if anything were to ever happen to Bryce because of me. I shake my head trying to dismiss the thought.

We take the guys out for lunch at a restaurant nearby. We talk, eat, and laugh and enjoy each other's company, having a good time together.

Bryce holds my knee the whole time and when I tense, he notices. "What's wrong?"

"I'm getting that feeling. He must be around here."

I feel Bryce tense instantly.

My eyes search over everyone in the restaurant and when I'm satisfied that he's not in here, I turn toward the windows and notice my stalker sitting in a blue pick-up truck watching us.

"I knew it. That's him, blue pick-up."

Bryce and Austin shoot up out of their seats and hurry toward the door, but an elderly couple are taking their time exiting in front of them. By the time they get outside he's long gone.

I can see Bryce swearing, he's so mad. They look around the building in the parking lot.

My adrenaline is pumping and I'm so scared that Bryce will catch him. I don't want him to get hurt.

We pay for lunch and then meet them outside.

Bryce is still pacing, and running his hands through his hair.

His natural reaction and coping mechanism, whenever he's frustrated and mad.

Bryce glances over, then turns abruptly, strutting toward me, but he physically relaxes as soon as he wraps his arms around my shoulders as he holds me and kisses my forehead. "We didn't get the license plate."

I guide him toward his pick-up, "Let's go drive around. Maybe we'll see his truck."

Bryce calms down as we're walking, then unexpectedly, he spins toward the restaurant. "We have to pay."

"I did."

"Angel, I'm paying you back."

"You bought me that beautiful dress."

"You won't win, Angel. I'm always paying."

"Stubborn!"

"You have no idea."

We drive around town for about an hour and then head back to my house, not seeing my stalker anywhere.

Sitting around the kitchen table, we try to figure out a game plan. Occasionally, I'd think about me and Bryce having a quickie on my table; I squirm in my seat.

Bryce glances sideways at me, then tightens his grip on my knee, a sign he knows what I'm thinking.

Austin and Bryce think that if my stalker is going to do

anything, he'll probably come at night. So we agree to go to bed early, then during the night, we hope we'll hear something, or the motion lights and cameras will detect movement if he comes around.

While I was at Gramps, I had a security company change the locks and install a digital key pad at the back door. Cameras are strategically placed throughout my yard and they set up a monitor in my bedroom, so I can see it from my bed and I also have one in my kitchen.

Both Bryce and Austin are quite impressed with the new system.

We say our goodnights and head to the bedroom hand in hand.

Bryce goes straight for my bag sitting on my bed and pulls everything out of it.

"Excuse me? What do you think you're doing?"

"I've been dying to know what you bought."

Jeez…He really doesn't have any boundaries when it comes to me. But he's so cute he looks like a little boy opening a present.

Oh, shit, he's going to find my new vibrator.

I try to distract him by plastering myself up against him. Lifting his shirt, I run my hands up his perfect abs to his meaty pecs. I look over his shoulder. Crap! Too late!

"What's this? I knew it. I knew you'd buy one."

"Well, seriously, it's okay for you to masturbate, but not for me?"

Irritated, I feel my face getting warm, and he's grinning at me, making me angrier.

"Calm that red headed temper down. I thought about it later that night and it was selfish of me."

"Ya think?" My voice rises a couple notches.

Bryce holds me and pulls my hair behind my ear, then he

gives me a hug and a kiss, trying to calm me down I think. Well, it's working.

He looks deep in my eyes. God, he's gorgeous! How does he do that? He's melting me to my core. I'm like putty in his hands. Distracted again, as I lose my train of thought. I can't stay mad for long.

"Wow! That's sexy!"

We both look down on the bed.

"You like?"

"Oh yeah, I want you to go put it on."

And just like that, I'm not mad anymore. I go into my bathroom, brush my teeth, clean up, and put some perfume on. When I'm done getting dressed, I look in the full length mirror. Very nice. I hope he likes it.

I'm wearing a white lace bra with a tiny bow and one pink diamond fastened between the breasts. I chose a lace garter belt to match, knowing that's all Bryce has in the kinky cabinet, along with the silk stockings. He obviously likes this look. The thong I'm wearing is soft white lace, with a bow and pink diamond, but he hasn't seen that it does up with a string of pearls from the crotch, all the way up to the back.

When I come out of the bathroom, Bryce is lying on my bed, totally naked with his legs spread and his hands clasped behind his head, showing every gorgeous muscle he has with that sexy pose.

Stopping dead, I almost stumble over my own two feet. "Fuck me!" I swear to God I'm drooling. My eyes rake greedily up and down his sexy body.

"Oh, I plan to." Bryce bolts out of bed and prowls toward me with hungry eyes that say 'I can't wait to fuck you'. He circles, completing a full inspection, eyeing me up and down. The look of scorching possessive need. I couldn't have asked for a better reaction.

Bryce drops to his knees behind me and rubs my butt cheeks, then I feel his tongue running over the pearls, that are strung tight from the crotch of the thong up the crack of my butt. "I like these."

I giggle and squirm. "It tickles."

"We'll have to work on keeping you still, Angel."

He holds me by my hips, and I try not to wiggle. He kisses me gently and I feel him speak against my butt cheek. "So sexy."

He runs his finger behind the pearls. "The things I could do to this sexy little ass."

My eyes widen. Uh oh. What's going through that kinky head of yours? I tense, but then relax thinking of all the possibilities.

He stands abruptly pulling my hair to one side, and I feel the heat from his warm body plastered behind me. He tips my head and kisses my neck. I feel his cock pressing hard against my butt. He sends delicious tingles throughout my whole body; I'm rendered speechless. I can't move, I'm frozen with my eyes closed, enjoying every sensation, lost in the intimate moment. He snakes his arm around me and I feel his fingers slip inside my bra, onto my nipple. He pinches and tugs on it, then switches to the other one.

Bryce stops and I sigh. When I open my eyes he's standing in front of me.

"You like that, don't you Angel?"

"God yes, you can do that to me any time you'd like. That turns me on. You render me speechless and immobile. I'm a puddle."

Bryce smiles. "I see that."

His cock pokes me and I look down. His cock is so hard, it's protruding straight out. I wrap my hands around the shaft and run them up and down stroking him.

He closes his eyes and moans from the sensation as I work him over.

I drop to my knees, lick my lips and then lick from the base to the tip. I then take his cock as far as it can go into my mouth.

"You feel so good on my cock, I've been dreaming of you doing this all week."

I ease him out of my mouth, slow. "Mmm you taste so good. I've been having wet dreams about you and in my dream I'm doing this to you."

Licking my lips, I look up at him, then take him deep in my mouth. I want to see his reaction because giving him pleasure and satisfaction is such sweet ecstasy and a huge turn on for me.

"Angel!"

I'm taking him in and out of my mouth, faster now. I can tell he's enjoying it immensely because he's moaning and rocking his hips to meet my mouth.

His hands reach around the back of my head and he's guiding my mouth at his pace onto his cock. "You suck cock good. Too good, you're going to make me come."

Abruptly he pulls out and we hear that smacking sound that my lips make. I'm left leaning back on my heels, wiping my mouth and looking like someone snatched my lollypop.

He lifts me up by my arms from my kneeling position, "Come here. I owe you something." He pulls me toward the bed, he sits, and then it dawns on me and I realize what he owes me.

Before I can protest or say anything, I'm tugged across his knee. Crack! On my left butt cheek.

"Ouch!" I cry out. And then he rubs it so gently. Soft, circular motions. Then he slides his finger deep inside me. In and out. I want to moan it feels so good.

Smack! On my right butt cheek. Then he rubs again, round and round. Then I feel him slide his finger in me again, in, out, in, out.

What the hell! Is this because I was driving too fast and I was a little too bold when I text him?

"You like being a bad girl. Don't you?"

Smack! Then a rub. Then his finger probes deep inside me.

I'm determined not to let him know that it hurts or feels good. Or crap, I'm not sure how I feel about this.

"I like it when you're a bad girl."

Smack! And a rub. He switches cheeks. Then he slides his finger inside me again.

"Do you know how horny I've been thinking about doing this to you?"

Smack! And a rub. I'm tensing more with every blow. Then I feel the sensation of his finger going in and out of my pussy. These feelings are so intense, pain and pleasure all at once. It's hard to wrap my brain around it.

"I want you to defy me."

What the heck, is this reverse psychology? I knew there was another side to him.

Smack! A rub and a finger, "See how wet you are?" His voice is filled with wonder. "Okay, that's it, I'm done." He demands.

"I think you've been punished enough."

Six in total, and I didn't let him know it hurt or that it felt good.

Bryce lifts me up, spreads my legs so I'm straddling his and we're facing each other as I sit on his lap.

He caresses my behind. "You did so good, Angel. You're amazing." He kisses my temple, then hugs and rocks me like a baby, rubbing my butt cheeks. We stay like that for I don't know how long, both lost in our own thoughts. And my thoughts are, does he not see how fucked up this is? What other weird shit is he into?

"Remember when I told you I wanted to fulfill one of my fantasies?"

I tense. Oh, Jesus, here we go.

"Yes."

"That was one of them. But the one that tops my list, we'll have to wait until we get back to the cabin for. So I thought we'd try something else. And no it doesn't consist of pain, just pleasure."

"Why do you like to spank me?"

"It turns me on instantly. You'll like it too, in time. I can see how you're a little reluctant right now, but trust me, you will like it. I can see how your body reacts to it."

Bryce stands and I slide down his muscular body, until I'm standing, too.

He pulls back, the duvet cover and sheet then turns back to focus on me.

Bryce runs his finger along the lace of my bra and my breast. "We're going to get you naked. I don't want to ruin this." Bryce stands in front of me looking down with his dark eyes staring deep into mine. He reaches behind me, I feel a little tug and in one swift motion my bra is off and he tossed onto the chair.

Cupping each breast with his overly large hands, Bryce runs his thumbs across each nipple, making them pucker and harden on command. "These are so beautiful, their perfect!"

Gracefully, he lowers onto his knees and unclasps the garter from the silk stockings and then runs his finger inside my thong, skimming my enlarged clit. "Look what's popping out for me." He opens my legs wider and slides his finger deep inside me. "Ah, just the way I like you. Wet." Then he sticks his finger in his mouth. "Mmm, so sweet."

What I feel for him in this moment, seeing him in front of me on his knees, undressing me, intimately has me wild for him. Even though he took me over his knee and spanked my butt. Why do I feel this way? What is it about him that makes me lose my mind?

He spins me and he must see how pink my butt cheeks are so he kisses them. Gentle little butterfly kisses and I've forgotten about the pain. It's gone when he does this to me. He unclasps the garter at the back and slides the silk stockings down skimming his fingers down my legs, one at a time, slowly. He holds my hand and helps me out of them. The garter and thong are the last to go.

"Climb in, get on your back." Bryce demands

I do what he wants because I'm excited for the pleasure.

He saunters over to his bag of goodies and I watch his totally naked, muscular body flex when he pulls something out. Holy shit, he takes my breath away. I can't take my eyes off of him. He turns to see me almost drooling. "Like what you see?"

I lick my lips. "Mmm. Yes, I do."

I see that he's holding some ropes and a blindfold as he turns toward me. "I thought we'd have some fun."

"Yes, please." I say anxiously.

I watch him intently as he gently takes my hand, sliding his fingers over my wrist, sending delicious tingles straight down there. He's hardly touched me and, yet, I'm putty in his hands.

Bryce wraps the rope around my wrist and ties his famous knot to the post of the bed. I watch his gorgeous body move to the foot of it. His finger slides down the instep of my foot and I twitch, my foot moving out of his grasp.

I giggle. "That tickles."

"Give me that foot back! You don't want to be spanked again, do you?"

I give it back to him reluctantly.

He grabs my ankle and wraps the rope around it, then ties it to the bed post.

He saunters around the bed and repeats the same on the right side.

When Bryce is done he says, "How's that? Can you get out of them?"

I pull on my restraints, "No."

"Good. Now I think you've seen enough." He slips the blindfold over my eyes, making my other senses hyperaware.

There's slight movement, I feel on the mattress next to me. "I'll be right back. Don't go anywhere."

I giggle.

"God I love that sound."

I hear his feet walking across my hardwood floor. I hear the door open and then I hear faded footsteps.

Holy shit! He left my bedroom totally naked. What if Leena's out there?

I listen intently. I hear the fridge open and I hear him clanging around in there, then he closes the fridge door. I'm grinning. What is he up to?

I hear his feet pattering on the floor again. He's back and I hear him close the door. Bryce places something on the table next to my head. I feel the bed dip on each side of me.

Clearly, he's standing over me. I wait, listening for a sound or movement, but there's nothing for at least a minute. I squirm, feeling a little self-conscious and uncomfortable.

"Angel, you are so fucking beautiful. I can't stop staring. I wish I had my phone right now. Where's yours?"

"In my purse."

I feel him jump off the bed. "Don't move, Angel." And he's back standing over me again. I hear the clicking of the camera.

"Bite your lip, Angel."

"Are you serious?" I can't hide my smile.

"Yes, I want a picture of you biting that lip."

"Fine." I bite my lip.

He snaps the picture.

I feel his full weight on me as he straddles and sits on my hips. Leaning to one side, I feel that he's either grasping something or placing something on the table.

"Smell this."

I inhale sharply. "A strawberry?"

"Take a bite." Bryce says in his deep sexy voice.

"Umm."

He waits until I'm done chewing and I swallow.

"I want you to trust me, Angel. I want you to smell it when I put it against your lips and I want you to take it in your mouth. No talking, no moaning. Got that?"

I shake my head, yes.

Feeling it against my lips, I smell it, then take it in my mouth. Cantaloupe. He waits until I swallow.

Another. I smell it and take it in my mouth. This one is watermelon. He waits until I'm done again.

Bryce is silent.

Again, he does the same. A banana with chocolate on it. Why is this so erotic? I've never been fed before. Oh yeah, the first day we met when I was tied to the bed. That was pretty hot…if I wasn't so scared.

I wonder if he's getting as excited as I am, it's hard to tell with his silence.

My nipples feel like they're standing straight up. And as I'm thinking how hard they are, Bryce rubs something across both of them, teasing and taunting each one.

It's like he can read my mind. I feel something wet, leading down my abs, to my belly button.

Then he licks it all the way up. I pull on my restraints, because I'm on fire with this agonizing torture.

"Don't move Angel!" Bryce warns.

He rubs different textures, over various parts of my body to see how I react, then he licks the juices off with his skilled tongue.

Not knowing and seeing what he's going to do next is driving me insane.

I try not to move, but my body quivers and trembles all over from his touch.

Our quickie this afternoon wasn't enough to pacify me. I want him right now.

Bryce nibbles my hips and takes his time going lower.

"Bryce please, I need you."

"I know Angel, I'm almost there."

Something cold rubs across my pussy lips, then I feel the warmth of his tongue.

I pull on the rope, so I can open my legs wide and it bites into my ankles tightening more, but I gain a few more inches.

His finger probes deep inside me. "How's that Angel?"

I moan. "Mmm, yes I like that."

Then I feel his tongue leisurely sliding up one side, then the other of my pussy lips.

"You like this too, don't you?"

"Yes."

He's been teasing the hell out of me all this time. I'm wound tighter than a rubber band. I don't think my body and mind can take much more.

My skin is misted with sweat, my breathing has slowed and I tug on my restraints. He's so talented with that damn tongue of his.

He thrusts his finger in and out faster. He knows exactly how and when to set me off. I'm so close, I can feel it, I pull on my restraints harder now, my legs start to shake and I come undone falling apart underneath him. My aftershocks ripple through me and I'm vaguely aware of Bryce untying the ropes as he slips my blindfold off. I blink from the light.

"Welcome back Angel. How was that?"

"Frickin' amazing! I would've never lasted if we didn't have that quickie."

"I know that's why I took care of you. Now I want you to turn facing the end of your bed and lower yourself onto my cock."

Eagerly, I do as I'm told. I turn so I'm facing away from him. Straddling Bryce's hips, I lift his hard heavy cock and lower myself down onto it, inch by inch.

I gasp. "Oh my, it's so hard."

"Yes that's what you do to me."

Jeez you don't know how big and hard that thing is until you get it inside you, then it takes your breath away.

I inch my way down, until I can't take anymore.

He fondles my butt cheeks. "I love this position I get to play with this fine, fine ass."

I raise and lower myself up and down. "Babe, I feel everything, it's so sensitive this way."

He holds my hips guiding me. "Christ, Angel you'd better go slow."

I can see he's close, so I maneuver up and down slowly to savour this exquisite feeling. I circle my hips while I hold onto his strong thighs for support. I lean forward rubbing my clit on his balls.

Without warning he pulls out, flips around and has me pinned to the mattress by my hands.

"Damn, you're fast! You've got ninja skills."

He grins at me with his half wicked smile, amused by my comment obviously. I see him quickly glance at the security monitor.

"Yes, I haven't showed you all of my skills yet."

"I can't wait."

"Up on your knees, facing the mirror." Bryce demands.

Then he gets off the bed and walks to my bathroom.

I hear him opening drawers, while I stare at myself in the mirror on the back of my door, up on all fours. I'm left wondering what the heck he's up to now.

He's back and kneeling on the bed beside me. He pulls my long hair to the back of my head, and slips a hair tie in with expertise.

Okay, obviously he's done this before.

Bryce positions himself behind me and slowly sinks into me, then he twists my hair around his forearm and pulls gently, tugging my head back. "Look how hot this is…"

"You. Are. At. My. Mercy." He says slowly, then he leans over my back and holds onto my throat like he's going to choke me and whispers in my ear with that husky voice. "Look how fucking erotic this is. I love seeing you like this. Mine to do with, whatever I please."

I watch as Bryce lifts himself off my back, his hand grips my hip and he pulls out to the head of his cock, then he sinks slowly into me while he has my hair wrapped around his forearm pulling my head back slightly. He pulls out fractionally again. "Do you want it hard?"

"Yes, fuck me hard!"

Bryce grabs my left hip and slams into me, while tugging my hair back gently. It makes me gasp from the fullness and the intense feeling from hitting the sensitive tissues inside.

So turned on, and hot for him, that I'm almost shaking with need and greediness. I'm going to explode.

Bryce passes my new vibrator to me. "Put this on your clit."

Revving it up, I lean down on one shoulder, placing it where he wants me to. The sensations are phenomenal.

"Angel I can feel that vibrating my balls."

With an expert shift of his hips, he shoves his cock deep and hard filling me to the end, pushing me forward, but I hold on, pushing back. He always starts out gentle and as he loses control his aggression grows, but not that he's hurting me. He knows, he's my perfect lover.

"Come for me Angel."

Letting go at his command, I unravel. The moment he realizes, he lets go, thrusting into me, one, two, three more times.

I can see him in the mirror tensing, then he relaxes and tenses again as he spurts long and hard, filling my insides with warm come.

While the tremors rip through us, I'm vaguely aware of a text coming through my phone.

Bryce falls and pulls me so we're spooning, his cock stays securely lodged in me. "Wow! You rock my world, Angel."

"You do the same to me, but more intense I think. I'm curious. How do you hold out so long?"

"I've trained my body to have control." He holds me and gently kisses my neck.

"Oh." I say softly, thinking I should really try that. Try to have a bit more control.

We hear my phone again. Bryce grabs the phone and reads the text.

"Who is it?" I ask.

"Do you really want to know?"

And somehow I know it's Lindsay. Again.

22

"LET ME READ it."

"Angel, you don't need this crap in your head."

Bryce always tries to protect me, but with what I've been through, I think I can handle it. I'm pretty strong.

He pulls out of me, reaches for some Kleenex, stuffs it between my thighs and then gives me a kiss. Bryce sits up against my headboard and reads all the other text, we've exchanged.

I see him smirking a little. "Holy shit, Angel, remind me not to piss you off."

Smiling back at him, I feel a rush of energy and I am quite pleased with myself. "Aren't you going to text her back?"

"No, Angel, that'll make things worse."

She sends another one.

Now I'm really curious, but he has my phone in his hand and he's reading it.

His facial expressions change. Bryce looks upset. Shit, I don't like that look. It's like he's struggling with his emotions. Almost like…he still loves her. Fuck, I hope I'm wrong. God, please.

Bryce glances at the security monitor again and then he bolts out of bed and pulls his pants on. "That fuckers here!" He yells, as he throws his shirt over his head.

I lunge out of bed and scramble to get my clothes on, while I stare at the security monitor. The motion lights are turned on, but I don't see anyone outside in camera view.

Bryce is already out of my room and he's banging on my spare room door. Boom. Boom. Boom. "Psycho's here!"

Just as I walk out of my room, I see Austin flying out of my spare room, pulling his shirt on and doing up his pants.

"Bryce is outside already." I say quickly.

"He's supposed to wait for me." Then he darts outside.

My heart's racing, but part of me is thinking, is Bryce paranoid, or is my stalker really here?

Leena comes out of the bedroom and I grab her arm, pulling her toward the door.

"Come on, let's go with them." I say excitedly.

When we get outside, I see that Richard's garage next door is a fire ball of flames and Bryce is scrambling to get my hose at the side of the house. "Call the fire department!" Bryce yells.

I run back up the steps of my deck and into the house for my phone.

Jeez, this is the second time in one day that I've called to report a fire. They're going to think I'm the pyromaniac.

Bryce is trying to put the fire out, but it's an inferno, and he doesn't have enough water pressure with a small garden hose.

My eyes are glued to Bryce, watching his every move, watching him take control of the situation and it's so frickin' hot. I have such pride, love, respect, and admiration for him right now, it's almost overwhelming.

Leena appears beside me, grabbing my arm, returning me from the lust filled trip I'm on to the here and now.

Our eyes follow Austin as he runs to the side of my neighbors' house, to unravel his hose, pulling it toward the garage so he can assist Bryce.

Hearing the sirens as police and fire roll up to the scene, I relax, realizing I was worried and tense during the whole ordeal, because I don't want Bryce or Austin to get hurt.

The firefighters pull the hose off the truck, and get into position, ordering different commands back and forth.

Bryce and Austin appear beside us and we stand out of the way, watching intently as the water sprays hard onto the fire and it's quickly extinguished.

The chief of the fire department and the police are in deep discussion and when their finished talking they come over to us. "We're thinking your stalker and our arsonist is the same guy." Constable Grant states. "We'll set up twenty four hour surveillance a few doors down in a black van. If you need to go out, I want you to call this number, but we don't advise it; we only have one unit and it has to stay here. We can't protect you if you leave." He hands Bryce a card. "We're going to catch this guy before he does any more damage, but in the meantime, keep a close eye on each other. This guy is very dangerous and unstable; don't put anything past him. He's unpredictable."

When the commotion dies down, we go back inside and sit around the table discussing the day.

"Don't you think it's strange he hasn't tried to burn Keera's garage?" Leena gives her observation.

"He doesn't want to piss her off. He wants her to love him." Bryce snarls.

"Her stalker wants to get her attention, but he doesn't want her mad at him." Austin replies.

"See, we have to start thinking like him." Bryce counters. "I want to catch this psycho more than ever."

"Good, let's all go to bed. Get some sleep while we can. He'll most likely lay low for the rest of the night." Austin adds. "But if you hear anything, wake us up."

"Come with me, Angel, you look tired. Let's get you to bed."

In the bedroom, I watch him with lust and hunger in my eyes

while he gets naked and as I start to undress, a scorching predatory gleam in his eyes surfaces, that has me weak in the knees. The way he looks at me when I take every piece of clothing off slowly, makes me feel loved, cherished, very sexy. His eyes melt me to my core with his seductive gaze and that sexy half smile.

Oh my. He's licking his bottom lip. He's so damn sexy and such a tease. The sensation arrows all the way down. God, I hope that look never fades.

Bryce comes closer and circles behind me. He runs his hand around my waist, leaving trails of fire. I'm so exhausted, but I don't care, I want him. Again.

After seeing him take control of that fire, the way he takes control of every situation gets me insanely aroused and I want him to take control over me.

"Come. Let's get you to sleep, Angel."

"What?" I sigh disappointed.

He leads me to the bed, but as he turns I see his dimple.

Oh, he's enjoying this. He's teasing me…I hope.

Bryce pulls back the duvet and sheet. "Climb in Angel."

I do and Bryce climbs in next to me. He pulls the duvet up and gives me three quick kisses on my lips. "Goodnight Angel, sleep well."

"Goodnight." I say with a heavy sigh.

He turns the light off beside him.

I'm lying with my eyes open. I can't believe this. He doesn't want me? The honeymoon's over, already?

What the hell did Lindsay say in that text to make him not want me? I didn't get a chance to check it, with all the craziness going on around here.

I roll over in a huff, onto my side.

Bryce rolls on his side too, so we're spooning, and then, I feel how hard his cock is up against my butt.

He does want me! That's one thing he can't hide from me.

His hard cock grinds up against my butt as he wraps his arm

over me and cups my breast. I push back on his cock and rotate my butt. Right away our breathing changes.

When we have our hands on each other neither one of us can resist. We both know this is where we want to be, nowhere else, just him and me, lost in this moment, lost in each other.

My body jerks awake violently, and I sit up quickly, trying to clear the fog from a deep sleep. But then it all comes back to me as I remember bits and pieces of a bad dream I had.

"Angel, are you okay?" Bryce coaxes me to lie back down, rubbing my arm to calm me.

"Yeah, just a bad dream. I'm okay."

My mind wanders and I remember a house on fire and Bryce was inside, trapped. I could hear Bryce banging on the door and yelling for someone to hear him. My stalker had a gas can by his feet and he was swinging a set of keys around on his finger, showing me Bryce was locked inside and my stalker was the one who locked him in there. The expression on his face was pure evil and it woke me out of a dead sleep.

Bryce wraps his arms around me and holds me tight. Then he runs his hand up and down my back and kisses my forehead, waiting patiently for me to tell him.

I tell Bryce what I remember.

"Angel we can't let this lunatic get to us, he wants us to lose our minds and we're not going to let this happen are we?"

"I can't help what I dream." I say softly.

"I know you can't, Angel. I think you're having bad dreams because he threatened me, but don't worry. I'm not going to let anything happen to us. We'll be together forever."

He always knows exactly how to calm me down.

Bryce hugs and kisses me tenderly, one thing leads to another, burning lust and desire consumes us and we can't keep our hands off each other. We make mad passionate love again.

I feel more secure with the police camping out down the road. We don't have to constantly stare at the monitors like we were.

The police advise us to stay home as much as possible, so they can protect us, but Bryce has other ideas. He wants to work out and grab a few things from the cabin.

I watch Bryce glancing in the rear view mirror quite often for any signs of my stalker following us. He wants the cabin to be my safe haven, and it is, I always feel safe there.

Last night after we made love he told me that he wishes he could take me away from all of this. It melted my heart.

I told him that he's too sweet, but I've only known you three weeks. I can't pack up and move away with you. I think he understood because he dropped the subject right after.

At the cabin, both Bryce and Austin work out with low hanging shorts and their shirts off, and I try, I mean, I really try not to look at Austin, knowing Bryce will get jealous, but they're so goddamn gorgeous. I mean, seriously, I'm not dead yet. He's going to have to suck it up and get over it.

Leena checks out Bryce, then Austin, then back to Bryce. She's probably doing the comparison thing like I did. God, we're lucky women.

On our way out of the cabin, we grab some venison out of the freezer to cook over the weekend at my place. I feel bad because I'm taking them away from their beautiful cabin to deal with the crap in my life, but Bryce is on a mission to catch my stalker so we can finally relax and enjoy life and be in a normal relationship with no worries. I want that too, but realistically I think it's going to take some time.

We get in the truck and Bryce says, "I'll be one minute." He walks back to the garage and when he emerges he's carrying two rifles.

"Bryce, what are you doing with those?" I ask.

"Well, if he's dumb enough to come into your house, this thirty odd six will do the job. And if he's in the yard, I'll pop him in the ass with this pellet gun."

"Bryce, you're not serious, are you?"

"Fuck yeah, I'm serious. He's fair game if he comes in your yard."

"Austin, help me out here. You have to reason with him."

"I've learned a long time ago, once Bryce gets something in his head, there's no changing it. Look when he kidnapped you. I tried to reason with him then."

"I didn't kidnap her." Bryce says in his deep voice.

"I was keeping her safe." Austin and I finish off the last part of the sentence with Bryce, and we all laugh.

Bryce stows the guns behind, in the back seat at Leena and Austin's feet.

Hopping in the driver's seat of his truck, Bryce tries to reassure me with a squeeze to the knee. "You need to relax. It's not like I'm going to kill him. I'm only going to wound him. You know, use him for target practice."

When we get back to my house, we call the cops to tell them that we're back. Bryce brings the guns into the house, and we make a late breakfast.

We need to take a shower after our good workout, and get ready for our big night out, dancing.

While we get undressed Bryce prowls toward me, smiling with something behind his back.

"Will you do something for me?"

I smile and answer back apprehensively. "Yes."

He opens a box with two metal balls inside. "Will you wear these for me tonight? They're Ben-Wa balls."

I look down at them and then back at Bryce as I'm still smiling. "Sure. How do I wear them?"

Bryce laughs. "I insert them inside you."

My eyes get big. "What?"

He laughs harder. Then he takes them out of the box and places them in my hand.

"Hmm they've got some weight to them. Don't they fall out?"

He chuckles. "No, you'll tighten your muscles. Trust me, you'll love how they feel."

"Have you done this before?"

"No, the guy's at work were talking about them."

"You talk to the guys at the station about this stuff?"

"You wouldn't believe the conversations we have."

"Oh." I hesitate thinking. "So I've got another stupid question. How do we get them out, when they need to come out?"

He smiles this time. "You push them out or I'll slide my finger inside you and pull them out."

"Oh, okay." I say softly.

"Talking about this is getting me hard." Bryce pulls his shirt off, drops his pants and boxers and his cock springs out.

I grab him by his cock and pull him to the shower. "You like laughing at me because of my inexperience."

"I'm not laughing at you, you're so cute. I love seeing your face when I tell you or show you something new. And I love it when you pull me around by my cock. You're my little dominatrix."

We climb into the shower and I close the door.

"On your knees!" I demand.

And he does it.

Hey, I like this. "Lick here." And I point to where I want to be licked.

And he does it without saying a word.

I lift my leg over his shoulder to give him better access. "Slide your finger inside me. Fuck me with your finger."

And he does it. Jeez, I wish I had that riding crop of his so I can spank his butt.

My back presses hard against the wall of the shower and my fingers claw their way into his jet black hair. I hold him so his mouth stays firmly on my clit, while circling my hips shamelessly and I feel the pounding from his finger thrusting inside me.

He runs his teeth from the top of my enlarged clit, all the way down until he hits that very sensitive spot making my body jerk with pleasure. Bryce looks up at me through his long beautiful lashes, taunting and teasing me scraping his teeth downward. "Look, how fucking beautiful this is. It's so big. You like this, don't you?"

I moan with satisfaction and my unspoken words and actions tell him everything. I grasp his hair tighter, so it's almost painful.

Fire curses through my veins, and I feel myself getting warm. My breathing has slowed and whimpers escape from deep within. Pleasure ripples throughout my body.

Bryce flicks my clit with his magical tongue quickly, his finger thrusting inside me, pressing on that perfect spot and my body starts to quiver almost immediately.

"Babe, don't stop."

He keeps going until I finish grinding against his talented beautiful mouth and my body goes limp.

My leg slides off his shoulder, and he pushes me up against the ceramic tile, to steady me, and then climbs up my body, ensuring I don't fall, because my legs feel like jelly.

He holds my face in his hands and stares deep in my eyes, "How was that for my little dominatrix?"

I smile. "Wow! Hey…know what they say about the shy ones…sometimes they'll surprise you."

"I was rock hard when you told me what to do. I like it when you're demanding."

I grab his cock with both hands, his body jerks and he moans.

"Christ, Angel, you send tingles through my cock."

Dropping to my knees, I lick my lips and take him in my mouth. I ease back out and then run my tongue from his tight balls to the base of his cock, all the way up to the very tip. I lick him like he's my favourite lollipop, thoroughly soaking him. I watch his reaction as I look up.

"That's it, Angel, get me wet, let it run down my balls."

I then take him to the back of my throat.

"That's deep." His fingers snake through my hair grasping the back of my head, holding me in place. I relax my throat muscles taking him deeper inside. I slide my finger on the soft spot under his balls and I don't think they can tighten any further, but to my amazement they do. I fondle them and he moans. Bryce thrusts his cock into my mouth aggressively harder now, fucking my mouth.

"That's the prettiest little mouth sucking on my cock." Bryce says in his husky slow drawl.

I gaze up through my eyelashes at him and he at me with dark eyes, filled with desire watching me suck.

Something strange happens to me every time he looks at me that way.

When I reach under his balls again, I caress the soft spot. He moans and his body jerks violently.

I think he likes this, so I do it again. But this time I pull his cock out of my mouth and lick the seam of his balls all the way up. Then I run my tongue round and round getting them wet.

"Holy fuck, Angel, does that feel good!"

I resume sucking his cock and I taste a droplet of pre-cum against my tongue, my moan of pleasure vibrates against his cock.

"Can you taste that Angel? My come will be dripping out of that pretty little mouth, in a minute."

I'm cupping his balls, sliding my finger on the soft spot and sucking his cock all at once. I've never seen him so hard.

"Fuck! Fuck! Fuck!"

Bryce empties himself into my mouth, while he thrusts aggressively a couple more times and I take it all and swallow. When his body stills from the tremors, he lifts me by my arms.

"Come here. You're so beautiful! As usual, you always amaze me. That felt so good. I like that."

"I can tell." I say in my soft voice.

He's searching my eyes, and then kisses me long and hard.

I'm the first to pull away, and look deep in his eyes. "Oh, and I had better be the only pretty little mouth that's sucking on your cock. My cock! And only my cock." I say possessively.

"Yes, your cock." Bryce repeats. "I love it when you talk dirty to me. And when you're demanding. And you don't have to worry, Angel, you're the only one I want. You, and your pretty little mouth." He runs his finger along my bottom lip, and with him doing that, I want him again. I'm turning into a nymphomaniac.

Bryce shields me from the cascading water as he turns the knob, adjusting the temperature to warm and we quickly wash up after our sexcapade.

Bryce and Austin make us a quick snack while we curl our hair, apply our makeup and paint our nails.

With Bryce in the kitchen, I finally get to look at my phone to see the text Lindsay sent. Leena reads it with me. The first one reads:

I'm sorry to bother you. I was just wondering if you know where Bryce is? I can't find him and I'm worried.

The second one reads:

If he's with you, can you tell him to call me, please? Don't do this. I love him. He's my whole life and without him, I can't live. Please Keera, you don't love him like I do. Let him go, please have a heart.

"That's why Bryce looked so upset after reading this." I say to Leena.

"She sounds pretty normal to me, not at all like the psycho Austin says she is." Leena states.

"Oh yeah?" I disagree. "You've got to see the other ones."

I have to show her even though there are some pretty explicit things in the earlier text sent from Lindsay.

Leena reads them. "Holy shit. It doesn't even sound like the same person."

"I know, eh?"

"Damn girl. I'm proud of you. It's about time you stand up for yourself and quit taking crap from others."

"Yeah, I couldn't take anymore shit from her."

"By the way, I'm looking at you and Bryce differently now." Leena teases. "Kinky fuckers."

I bump her shoulder and smile.

"Austin's quite the kinky fucker, too, and I love it."

"Really? Austin?"

"Oh yeah, and he's hung like a horse."

"So is Bryce." My head tilts to my shoulder in a shrugging motion and I raise an eyebrow.

Bryce comes in. "Munchie session is ready."

His eyes widen and he smiles wickedly when he sees me and Leena hugging. "What's going on in here?"

Leena pulls away, walks over to Bryce and shoves his shoulder.

Bryce rubs it. "What's that for?"

"Because I know what you're thinking, Mr. Kink. And you can forget it. It's never going to happen."

I look at Bryce, my confusion showing on my face and I almost see him blush. He comes to me and hugs me.

Leena must see the confusion on my face, too.

She stands at the door leaning against the frame. "Don't you know it's every guy's fantasy to watch two women have sex."

I smack Bryce's shoulder and smile. "Sick."

"What?" He says as we walk to the kitchen. "Austin, I'm getting beat up by these two, for smiling."

"Tag teamin' ya, eh?" Austin drawls.

Leena pipes up. "We were hugging and Bryce came in with his wicked grin."

"Yeah that's in my spank bank too." Austin chuckles.

After our munchie session, Bryce and I go into my bedroom to get dressed. Bryce wears a black suit that fits to perfection with a dark purple tie. "I wanted to coordinate with your dress, but it's pink. I'm not wearing pink. Sorry, Angel."

I walk up to him with my seductive look wearing my thong, and run my fingers up and down his tie. "If I really, really wanted you to…you'd do it for me, wouldn't you?"

"Fuck, Angel, quit doing that you're making me hard. And yes, I'd do it for you, but I know you wouldn't want to torture me. Right?"

I smile at him, and then slip my dress on.

"You're not wearing a bra?"

"Can't with this dress. Can you help me with this button?"

"I'd rather let this dress drop to the floor and get you back in that bed."

He stares down at my tits and then pulls on my nipples through the fabric. "Look at these fuckers. They're going to be hard all night. Just like me."

"Yeah, going without a bra does that to them." I say as I look down.

"And I love it."

I slip on my light pink high heel shoes that match perfectly with the dress and ask Bryce if he can help me with my necklace.

After he secures it with the clasp, he stands back and stares, "Look how beautiful you are. I can't wait to show you off. You'd better stay right beside me tonight."

I smile, liking his overly possessive comment.

"And look how gorgeous you are. You're going to dance with me, right?"

"Definitely." He holds out his hand with the Ben-Wa balls. "I want you to go over to your bed and bend over, ass in the air."

I'm so excited. I hurry over to my bed, assume my position and wait for my next instruction.

Bryce lifts the back of my dress and pulls my thong down, skimming his fingers along my sensitive skin.

"Step one foot out of them."

"Holy fuck, Angel, so sexy in that position. Dress up, legs spread, ass up in the air, with fuck me high heel shoes on, ready and waiting for me. Where's your phone?"

"You're taking a picture again?"

"I'd like to. Where's your phone?"

"Table."

"Don't move, Angel."

He takes the picture and then stands back admiring. "Damn! So sexy."

I hear the balls clang against his teeth. Assuming he stuck them in his mouth to get them wet.

"Ready, Angel?"

"Yes."

He inserts one with such gentleness and care, pushing it up as far as he can. "How's that feel?"

"Good."

"One more." He purrs and he inserts the second one so slow it makes my pussy clench. I rotate my hips as my butt moves with a sexy sway and I try to suppress my moan against my arm.

"You're trying to kill me, aren't you Angel. Your pussy just clamped down on my finger and I love it."

He bends and kisses my butt cheeks, then I feel him speak between kisses. "Do you like them?"

"Oh yes."

"Good, now step your foot back in your thong." Then he

pulls it back up, skimming his fingers against my sensitive skin, leaving a trail of goose bumps. He pulls the bottom portion of the dress back down and smacks my butt. "How's that feel? You can stand now."

Bryce pulls me into his embrace and grinds his hard cock against me.

"They feel good. Are you sure they won't fall out?"

"Just tighten your muscles like your pussy does when it's sucking on my cock."

"How do you know so much about this stuff?"

"I read a lot."

"Good answer." I say sarcastically.

Somehow I think it's from experience, but for now I think I'll dismiss it out of my mind and think of how he's enjoying himself with our new toy.

Bryce leads me into the kitchen, hand in hand, where Austin and Leena are leaning against the counter. "Wow, what a good lookin' couple you two are." I state.

Sitting around the kitchen table, we have a drink and then call the police to inform them we're going out for the evening. And of course, they advise us that it's not a good idea because they're stationed at the house, so they won't be able to protect us.

Just as I'm reaching to get up into the truck, Bryce whispers in my ear, "I want you to tell me every once in a while how they feel."

I glance at him and smile. "Okay," I adjust my dress and coat so I'm comfortable when I sit on the front seat beside him.

When we enter the Royale Inn, it's beautifully decorated with elegance. The tables are covered with crisp white eyelet lace edged linen and the chairs match precisely, tied back with big eyelet lace bows.

The centerpiece in the middle of the table is an oversized clear fish bowl vase, with dark purple crystals lying at the bottom and dark purple flowers floating on top of the water. There's a dark purple, three wick candle lit in the middle. It's absolutely beautiful. The twinkling lights are meticulously strung across the ceiling and look fantastic. I feel a sudden rush of excitement run through me.

There is quite a few people already dancing and when the hostess shows us to our seats, we notice the atmosphere looks promising. I elbow Leena and she does the same to me as I see her blinding smile light up the room.

Leena reserved us a table the moment we said we wanted to go. Leena loves taking care of things like this. She's always been very organized.

We sit down and our attention is diverted over to two waitresses fighting over our table.

The pretty petite brunette wins, and the first thing out of her mouth is, "Bryce, where have you been?"

23

I GLANCE AT LEENA and mouth 'what the fuck?' We're both thinking the same thing — Bryce and the waitress must have had a relationship before.

The waitress focuses all of her attention to Bryce and Austin, flirting and blushing. She finally leaves to get our drinks.

The manager comes over, shakes Bryce and Austin's hand and asks, "And who are these two lovely ladies?"

Bryce smiles, "This is my girlfriend Keera, and Austin's girlfriend, Leena. Ladies this is Trent, he's the Manager."

I hold out my hand to shake Trent's, and he shocks me by flipping it and kissing the back of my hand. "Pleased to meet you." I say, blushing a bit.

"Oh, the pleasure is all mine." Trent drawls and then does the same to Leena.

Trent pulls a chair up and sits between Bryce and Austin. They talk like they're really good friends and I find myself moving closer so I can hear more of their conversation.

I hear Austin giving Trent directions to their hunting camp. "You're more than welcome to use it."

"Thank you, I will and if there's anything you need tonight, don't hesitate to ask." Trent glances at Leena and me. "It was very nice meeting you ladies. Keep these two out of trouble."

Simultaneously, we say that we will.

Trent leaves our table to take care of business.

"So you know Trent from hunting with him?" I ask.

"Yes, he hunts on our land. We've had a couple of hunting trips with him and his buddies. Good times." Bryce says with a smile as he remembers back.

The waitress brings our drinks and now she's really focusing on Bryce.

She asks him, "Why haven't you come into the bar? It's been a long time. At least a year."

Obviously someone's been paying attention to my boyfriend.

Then she touches his shoulder and his back. The whole time she smiles and blushes.

Christ, why doesn't she just sit on his lap. I glance at Leena and she glares back at me.

"Time to hit the john?" Leena blurts out.

"Yeah." I push my chair back and Bryce tightens his grip on my knee. I place my hand on his, "Ladies room." I say then he lets go.

When I get up he spins grasping for my hand and he holds it tight. "When you get back, I want that dance you promised me." Bryce says it loud enough so the waitress can hear him.

"Okay I won't be long." I bend down and slap a lush wet kiss on his lips.

When I get up I feel the Ben-Wa balls moving inside me. I bend back down and whisper in his ear, "I felt them move when I got up. I tightened my muscles like you said, wow! What a sensation. They're making me so hot, I can't wait to have your cock inside me."

I stand back up and glance sideways. I think she gets the hint because she backs up, and disappears.

I'm relieved that she's gone. I guess what I'm feeling is jealousy and I don't know how to handle it. I don't like feeling this way. I can see Bryce feels uncomfortable when she hits on him.

Entering the washroom, we both bend down to see if anyone is in the stalls before we start slamming the waitress.

Leena has a few choice words for her and I agree. I don't want to be catty, but she's really pissing me off.

When we venture back out to the dining room, I see the waitress with her hand on Bryce's shoulder again.

Seriously, am I going to have to deal with this shit all the time because he's too irresistible?

He sees me walking toward him and stands, holding out his hand for me.

Her hand falls to her side and she backs up.

Bryce takes my hand and leads me to the dance floor. He whispers in my ear, "I'm sorry about that."

I reach up and he bends until I'm close to his ear, "It's not your fault."

He searches my eyes to see if I'm angry. He slaps a long tongue on tongue passionate kiss on me.

A little part of me hopes the waitress is watching, so she knows he's mine.

The music starts to play and Bryce holds me close, swaying his hips to the beat perfectly.

He moves with grace and expertise, he's so good at this, I have to ask, "Who taught you to dance like this?"

He looks deep in my eyes and smiles. "Don't laugh, okay? Our mom taught us. She always said she wanted all of her children to know how to dance. She says dancing makes you happy."

"I can't wait to meet your mom. She sounds like an amazing woman."

"Yes, she is." Bryce says proudly.

We bump into Leena and Austin on the dance floor and I smile at Leena. She says "Wow, eh?"

"I know." I can't believe this. We were hoping they would dance with us, but they're expertise is such a surprise and an added bonus because they're so talented.

Leena, Katie and I took dance class together until we got into high school and then we were too busy, but we still love to dance.

We're dancing so close I feel Bryce's cock rub against me. I look down then back up and he smiles with that mischievous smile. "Yeah, I've been like this, ever since I put the balls inside you. And when you told me how they felt, I thought I'd explode. Could you tell I was pretty uncomfortable with the waitress standing there?"

"Yeah, I could tell."

A tap on my shoulder has me turning around to see a tall blond Greek god with the bluest eyes I've ever seen. "May I cut in and have this dance with you?"

"Oh I'm sorry, all my dances are saved for my husband." I say, quite proud of myself I thought of an excuse so quickly.

"Oh so sorry, I didn't see a ring."

I look at my finger, "Oh, it's in getting sized."

He backs up and leaves.

"Husband eh? I like the sound of that."

"You do eh?" And a part of me is ecstatic knowing he's not against marriage.

"Good thing you got rid of him, I was going to deck him."

"Have you been in a few brawls over a woman?"

"No. I don't know how to explain it. I wanted to kill him."

"I know exactly how you feel. It's jealousy. That waitress was pissing me off, putting her hands all over you."

"I've been jealous before, but not like this. It's extremely heightened. It's ten times worse with you than with any other woman I've been with. I get so enraged instantly, I have to tell myself to calm down."

"I guess we'll have to learn how to control this. We wouldn't want an assault charge laid against us, would we?"

"No, so you keep me in line and I'll do the same for you."

"Deal!" I discreetly grind against him. "You know, it's a good thing I have a thong on, because I'm so wet, hot and horny, I wouldn't want these babies dropping out on the floor right now."

Bryce breathes deeply and then I feel a gust of breath against my ear. "Follow my lead."

We dance our way to the hall with a sign overhead that says restrooms, banquet hall, and Manager's Office. We walk hand in hand with Bryce impatiently pulling me down the hall to the second last door on the right.

Bryce sticks a key in the lock. "Trent told me to lock up after I'm done." We slip inside and Bryce locks it behind us.

Standing in the middle of the room, I look around. It's very clean, only the laptop on his overly large dark cherry mahogany desk. Big scenic pictures scatter across the walls and smaller ones on the shelves of the wall unit that match the desk behind his large, overly stuffed leather chair.

I move over to see a few pictures of Trent and his hunting buddies. As I look closer, I notice Bryce and Austin in some of them.

"Nice pictures." I say as I place it back where it was.

Bryce moves the laptop out of the way. "Yeah, we were hunting in New Liskeard."

Spinning, I see Bryce prowling toward me with dark eyes. He kneels down in front of me, lifting my dress and places it on his head, then he skims his fingers along my sensitive skin as he slides my thong down, setting my skin on fire. I'm leaning against the desk with my fingers gripping the edge. Before Bryce gets up he flicks my clit with his finger.

"Whoa!" I say as he startles me.

Bryce pulls my dress off of his head as he stands and straightens it. He stares down into my eyes, and then his eyes move to my cleavage.

"You like it when I spank your clit, don't you?"

"Yes."

He runs his finger between my breasts. "I love this dress but I think it's going to get in the way."

Bryce tugs on the button at my waist, slides it down off my shoulders and it pools at my feet. He picks it up and hangs it neatly on the chair.

I resume the position of leaning on the desk when he turns to look at me.

"Holy fuck, look at you. So sexy. Now up on the desk." He lifts me so my butt is on the edge of the desk.

Unexpectedly we hear voices at the door. "I think he's in here."

Both our heads turn to look at the door.

We hear someone trying to open the door. "It's locked, but the lights are on."

"Someone's in there and it's not Trent. He's at the bar."

It's the waitress again. I can tell by her whiny voice. Jesus, will that little bitch in heat give it up?

I don't say it out loud, because I don't want Bryce to know I'm being catty. This is a whole new side of me and I don't like it either, but she won't give up.

"Did you fuck her?" I ask bluntly.

"No, Angel, I used to come in here to see Trent, but she kept hounding me, so I stopped coming. I thought if she saw me with you, she'd give up."

"Somehow I don't think she's giving up." I say under my breath.

"Forget about them. Let's focus on this sweet pussy."

Despite my irritation over the waitress, I let my frustrations go focusing my attention on Bryce sliding his finger slowly inside me, unhurried strokes, as far up as he can go, then slowly he withdraws. "Such a sweet pussy and so wet for me."

I moan as he probes around in there, trying to find the balls and it feels so good.

"You like my balls?"

I smile, "Yes, both sets of them." I say with my seductive purr.

Bryce circles my clit with his thumb and I lean back on my elbows, shamelessly opening my legs wider, circling my hips.

Bryce leans and whispers close to my ear. "You like fucking in different places, don't you?"

"Yes."

"You like being naughty with me."

"Yes."

"You like these balls moving inside your pussy getting you wet, don't you?"

"Yes, holy fuck, Bryce." And my legs start to shake, I'm quivering on the desk and my pussy clamps down on his finger.

"Oh, my sweet Angel, you're so tight."

"Bryce. Please!"

"Oh no. Not yet, but I do love it when you beg."

He pulls the balls out and sticks them in his mouth, "Mmm you taste so sweet." Then he pops them out of his mouth and slips them in his pants pocket.

I can't believe he did that, but then I instantly focus on Bryce going down between my legs and licking slowly up one side, and then the other of my wet pussy. He leisurely slides his finger deep inside me, driving me crazy with his slow thrusting motions.

"Bryce please. Faster."

He looks up at me through his beautiful long black lashes thrusting faster and his tongue flicks wildly on my clit with precise expertise.

My elbows slide out from underneath me and I fall onto my back. I grasp two handfuls of his silky jet black hair and hold him in place. My breathing is slow and measured, my skin has a slight sheen of perspiration and I'm circling my hips to the rhythm of his talented tongue.

"Bryce!" I cry out.

My legs start to shake uncontrollably and I tighten my grip

on his hair. When I realize I'm pulling too hard, I loosen my grip as my head thrashes from side to side. I'm coming apart piece by piece, enjoying the intensity of one of the strongest orgasm's I've ever had. I'm vaguely aware as I hear his zipper, then he pushes deep inside me in one swift movement, making me gasp because he's so big and hard.

"My Angel is so tight." He pulls out to the tip, and then slams back into me. "Do you want it hard, Angel?"

"Yes."

"Do you want me to fuck you senseless in Trent's office?"

"Yes, please."

"Or do you want me to tease you with my cock? Giving you a little at a time."

He pulls it out to the tip and then he pushes it back in just until I feel him stretching me a bit, then he pulls back out again.

"Bryce please. Fuck me hard!"

He slams into me balls deep, slapping them on my ass. He pounds me hard, giving me everything he has, and it's Heaven. "Play with your clit. I want you to come again."

I do and Bryce keeps up the relentless pace, until he sees me losing control and then he follows, slamming into me two more times, losing his breath, closing and opening his eyes, rearing up, pouring his load in me as far up as he can get it.

His full weight falls down on me, shuddering and his mouth gently caresses my shoulder. A muffled groan escapes his mouth. "Jesus, Angel you fuck me so good."

"I should be saying that. You did it all."

Bryce and I both laugh. He takes a soft napkin out of his pocket, and when he pulls out of me, he hurries to collect any drops before they hit the desk. He takes his time intimately cleaning me up.

The way he takes care of me fills my heart with overwhelming love.

I hope he never breaks my heart. It would crush me.

My mind does a flip. What if he discards me one day and tells the next replacement that I'm a crazy bitch. Although Bryce never has said Lindsay's crazy or psycho, it's always been Austin claiming that, but after getting the nasty texts from her, I'm swaying to crazy. I don't know what to think.

After Bryce is done cleaning me up, I take the napkin from him and intimately clean him up. When I look up, his dazzling gaze fills my heart with love. He reaches into his pocket and pulls out the Ben-Wa balls, holding them in the middle of his palm. "I want to put these back inside you."

"Are you kidding? They make me so horny. I'll want to fuck you again."

"That's okay. You'll be wet and ready for me when we get back to your place."

Bryce bends me over. "Spread your legs." Then he pushes the balls back up inside me as far as they can go.

I circle my hips and moan. My movements are slow and seductive.

"You're looking to get fucked again, aren't you?" He smacks my ass.

"Ouch." I say.

Bryce smiles as he moves in front of me. "Tease! Shaking that ass in front of me."

He lowers to help me put my thong back on, skimming my legs with his fingers all the way up. His mouth slowly curves up into a wicked smile, while he adjusts the lace on my thong. He gently flutters his fingers along each hip, sending a shiver through my body. He then takes my dress off the chair and slides it over my shoulders, running his fingers ever so slightly over my sensitive skin so I can feel him.

"You're a tease. No wonder you've got women hanging all over you. You're too irresistible."

"Well thank you and, no, I don't have women hanging all over me. Just you, Angel."

"Oh yeah? What about your stalker out there?"

"You're not going to leave my side, you hear me? She can't bother us when we're on the dance floor. She's not going to ruin our night. Technically our first date. You do want to dance with me, don't you?"

"Oh yes, I love the way you move."

Bryce buttons my dress. "I'm going to show you some of my moves when we get back to your place."

"I can't wait." I give him what I hope is a mischievous smile by tipping my head to the right and showing my dimple.

"Come with me, my beautiful Angel." He holds out his hand and I put mine in his as we make our way out of the office. He closes the door and locks it. "Leena's probably wondering where we ran off to, unless Austin told her."

I give him a gentle shove at his shoulder, feeling a little embarrassed.

"What?" He says surprised. "Austin wants to use Trent's office next." He pulls me down the hall and onto the dance floor as we make our way slowly toward Austin and Leena.

"What took you so long?" Austin teases.

Bryce hands Austin the keys. "Some things can't be rushed."

"You didn't get that desk all wet did you, Blondie?" I smack Austin's shoulder.

"I love teasing you, Blondie, and watching you turn ten different shades of red."

Leena nudges my arm and gives me a smile. She and Austin make their way through the people on the dance floor toward the hallway.

The disk jockey plays a few slow songs while Bryce holds me close in a tight embrace. We're lost in the moment, swaying to the beat, lost in each other.

He lifts my hand to his mouth and kisses it, then tucks it against his heart. "Feel that? It beats for you and you only."

"Babe, do you have any idea what you're doing to my heart? You melt me. You make me weak in the knees."

"Good, I hope I'm capturing your heart, Angel."

"Oh, you are."

"Angel, I don't want to scare you, but I think I'm falling in love with you."

With those few words, I realize this is the happiest I've been since I was eighteen, before my parents died. "I think I'm falling in love with you too." I look deep in his eyes to see his reaction and the love I see, takes my breath away.

Bryce's lips find mine and we're lost in a passionate kiss, all sound and movement have disappeared and we're lost in our own little world, in our own private little bubble, just me and him.

When we come back to earth and separate our lips, Bryce looks deep in my eyes. "I was so nervous to tell you. I didn't want you to bolt. I didn't want to scare you off. I knew the first week we were together that this relationship was different from all the rest. I wanted to tell you then, but I stopped myself. You don't know how happy I am." His lips seal to mine and we're all tongues, kissing passionately again. "I don't want to spend a single second away from you."

"I know. It nearly killed me when you had to go back to work."

I feel someone staring, so I glance sideways and see the waitress gawking, her line of sight doesn't move beyond Bryce. She's leaning with her back against the bar and her arms crossed. She's sour faced and scowling, not looking too happy, but I think she finally realizes she's waited a whole year for nothing. Anyone can see the love and passion between us.

We finally sit down or I should say Bryce tugs me onto his lap. "Let's talk about the first thing that pops up." He says chuckling.

I look deep in his eyes. "See? You're too irresistible." Our lips lock again and then we hear. "Would you like another round?" We separate and look up to see a different waitress.

Bryce answers, "Just the blue and a bud light lime, this time thank you."

When the waitress walks away, I say, "I think she gave up."

"Good!" Bryce blurts out.

I feel something hard under my butt. He wasn't kidding.

Shifting on his lap, I look around to see if anyone's watching and then run my fingers along the outline of his impressive erection. "I can't believe you're ready to go again."

"With you, always."

Bryce moans in my ear and I smile wickedly at him. "Teasing my cock out in public."

We wait for Mr. Stiffy to go down and then we dance a bit more.

Later, I feel a nudge. It's Leena and Austin; they've danced their way over to us.

"What took so long?" I tease.

"Like Bryce said, these things can't be rushed and my baby's got no complaints." Austin hugs and kisses Leena. They're so cute together, it makes me smile when I see them showing affection toward each other.

We order something to eat. We drink and dance until our feet hurt. The whole evening is a great success, making tonight a memorable first date. Especially, when Bryce said he was falling in love with me. I can't stop thinking about it. I'm overwhelmed with happiness.

Along the way to the washroom, I tell Leena how Bryce expressed his love for me.

"Yeah, any idiot can see that. He can't take his eyes off of you. Or his hands for that matter. And what did you tell him?"

"I told him I think I'm falling in love with him, too."

"I knew the moment I saw you two together. I saw it in your eyes. Can't hide something like that from me." Leena grins.

We call it a night around midnight, because we're whipped from all the excitement of the night before. Besides, I still have the Ben-Wa balls inside me and I'm climbing the walls. Bryce needs to leave too after I whisper my naughty thoughts to him on the dance floor. He has a raging hard on which needs to be relieved.

After saying goodbye to Trent, we head outside where I have to stop and take my shoes off. My feet are killing me from dancing all night in these heals.

I hold Bryce's shoulders as he bends down to take them off. He grabs my shoes in one hand and hoists me up and over his shoulder and smacks my ass with the other hand. I squeal with laughter and smack his ass while I hang upside down.

Bryce sets me down gently on the chrome running board of the truck so I don't get my feet dirty and I scoot over on the seat when Bryce hands me my shoes. He's such a gentleman, always thinking of me, making sure I'm taken care of.

Standing on the running board, Bryce leans through the open door to look at the paper on his windshield.

"That mother fucker!" Bryce shouts as he jumps down without taking it off. "If he touched my truck, he's a dead man!"

24

BRYCE AND AUSTIN search the parking lot while I scramble to put my shoes on fast.

We look the truck over and don't see any damage, but it's really hard to see in the dark, it doesn't help with the truck being black either.

Austin finds a napkin in the truck. He lifts the wiper blade and takes the note off the windshield. Then we all stand around Austin while he reads the note.

> You don't know how much it killed me to see you dancing with him and sitting on his lap. The way you look at him is the way you WILL look at me. I'll be dancing with you, and you'll be sitting on my lap, looking deep in my eyes.
>
> YOU BROKE MY HEART!
>
> You're not listening to me when I told you

to get rid of him. I know you don't want me to kill him, so he better disappear.

I won't wait forever...I'll take care of the problem myself and then you'll be MINE!

We'll be so happy together...You'll love me until death do us part.

"He was here, watching you." Austin looks up from the note to Bryce and I.

"He's got balls walking in there." Leena comments.

"For him to stand there and watch you for quite a while." Austin mutters. "Yeah, he's getting bolder."

"I didn't notice him." I say alarmed. "I felt someone staring, but when I looked over at the waitress, she was staring at us."

"This fucker keeps slipping through my fingers and it's really pissing me off!" Bryce shouts.

"I'll take the note to the cops, once we get it in a bag at Blondie's." Austin says.

Before we leave, Bryce and Austin look over the truck with my phone and a flashlight Bryce always stores in the glove box.

Bryce glances in the rear view mirror all the way home, looking for any signs of my stalker, but he's disappeared like always.

When we get inside the house, I give Austin a bag to put the note in.

Austin takes the note to the cops in the van, so we get undressed into something more comfortable. Bryce in his t-shirt and black pajama bottoms that hang perfectly on his hips and I wear some yoga pants and a T-shirt. We wait at the kitchen table for Austin to return.

When Austin comes through the back door he's laughing.

"What the hell are you laughing at?" Bryce says with a smile.

"I scared the shit out of them. I made my way down the road

through your neighbours' yards and came up from behind them opening the back doors. Yeah, it was priceless seeing the expressions on their faces. I bet they'll be on their toes now."

"I'd give anything to see that." Bryce laughs.

"I gave them the note. They said they would hand it in to Constable Grant in the morning. I think they'll be watching the monitors a little closer now."

"You had to tell me that eh." I say in a huff. "Here I thought we were safe with the cops watching."

Austin squeezes my shoulder. "Don't worry Blondie, I told them I'd be back, so they'll be on alert, watching closely."

Bryce holds his hand out to me. "Come with me."

I put my hand in his while I stand, then he holds me and whispers in my ear. "I won't let anything happen to you." He kisses my forehead. I always feel safe in Bryce's arms.

We say our goodnights to Leena and Austin, as Bryce cocoons my back and we march into the bedroom.

Bryce kicks the door closed and he immediately has his hands on the hem of my shirt. "Let me help you out of this. I don't like all these clothes separating us. I want you naked as much as possible. I love looking at you. Every inch of you. Completely mine and only mine."

Every time we get a note from my stalker, Bryce's whole demeanor changes, he wants to claim me, possess me, dominate me, and show me that I'm his. Bryce bends to look in my eyes. "What's wrong?" He tugs me over to the bed and we sit. He waits patiently for me to answer.

"He's getting bolder. For him to come inside and watch us at the Inn…" I stop speaking as my mind wanders.

"This is exactly what he wants. He wants us to lose our minds over this, so we let our guard down. Ignore what he wrote in the note."

"I can't! He's threatening you. I'd die if anything were to happen to you."

Bryce holds me in a tight embrace. "Nothing is going to happen. He's a little weasel that needs to be taken down. He's going to get his, for making you worry. Trust me. I'll take care of it." Bryce lifts me up and finishes undressing me. "I don't want you worrying over this Angel. Okay?"

"Okay." I say softly.

He stands back eyeing me from head to toe. His gaze slowly covers every inch of my body. "So sexy." He licks his lips and pulls on my nipples, sending a shiver through me, leaving goose bumps all over my skin.

Bryce pulls back the duvet and sheets. "Middle of the bed, on your back."

That dominating voice arouses me in a heartbeat, doing the strangest things to my body, so I instantly dismiss thoughts of my stalker and hurry to get into position, waiting impatiently for his next instruction.

Bryce saunters over to the stereo and turns it on. He flips through the channels, until he hears the perfect song and then he stands in the middle of the room, so I can see perfectly when he starts shaking his hips, moving to the beat with expertise. I can't take my eyes off of him as he lifts his shirt slowly, allowing me to see the honed muscle of his hard abs, taunting and teasing me. He lets it fall back down as his fingers move to the waistband of his pajama bottoms. He tugs them down, giving me a peek of his happy trail, while he gazes deep in my eyes.

He's so sexy. I'm so hot and wild for him, I think I'm drooling a bit.

His hands move back to his shirt as he lifts it slowly, caressing his washboard abs with his expert hands, which I'm envious of and want them all over me. My attention draws to his cock growing thick and hard. He pulls his shirt up and off, holding it with one finger, swinging it around in a circle over his head, then he uses it like a sling shot, flinging it at me and I catch it.

"Ha! Ninja skills." I say, surprised that I caught it.

"I see that." He grins, amused, and moves his hips to the beat as one hand roams freely over his abs and his other large hand cups his meaty pec, squeezing his hard nipple.

Holding his shirt tight in my hand, I inhale the smell of his cologne, his deodorant and him. What an amazing mixture, an intoxicating scent.

Bryce spins so I see his ass shaking. He slides his fingers into the waistband of his pajama bottoms and slides them down so I see a quick peek of one cheek and then he pulls it back up. He's still shaking that ass to the beat while he lowers his bottoms, just a fraction, so I get a peek of the other cheek. In one swift motion he slides them down until they hit the floor giving me a side view of his hard cock springing out and he doesn't skip a beat as he kicks them away.

I watch intently as he keeps dancing for me now that he's totally naked, zooming in to his tight ass muscles flexing and his cock bobbing from side to side.

My cheeks are getting sore from me smiling, but he can see that I'm really enjoying his sexy as hell strip tease. Wild for him, my pussy clenches and I feel the balls inside me move around, leaving me needy and wanting. I squirm on the bed. "You're so sexy." I purr.

"I am eh." Bryce drawls. "So you like?"

"Oh yes, I love this. You can strip for me anytime you'd like."

I see Bryce's dimple as he turns to get something out of his bag on the chair. He pulls out ropes and a chrome bar with leather buckled cuffs attached to it.

"What's that for?" I ask inquisitively.

"I attach these to your ankles and I open this." He slides it open so it's about three feet wide. "And it keeps your legs spread wide for me, but you'll be able to lift your legs to your chest or over my shoulders instead of being tied to the bed. Giving me better access to my sweet, sweet pussy." He grabs a handful of my pussy, squeezing me as he licks his lips.

Bryce wraps the leather cuffs around my ankles and buckles them to the bar. I lift my legs in the air testing our new toy. I try, but I can't close my legs.

He wraps the rope around my wrists, and ties it to the post of my bed. Then he saunters over to my other wrist and does the same before brushing his fingers along my ribs, tickling me and I squirm, but I can't go far, I'm tied.

Bryce settles at my feet and kneels while he effortlessly picks up the bar and I watch his muscles flex as my legs lift, separated in the air. The bar rests on his shoulders as his finger probes the entrance of my moist pussy, then he slides it all the way in. "Can you feel that? I'm moving the balls around."

I moan and inhale sharply. "Oh yeah, babe. It's so good."

He continues torturing me like this for a little while, and then in a blink of an eye his mouth lowers and he circles my clit with his magical tongue. His finger pounding relentlessly into me at a very face pace working me into a frenzy instantly. When I clench down on him he stops. "I could drive you to orgasm over and over again until you're ready to scream and there isn't a damn thing you can do about it." A mischievous smile crosses his lips.

"Just remember, paybacks are a bitch."

"Oh really? You're saying you'd get me back?"

"You have to sleep sometime." I smile wickedly.

Bryce chuckles. "Christ Angel, what you do to me." He kneels up and I see his cock bob from the weight, it's so hard. It looks as if it could explode if it gets any larger. His full body weight falls down on me and he nuzzles in my neck. I've learned that this is one of his coping mechanisms to hold onto his control.

Gaining his control again, he reaches over me untying my hands. Guess he changed his mind about having my hands tied.

I reach, trying to wrap my fingers around him with one hand, but his cock is too big for them to go completely around. I stroke up and down.

Bryce moans. "You feel so good wrapped around my cock."

He pulls away and nestles back between my legs, lifting the bar over his head, resting it on his shoulders. "But right now I need to eat my sweet pussy."

He flicks his tongue across my clit and thrusts his finger inside me at a steady rhythm.

My pulse quickens and my breathing slows to shallow intakes, while my fingers snake through the silky black strands of his hair and I grasp tightly keeping his expert tongue in place. The delicious sensation I feel from the weight of the balls deep inside me and the pounding of his finger moving them around is going to make me lose control.

Torturing me, Bryce brings my body to the verge of orgasm letting it build and then letting it subside, over and over again. I'm mindless and begging. "Bryce, Please."

"Shh, I've got you." Bryce continues working me into a frenzy.

My orgasm rips through me at lightning speed sending me over the edge and I moan out his name. "Babe!"

My whole body tenses and quivers, but Bryce doesn't stop even when I grip his hair too tight, which is probably painful. He brushes his tongue across my clit one last time and my pelvis jerks a bit from the sensitivity of my explosive orgasm. My muscles go limp and I try to catch my breath.

My eyes open suddenly and I gasp at the fullness as he stretches the walls of my pussy sinking balls deep. I moan with pleasure and reach out to grab the sheets with both hands.

"How does that feel Angel, having both the Ben-Wa balls and my cock deep inside you?"

My back arches and my head falls back.

"Babe, it's so sensitive. It feels so good."

"I've got to go slow. You're so sexy. You're going to make me come already." Bryce stops moving and his full weight falls down on me and he whispers in my ear.

"I love that you let me try new and different things with you. It gets me so hot. I can't control myself."

He's not lying; he can't control himself.

And then my mind wanders. I've got to ask Bryce if he's tried new and different things with Lindsay. I know I'm torturing myself thinking about them having sex together, so I try to dismiss it out of my mind.

Bryce withdraws and then his cock slams hard into me. "He wanted you, but you're mine."

His comment is so random it throws me off a bit and then I realize what he's talking about.

"Yes I'm yours." Obviously it's still bothering him, when that guy came over to ask me to dance.

"Mine and mine only." There's a pause in his voice. "Unless you want another cock? I'd give that to you, if you really want it. I'd do that for you. It would kill me, but I'd do it."

What? His comment shocks me. I can't believe he said that. "No, I only want you. You only, Babe."

His cock slams into me with every word. "THIS… SWEET… PUSSY…IS…MINE." And then he picks up the pace and slams into me hard and fast.

Bryce slides me my vibrator. "Put this on your clit, I want you to come again."

I rev it up and do as he wants. What a sensation. I've got the balls weighing heavily inside me, my vibrator on my clit, and the spreader bar across Bryce's back holding my legs up and they're spread wide open. His cock fills me and he gives it to me hard. It's too much. Too many sensations. I let out a loud whimper of ecstasy.

"I love that sound. The sound of you enjoying every inch of my cock."

My hearts pounding and I'm wound so tight from all the sensations that I pulsate and clamp down around his cock.

"Your pussy is so tight. It's sucking me off."

I can't hold out any longer. His blunt words make me shatter into a million pieces and Bryce follows. His chest heaves for air and his skin is drenched with sweat. His groans are loud enough for me to hear over my own whimpers. His whole body tenses, releases and then tenses again as I feel his cock jerk inside, giving me what I'm asking for as he sends his warm come tunnelling deep inside me.

The metal O-rings clang against the bar when his full body weight collapses on top of me. His arms wrap around my back holding me, while his lips skim my neck and I feel him speak. "Holy fuck Angel, you'll be the death of me. But what better way to go."

"That was fun." I say breathless. "Yes, what a way to go. Making love to you."

His lips find mine for a few seconds then he holds himself up with his massive arms and hovers over me.

"You're so beautiful. I could look at you for hours, but you probably want these off."

Bryce pulls out, and lifts the bar at the same time, then hurries to retrieve a washcloth in record time so I don't drip on the bed. I hold it in place while I watch Bryce unhook my ankles from the spreader bar.

"Did that hurt you?" Bryce asks.

"No, not at all. It kept me from closing my legs."

"Just the way I like you. Restrained and spread wide open for me, so I can do whatever I please to this sweet juicy pussy of mine. I love driving you insane with my tongue, my fingers, and my cock. I could lick this sweet pussy all night if you'd let me."

"Babe, I love how you tell it like it is. You don't hold anything back."

"I get hot and horny talking dirty to you and I hope you get turned on too."

"Yes, please don't ever stop. I love it. You get the cutest mischievous grin on your face and, yes, it does turn me on very much. Babe, can I ask you something?"

"You can ask me anything, Angel."

"Did you get to try new and different things with Lindsay?"

He winces at my question, but he does answer me. "No, are you kidding. She'd have my balls. She wanted it the same way every time. Didn't like to try anything new and if I asked, I got the third degree on where I learned it and who I was fucking."

I laugh, "So where did you learn how to do all of this fun kinky stuff."

Bryce points to his temple and taps it with his finger. "It's all right here Angel, all in my mind. All the things I want to try with you."

"So you've never experienced this with anyone else before?"

"No, you're my first. Sex was pretty boring before you came along."

I'm quite happy with his comment.

Bryce holds his hand out for me to take. "Come with me. Let's get you cleaned up for bed."

And just like that the conversation is over. I can tell he doesn't like talking about Lindsay.

I put my hand in his and he leads me to the bathroom. Just as we enter the door the balls fall onto the ceramic floor, making a clanging sound. I giggle. "I forgot those were in there."

Bryce laughs. "You're dropping my balls all over the place." He gets this boyish grin on his face as he bends to pick them up so he can clean them with my vibrator.

He places them inside his bag. "We're going to need these." He says with a smirk. "I don't have any toys at my house."

"What! You're kidding? Mr. Kink has no toys?"

Bryce smacks my ass.

"Ouch!" I rub my butt cheek.

"My mom sometimes cleans my house and I don't really want her finding anything, so I keep them at the cabin."

I hear Bryce from my bedroom. "We should get to bed. You can pack your clothes tomorrow morning. We'll head out around ten." Then he walks back in the bathroom and wraps his arms around me from behind and hugs me tight. "I'm so happy you're coming with me."

"So am I." I hurry to say before he notices in my voice that I'm nervous to meet his parents.

Sunday morning, after closing my house up, we place our bags in the back seat of the truck and say our goodbyes as we hug and kiss Leena. She has to work, but said she'd book the time off and come with us next time.

We give Austin and Leena some privacy, knowing they'll be awhile saying goodbye.

Bryce and I get in the truck and call the police to let them know we're leaving for a week to Barrie and if they get more information about my stalker to call my cell.

We had a feeling they wouldn't keep the van at my house if we weren't there, but that's fine. The doors are locked, water and gas are off, and security cameras will record any movement around the perimeter of my house and at the road in front of my house.

Bryce and I look at Leena and Austin, still in a tight embrace, then he pulls back and gazes deep in her eyes to wipe a tear off of her cheek.

I swallow back the lump in my throat. "I think they're falling in love."

Bryce breathes deeply. "I'm so happy you're coming with me. That would be us if you weren't. It kills me to be apart from you."

"I know, it kills me too, it breaks my heart."

Austin's quiet when he gets in the truck and Bryce doesn't tease him like I thought he would.

We wave bye to Leena and head for Highway 11. I wait until I think Leena is home and then text her.

You home yet? How are you doing? Looks like you two are falling in love. We're going to miss you!

I wait for her to text back.

I'm home. I'm okay. And yeah, I think so too, it's so much harder saying goodbye this time. I'll miss you guys more than you know.

I show Austin and he smiles.

I'll call Katie this week. See what she's up to and you text me when you're not working. Bye sweetie ttyl.

Leena texts back. *Have a safe trip ttyl. Love you guys, bye.*

Austin starts talking after he sees the text. He's probably more at ease knowing she's okay and home safe.

"When does Leena have to work?" I ask Austin to get him to talk a bit more.

"Monday to Wednesday she's working from two to ten, Thursday and Friday is morning shifts, then she's off for the weekend, so I'm coming back." Austin says excitedly.

"Yeah, we're coming back too, but I think we'll go to the cabin this time so we don't have to deal with her stalker." Bryce groans.

I think Bryce has an ulterior motive and I'm thrilled with the prospect as I wonder what he has in mind. I shift on the seat restlessly and clench my muscles.

Bryce looks down at me with his wicked smile and somehow I think he knows what I'm thinking.

I give him a wink.

"Text me with a time and I'll meet you at your place, I'll drive this time." Austin mutters.

"It's about time. I thought you'd never offer." Bryce teases.

"You're the one that said he wanted to drive his shiny new truck and besides that, it's keeping the miles off of mine."

The ride to Barrie is very scenic, lots of trees, rock faces along the highway and Bryce stops on the side of the road when a moose and her calf saunter out of the tree line. I capture some great pictures of the magnificent animals and when more cars stop to check them out, they run back into the bush.

This is very exciting to me. The only time I get out of Huntsville is to see Gramps in North Bay, which is as adventurous as I've been.

I think Bryce senses it, because he looks at me and smiles. "I hope you like Barrie, it's a big city, but you'll get to know your way around. I'll have you drop me off at the fire station, that way if you want to go somewhere you can and I'll give you a tour of the station one day when we're not busy."

I want to meet everyone in Bryce's life, but I have to admit I'm a little nervous.

As we drop Austin off at his house, he slaps Bryce on the back and squeezes my knee. "I'll see you two sometime this week. Don't work too hard and be safe Bro."

"You be safe too, watch out for the lunatics." Bryce drawls.

Austin grabs his bag from the back seat. "Always." And we watch as he disappears into his house.

We pull away from Austin's and I ask Bryce, "Do you worry about Austin when he's on the job?"

"Oh yeah, I think my whole family does. I like to keep in touch with him during the week. He lets me know about the exciting things that happen at the cop shop and I tell him what's happening at the station."

"Do you have any friends that you're close to?"

"Yeah, Jax and Dante are really good friends of ours. We hang out and we've gone hunting together. I work with them. They've always got my back."

We drive three roads over from Austin's and pull into a driveway. "Speaking of my family. Would you like to meet them? This is their house."

"What? Right now?" Panic sets in instantly, and I tense against his arm.

25

"I CAN TELL YOU'RE nervous. So did you want to get it over with?"

"Umm." I'm in deep thought, talking to myself. Jeez Bryce you're a little pushy, don't you think? Crap. You're rushing me. Come on Keera, you can do this.

"They don't know we're coming, so they'll be thrown off a bit, too." Bryce tries to coax me.

Bryce opens his door, jumps down and holds out his hand for me to take.

"Okay." I say apprehensively and place my hand in his while he looks at me with a stupid grin on his face as I slide out of the truck. "You're enjoying this aren't you?" I spit out.

He wraps me in a tight embrace with his massive arms. "I don't want you worrying and I want you to sleep at night." He bends down to kiss me. "Come with me. Everything's going to be fine, you'll love them."

Bryce calls for his mom as soon as he gets in the door, but she doesn't answer, so he leads me through the living room from the front of the house to the kitchen at the back.

We find Bryce's dad in the kitchen, eating lunch. He stands as soon as he sees us and shakes Bryce's hand. "How've you been Son?" And then his focus shifts to me. "This must be the lovely Keera. I'm pleased to finally meet you."

I hold out my hand. "I'm pleased to meet you Mr. Hamilton."

"Call me Garrett." Then he wraps me in a bear hug and whispers in my ear. "We have you to thank for saving my boy."

Garrett pulls away. "I'll go find your mother. She can't wait to meet you." His gaze never leaves mine, as I stand frozen trying to figure out what he means by saving his boy. Then he's off to find Bryce's mom.

Bryce hugs me. "See that wasn't so bad."

We hear a distant loud squeal from another room. "Bryce is here…with Keera?"

"Yes, they're in the kitchen." I hear Garrett say.

Bryce's mom comes rushing toward Bryce with her arms wide open and hugs him as she keeps her stare locked on me. "Oh Bryce she's beautiful." She pulls away from him. "Hello dear it's so nice to finally meet you." Then she hugs me. She pulls back holding me at arm's length and looks me over.

"It's so nice to meet you too, Mrs. Hamilton." I say and smile.

"Call me Deana. Please. Mrs. Hamilton makes me seem old."

Garrett's big and husky, like Bryce and Austin, with salt and pepper black hair. He's still very hot for his age. I can see how much they look like their father. Bryce's mom is a little taller than me and has shoulder length dark auburn hair with perfect features and flawless skin. She's very beautiful and this is why her boys are so gorgeous, because they have good genes from their parents, I think. "Now I know where your boys get there good looks from."

"Well, thank you dear." Deana says proudly. "Bryce, I love her already."

I look around and notice their house is immaculate. "You have a very beautiful home." I state with a hint of shyness in my voice.

"Let me show you around." Deana takes me by my hand, leading me from room to room and I comment on how beautiful it is, or we talk about the décor.

I'm really trying not to be shy in making sure their first impression of me is a good one.

When we get to a door down the hall that's closed, Deana opens it and when Bryce's sister sees us, she jumps off her bed and rushes toward me. "Keera? I'm so happy you're here!" She hugs me. "We're going be great friends, I know it."

"So nice to meet you." I say breathless, because Ciara's hugging me so tight.

Ciara is beautiful like the rest of the family. She's thin and a couple inches taller than Deana. She has long straight as a pin dark brown hair. That's odd that she doesn't have black hair like her brothers. Her skin is sun kissed and flawless. Her eyes are brown with long, thick eyelashes, like Bryce's.

"Before Bryce comes in." Deana rushes to say, "We want to thank you. We've got him back now. Austin's told us he's really changed since he's met you and we've even gotten a couple phone calls from him, which Bryce has never done before and he came to see us last week when he had a chance from that crazy work week."

"Yeah, Lindsay really sucked the life out of him, to put it mildly." Ciara moans.

I get the nerve up to ask. "So what exactly did Garrett mean by you saved my boy? Bryce doesn't tell me much."

"Lindsay messed with his head, she controlled him." Deana winces remembering back. "He wasn't allowed to see us, his own family. And what kills me is that he listened to her."

"Until we had an intervention." Ciara interrupts. "And we told him that relationships aren't supposed to be that hard. We told him how she was controlling his mind and when it's easy, you know you've found the right woman. We also told him what a jackass he's been and then low and behold." Ciara raises her hands in the air and shrugs her shoulder. "He finally woke up."

"Bryce doesn't like to talk about it, so this is our secret." Deana says quickly because she hears a creak in the floor down the hall. She points.

Bryce opens the door and pops his head in. "Can I have my girlfriend back?"

Deana looks up at Bryce. "What day are you not working? I want you to bring Keera over for dinner."

Bryce looks at me. "Wednesday's good for us." His hand rests on my lower back and he leads me to the hallway.

"You're not leaving already?" Deana asks. "Have a drink with us."

"Okay, one drink and then we're heading to the grocery store. My house is a little bare." Bryce pulls out a chair for me to sit at the kitchen table and we drink, talk and laugh. Ciara sits on the other side of me to chit chat with us.

We say our goodbyes, then we walk to the truck with Bryce's arm wrapped around my waist and my hand in his back pocket. "Don't look now, but they're watching us through the front window." Bryce says as he opens the truck door for me.

And of course I have to glance their way. "Look at them. They're so cute, staring out the window at us." I wave bye to them and then hop up in the truck and snuggle next to Bryce while we drive to the grocery store.

"So, what'd you think of my family?"

"I think I was nervous for no reason. They're so nice and they made me feel so comfortable. I love them."

Bryce wraps his arm around me, squeezing me up against him and he kisses my forehead. "I knew you would."

We stop at a grocery store to stock up on a few things then

head to Bryce's house, which is only a few blocks away from Austin's and his parent's.

When we pull into the driveway, I notice the large windows at the front and the dark chocolate brown brick that surrounds the whole house.

"Wow! Nice house." I express.

"Thanks." Bryce squeezes my knee. "Stay right there." He gets out of the truck and runs around retrieving our bags out of the back seat and then he opens my door. "Come here."

"Babe, you don't have to."

"I want to. Now come here."

"Demanding, aren't we? Fine!" I say with a little attitude and a smile on my face, then I scoot over. "Why do you always want to carry me through the door?"

"Tradition." Bryce picks me up in his arms and carries me to the door and punches a code into the keypad. "I want you to remember this code."

"Okay, got it." I say with my smart ass voice.

Bryce smirks at me and shakes his head as he opens the door. He drops our bags and sets me down on my feet. He flicks the lights on. "Stay right here." Then he runs back to the truck to get the groceries out. I look up to see a beautiful chandelier hanging in the foyer. He has medium stain on his oak stairs that lead upstairs and down. I wonder to myself how many coats of varnish he had to apply on the stairs to get them so shiny. They're magnificent.

He's back in a flash. "Welcome to my house." Bryce says with the biggest smile. "Let me show you around." He holds his hand out for me to take.

We walk upstairs to the kitchen and drop the groceries on the counter then I follow him from one room to another. The living room to the left of the stairs has a fair amount of fireman memorabilia and blown up pictures of Bryce in action as a firefighter. The first picture which catches my eye immediately is of Bryce wearing only his bunker pants. He's bare chested, eight pack abs showing perfectly and he's opening a fire hydrant. I've never seen a firefighter look so hot.

I point. "Nice picture. Where was this taken?"

"My mom took that picture a couple years ago. We were at a firefighting competition in Toronto. She said it's her favourite and had it blown up, so I didn't want to upset her by taking it down."

"I'm glad you didn't. It's my favourite too." I rub against him.

My eyes glance over all the others and stop abruptly. "This is you?" I point and ask softly, but I already know the answer, wanting the full story of the picture.

"Yeah, we were venting the roof and someone took that picture at the right time, just as the fire flared up into my mask. It got a little hot, but I didn't get burned."

And that's when it hits me, seeing those pictures makes me realize how dangerous his job really is.

"Bryce. Oh my god! Holy shit…I…I knew it was dangerous but, seeing you in these pictures, I'm really going to worry now."

"I don't want you worrying." Bryce pulls me in for a tight embrace. "I'll be fine. We all watch out for each other."

There's another picture of him with the Jaws of Life, ripping open the door of a car to get the occupant out.

Another picture shows him inside a burning house spraying water on the flames. The name Hamilton is across the shoulders of his fire coat and helmet. Trying to distract me, Bryce points out a few pictures of Dante and Jax with him and I can see the tight bond they share.

He pulls me down the hall and into the bathroom to get my mind off of it, I presume, and then into the bedroom. He rushes over to the nightstand and throws a picture in the drawer.

I don't get to see it because I'm too busy looking around at everything else. "You have a beautiful house, Babe."

"Thanks. Can you tell my mom decorated it for me?"

"She did? She's got great taste."

"Come with me." He pulls me out of the bedroom and points out a few other things trying to distract me from the picture he shoved in the drawer.

After putting the groceries away we lie on the couch enjoying each other's company hanging out, all tangled up.

He asks me a few questions and I ask him a few to get better acquainted. We're still in the process of getting to know one another. We need to know what our likes and dislikes are.

"So did you live in that same house while you grew up?"

"Yeah, I still love going to my parents' house. How about you? Did you ever move growing up?"

"Been in the same house all my life. All our memories are there. I still see my parents all over the house at times."

Bryce holds my face in his hands. "I'm sorry." He hugs and kisses me. "It must be comforting living there with all the memories."

"Yeah. Everyone was telling me I should sell it when they died, but I couldn't. I got a job as a receptionist to help Gramps pay for it and when I got the settlement, I paid Gramps back and then paid the mortgage off."

"I wish I would've known you then. I would've helped you get through the tough times."

"Thanks Babe. Your parents are fantastic people, they're so nice. It's hard to believe they didn't like Lindsay."

Bryce physically tenses when I mention her name, unaware that I notice. "Yes they're the best. They did like her at first, but once they saw the change in me, they wanted her out of my life."

"What kind of change do you mean?"

"I don't know, they said I looked depressed. It was a constant battle. Every time I went to see my parents, Ciara would start in on me, nagging about Lindsay. My mom would make a few comments and then my dad and Austin would finish, letting me know how she's screwing with my mind. Then I'd go home and if I mentioned to Lindsay by mistake that I was at my parents' house she'd fly off the deep end and lose it. So I stopped going over there. Life was easier that way."

"Did Lindsay live with you?"

"No. She wanted to move in, but I kept putting it off."

"Why?"

"It didn't feel right. So what do think of my pain in the butt sister?"

And just like that the subject of Lindsay is changed. I can tell he does not like talking about her.

"Your sister is great. She's so sweet."

"Ciara? My sister?" Bryce says sarcastically.

"Yes your sister. I really like her."

"Good. I'm glad. So when and where did you first notice your stalker staring at you?"

"Back in April, I remember it was spring. It was at The Lodge when Katie, Leena and I were out one night, dancing."

"He's been following you around for six months now? Why didn't you tell Grant that?"

"That was the first time I noticed him watching and Grant didn't ask me that question."

"We've got to let him know next time we talk to him."

"Alright."

"Come with me. Let's make some dinner. I'm getting hungry." Bryce lifts from the couch, pulling me up with him.

"I can tell your belly's grumbling."

After we finish dinner and clean up, the sexual tension that crackles in the air is almost unbearable, starting with a light touch on my hip and then his hand would brush against my butt. Suddenly Bryce corners me from behind while I put leftovers away in the fridge. He pulls my hair to one side devouring my neck, peppering me with kisses as he whispers naughty promises in my ear while he grinds his hard cock on my ass.

I stand frozen with the fridge door wide open, enjoying every sensation. His hands leisurely caress my upper body, travelling over every square inch for quite a while.

When I push back and rotate my hips, Bryce pulls me away from the fridge and closes the doors.

He takes my hand and leads me down the hall, stopping abruptly to pin me against the wall, kissing me fiercely as his hand travels up my shirt grasping my breast. With our lips still fused, he attacks my clothing, scattering it down the hall as he pins me from one wall to the other, sliding us further down until we reach his bedroom, naked. We make love and we can be as loud as we want, it's just me and Bryce and we don't hold back.

Monday morning, I wake to the startling sound of a fire truck and it makes my body jump, but with Bryce's big strong arms wrapped around me, I hardly move. His alarm is whaling away so he reaches over and shuts it off.

I roll over to get out of bed and Bryce pulls me back in, confining me in a bear hug with my back to his front.

"Oh hell no. I want to feel your naked body beside me before I go to work."

"I was going to make you a coffee and bring it back to bed with me."

"You can do that tomorrow, right now I want to feel this sexy body and your soft skin against mine."

Bryce pulls my hair to the side, then wraps his arms around me grabbing handfuls of my breasts and I feel slabs of hard muscle against my back and his hard cock grinding into my butt.

"I'm happy to see you too." I purr.

He nuzzles his nose in my neck and tugs on my nipples then whispers in my ear. "I want you to think about my hard cock buried deep inside you, fucking you hard." His warm breath gusts against my ear. "I want you to think about my tongue sliding between your pussy lips, lapping up your juices and my tongue licking and flicking your clit until you can't take anymore and you fall apart squirting in my mouth." He kisses my neck in several spots and that's all he has to do, I'm rendered speechless and immobile, I'm a puddle. I close my eyes and the intensity of every sensation heightens. He gets me that damn hot in a nanosecond and I moan with pleasure.

I push back against his cock wanting and needing more.

Bryce rolls over, turns the light on and gracefully climbs out of bed.

I fall onto my back and sigh heavily. "You've got to be kidding me, you're going to leave me like this?"

His laughter fills the room. "I'll be thinking of you all day and I want you thinking of me."

Staring at his huge cock, I lick my lips. "You're such a tease." I whisper.

"You don't know how bad I want to climb back in that bed and finish you off." He pauses staring down at me, shaking his head. "I'd better go, but I want you ready and waiting for me tonight."

His sexy tight ass saunters straight to the bathroom and I hear him say, "I better take a cold shower…that's the only thing that's going to get this fucker to go down."

I proudly smile, knowing the effect I have on him.

Lying there for a minute, I let out a heavy sigh listening to the water start in the shower, then I roll out of bed hesitating as I pick up and throw back down my silk pajamas. I was going to get dressed, but I think since I'm sexually frustrated, then he should be, too. I strut into the kitchen totally naked and make myself a tea and Bryce a coffee.

The water shuts off as I walk into the bathroom, and when Bryce opens the door of the shower, his eyes almost pop out of his head when I hand him his coffee.

"I took a cold shower; I don't want to take another one. You've got to go put some clothes on."

I put my tea on the counter and smile. "I think that's a first." I lift my eyebrows mischievously. "You telling me to put clothes on."

"Such a tease." He says huskily. And then he smacks my ass as I turn to walk out.

Bryce's voice filters from his bathroom into the bedroom. "Are you sure you don't want my truck, so you can go somewhere today?"

"I'll use it tomorrow. Today I'm going to exercise, clean your house, call Katie and Gramps and make you dinner."

He joins me in the bedroom. "You're going to be busy." He runs his fingers down my back, awakening every sensitive nerve.

"What time do you think you'll be home?"

"Five, unless we've got something major, like a house or a building fire." I watch intently as Bryce gets dressed. "So if I'm not home, then you know something's up. Just keep it warm for me."

"Okay, will do."

This is the first time I see Bryce in his uniform and I can't take my eyes off of him. My eyes float up and down his perfect physic. "Wow!" I shake my head and smile. "Jesus Babe, you are way too yummy. I've never seen a fireman look as hot as you do in their uniform."

He takes my hand and pulls me down the hall. "You like my uniform?"

"Very much. And the gorgeous hunk of a man inside it. Too hot baby, too hot." He pulls me to the foyer and dips me at the front door giving me a long toe curling kiss that tightens everything from the waist down.

He tries to leave three different times, but comes back for another molten kiss, revving up our hormones. "Think of that Angel."

"Oh I will." I smack his ass. "Get. You'll be late."

When he finally leaves for work the first thing I do is check the nightstand for the picture that he rushed to put away yesterday. I thought he would have moved it, but it's still there.

Sitting on the bed, I study it as my heart drops to my toes. The picture is of Lindsay and Bryce, or I presume its Lindsay. They're dressed up on a dance floor, holding each other and they look very happy together. She's taller than me, thin, mid back brown strait hair, hazel eyes, and perfect features. She's beautiful.

I close my eyes and shake my head. "You had to look at this eh?" I shove it back in the drawer of the nightstand. Glaring at the bed, my mind pictures them rolling around on the mattress in a tangled mess. That mattress has got to go if I'm going to be staying here. "Time to exercise." I demand, to get my mind off of her.

When I'm done I start cleaning Bryce's house and my mind wanders. Now seriously, if I had an ex, I'd get rid of everything that reminded me of him long before Bryce came over. Now either he's not thinking straight, or their not done yet, and he's still holding on.

But how can he act the way he does with me? He said he was falling in love. I'm so confused I don't know what to think.

Katie calls me back on her way to another class. She's got a new boyfriend, university is going well and she's happy. I tell her about me and Bryce and Leena and Austin. Katie's coming home for Christmas, and I tell her I can't wait to see her. She says she feels bad for not calling Leena, but I tell her not to worry, I'll text her to let her know how you're doing. We say our goodbyes as she's entering her next class.

I start to clean and the phone rings. I look at the caller I. D. and it says Barrie Fire.

"Hello."

"Hi, Angel. How are you doing?" Bryce's voice is low and sexy.

"I'm good. How is your day going?"

"Good, but I'm constantly thinking of you and your hot body teasing me this morning."

"You're the one that started teasing me and then you left me like this."

He chuckles in my ear. "Yes, I want you naked and wet when I get home. I'll call when I leave here."

"Okay, I'll be wet and waiting." I say excitedly.

"Just what I want to hear."

Every time I see him or talk to him on the phone, I get a giddy school girl crush feeling and it sends me into a euphoric high. Obviously I should let the picture thing go. After hearing what Bryce's mom, dad, and sister have to say about Lindsay, I would think I'm the best thing for him and I should stop overthinking everything and get her out of my head.

Taking a shower, I do the normal grooming so everything's nice and smooth. When I get out of the shower, I inspect my pubic area to make sure I've done a good job, thinking about Leena trying to convince me to go with her for her next Brazilian wax job. It puts a smile on my face when Leena told me her beautician smacked her ass when she was up on all fours and told her she's got a great ass. I finish getting ready, curling my hair and applying minimal makeup on my face.

When I get the call from Bryce I get so excited, I run up to his bedroom and grab his dark purple tie out of his closet, dropping my towel to the floor. It's still tied, so I slip it over my head and adjust it, letting it hang between my breasts. I sit on the oak stairs, so my naked body will be the first thing he sees as soon as he walks in the door. I wait patiently for him to come home.

I hear Bryce's truck pull into the garage and I swear to God my heart skips a beat, I can't wait for him to get in the house. The anticipation is making me antsy.

He comes in and closes the door. His eyes rake greedily up and down my almost naked body. His eyes darken.

26

"YOU LIKE?"

"Fuck, yeah, I love. I'm hard already."

He closes the gap between us and runs his fingers along his tie in between my breasts. My nipples pucker and I inhale sharply at his gentle touch.

"I love coming home to you like this. You don't know how much this means to me. And I love this tie on you."

"You do, eh?"

Bryce stands on the bottom stair and grabs the tie, pulling me up gently toward him so we're face to face. "I want you to stay like this while we're eating dinner. I'm going to take a quick shower and shave so I'm smooth and then I'm going to tie your hands up behind your back with my tie and fuck you senseless over the side of my couch."

He gently pulls me up the stairs by his tie.

You've got to be shitting me. I have to wait until after dinner. What the…?

He kisses me hard, taking my thoughts and breath away. He then pulls back suddenly, leaving me hanging again as he turns and smiles strutting down the hall with that sexy walk, shaking that ass a little more than he usually does pulling his shirt off so I can get a peek of what's to come.

"Tease!" I call out to him.

He turns so I can see his mischievous smile before he rounds the corner for the bathroom.

I sigh and go back to the kitchen with a stupid grin plastered across my face.

Preparing the finishing touches on our dinner, I hear the water shut off, so I quickly arrange our food on our plates and place them on the breakfast bar. I rush over to the swivelling high back bar stool and perch myself in a sexy pose, waiting patiently for Bryce.

My gaze slides over his amazing body as he struts toward me from the hallway. He's totally naked, shaved smooth and so sexy with that wet hair. The smell of his cologne and body wash manipulate my senses, and as usual the sight of him takes my breath away. Damn, I'm one lucky woman.

Bryce closes the gap strolling toward me with dark eyes and that sexy walk of his.

"Look at you, Angel." He eyes me and the food, then opens my legs and settles between them. His fingers glide along his tie fluttering against my sensitive skin sending a shiver throughout my whole body.

"Do you know how many guys would kill to have you? To have what I have with you. I can't believe somebody hasn't scooped you up before me. But let me tell you…I thank God every day, I saw you in that grocery store."

"I was just thinking what a lucky woman I am to have you. That was fate. Us seeing each other that day."

"Yeah, and then I made it reality by following you."

His finger finds its way between my moist pussy lips, and he slides one deep inside me.

I shamelessly open my legs wider and tilt my pelvis, giving

him easy access as he probes around, touching my sensitive wall. I moan and my head falls back from the intense feeling.

Then he suddenly pulls his finger out.

I watch his every move.

His finger slowly inserts in his mouth and he sucks on it. "Dessert before dinner. You're definitely wet for me and I love it."

Bryce climbs onto the bar stool next to me, leaving me once more on edge.

"Mmm, this is good, Angel."

"Thank you."

Spinning in my chair, my eyes float over his gloriously naked body, his beautiful meaty pecs with the smattering of hair between them. His nipples are still hard from the climate change of the warm shower to the cooler kitchen. The bulging muscles in his arms and thick veins running through them.

My gaze levitates over his large thighs and then stop to see that his cock is rock hard and standing at attention. I clench my muscles trying to alleviate the ache I feel.

Bryce does the same inspection of my body. The way he looks at me with lust and love in his eyes sends that delicious tingle everywhere. The electricity crackling between us is unbearable.

He runs his hand between my thighs setting my sensitive skin on fire. "Such beautiful skin. So soft."

I want him to keep touching. I want his hands all over me, I can't believe how greedy and needy I've become.

An idea pops in my head to get this moving a bit faster. I pick up a big long carrot from my plate and take it deep in my mouth, wrapping my lips around it.

I've got his undivided attention now, his eyes widen, and he focuses on my mouth. I swirl my tongue around it, then slowly deep throat it again. His breathing hitches as he watches me intently while I suck on the carrot like his cock. "Oh, Angel, you're asking for it."

I mischievously smile and bite it in half.

"That's it! Over the couch!"

"Whoo hoo!" I say as I jump off the stool and eagerly hurry over to the couch, waiting for my next instruction.

Bryce stands in front of me, loosening the tie from my neck. "You've been teasing my cock all day."

"And who started it this morning?"

He pulls the tie up and off my head, then turns me toward the couch and ties my hands behind my back with it.

"Over the couch." He places his hand in the middle of my back and guides me down. "I'll be right back." And then he's gone again.

"Unbelievable. He left me again. You've got to be shitting me." I mumble into the cushion.

I hear him go into the garage then I hear his truck door close. What is he up to now?

The garage door slams and I hear Bryce's feet pattering across the ceramic tile and up the stairs, closing in on me.

He throws a bag on the couch, and reaches inside pulling out a riding crop. "We went shopping for toys on our lunch."

My eyes widen. "Who's we?"

"Me, Jax, Dante and George."

"Bryce! I'm going to be so embarrassed meeting your friends."

"Why? They were the ones that suggested we go, since I've got no toys in the house."

Men. They're clueless.

I have a few things I want to say, but he startles me with a crack on my ass with the riding crop and all thought is out the window.

"You don't like this?" He kisses the spot that he hit and pushes his finger deep inside me. Slowly.

I try not to moan because I'm still irritated with him.

He bends over my back and whispers against my ear. "I think you do like it. Your body's telling me it does." His voice a sexy purr.

Bryce withdraws his finger and I feel another snap on the other butt cheek, a kiss follows and then his finger probes around inside me.

I've lost all train of thought from the pain and pleasure mixture. I can't help but moan and circle my hips.

How can I be enjoying this? It's so wrong but it feels so right. I anticipate the next crack of the riding crop. Bryce alternates between different spots on my butt cheeks, so it doesn't hurt as much, and what follows has me moaning and circling my hips.

Bryce leans over my body again and whispers in my ear, sending a shiver down my spine. "You've wanted to come all day. Haven't you, Angel. It'll be worth the wait." He says in that deep sexy tone.

He cracks my ass again and when he kisses my butt and sticks his finger in me, I roll my hips and whimper. "Please" escapes my lips.

"Fuck, Angel, any restraint I did have is now gone."

Bryce pulls me up and off of the couch with one hand supporting my chest and the other by my tied hands. He quickly unties me, then slides it back over my head skimming my breasts with his fingers. "I like you wearing my tie. Now come here." He pulls me by his tie around to the middle of the couch. "I want you to lower yourself on my face." He says while he positions himself, lying down.

He then holds out his hand to steady me while I straddle him. I hold onto the arm of the couch as I roll my hips and ride his mouth.

I find the perfect rhythm where my clit bumps against his nose. It's enormously large and when Bryce swipes his tongue across it, flicking wildly, it has me almost losing control.

Bryce must sense it, because suddenly, he pushes me back onto his legs. "Roll over. Sixty-nine, Angel. I want you sucking my cock while I'm eating this sweet, sweet pussy."

I do but, seriously, is he ever going to let me come?

His cock glistens with pre-cum as I take hold of his hard shaft trying to wrap my fingers around it. I lick my lips and deep throat him.

"Holy shit, Angel, that's deep."

His moan vibrates against my pussy and I keep doing the rocking motion, knowing he likes it.

We feast on each other, for quite a while, giving the ultimate pleasure and taking it all the same, until I start to quiver on top of him, but Bryce holds out. He has such unbelievable control. I tasted his pre-cum a while ago, and yet, he still holds out.

He waits for my aftershocks to subside, then he taps me on the butt. "I want you standing at the end of the couch, facing me." He demands.

I maneuver myself up and off of Bryce and go to the end of the couch, while I watch him take a new vibrator out of the package. He places it on the couch.

His fingers gently skim my neck as he pulls the tie up and over my head. "I'm going to give you what I promised, with a cherry on top."

I don't know exactly what he means by that, but I feel a chill of desire and my insides clench from delicious anticipation.

Bryce spins me tying my hands behind my back once more and guides me down so my butt is up in the air and my cheek rests against the cushion.

I hear him open another package but I don't get to see what it is.

"Look at you, so beautiful, bent over, ass in the air." He opens my legs, separating them with his. "And spread wide open for me."

I feel his cock probing my entrance, then it slides in, filling me to the hilt.

Taking it all, I gasp. There's nothing I can do, but take it all. Take whatever Bryce gives me.

He withdraws to the head teasing my entrance by pushing

in fractionally, in and out. "Do you want my little cock?" Bryce slams into me hard. "Or do you want my big cock?"

"Big!" I cry out.

Withdrawing, Bryce then slams into me again, harder this time.

He unties my hands. "When I tell you, put that vibrator on your clit."

Holding it steady in my hand, I position it getting it ready. I feel something cold squirt on the entrance of my ass. Is that anal lube?

He penetrates me at a steady rhythm. "Now, Angel! Put it on your clit."

Firing it up, I place it on me, then I hear another vibrator behind me and something foreign invading my ass.

"That's it, Angel, take it. I'll go slow. Almost there. Good. You did it. How does that feel, having both holes filled?"

"Babe!" escapes from my lips, and I don't know why.

"I know, Angel. It feels so good, doesn't it?"

"Oh god!"

"Did you feel how hard you made my cock by taking that in your ass?"

"Yes."

"I can feel it vibrate against my cock. Angel, I'm not going to last much longer."

"Do it now, fuck me hard! I need your cock."

He slams into me, fucking me hard.

I'm already falling apart, a quivering, whimpering mess, grasping onto the cushion for support, while my intense orgasm shatters me and I come unglued.

I feel Bryce slam into me one more time, then he rears up and back, tensing as I hear him gasp for air. His come shoots deep inside me.

He pulls the vibrator out of my ass and falls down, draping my back. "I'm telling you, Angel. You're going to kill me."

He holds me for a minute while we catch our breath. "How was that, Angel?"

"Intense, very intense."

"Did I hurt you?"

"No."

"You have no idea how fucking hot that is seeing you filled like that."

He lifts and pulls out slowly, then helps me up from my bent over position. He quickly sticks a wash cloth between my legs then wraps his massive arms around me holding me tight. "Thank you Angel, you're amazing, and your mine. All mine."

I look up at him and the gratitude that he shows, fills my heart, but he should've asked me first.

Bryce holds my face in his hands. "What's wrong? Don't lie to me. Did I hurt you?"

"No." I hesitate for a second. "Don't you think we should've discussed this? This is my body. Did you ever think for a second that I wouldn't like it?"

"Are you mad at me?"

"Some things need to be discussed with me. Not your friends. Especially something like that. Can we keep our sex life to ourselves?"

"I fucked up. I'm sorry Angel." He runs his thumbs along my jaw line caressing as he searches my eyes. "We'll discuss it together for now on and I'll go shopping for the kinky toys with you. Okay? I'm sorry. I don't want to mess this up. I need you to tell me when something's bothering you, so I can fix it. Do you forgive me?"

I hesitate. "Yes."

We hold one another for a bit more and then Bryce grabs my hand. "Come with me. We'll get cleaned up, then we'll clean the kitchen and watch some T.V."

Tangled together, we lie on the couch in a comfortable position. Then Bryce bares his soul. "Angel what we have together, you and me, it's like nothing I've ever felt before. What you do to me. What you let me do to you. You're amazing. You're what I've been waiting for. What I'm trying to say is…I can't live without you."

I turn to look at him. "I feel the same way about you. I can't live without you, either."

"You've got my heart, Angel."

"And you've got mine."

I think he's so overwhelmed with gratitude, because of what I let him do to me, but he's getting majorly sentimental and that's not like him.

"Isn't this nice. Just you and me. No worrying. No ex-girlfriend. No stalker."

"Yes this is how our life is going to be very soon."

We talk a bit more then fall asleep on the couch with Bryce holding me.

A few hours later, I feel Bryce scoop me up in his arms, carrying me to his bedroom, lying me down on the bed. He kisses my forehead and climbs in beside me.

Tuesday morning, I drive Bryce to work then come back to his place. After my shower, I head to the mall with Bryce's truck and strict instructions to park away from other vehicles.

Inside the mall, I walk from store to store in search of a few more outfits, snatching up good deals. Suddenly, I get a strange feeling like someone's watching me, so I'd quickly look around, but don't see anyone staring, so I ignore it.

Later, that feeling of uneasiness creeps up on me again, so I make my mind up to go to another mall. Walking down the hall toward the exit, a sudden yank of my hair from behind stops me dead in my tracks. Pain shoots through my scalp and I wrench my head away quickly in an attempt to stop it.

Turning around, I see Lindsay, hysterical. She's waiving her hands around in the air and calling me every name in the book.

In her right hand is Bryce's phone, in the other is a few strands of my long hair.

I lose it.

Dropping my bags in a rush, I shove her back and drop kick her to the chest. She gets some serious air and falls back on her ass, hitting her head on the marble tile. Bryce's phone flies out of her hand and skitters across the floor.

She finally shuts up, due to the shock that I kicked her, and when I realize it myself, I rush over to pick up Bryce's phone. Then I hurry to pick up my bags and high tail it out of there.

A small crowd gathers when I look back. Lindsay's screaming for security and pushing away anyone who tries to help her up.

I walk fast to exit the building. How embarrassing was that? But I did get Bryce's phone back.

When I pull up to the fire station, Bryce comes out to the truck knowing I'm too shy to go in there alone. Instantly aroused, I drink in the sight of him in his uniform strutting toward the truck with his sexy walk. I open the door to get out and he stands between my legs.

"Hi." I say softly.

"Hi Angel, how was your day?"

"Good and yours?"

"I've been looking forward to seeing you all day." He says in his deep sexy tone.

"You're quite the romantic. You know that?"

"I am eh?" He puts his finger down my cleavage. "I like this top on you."

"You do, eh?"

"Yes, so sexy." He runs his finger along each side of my breasts.

My nipples pucker instantly as I hold my breath and watch him.

"Look what you're doing to me already. I'm a walking hard on with you."

"You want me to take care of that for you?"

"If you only knew the things that are going through my mind right now. And yes, I'll take you up on that offer."

I smile. "Oh, I almost forgot." I hand him his phone.

His eyes widen. "How'd you get this?"

I smile mischievously. "Can you text Austin and see if there's an arrest warrant out for me?"

"Keera, what'd you do?" He says in a stern voice.

"Jeez, no Angel? Just Keera."

"Are you going to answer me?" He says in a raised voice.

I feel like a child being scolded by my father for doing something bad.

"Well, this is what happened..."

When I tell him about my hair, he moves me so he can see the back of my head. He rubs it.

"I'm sorry, Angel. She loses control sometimes."

"No one pulls my hair! Except you."

He smiles and I finish telling him how I got his phone.

"Holy shit, remind me not to piss you off, but you are a wild one when you finally do get pissed." He offers his hand for me to take and I slide out of the truck. Bryce clips his phone on his belt and then guides me with his hand on my lower back. "Now let me give you a tour."

Just as we walk in the door to the fire station, Dante and Jax rush toward us and Dante halts right in front of me. "I want to meet the woman who's got this big guy crumbling to his knees."

I smile and hold out my hand. "I'm Keera, pleased to meet you."

But he grabs me in a tight embrace and won't let go.

He whispers in my ear. "I'm Dante."

Jax grabs his arm. "Back away asshole. My turn."

"It's so nice to meet you guys." I say still in Dante's embrace.

"Hey, jackass, back up and give Jax a chance to meet her." Bryce grumbles.

Dante backs up and Jax hugs me. "So nice meeting you and thanks for straightening him out. He's acting normal again." Jax whispers. "He's not moody. He's happy."

It makes me smile how concerned they are for Bryce. I remember the tight bond they have together from the pictures Bryce showed me at his house of his friends. They're a few years older now from the pictures. Both Jax and Dante are tall and muscular, but not as big as Bryce. Jax has light brown hair and Dante has dark brown hair. Both are very good looking men.

Bryce pulls me away from Jax. "Can I have my girlfriend back?" He wraps his arm around me. "Come with me, Angel."

Dante follows.

Bryce looks back and snaps. "Don't you have something better to do?"

"Yeah, I'm doing it." Dante says with the biggest grin.

Bryce shakes his head and ignores him.

Leading me around by that simple touch at my lower back, Bryce shows me the fire trucks, their name tags above their fire gear hanging up ready to go for the next call, their laundry room, work out room and the kitchen.

Bryce finally gets pissed at Dante when he gets a little too close. Bryce raises his voice. "Back the fuck up, man. Quit sniffing around my girlfriend!"

Dante laughs and finally leaves us.

We finish the tour of the offices, the meeting room, and their sleeping quarters.

Bryce ushers me into his smoked glass cubical, and in it is a single bed with a nightstand, lamp, and tall wardrobe. His wardrobe sparks thoughts of all the toys in the kinky cabinet that Bryce has used on me and it revs up my libido. I look down at the bed and envision him sniffing my thong, playing with his cock. I shift restlessly.

"You've got your fuck me look on your face." Bryce says in his sexy tone.

"I was thinking about when you called me that night. You were playing with your cock." I point to his bed. "Right here?"

"Yes, does that turn you on?" He wraps me in a hug.

"Yes, it does." So does the way you're looking at me. Like you want to eat me alive.

"You know what turns me on?" He sticks his finger down my cleavage again. "You, and how hot you look right now. And you envisioning me playing with my cock." Bryce grinds against me on that perfect spot. "Feel that. See what you do to me?"

Bryce kisses me hard, leaving me breathless and panting. Abruptly, he pulls me around the maze of cubicles into the washroom, closing and locking the door behind us. "Strip!"

"Right here in the fire station? What if…?"

Bryce shuts me up with another hard kiss, then suddenly he pulls away. "I've always wanted to do this."

He unbuttons my shirt, then starts on my pants. We both quickly take over stripping out of our own cloths to be efficiently faster.

Pushing me hard to the wall, Bryce spreads my legs with his, sticking his finger inside me. "Good, you're ready for me." He slowly inserts the same finger into his mouth, sucking it. "So sweet."

That longing ache at the apex of my thighs, is back.

He lifts my leg and drapes it over his arm, leaving me with one leg on the floor and shoved against the wall, spread wide. He pushes his cock into me hard, making me gasp. He whispers in my ear. "This is going to be rough, hard and fast, Angel. Play with your clit and if it's too much, you'll have to tell me to stop."

Oh my, really? Seeing how hot Bryce looked in his uniform one moment and how he quickly stripped out of it, tossing it to the floor with no regard, so he can have me, turns me on to no end, as does his aggressive movements with his muscles bulging and straining.

This is what every woman fantasizes about. Having a hot fireman fucking her in every room or fire truck imaginable at the station. And I've got him. He's all mine. Silky black hair falling down in front of his eyes as he shoves into me harder than the time before. My hands reaching to his nape to grab a handful and I tug gently. Then my hands follow down his neck to his shoulders, then down his muscular arms. I squeeze, feeling the thick veins pumping blood through this miraculous body that I hold in my hands.

He bangs the hell out of me against the wall with such ferocity and deep desperation, I wonder what's bothering him, but now is not the time to ask. I enjoy being naughty, fucking at the fire station, and knowing we could get caught at any moment makes it that much more exhilarating.

Bryce pins my hands against the wall and bends his knees, changing the angle of his pounding. His cock hits the right spot as he ferociously rams me into the wall.

I pull my hands away and hold onto his shoulders.

His hands move to my hips and his fingers dig into my skin, shoving me down onto his cock matching every thrust and keeping perfect rhythm. His cock is hard as stone. His skin, damp with sweat. His heart pounding, like it could beat right out his chest.

My finger slides between us and I swirl my finger around my clit. I clamp down on him, milking his cock.

"Babe. Oh god. Right there. Don't stop!"

I watch every expression on his beautiful face as we fall apart together. His cock jerks inside me, once, twice. He's filling me. He nuzzles in my neck and then gently bites.

When we catch our breath, Bryce whispers. "When I'm lying in that bed." His head motions toward his bed. "I'll be thinking of us, in here, fucking."

"See, you're so romantic." I tease.

"Are you being sarcastic?"

"Me? Nooo."

He wraps my legs around his waist and carries me over to get some toilet paper, then he puts me down. We clean ourselves up and get dressed.

My face turns beet red with embarrassment when I see Dante with his ear pressed to the door when Bryce opens it.

Dante stands quickly. "Damn, you guys are quiet."

Bryce shoves Dante's shoulder. "Asshole, don't you get the hint."

Dante stumbles back, regains his footing, and then quickly runs down the hall yelling. "I knew you were fucking in there."

Bryce turns to look in my eyes. "I'm sorry about that, Angel. He likes screwing around."

"That's okay. He's quite the character."

"Yeah, jackass is more like it."

We walk back to Bryce's bed and I pick up his pillow, inhaling his scent. "Mmm, smells like you and your cologne."

"Shouldn't do that, Angel, I'm going to want to take you back in that washroom and bang the hell out of you again."

I smile, loving how I affect him that much. I look around noticing that most of the guys have pictures of their loved ones on their nightstands.

"I want a picture of you, Angel. Right next to my bed, so you're the last vision I see at night and the first beautiful face I see when I wake."

"You're so sweet. I'll see what pictures I can find. I'll work on it."

"I'm glad you came here today."

"So am I." I give Bryce my seductive look and rub against him.

We venture back to the fire trucks with Dante following closely behind.

Bryce whispers in my ear. "Another fantasy I want to fulfill is you and me fucking on this fire truck." He runs his finger down my cleavage again and when I look up he has his mischievous grin on his face.

I giggle as he kisses my neck.

We hear Dante comment. "Jesus, didn't you guys get enough in the washroom?"

Bryce is about to blurt something out to Dante, but a loud beeping sound comes over the speakers throughout the station, silencing Bryce.

The dispatchers' voice resonates over the loud speaker. "Barrie dispatch to Barrie fire station 2, we have a report of a house fire, possible entrapment at 109 Dalton Street. Cross street Bayfield. Time of dispatch, sixteen fifteen hundred hours."

Bryce kisses me. "Gotta go, Angel. I'll have Jax or Dante drive me home."

"Be careful!" I yell as he turns and runs to his gear.

I stand out of the way and watch them jump into their boots, slinging the straps of their pants over their shoulders. They quickly grab their coats, helmets, and gloves and run for the truck.

27

*E*XITING THE SIDE door, I saunter over to Bryce's truck and watch as each truck leaves the station. Dante rolls the window down, sticking his head out to wave at me. "Bye Keera."

I wave back. My adrenaline is pumping from watching how efficiently fast they're moving. I want to see them fighting a fire and this is my perfect opportunity, so I hop in Bryce's pick-up and drive behind the last fire truck.

I park Bryce's truck down the road from where the house is burning so I'll stay out of the way and walk down to where a small crowd has gathered to watch.

It's hard to see who is who with their gear on, until my eyes glance over the name Hamilton on the back of Bryce's helmet and coat.

Every move he makes commands respect and attention from the men he works with. How he controls the situation and takes over with dominant confidence has me in awe as I watch intently.

His efficiency and self-confidence oozes out of every pore as he barks out orders to the crew. His leadership works for them and they quickly take control of the situation. They break open the front door and several of the firefighters enter the house, including Bryce.

Watching him in action is awe inspiring. It fills my heart with such love and admiration. I'm scared for him, but I also can't believe how turned on I am. I'm having visions of him with his gear on, shirt off and him hoisting me up and over his shoulder to throw me on the bed. Dang, we might have to try this.

I shake off my sex filled magical spell and come back to reality as one of the firefighters carries a screaming woman out of the house. She's yelling. "My baby, my baby!"

After they place her on the gurney, Bryce emerges from the smoke, cradling a baby. Bryce places the baby in the mothers' arms and the ambulance attendants go to work strapping them down and loading them inside. Once I see the mother and baby are taken away by ambulance and the fire is extinguished, I finally relax. As they clean up, I see Bryce is safe, and that's when I head out on a mission to have a few pictures made for Bryce to place on his nightstand at the fire station.

The frame I purchase holds three five by seven photos. The one in the middle is me sitting on Bryce's lap, in my pink dress Leena had taken when we went out on our first official date. The one on the right is me in my bikini, when Katie, Leena and I went to Algonquin Park camping in the summer. The one on the left is a picture of me in my black bustier Bryce took, catching me off guard, but he says he loves it, so I put it in the frame, too. I wrap it up and put a bow on it, then walk to the kitchen to put the finishing touches on our salad for dinner.

I want to be sitting on the stairs naked so I will be the first thing he sees when he walks through the door, but he's being driven home by Jax or Dante and they might come in with him, so I think it would be best to keep my clothes on even though I want to jump his bones as soon as he gets through the door.

The door closes and I hear, "Angel?"

I walk to the stairs as he's coming up.

My pulse quickens and I feel that familiar tingle everywhere.

"Hi." I say softly.

"Hi, Angel." He comes close to me and sticks his finger down my cleavage. "I want to hug you, but I stink."

"I wanted to be naked for you, but I didn't know if you'd be alone."

"Yeah, Dante wanted to come in to see you, but I told him to go home. I don't know what's wrong with him; he's obsessed with you. He said he saw you at the house fire?"

"Yeah, I followed the fire truck. I wanted to watch you."

"And?"

"You're very good at your job. I was worried about you, but very proud of you at the same time. I think every emotion flowed through me from adrenaline laced fear to extreme admiration to erotic anticipation but right now, all I want to do is fuck you senseless. Watching you got me so hot." I grab for the hem of his shirt and he stops me, holding my hands with his.

"Hold that thought, Angel. I have to take a shower." He hugs me and kisses my forehead, then heads down the hall.

Eating dinner together, totally naked, is an exercise in surviving acute sexual tension. We learn that neither one of us has that much self-control. Half way through dinner, we end up lunging at each other, not able to resist another minute and make love for quite a while. Later, we cuddle on the couch with our legs and arms entwined watching T.V.

I finally get the courage to give him his gift. I move to get up and he pulls me back down.

"Where do you think you're going?"

"I want to give you something."

"Oh." He lets me go.

I pad into the kitchen, get the gift and hand it to him.

He looks at me wide-eyed and he grins from one ear to the other. "What's this?"

"Open it." I say smiling.

"Come here first." He opens his arms wide.

Lying back down on the couch with Bryce, I snuggle into him anxiously awaiting for him to open the gift. He inspects the three five by seven pictures of me I put in the frame.

"I love it." Bryce points to the one with me in my bikini. "I really like this one. Where were you?"

"Katie, Leena and I went camping in Algonquin Park, so I could face my fears."

"Fears? What do you mean?"

"Something happened to me when I was camping in Algonquin Park when I was a teenager, but when the girls went, we had a great time and I got over it." I answer vaguely because I'm not ready to share how Jake almost raped me. I keep that horrible memory tucked away, still unable to talk about it.

"I'm glad you faced your fears. Thank you. This is going on my nightstand at the station." He hugs and kisses me.

As soon as we start watching TV on the couch, I notice how Bryce is nodding off to sleep, so I move slightly and he awakens. "Let's go to bed, Angel."

Bryce guides me down the hall to the bedroom where he flops down on the bed from total exhaustion. I come around the bed and hoist his legs up onto it and cover him up, tucking him in. He grumbles. "I love you." And then quickly falls asleep.

"Did I hear what I think I heard?" I whisper.

Lying down beside him, I stare up at the ceiling replaying what Bryce said and that's exactly what it sounded like. I didn't imagine it. He loves me. Warmth fills my heart and I fall asleep, cuddled next to Bryce.

Wednesday morning we wake early, and have plenty of time to get ready together. After our shower, I watch intently as Bryce shaves his face and I comb out my hair. "What are you looking at?" Bryce looks sideways at me, halting for a second between strokes.

"You. I like watching you shave."

"You do eh?"

"Yeah, it's turning me on."

Bryce chuckles. "Hold that thought until tonight." He rinses his face thoroughly and then closes the gap. "Having you here with me feels right. I don't want us to be apart."

"I'm enjoying it too. It does feel right when were together. I love going to bed with you at night and waking up to you. No place would I rather be."

"Come with me." Bryce pulls me into the bedroom and we get dressed, then we saunter down the hall to make a quick breakfast.

As I'm cleaning up, I hear our favourite song begin. Bryce takes my hand, pulling me to the living room. "Dance with me."

It takes me by surprise, having me hesitate for a second before answering. "Sure, I'd love to."

We hold each other tight, lost in our intimate moment, dancing slowly. Silently. This is where I want to be. Forever in his arms. So many emotions I feel, it's hard to distinguish between them all, but I do know this, I've never felt more alive. I don't think I've ever been this happy. I don't want this to end.

The song ends and I sigh.

"I promise, we'll continue this when we get home tonight, after we go for dinner at my parents."

Bryce gives me a long hard kiss, leaving me wanting more when I drop him off at the station.

Dante comes running out, heading for the truck, but Bryce cuts him off and pulls him back.

"Fuck you man, she's mine."

"What? I want to talk to her." Dante looks back and smiles at me, while Bryce waves and hauls him back inside.

It makes me smile how great they get along to be joking like that.

My first stop is to the dollar store and then head to a different mall, hoping this shopping experience will be better than the last.

Back at Bryce's as I'm wrapping his new shirt and jeans, I hear banging on the front door, the doorbell is ringing and there's yelling from outside. "What the hell?" I look out the front window to see Lindsay throwing her arms in the air, pacing and yelling hysterically again.

"Fuck's sake! Will this bitch just leave us alone?" I run to the front and back doors to make sure they're locked, then I get my phone and text Austin.

Are you at work?

Yeah, why?

Lindsay's at Bryce's front door. She's hysterical again, and if I go out there, I might get charged with assault.

DO NOT go out there! I'm sending a car over right now.

Thank you.

I watch out the front window. She comes into view every once in a while, yelling my name, calling me every word in the book that she can think of. She bangs on the door, rings the doorbell, and tries the key pad. I glance across the street and notice the neighbor's looking out their front windows. I look back down at Lindsay who is still throwing a conniption. "Bet that pisses you off that Bryce changed the locks and you can't come in whenever you damn well please." I say, mostly to myself, with a smirk on my face.

She's yelling at me to get my ass out there, saying I'm scared and a chicken shit for not facing her.

I'm not scared, if I kicked your ass once, I'll do it again. And as I make my mind up to go out there, I see her punch the brick wall. "This bitch is bat shit crazy. Now I don't feel so bad for drop kicking her."

The police show up ten minutes after I text Austin. And as soon as she sees them, she beelines it for her car and locks her doors. Immediately, they pull the police cruiser right behind hers.

I crack the front windows open, so I can hear what's going on.

They tell her to get out of the car, but she doesn't listen.

I commentate out loud. "I can't believe you just did that." Or, "Don't be a dumb ass, Lindsay, just cooperate with them."

The police officer that pulled the car behind hers walks around to her passenger window and breaks the glass.

He opens the door and pulls her out placing her face down on the concrete, cuffing her.

I wince. "Oh shit, that's gotta hurt."

They lift her and place her in the back of the police cruiser.

The police come to the front door. "She won't be bothering you anymore Miss Johnson. We've had problems with this one before. Officer Hamilton said he'd fill out the report. We'll send a tow truck to pick up her car."

"Thank you." I shut the door and then run back up to the front window to watch Lindsay as she thrashes around in the backseat.

I close the window and watch them pull out of the driveway. "Well, that was way too exciting."

When I get to the fire station, Bryce, Jax and Dante are standing just inside the door and when they see me pull in, they come walking toward the truck.

I scoot over so Bryce can drive.

Bryce gets in and Jax hangs on the driver's door when Bryce rolls down the window to talk.

Dante jumps into the passenger seat, next to me. "Hi beautiful."

"Hi, Dante."

Jax teases Dante. "Hey, jackass, keep your hands off my girlfriend."

Dante places his hand on my knee. "Fuck you, I've got her all to myself."

"How 'bout fuck ya both. She's mine." Bryce groans and looks at me sideways. "We've got to drive Dante home. For some reason he had to take his truck in to the dealership."

"Okay." I say softly.

"So what's this I hear you had an exciting day?" Jax says grinning.

"I'm dying to know. Did you kick her ass again? That's so frickin' hot watching two women roll around. In mud or Jell-O, preferably." Dante says with a gleam in his eye.

I smile at his comment. "No, I thought it would be best if I stayed in the house."

"Smart thinking." Jax says. "She's crazy. Let me know what happens." He pounds on the door panel. "See you Friday."

And then I remember Bryce has Thursday off to spend the whole day with me.

"Now I've got you to myself." Dante squeezes my knee again.

Bryce pushes his hand away. "Hands off, fucker!"

Dante leans forward to look at me. "Touchy, isn't he?"

I smile at the amusement in his voice.

We drive Dante home and he has to get one last squeeze in before he says goodbye.

As we pull away Bryce apologizes for his friend. "Sorry about that, Angel. I don't know what the hell's gotten into him."

"He's harmless. I think he likes to bug you."

"Yeah." He huffs out a breath.

When we pull into Bryce's driveway Lindsay's car is still there. Bryce sees the broken window and asks what happened.

The expression on his face after I finish telling him is one I've never seen before. Is it worry? Is it sadness? I can't tell, but I let it go so his good mood returns.

After we're inside for a bit, I notice his mood does change for the better and I bring out his gift for him. "Open it."

"You've got to quit spoiling me."

He opens it and smiles. He looks at the size of the pants. "How'd you know my size?"

"I looked at your old ones. I hope they fit the same because I love how you fill them out." I look him up and down, then zoom in to his abundant package.

"Oh, Angel, if you keep looking at me like that, we're not making it for dinner."

I smile.

"Come here." He pulls me into a tight embrace and kisses me passionately. "Thank you, Angel. We'll continue this after dinner."

"You're welcome."

He picks up his new shirt and pants. "Do you want me to wear these tonight?"

"If you want to. If they don't fit, I'll take them back."

He turns and heads for the bathroom. "I think they'll be fine."

I head to the bedroom and change quickly, then saunter to the bathroom to brush my teeth, spray some perfume on, comb my hair and fix my makeup, not that I need to, but since I'm meeting Bryce's parents again, I want to look nice.

Bryce wears the jeans and Henley shirt and he looks amazing. The jeans fit perfectly with a pronounced bulge at the crotch and his ass is a sight to be stared at constantly. His shirt is tight enough to show every muscle underneath.

Deana and Garrett are waiting for us at the kitchen table when we come through the door, Ciara sits next to me on one side. Bryce on my other side, and we talk and drink waiting for Austin to show up.

Austin glares at Bryce when he comes into the kitchen. "Sorry, I'm late. I had a disgruntled prisoner I had to deal with."

Bryce looks at Austin, but doesn't say a word.

"Yeah, that would be your crazy ex-girlfriend. She kept lunging at me and I had to handcuff her to the table. I'm telling you, she's getting worse. I guess there's no love lost between us two."

Austin gets a beer out of the fridge and sits down with us. "She wasn't cooperating with my officers. She got in her car and refused to open the door, so they pulled her out, dropped her to the ground and handcuffed her."

"See that's one crazy bitch." Ciara comments.

Deana corrects her. "Ciara. You don't talk like that."

Ciara whispers. "Sure I do, all the time."

"Yeah, my guys had to listen to her rant all the way back to the station. Then, when they pulled her out of the car, she tried to escape."

Garrett shakes his head. "Now, why wouldn't she cooperate?"

"Did you charge her with anything?" Deana asks quietly.

"I told her if she bothers Keera, Bryce or anyone of us, I'm throwing the book at her, charging her with whatever I can. I told her I'm going to convince Bryce to fill out a restraining order against her. I'll tell you, if looks could kill, I'd be dead."

He looks at Bryce to see his reaction.

I think we all do. But there's nothing. Bryce is straight-faced, not giving anything away. He sits and drinks his beer.

Why is he so silent? Why isn't he reacting to this? In his defence he doesn't like talking about her. Suddenly my last comment makes sense.

He still cares for her. Oh god!

Austin continues speaking, pulling me from my thoughts. "Oh ya, I'd say she really hates me now, especially when I called her mother to pick her up."

I look at Bryce periodically to see what his reaction is, if any to all of this, but he shows no emotion, he doesn't speak, he just sits there.

Feeling a little uncomfortable with all of this talk about Lindsay and my wayward thoughts about him still caring for her, I ask Deana if she needs any help.

"Thank you dear. I'll set you up to grate the cheese and we'll make some garlic bread."

Austin glares at me and keeps talking. "Oh yeah, she said if anyone should be charged its Keera for kicking her at the mall."

Oh, shit. Everyone turns to look at me.

I stiffen and feel heat rush up on my face as I turn a beet red.

Ciara comes over to pat me on the back. "Way to go. She must have really pissed you off?"

"She caused a scene. She was hysterical and ripped a handful of hair out of Keera's head." Bryce says defending me.

Austin gracefully rises from his chair and comes closer, settling with his hip against the counter, leaning to look in my eyes as he holds his beer. "So she fell on her ass, hit her head and you stole her phone?" He says with a devilish smile.

"It was Bryce's phone and she stole it from him." I say softly, breaking my silence.

I feel like I'm being interrogated by the police. Oh, I am!

Austin stands directly in front of me and I look up at him. "You can't go around assaulting people, Blondie." He hugs me with the biggest grin on his face. "But I love you so much right now. You don't know how many times I've wanted to kick her ass for her tantrums and childish outbursts, but I can't."

After he says that I hug him back. He kisses my hair, then saunters back to sit in his chair.

"Seems like we have a feisty one here." Austin looks over at me with the biggest grin.

I smile, but I could kill him right now for telling his parents about what happened.

Deana wraps her arm around my shoulder and tugs me close. I think reassuring me. "You can put the garlic bread in, dear. Five more minutes and we'll eat."

Austin thankfully stops talking about Lindsay and I relax. He tells us a few other things that went on at the police department and then he drills Bryce about a few things that happened with police and fire.

My mind wanders off, occasionally thinking of Bryce still having feelings for Lindsay, but how, when he says he loves me? How can he treat me with such care and compassion and still love someone else? He can't. So stop thinking about it.

We laugh, eat, and drink as Austin and Bryce tease Ciara. She teases them back with, "I'll get Keera to kick your asses. She's on my team now."

Our conversation flows freely, now that Austin isn't harping about Lindsay, irritating both me and Bryce. All is forgotten and we have a great time.

I really enjoy the way they joke and tease each other and the way they react when a humorous insult flies over. I've never really had that, being an only child.

After we clean up the kitchen, we say our goodbyes and I'm surprised that I get a hug from everyone and they want us to come back Thursday night. So I take it they're not too upset about me kicking Lindsay.

When we pull into the driveway, we notice Lindsay's car is gone, so Bryce maneuvers around the broken glass to get his truck into the garage.

He lifts a broom off the wall, then sweeps the glass into a small pile. I grab the dust pan that hangs next to some of the other tools and bend down in front of Bryce so he can sweep it up.

"Thanks, Angel."

"No problem."

That's the first thing we say to each other since we left his parents.

I was deep in thought about how the night went and I wondered since he wasn't saying much if he was deep in thought about Lindsay.

He must sense I'm a little worried.

He places the broom and dust pan back on the wall, then tugs me close, gently holding the small of my back, guiding me into the house.

"My family loves you."

"They do?"

"Oh yeah, they told me when you went to the washroom. And of course Austin had to put his two cents in. He said you're a little shy now, but once she gets to know you. She won't shut up."

"No! He didn't?"

"They laughed and said they want me to bring you around as much as possible. They want you to feel comfortable like you're one of the family."

"I do. I had such a good time. I love how you guys tease one another. I never had that growing up."

"Well you do now."

He hugs and kisses me, then pulls me over to the stereo still wrapped in his strong arms. I watch him slide Brantley Gilbert's disc in and he flips through to our favourite song, "fall into me." We dance holding each other tight.

The way he moves. His hips turn me on in an instant.

The man can dance.

We both get lost in the song, lost in each other's eyes, lost in our intimate moment.

When the dance ends, I look deep in his eyes. "I wanted to tell you how hot you look tonight but someone was always around us."

"I could tell, by the way you were looking at me, Angel. I had an awful urge to drag you into my old room and make love to you, but they wouldn't leave us alone for two seconds. Someday, I'll make love to you in there."

Oh my. Really? The promise makes me shiver. He can tell what he's doing to me. His finger slides down my shirt between my breasts, and by my bra, he pulls me down the hall.

"Come with me, little girl. I've got something I want you to see." He flashes his mischievous smile at me and that's all he has to do with me and I'm putty in his hands.

He spins me around by my bra when we enter his bedroom and he shoves me against the wall. Desperately, his mouth covers mine in a heated rush. There's an urgency in his touch a ravenous greed when he undresses me, the way his hands tremble, the way he looks in my eyes. He needs me, needs me bad.

I try to think quickly why he feels this way and the only logical explanation that pops into my head is Lindsay.

I pull away quickly. "What's wrong?"

"Nothing. What makes you think something's wrong?"

"Don't lie to me Bryce. We don't lie to each other remember?"

"Fuck." Bryce runs his hands through his hair, frustrated. He hesitates collecting his thoughts. "Whenever something or someone gets in the way of our relationship, I need to show you how much I need you and that you are mine."

"Someone? Meaning Lindsay?" Oh, struck a nerve talking about her again? "I see the way you cringe whenever someone mentions her name. Why Bryce? Do you still care for her?"

"You've got to understand she's got some mental issues that need to be worked out." Bryce closes in on me and I back up against the wall, letting him know I need an answer without his distraction.

"You didn't answer my question. Do you still care for her? Yes or no?"

"That's my problem, I care too much about people. So yes, I care what happens to her, like every other person on the street. I don't want her to hurt herself."

I look down at the floor lost in thought.

Bryce lifts my chin, forcing me to look at him. "Look at me please."

"So Lindsay's the someone that you're talking about who will get in the way of our relationship?"

"No. We won't let her."

"But she is Bryce. I feel it already."

"Angel, we will not let anyone ruin our relationship." Bryce holds my face in his hands caressing my cheeks with his thumbs. "Listen to me. The love I feel for you is…too much. I don't know how to rein in my feelings for you. It overwhelms me at times."

I swallow down the lump in my throat so I won't cry.

"Angel please believe me, my mind is wrapped around you day and night, thinking of nothing else, but you. Don't let me fuck this up. Please, I need you. Like the air I breathe."

Tears fall and I turn away because I don't want him to see how weak I am. Weak because of him.

"Please don't cry. It tears me to pieces, knowing I caused you pain." Bryce wipes away the tears. "Angel, let me show you how much I love you." Wrapping his strong arms around me, Bryce holds me tight, almost too much. His hand snakes through my hair and he holds me steady as he lowers his mouth to mine, tasting the salt from my tears, but he doesn't seem to care, he kisses me with a need so strong it makes me ache.

The emotions flowing through me at this moment has me hesitant, still. The love and need for him, overwhelms me too, to the point where I can't breathe sometimes. The anger and pain I'll feel if he breaks my heart. The fear of losing him to Lindsay has my heart constricting in my chest and it's a pain I'll never recover from.

"Angel, say something please. Talk to me. We have to communicate."

"I have a feeling you're going to break my heart."

"Never. I love you too much." He kisses me again in an attempt to soften me. "Don't you see how much? Fuck I'm obsessed." His pain filled eyes search mine rapidly.

Giving in, I lift my mouth to his and we kiss slowly at first, until the greed and need takes over, too impassioned to care about anything, but us in this moment.

I want to be the one that makes him forget every single memory about her. For the next couple hours or so I let go surrendering my heart, body, and soul.

28

THE SUDDEN BRIGHTNESS from the lamp hurts my eyes when Bryce flicks the light on waking me from a deep sleep.

"Are you awake?"

"Not really."

I roll onto my back, stretching and squeaking.

He climbs onto the bed and huddles over me, kissing my neck. "Wakey, wakey."

"What time is it?"

"Seven."

"I thought you wanted to sleep in on your day off."

He kisses my neck because I dose off.

"I want to show you something."

"You showed me last night. Remember, ya sex fiend."

I feel him smile against my cheek as he kisses me.

"No I want to show you something else. Look."

I open one eye and peek up at him.

He's holding a tiny little box with navy blue metallic paper and a pink ribbon and bow.

"What? That?" I ask, still not wanting to get out of bed.

"Come with me and you'll find out." He pulls me up gently then tugs my legs over the bed.

I bend down to pick my silk pajamas up off the floor.

"No clothes. I want you naked."

"All righty then." I say as I stand.

He holds my lower back until we reach the kitchen. "Sit."

I climb onto the bar stool smiling, because I realize he's cooked me breakfast. "What time did you get up?"

"Six. I watched you sleep for a bit, then thought this would be the perfect opportunity to give you your gift."

I keep eyeing the beautiful wrapping on my gift in the middle of the breakfast bar and wonder when he found the time to go shopping.

He places my tea and my plate of bacon, eggs, home fries, and toast in front of me. I dig in immediately.

"Hungry? Worked up an appetite?"

"Yeah, from all that sexercise you gave me."

"I didn't hear you complaining last night."

"I'm not complaining. That was amazing."

He kisses my cheek and squeezes my knee. "You rocked my world, too."

He leans over the counter, picks up the box and hands it to me. "Open it."

I rip through the ribbon and paper, opening the tiny box, then I stare down at it for a bit.

I look up at him smiling, "Babe, it's beautiful." I touch it, running my fingers over the diamonds.

Bryce bought me a two heart gold and diamond necklace.

He pulls it out of the box, and gently touches my neck as he clasps the back, then he comes around to face me.

His finger runs along each heart. "This is your heart and this is mine. We'll always be connected by our love."

Tears run down my cheeks and I raise my mouth to his and we kiss, a slow savouring kiss. "Thank you, it's beautiful. I love it."

"You're welcome. Now let's finish our breakfast, then we'll take a shower. I want to show you around Barrie."

It's a beautiful October day driving along Lakeshore Drive looking out at Kempenfelt Bay. Stopping at the marina, we get out and walk along the scenic trail holding hands. The sun makes it warmer than it should be and when the wind gusts, it makes me shiver. Bryce holds me in a tight embrace against his warm body.

Back in the truck, we drive past the mall. The incident with Lindsay still leaving a bad taste in my mouth, but then Bryce shows me the O.P.P. station where Austin works, and I forget all about it.

He shows me a few other points of interests in Barrie, then we stop for lunch. We talk, laugh and eat. It's a perfect day enjoying each other's company. We later drive to Bryce's parent's house.

Bryce's mom and dad are working, and Ciara is either in class at college or at her part-time job.

After Bryce searches the house to make sure no one's home, his face lights up like a Christmas tree. "We're alone."

He pulls me toward his old room and I know exactly what he has in mind by his wicked smile.

"What if someone comes home?"

"We'll hear them. Don't worry. There's a lock on the door."

He pulls me inside and I look around, noticing his mom and dad have left his room the way it was, when he moved out.

Bryce doesn't give me much time to check things out.

His hands reach up sliding my coat off my shoulders and he lifts my shirt up and off my head immediately. He spins me around so my back is to his front. He pulls my hair to the side kissing my neck a few times sending chills and a tingle through me to all sorts of interesting places.

Bryce's fingers work fast undoing the clasp on my bra, then they slide under the straps, letting them slide down my shoulders until he gets it off, and he flings it across the room. He resumes kissing my neck.

His big hands cup my breasts and he pulls at my nipples making them tighten to large peaks. His cock presses against my jeans and I can feel how aroused he is.

Suddenly he spins me around again so I face him.

"When I was a horny teenager, I always dreamt about having a girl in my room and the things I'd do to her." He cocks his head and smiles mischievously. "God, the things that went through my mind back then. I thought there was something wrong with me until I talked to Austin, and he said I was normal. And look, here you are, making all my fantasies come true."

"You've never had a girl in here?"

"No. You're my first."

I have to ask. "Lindsay hasn't been in here?"

"No, I never brought her around. She didn't get along with my family."

My mind wanders and I have a rush of immense satisfaction spreading through me knowing that I'm his first and Lindsay is not.

"Now back to what we we're doing. Me seducing you."

Short and sweet answers—whenever I ask about Lindsay. He always changes the subject. He doesn't like to talk about her at all and it makes him very uncomfortable when anyone else talks about her.

I don't want to be pushy at the moment, so I let it go. Our discussion last night about Lindsay wasn't enough but one day soon we'll have that conversation and I will get him to talk more. I hope to pull everything out of him.

He tugs at the button and zipper on my jeans. I hook my thumbs in the waist band and shimmy out of them.

I reach for his shirt and pants and we quickly get them off, flinging them somewhere in this room.

We stand there naked, hesitating for a few seconds, staring at each other's body. We both lunge, greedily sealing our mouths hard against one another with a firm demanding kiss.

Bryce backs me up until I feel my knees hit the side of his old single bed and I expect him to push me down but he gently lowers, keeping his lips sealed to mine until I lay flat on my back and his big hard body is on top of me.

The kisses start out slow and sensuous and as his arousal heightens the kisses become aggressively firmer.

We suddenly separate, panting, trying to catch our breath.

"I wanted to make out with you for a while but you get me so fucking hot. I swear to God you could make me come by kissing you."

"I feel the same. God, Babe…what you do to me."

His mouth finds mine once again while he spreads my legs apart with his. He kisses his way down, then alternates between running his lips over my skin and nipping gently down my belly. Driving me insane.

I beg him. "Babe, please."

I feel him smile against my thigh, then his gaze floats to mine. "So impatient." He lowers his mouth and resumes the torture.

"Yeah, and you're such a tease."

I feel him smile again before his tongue slips deep inside me.

His tongue feathers along each side, licking upward. His finger circles my opening relentlessly. I push my hips toward his finger so he'll insert it.

"Nope, not yet." He says in a teasing voice.

I sigh in frustration.

He teases me a bit more, but then gives into me like he always does. I guess he has to show me who's in control.

His tongue zeroes in on my clit and his finger thrusts at a steady pace.

My breathing slows to almost nil and my fingers latch onto his jet black silky hair and I hold him tight, so he'll keep the exact pressure I need.

His teeth scrape over my swollen clit, enlarging it and then he latches on and sucks.

When he knows I'm close to orgasm, he rapidly flicks and thrusts his finger hard into me.

"Babe!" I cry out, then soft whimpers escape my lips.

I claw at the sheets and buck my hips. My hands snake back into his hair holding him in place not wanting to let him go. My legs shake uncontrollably. I'm arching my back and my vision blurs as my explosive orgasm tears through me. I distantly register Bryce pulling me into the middle of the bed. I feel him poke at my entrance, then he slides deep inside me.

My eyes fly open and I gasp quivering around him from my subsiding aftershocks, but I'm ready for more.

"Do you feel how fucking hard you make me?"

"Yes." I say breathless.

My nails rake down his back to his tight butt cheeks, pulling him into me. "Give it to me, Babe. I need you. Need your body. I need your cock."

Bryce holds my hips and thrusts his cock hard into me over and over again with his punishing lunges. With every push into my body, I can see him losing control and how he aggressively drives deeper than the thrust before.

His hair and skin are damp with sweat. Eyes closed, his jaw and neck strain as he lets out a groan of pleasure. "Come with me Angel, I need you with me."

I reach down fondling my clit and my muscles clamp down around his cock, spasms shoot through me, uncontrollably. "God, Babe, you're going to do it to me again." My orgasm rips through me like a freight train. "Babe!"

Shuddering, Bryce lets out a throaty groan. "I'm with you. Let go."

His powerful thrusts drill me hard two more times and then I feel his cock jerk inside me, spilling his warm come.

Grabbing hold of his ass cheeks, I pull him farther into me as he rears up and groans, knowing I'll be sore from having him so deep.

I feel his heart pound as he collapses on top of me. We both smile at each other and try to catch our breath.

The front door slams and our eyes widen.

"Oh my God, Bryce, someone's here."

His mouth curves wickedly. "Shit, I didn't think they'd be home so soon."

Bryce slides out of me, then reaches for some Kleenex on his desk. He quickly places it between my legs and then scrambles to find our cloths we flung around the room.

I clean up, quickly get dressed and run my fingers through my hair to fix the just-fucked look. I check in the mirror and then give up, and instead straighten the covers on Bryce's bed.

We hear the door close again. "Honey, I'm home."

"I'm in here, dear."

Shit, both his parents are home. I listen intently.

"Where's Bryce and Keera?" Deana asks.

"I was thinking the same thing. I saw his truck in the driveway." Garrett says in a husky voice.

We hear footsteps and the floor creaking down the hall, just as I get the bed made to perfection.

Bryce's mom peeks her head in. "There you two are. Showing Keera your old room?"

"Yeah, she wanted to see it."

"Did you show her all your hockey trophies and pictures?"

"Yeah, Ma." Bryce says a little embarrassed.

"Keera, you have to watch him play hockey someday. He's something else. He's fascinating to watch. I miss that."

"You can come watch the fire department verses the cops. We start next week."

"Austin's playing, too?"

"Yup, he says he can't wait to kick our asses."

Deana clasps her hands together. "Your father's going to love this. I think he misses it, too." She says with a whisper. "I'll go make us some dinner, give you two some privacy."

"Thanks, Ma."

She closes the door behind her.

My breath leaves me in a rush and I smile. "Holy crap, that was close."

Bryce pulls me to him and holds me in a tight embrace. He bends and kisses me. "Boy, that'll get the old heart racing."

I slap his shoulder, embarrassed. "You're so bad."

He laughs. "What? You know you like me bad."

"Oh, I do. I thought you locked the door?"

"I did, but I unlocked it before she entered, so she wouldn't be suspicious."

It takes a few minutes to calm down and then I look around Bryce's room.

My eyes inspect all the pictures of him with his teams and single pictures of him holding his stick. "Bryce, look how cute you were when you were little. Look at that baby face. How I wish I would've known you back then."

"I wish I knew you back then, too. I could have made out with you in my room. I would've been as hot for you then as I am now. When we get back to your place I want to see pictures of you when you were young."

I glance over to the posters of girls with their bathing suits on. "That one there is a classic." I point to the iconic Farrah Fawcett poster.

"Yeah, she's my favourite. Beat off to that poster, quite often. That's how big your nipples get. Fuck, it's getting me hard thinking about them."

"Everything gets you hard. Remember?"

"Only when it comes to you, Angel. Just you."

I smile and then my focus shifts to his hockey trophies. "Wow, you must have been collecting these for a while. You must have been really good."

He comes up behind me, pulling my hair to the side and kisses my neck. "Oh, I don't know, I think I still have it." He circles his hips and pushes his cock against my butt.

I turn a bit to look at him. "Are we talking about hockey or sex? Because I know you're great at sex."

"Well, thank you, Angel. You're pretty damn good yourself."

"I've got a good teacher."

He spins me around and hugs me. "Will you stay with me next week so you can watch the game Wednesday night?"

I do enjoy staying with him at his house, but I have my own house and haven't been there much since we met.

Although when I'm here, I totally forget about my stalker. The only worry here is Lindsay.

I shake my head. "Yes, I'll come back with you." I love making him happy.

He kisses and holds me in a tight embrace.

"You don't know how much this means to me. I want you with me. Always."

"I need to check out my house, to make sure everything's fine."

"Yeah, we can do that."

I like how he says we.

"Babe, I forgot to tell you, when I text Leena she said there were two fires in town that the police are investigating."

"They're supposed to call us if they have any new information." Bryce groans.

"They're probably busy investigating."

"That's no excuse. They said they'd keep us updated." Bryce says raising his voice a bit.

I should have never said anything. He's in a mood now.

His mom gives a quick knock then pops her head in. "Dinner's ready."

Bryce holds my hand behind his back as he tugs me along to the kitchen. We sit beside each other and Bryce places his hand on my knee.

I love how he always touches me. If it isn't his hand on my knee, or his arm wrapped around my shoulder, then he's rubbing our feet together.

"Where's Dad?"

"He's in the garage working on his truck."

"What's he doing to it?"

"Lord only knows. Here, take him his dinner."

Bryce looks at me and squeezes my knee. "I'll be right back."

"Okay." I say softly.

He picks up the plate of food and then walks toward the garage, just missing a collision with Ciara, who is entering the back door.

"You're so lucky I didn't wear that." She says with a straight face.

Bryce smiles. "Next time, I'll make sure you wear it."

"Bite me, jackass. Don't you have a house to go to?"

"Just because you said that, I think I'll come visit more often." Bryce gives Ciara a devilish smile.

"Hi, Ciara."

"Hi, Keera."

"How was your day?" I ask.

"Good until I saw him. God, he's a pain in my ass."

I remember when Bryce said the same thing about her. Oh, brotherly and sisterly love. It's cute. I enjoy sitting back watching them throw humorous insults back and forth at each other. It makes me smile. But deep down they really love each other. I can see it.

Deana pipes up. "Someday you'll miss him."

"He's been gone for three years now and I still don't miss him. Don't think it's going to happen, Ma."

"Oh, Ciara." Deana places a plate of food in front of me and Ciara.

"Eat up girls, before it gets cold." Deana demands.

Bryce comes back in, just as I finish rinsing my plate, and I place it in the dishwasher.

"Dad's checking his brakes, rotating his tires and doing an oil change. He might be out there for a bit."

Deana places a plate in front of Bryce. "Is he eating before it gets cold?" Deana inquires.

"Yeah, he knows how you get, Ma. He ate and talked, then got back to work."

Bryce eats and I watch as he devours it. "Mmm, that was good Ma. Thanks."

"Yes that was delicious thank you again." I say.

Suddenly, our attention is diverted to someone banging on the front door. We all leave the kitchen to look out the front window.

It's Lindsay. She's yelling something about a whore.

29

"FUCK'S SAKE!" BRYCE lets out a heavy sigh as his body stance and expression changes.

"Tell her to take a hike." Ciara groans. "No one wants her around here."

Bryce walks to the door then turns to look at me. "Don't come out here, stay with Ciara and my Mom."

"Bryce, you make sure to tell her not to come here again." Deana's voice is stern.

Bryce opens the door and I hear his voice change to caring. "Lindsay what are you doing here?"

Lindsay angrily blurts out. "I'm here to kick the home wrecker's ass." She tries to push past Bryce, but he holds her by her arms, then closes the door behind him.

I'm glued to the front window watching their every move, and so is Deana and Ciara.

She's having another hysterical fit and Bryce is trying to defuse the situation.

"Jesus would you look at that nut job? I'm telling you she's out there." Ciara comments.

Lindsay will not leave the front porch when Bryce urges her to.

Bryce faces us, trying to talk reasonably to Lindsay, then all of a sudden, I see his expression soften and change to…

My heart drops and my eyes glaze over from the look on his face. I've got such a lump in my throat, I can't swallow it down, but I tell myself I'm not going to cry in front of Ciara and Deana.

When he looks at her that way, her body physically changes. She wraps her arms around his neck and hugs him, then she takes his face in her hands and kisses him. She takes his hand and they walk to his truck. He opens the door for her and she climbs in. While he's walking around to get into the driver's side she looks directly at me with a big evil grin.

My face turns beet red from anger. I want to kill her.

"What the fuck does he think he's doing?" Ciara blurts out.

"Watch that mouth there, missy." Deana then turns her attention to me with a look of concern on her face. She rubs my back then walks to the archway between the living room and kitchen. "He'll be back. He just has to drive her home."

I think she's trying to smooth out the situation.

Ciara and I stare out the window as we watch Bryce climb into the driver's seat, then he backs up and pulls out of the driveway.

I stand there with my finger nails clenched tight in my fists.

That look is the look he gives to me.

My mind keeps replaying it in my head as I stare out the window.

I can't believe he left me for her.

My head turns, glancing over to Ciara and Deana who are talking, but I'm not paying attention, I'm in a daze. They stop talking and look my way. Sympathy etched across their faces tells me I need to get out of here before I start to cry.

I hurry to put my boots and coat on mechanically, almost forgetting my purse. "I'm sorry. I've got to go. Tell Bryce I went home."

Why I care to tell Bryce where I'm going is beyond me. He obviously didn't give a shit about my feelings when he left with her.

I open the door and step outside before they can say anything to keep me here. The cool breeze, is a welcome feeling on my heated face.

The moment I close the door the tears start to flow and I can't stop.

I walk through the streets delirious not knowing where I'm going. I walk, thinking about what happened. Replaying that same look he gave her in my head over and over again, torturing myself.

I come to the conclusion…*he still loves her.* And it breaks my heart.

Time passes and when I finally come back to reality, I don't have a clue of where I am.

"Get a grip Keera, think. You don't have a car. Maybe I could take a bus? Leena. I'll call Leena."

I dig out my phone, flipping to her number. "Hi, you're not working?"

"No."

"What are you doing right now?"

"Nothing. Why?"

"Can you come pick me up in Barrie?"

Leena's voice goes up a few notches with panic. "Where's Bryce? What happened?" She senses something's wrong; she can hear it in my voice.

"I'll tell you when you get here. Can you come right now?"

"Yes, yes, I'm on my way."

"Leena? Don't talk to Austin or Bryce about this, okay? I need some time to think." I say in a shaky voice because I'm starting to cry again.

I hate how weak I am when it comes to Bryce. I have to be stronger.

"I won't."

"Promise me."

"Okay, I promise. Now, where are you?"

"I'm walking. I'll call you and let you know where I end up."

"I'm already in my car. Call me."

I knew I could count on Leena, she's always there for me.

Spinning around in a circle, disoriented, I try to decide which way to go, then an idea pops in my head.

There's an app on my phone that gives the location of all the Tim Horton's in the area.

With my mind clouded the way it is, I impress myself that I actually think to use my phone as a tool.

I walk until I reach the Tim Horton's, then call Leena to let her know where I am.

My phone rings as I'm putting my French vanilla on the table and I hurry to silence it because my Moves Like Jagger ring tone has everyone staring at me.

It's Bryce.

I shake my head. He's got a lot of nerve calling me. Shouldn't he be with Lindsay?

I'm being petty, but at this point I don't give a shit. I don't answer it. I'm angry and hurt and getting more pissed off by the minute.

Furious, I tap away changing my phone so it vibrates in case Leena needs to get a hold of me, then I quickly glance at a really long text from Bryce, but I avoid reading it.

I don't care what he has to say because it's all bullshit anyway. I know what I saw and he wants to change my mind.

Every memory of Bryce and me together flashes in the back of my mind. The first time we had sex. When he took my virginity. All the beautiful love making and kinky sex, plays like a movie in my head. My hand automatically reaches up and I run my finger along the diamonds of the two heart pendant Bryce gave me this morning. His sentimental words replaying in my head. 'This is your heart and this is mine. We'll always be connected by our love.' "Bullshit!" I whisper and shake my head. I think about all the intimate moments we've shared together. The only time we fought was when I called him an asshole for kidnapping me, before I understood what was really going on and recently when I confronted him whether or not he still cares for Lindsay. That was a lie obviously. The thought of not being with him ever again makes my chest tighten and ache. How am I going to live without him? You'll learn to live without him. He loves someone else. Yes, he does. So that's why I have to be tough. I have to be strong. There's no way in hell I'll be with a man who loves someone else.

Regret overwhelms me for giving up my virginity. What a fool I am?

My phone vibrates. It's Leena. "Hello."

"Bryce is calling my phone and texting me. Is he calling you?"

"Yes, he called and sent a text. I didn't answer and I haven't read the text."

"God, Keera he's frantic. I feel so bad for him. You've got to talk to him."

"No! I need some time."

"Jesus, what the hell happened?"

"Leena, do not answer that phone if it's Austin or Bryce. Promise me."

"I promise. Now, tell me what happened?"

"I'll tell you when you get here."

"Christ, okay, I'm getting back on the road. I'll be there in fifteen minutes. Bye."

A very small part of me thinks I'm over reacting that I didn't see what I think I saw.

I replay the look over and over in my head.

No! I know what I saw; there's no denying it. Leena pulls up and I go outside and get in the car.

I let out a heavy sigh as I slouch in the seat. "Okay, let's get out of here."

"Oh, honey, look at you." She gives me a hug because I probably look like shit.

"You're going to make me cry again."

"Okay, I'll drive and you talk."

We drive through the streets of Barrie and then get onto Highway 11 and head north back to Huntsville.

I tell her everything, step by step, then she stares at me, probably trying to find the right words.

"Don't you think this is all a misunderstanding?"

"I knew you'd side with him. You weren't there. If you were, you'd be pissed, too."

"I'm not siding with Bryce. I think there's a logical explanation for all of this. But I do know he loves you."

"Okay, let's say Austin had an ex that wouldn't give up. Kept sucking him back in and then you hear from his family and friends that he was very messed up after they broke up. And when you go to his house for the first time and he shows you his bedroom, he hurries to put away a picture of them both looking very happy together, I might add, in the drawer of his nightstand, so I don't see it. But it sat there next to his bed for how long? We've been together for over a month. Ya think he could have gotten rid of it? And whenever someone mentions her name, he physically cringes and clams up not saying a word. So I confronted him. Asked him if he still cared for her. He said yes, like anyone else on the street. But that look he gave her. That's how he used to look at me, with love in his eyes. I'm telling you, Leena, he still loves her."

I look at her and, for the first time ever, she's at a loss for words.

"I've got to protect myself. I've been through too much distress in my life. There's no way in hell I'm going to be with a man who loves someone else. I can't let this drag out. It's best for both of us to end this right now. IT'S OVER!"

Coming soon!

Look for book two of the Unforgivable series.

Unforgivable Lust & Restraint.

If you like the Unforgivable series, help spread the word. Authors need reviews, so please, take the time to write a review on, GoodRead's, Amazon, Indigo/Chapter's, Kobo, Google, iBooks, and Barnes and Noble

Thank you for buying the Unforgivable series.
I appreciate it more than words can say.
I would love to hear if you like it. Please find me on Facebook, Twitter, Pinterest and Instagram or check out my website @ www.shayleesoleil.com for more information and upcoming news.

Lots of love from Shay Lee Soleil

CPSIA information can be obtained
at www.ICGtesting.com
Printed in the USA
LVHW02s1732150818
587066LV00002B/182/P